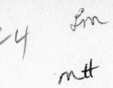
P9-DOF-018

The
LOVE LETTERS

Books by Beverly Lewis

The Love Letters
The River

HOME TO HICKORY HOLLOW
The Fiddler
The Bridesmaid
The Guardian
The Secret Keeper
The Last Bride

THE ROSE TRILOGY
The Thorn • *The Judgment* • *The Mercy*

ABRAM'S DAUGHTERS
The Covenant • *The Betrayal* • *The Sacrifice*
The Prodigal • *The Revelation*

THE HERITAGE OF LANCASTER COUNTY
The Shunning • *The Confession* • *The Reckoning*

ANNIE'S PEOPLE
The Preacher's Daughter • *The Englisher* • *The Brethren*

THE COURTSHIP OF NELLIE FISHER
The Parting • *The Forbidden* • *The Longing*

SEASONS OF GRACE
The Secret • *The Missing* • *The Telling*

The Postcard • *The Crossroad*

The Redemption of Sarah Cain
Sanctuary (with David Lewis) • *Child of Mine* (with David Lewis)
The Sunroom • *October Song*

Amish Prayers
The Beverly Lewis Amish Heritage Cookbook

www.beverlylewis.com

BEVERLY LEWIS

The LOVE LETTERS

BETHANYHOUSE

a division of Baker Publishing Group
Minneapolis, Minnesota

© 2015 by Beverly M. Lewis, Inc.

Published by Bethany House Publishers
11400 Hampshire Avenue South
Bloomington, Minnesota 55438
www.bethanyhouse.com

Bethany House Publishers is a division of
Baker Publishing Group, Grand Rapids, Michigan

Printed in the United States of America

All rights reserved. No part of this publication may be reproduced, stored in a retrieval system, or transmitted in any form or by any means—for example, electronic, photocopy, recording—without the prior written permission of the publisher. The only exception is brief quotations in printed reviews.

Library of Congress Cataloging-in-Publication Data

Lewis, Beverly.
    The love letters / Beverly Lewis.
      pages ; cm
    Summary: "Marlena Wenger, a young aunt from the Beachy Amish caring for her infant niece, finds comfort and hope from an Old Order Amish mother and her family who extend friendship to a homeless man, whose few possessions include a collection of love letters"— Provided by publisher.
    ISBN 978-0-7642-1321-2 (hardcover : acid-free paper)
    ISBN 978-0-7642-1246-8 (softcover)—
    ISBN 978-0-7642-1322-9 (large-print : softcover)
    I. Title.
    PS3562.E9383L68 2015
    813'.54—dc23
                                           2014041311

Scripture quotations are from the King James Version of the Bible.

The poem in chapter 22 appears on page 65 of *A Selection of Sepulchral Curiosities, With a Biological Sketch on Human Longevity*, edited and published by Thomas Kinnersley in 1823 in New York. An epigraph on a tombstone in Malvern Church, Worcestershire, England, it reads in its original form:

"They were so truly one, that none could say
Which of them rul'd, or whether did obey:
He rul'd because she would obey; and she,
In so obeying, rul'd as well as he."

This story is a work of fiction. With the exception of recognized historical figures and events, all characters and events are the product of the author's imagination. Any resemblance to any person, living or dead, is purely coincidental.

Cover design by Dan Thornberg, Design Source Creative Services
Art direction by Paul Higdon
Back cover photograph of the Brownstown Mill by Sarah Shanely

15 16 17 18 19 20 21   7 6 5 4 3 2 1

To
Kathy Illum,
longtime friend and devoted reader.
Your insight and love are incomparable gifts.

O my love's like a red, red rose
That's newly sprung in June:
O my love's like the melody
That's sweetly play'd in tune!

—Robert Burns

PROLOGUE

*M*y world tilted when *Dawdi* Tim passed away last winter; then it spun off its axis when my parents sent
me away from my beau to be with my widowed grandmother
for the summer.

"My Mamma *needs ya, with Dawdi gone,*" my mother urged.

While I dearly wanted to help my sorrowing grandmother in
rural Brownstown—far from my family's home in Mifflinburg—
the timing was just awful. Being gone for the summer, I would
miss out on my baptismal instruction, and without it I couldn't
marry Nathaniel Zimmerman this November. An entire year
would pass before the next wedding season rolled around for
my beau and me.

Nat wasn't very happy about the arrangement, either, yet
he tried to soothe my fears and took me for a ride in his black
courting carriage before I left. We stopped at Dairy Queen and
had ice cream garnished the way Dawdi had liked his—with
chopped nuts and oodles of whipped cream. I still cherish that
memory and Nat's efforts to console me, especially since it was

obvious he had his own worries, what with my parents having joined the Beachy Amish-Mennonites, and *Mammi* Janice a black-bumper Mennonite. Such a combination, to be sure.

I had assured Nat I was Old Order, skin to bone, despite where my parents or grandmother attended church. Looking mighty relieved, he'd reached for me and kissed my cheek, and then, after more tender words, he took me home.

Watching his buggy rumble down the road, I promised myself: *If anything, the separation will make our love stronger.*

~ ⁀ ⊙

So here I sat, a week later, in the grand white gazebo my grandfather built years ago, surrounded by the sounds of tree frogs and crickets. I reread Nat's first letter since I'd come, a newsy account of taking his courting-age sister to Singing, and of opening several new beehives, as well as cutting the first hay of the season with his father and brothers.

Memorizing his sign-off, *With all my love,* I dismissed my loneliness to the balmy breeze and contemplated the wall telephone in Mammi's kitchen, dreaming of my beau's voice in my ear. But Nat was much too conservative to ever call me. The phone in his father's barn was used strictly for contacting an occasional paid driver, clear up there northwest of Harrisburg, in what had been called Buggytown, USA, back in the 1800s.

In those days, there were fifty carriage and sleigh factories, and my own father could trace his ancestry to one of those original buggy makers. So that's where my parents had put down roots as Old Order Amish when my mother left Brownstown and the Mennonite church to marry *Dat.* Then, after attending the more traditional Amish group for many years, they joined the Beachy Amish two years ago, after getting written permission from our Old Order bishop. Out of respect, I halfheartedly followed in their footsteps, but only until I could become a member of the church of my childhood—the church where I would eventually marry Nat.

The scent of lilacs filled the air, and I spun a loose strand of hair from beneath my formal prayer cap around my slender fingers. In my memory, I could almost hear Dawdi's harmonica drifting out over the pastureland in the still of the night. *So many visits here through the years . . .*

The back door opened and Mammi, round and graying, stepped out. Her white cotton duster shimmered against the dusk. "You all right, Marlena?" Her frail voice pushed into the stillness.

"Just thinkin', is all."

"Want some company?"

I nodded in the fading light. *She's lonesome, too.*

Mammi wandered out to join me in the shelter of the gazebo and sat there, holding my hand, linking our collective grief. We took our time sharing personal memories, slow and sweet. "Remember how Dawdi would hoist me onto his big shoulders?" I said.

"And let you wear his holey brown hat, too. No one else was allowed to touch it."

I turned to look at her, interested in what she remembered. "Whatever became of that ol' thing?"

"It's round here somewhere . . . like so many reminders." Her pain mingled with her words.

After more shared recollections, Mammi said she felt chilly and headed back to the house, disappearing inside.

I remained there, moving my bare feet back and forth over the smooth wood, giving way to further daydreams. Dawdi was always playing his mouth organ or humming church hymns such as "In the Sweet By and By" and "Jesus, Lover of My Soul" while doing his farm chores. He hummed all the time, really. And there were the clever tunes he readily created, too, with lyrics to make a point, funny and otherwise. Like a doting old dove, he'd coaxed me right under his reassuring wing when my big sister, Luella, left the Old Order, along with any form of Anabaptist faith, far as I knew. She'd caused a terrible stir when she fell for a good-looking man outside our Plain community—with the emphasis on *fell*, according to my distraught parents. Where Luella's actions were concerned, *der Deiwel* had never been mentioned, but that dark spirit certainly came to mind when I considered Luella's choice to leave us far behind.

Then, a year or so after their wedding, Luella's soldier husband was sent to fight in Vietnam, in a war we did not support—like the rest of the Plain community, we were staunch pacifists. Just as worrisome, Luella had refused to return home to the farm to be looked after during the final weeks of her pregnancy, which only deepened the estrangement.

"*I miss her,*" Dawdi Tim had confided when we visited him and Mammi last Thanksgiving, before he took so ill in the depths of winter. His pale blue eyes filled with tears, and I knew our dear grandpa had not turned his back on Luella, unlike others in the church . . . including me, although Dawdi never would have pointed this out. Truth was, I loved Luella, but we'd never meshed, even though we'd made repeated attempts. We simply didn't see eye to eye. After she broke our mother's heart, I had even less reason to stay in touch.

I spied the spot in the backyard over by a stand of poplars where, as a child, I'd planted little rocks in the dirt, going over them each day with Dawdi's green watering can. Luella had mocked me for my efforts and hurried off to the hen house to talk to the chickens instead. But I didn't mind. I figured if everything else grew and thrived so effortlessly with Dawdi's loving care, then maybe my pebbles might sprout and blossom, too. They never did, of course, as Luella was quick to remind me, her hand on one hip.

Mammi's vegetable garden and flower beds were only one testament to the vibrant farm she'd built with my grandfather. Canning season was forthcoming—one of the reasons Mamma had sent me here this sunny month of June. Yet, truth be told, I suspected she and Dat also hoped that either Nat or I might find a new future mate while apart . . . one that would not tie me to the Old Ways.

Nevertheless, a single summer away couldn't keep me from eventually marrying the dearest boy in all of Mifflinburg, the only fellow I'd ever dated.

Rising from my cozy spot, I looked toward the adjacent Amish farm, its green borders bumping against Dawdi's newly rented land. I actually expected to see the Bitner boy out there with his yellow-and-white barn cat turned house pet, catching lightning bugs in a Ball canning jar with holes punched in the top, a makeshift lantern. Roman and Ellie Bitner's only son suffered from a bad limp and was considered slow for his fourteen years, but what he lacked in mental abilities, he made up for in kindness. In fact, there was something real special about the young fellow whose given name was Jake, though most everyone called him Small Jay.

Nearly all of the Brownstown Plain community knew of the youth's disabilities . . . and understood. Everyone but his father. But then, that might've been because Small Jay was

Roman's only boy, and what a farmer needed most was a robust and energetic son.

It was time for me to head indoors, into the stifling house that Dawdi had built with his own callused hands nearly five decades ago. I pictured Mammi sitting near the open kitchen windows, fanning her hot, sticky face with one of the round fans the ushers at her Mennonite meetinghouse gave out during the dog days of July and August. *Jah*, even the four walls of Mammi's kitchen, with its black-and-white-checked floor, were a stark reminder of Dawdi, as well as of Luella's and my summer visits here, often for a month at a time.

I stared up at the second-story door, which opened to a small white balcony. It was Dawdi's favorite spot to sit and hum after supper. That space had given me opportunity to hear him tell of "the *alt* days" when he was a farm boy. From that high perch, we could spy on everything, including Luella, who liked to count in her uppity-sounding French as she tossed feed to the hens . . . always pushing the limits of what was expected of a devout Amish girl. Luella seemed too busy with her own thoughts, and later, her own friends, to glean much of anything from her Plain family, Dawdi included.

All this pondering the past. Something stirred in me, and I was surprised to realize that I missed my older sister—her years growing up, living at home, and seeing her every day. After her marriage to Gordon Munroe, she'd basically disappeared from our lives.

On nights like tonight, I wished Nat were within walking distance. I longed for his firm and loving hand wrapped around mine, but I tried to encourage myself, knowing that in just three months, I would be home again.

As if I'd never left . . .

CHAPTER 1

*M*arlena Wenger was a knot of nerves as she pushed the iron over her grandmother's white pillowcase. She'd dampened it earlier, using a bottle with small holes drilled into its metal lid to sprinkle the water, and then rolled up the blouse to evenly distribute the moisture. Once it was ironed to her satisfaction, Marlena hung it up and reached for the next rolled item, a floral-print cotton dress.

Even though she dreaded the chore of ironing on this humid Tuesday, she'd gotten up earlier than usual, prior to the intense heat of the day. Already, her back ached and her legs had locked—something her mother warned her against. *"You can stand much longer if ya keep both knees bent,"* she could hear Mamma saying. But it took effort to remember, and there she stood, stiff-legged, her back arched.

Wishing for a breeze from the nearby open windows, she wondered why Dawdi Tim had never purchased a freestanding fan for the kitchen, considering the amount of electricity swirling through the walls of this house. *Makes no sense for Mammi to suffer in such heat.*

She let her mind drift back to her hometown of Mifflinburg. There, some of the older farmhouses had second-floor doors that opened outside to nothing but air. Nat Zimmerman's father once told her that such an exit could be the quick end of a sleepwalker. Her Dat, however, had explained that the doors, if propped open, circulated stale air when the upstairs was too oppressively hot for sleeping. But a doorway with no place to land? That was nothing short of peculiar.

Marlena thought now of her wonderful beau, as she often did during wakeful hours. Even her grandmother had mentioned Nat a few days ago, though not in such a positive light. *"He might be worried you'll grow accustomed to electricity and other conveniences."* But Marlena was quick to quell her seeming concern, though she doubted Mammi Janice would truly mind if things went awry with her conventional Amish beau.

Nevertheless, Marlena had assured Nat in her most recent letter: *I'm eager to return to the simplicity of the Old Ways. I miss the gas lamps and traveling by horse and buggy. And I am always glad to have the chance to chat with Mammi's Old Order neighbor Ellie Bitner.*

Presently she glanced at her grandmother, who was sitting hunched over her sewing beneath the table light, needle and thread poised in her fleshy hand. *More and more Beachy folk back home are yielding to the temptation of electric,* Marlena thought, pressing the facing flat on her grandmother's modest dress. How long before Dat and Mamma also gave in to the temptation of electricity and gas ranges and ovens? Of course, they were still considered new converts to the more progressive Amish fellowship, but Marlena was fairly sure her father had privately considered the notion of owning a car someday. The stringent dos and don'ts of the church ordinances had begun to ease up some since many of the formerly Old Order Amish church members had first split away.

"Will ya run next door for some fresh eggs this morning?" Mammi looked up from her sewing. "There's a-plenty of egg money under the cookie jar." She offered a small smile. "If ya don't mind."

"Once I'm finished here, *jah.*" Marlena was glad for an excuse to pay Ellie Bitner a visit. The kind and outgoing Amish-woman had always been someone Marlena yearned to spend more time with.

"Why not take some of your warm raisin bread along, too, dear? Surprise Ellie."

Marlena agreed, happy to ease her grandmother's load. Just how long before her grandmother could manage without help was unknown. For now, there were quarts of sweet strawberries to be picked and washed for this Saturday's market, and for the table. Soon, the juicy black cherries would be coming on, as well as the bulk of the garden produce. Weeding alone filled up Marlena's morning hours several times a week. Summer had always been a paradise of abundance at Dawdi Tim's beautiful, sprawling farm.

Mammi rose to get herself some meadow tea from the icebox, a newfangled convenience she'd splurged on after Dawdi Tim's insurance paid out. According to the circle letters, Mammi had ordered hers the same week as her Mennonite cousin out in Indiana. "I noticed young Jake Bitner out walking his cat earlier," she said.

"Sassafras?"

"Mm-hmm," Mammi said. "Sometimes he practically wears that cat around his shoulders when he sits near the pond in the willow grove down yonder."

"That cat obviously loves Small Jay."

"Well, but he keeps the poor creature on a leash, of all things. Restraining a cat is downright odd, if ya ask me."

Marlena couldn't conceal her smile. "Does Sassy also heel and sit on command?"

"*Ach* now, for Small Jay that cat might just do anything."

They laughed.

Mammi had relayed that from the time Sassafras was just a kitten, she'd sought out Small Jay in the most peculiar way, following him around and meowing and carrying on when he left her outside. And this was even before Small Jay had miraculously nursed the kitten back to life, after Sassy was stepped on by one of the mules. Ellie had called her son an angel of mercy at the time. The end result was that the cat eventually moved into the Bitners' house, where she enjoyed store-bought cat food and occasional crumbs from the table.

Finished with her task at last, Marlena unplugged the iron and set it on the counter to cool, then returned to fold up the wooden ironing board covered with a thick terry cloth towel secured beneath by thumbtacks. She carried it into the large pantry off the kitchen. "I'll run over to Ellie's now, Mammi."

"Don't forget the egg money, *jah*?"

Marlena retrieved the money and waved. "I'll be back right quick."

Her grandmother let loose a chuckle. "I've heard that before, so just take your time." She paused and looked wistfully at the ceiling, smile lines gracing her face, then looked back at her. "I daresay something 'bout that big farm calls to ya. Ain't so?"

Marlena shrugged. She couldn't deny feeling drawn to other Amish folk there in Brownstown, like Ellie and her young girls, and Small Jay, too. But this particular summer—right this minute, in fact—she'd much rather be hurrying off to see her darling beau.

CHAPTER 2

*E*llie tensed when her broad-shouldered husband snapped his black suspenders and turned to stride off toward the barn. She stood watching at the back door and saw Small Jay in Roman's path, near the latticed pump house, waiting to ask the same question he asked almost every day.

"*Guder Mariye!*" Small Jay called out to his father.

"Hullo there, Jake." Roman tousled the boy's cropped blond bangs.

"Could I help ya, Dat?" Small Jay asked eagerly. "I could water the mules or groom Razor, our pony, or even—"

"Not today," Roman replied, hustling past him.

Small Jay's shoulders visibly slumped. "All right, then."

"That's a *gut* boy," Roman said over his shoulder as he headed to the barn.

Ellie sighed and returned to the kitchen counter, where she was rolling out two crusts for tonight's strawberry-rhubarb pie. No matter how shorthanded Roman was outdoors, he continued to refuse their son's offer to help. "*It takes more time with him than without him,"* Roman had claimed to her in the privacy of their bedroom.

She was weary of their ongoing disagreement about the same thing. Certainly she understood, at least to some degree, why Roman stood his ground on this. Even so, she had pleaded with him numerous times to find *something* Small Jay could do. *"He's becoming a young man, after all,"* she'd urged.

And she heartily disagreed with Roman's recent suggestion. She would not consider having their daughters help with farm chores in Small Jay's stead . . . out there in the hayfield, or cultivating potatoes, or carrying wood to mend fences, or whatever else her husband had in mind. Girls' work was alongside their mothers, and there was no changing her mind otherwise.

On top of all the regular daily chores, she and Roman were scheduled to host the Old Order Amish Preaching service in a mere two weeks, which meant a thorough cleaning, washing ceilings, walls, windows, and windowsills. Every plate in her kitchen, all the glassware, and every single teacup and saucer, too, had to be washed and dried and put away—all essential duties to ready their home for its transformation into the temporary house of worship.

Straightening her long black apron, Ellie scuffed her bare toe on the wide-plank floor on her way to the front room. At the southernmost window, she stopped and squinted into the sunshine, wondering where Small Jay would take Sassy off to this morning—what private adventures they would encounter. Then, hearing the cat's meowing, she saw her son sitting right under her nose, there on the front porch steps, just grinning and talking *Deitsch* to the small cat perched on his shoulder. She listened more closely and was taken aback to realize Small Jay was singing his father's praises.

"Dat's best friends with the bishop," Small Jay bragged to Sassy. "And Dat's so strong. Why, he could lift a buggy with one hand if he wanted to."

Just imagine, Ellie thought, tears coming.

She watched as Small Jay lovingly stroked his cat. Truly, Sassy was about the only thing that could put a smile on those cheeks anymore. Her son had walked that cat all over God's creation ever since school ended back in May and Small Jay graduated from eighth grade. Forlornly, Ellie wondered when it would fully dawn on Small Jay that he really didn't fit in on the farm, or with his father. *Will he ever?*

What could she do to help him become stronger, if not smarter? Was there anything? Thus far, not a single medicinal tea or herbal concoction had healed his mind, or the unique way he perceived his life and surroundings. Truth be told, Jake was a special gift from the hand of almighty God, and neither Roman, nor anyone else, had the power to alter the truth of the matter.

Our lives never returned to normal after he was born, she thought, slipping down into the hard chair near the window. She'd never forgotten the look of sheer dismay on Roman's face the day their Jake came into the world. Quickly, they both had realized something was amiss, even without the midwife saying so. Their son was born alive, but he'd held on by an unraveling thread, not taking his first breath quickly enough or wailing like healthy newborns. And oh, the frighteningly sallow color of his tiny angelic face.

She recalled their son's babyhood, the odd way his eyes were always wide open when nursing, or how difficult it was for him to sit up without support, long past the time when most babies' backs were strong. Jake had walked late, too, not till he was nearly twenty months old. And when he had cried, it sounded like a bleating lamb.

With all of her heart, Ellie had hoped Small Jay had not retained a mental record of her and Roman's tentative looks in those early days . . . nor the choked words uttered by his father. Just how many memories were locked away in Small Jay's innocent mind before he could even speak?

Yet, what of now and the daily disappointment Roman scarcely concealed from their son? Oh, what Ellie wouldn't give for her husband to be proud of this dear boy who believed his father walked on water.

Ellie jerked to attention when she heard a knock at the back door. She guessed it wasn't one of Roman's brothers. No, the menfolk who helped her husband typically came and went as they pleased, tracking into her tidy kitchen for hot coffee or cocoa in the wintertime, and homemade root beer or iced meadow tea the rest of the year. She'd quickly learned as a young bride that this was the way things would be, and she'd trained her daughters, Dorcas, Julia, and Sally—twelve, ten, and seven, respectively—to help with the constant redding up. Ellie so disliked a messy house.

Making her way to the back door, she perked up to see their neighbor's granddaughter. There was no getting around the fact that Marlena Wenger could turn any man's head. She was tall and willowy, truly beautiful when she smiled, a hint of what looked like scattered sunbeams in her light brown hair. "Hullo, Marlena! You never have to knock," Ellie said, pushing the door open, pleased for the company. "*Kumme* in for a spell, won't ya?"

"*Denki.*" The young woman gave her a winning smile and offered a wrapped loaf of bread. "Mammi's out of eggs. And I brought you something."

Ellie looked at the warm bread in her hand and thanked her. "Ain't you nice."

"It's the raisin bread you enjoyed last time," Marlena said, following her into the kitchen.

"*Meindscht sell noch?*—Do you still remember that?"

Marlena nodded. "It's right moist, too. Saw to that myself."

"Let's have ourselves a buttered slice," Ellie remarked, placing the loaf of bread on the counter and opening the utensil drawer for a knife. "What do ya say?"

"I shouldn't stay long. . . ."

"Your grandma won't mind, will she?" Ellie said, feeling the urge to go overboard to welcome her. "I can pour you some cold meadow tea if you'd like."

"*Denki.* Tea's fine."

"*Gut*, then, we'll have us a chat." Ellie sliced the warm raisin bread, which smelled heavenly. The luscious aroma brought back memories of her girlhood visits to her maternal grandmother, half a mile away.

"We've seen Small Jay out walkin' lately."

Ellie glanced toward the window. "Have yous noticed how he always heads in the same direction, down the road toward the old Brownstown Mill and the bridge?" She placed the bread slices on an oval plate and carried it to the table, setting it near Marlena. "I have to say it worries me a bit. But at his age, I need to give him what freedom I can." She sighed. "How's your Mammi doin' these days? I need to go an' visit her again soon."

"She'd really like that." The young woman stopped talking, glancing toward the pond out the window.

"Is there anything I can do for her?"

Marlena shook her head slowly. "Not sure there's anything

that'll heal her broken heart, ya know. She still
she'll get along without my Dawdi."

"*Nee* . . . can't imagine how she must feel."

"Seems to me she's waiting to . . . you know . ...g for
Dawdi . . . to see him again."

Ellie nodded and felt sorry for her neighbor. "Maybe in
time, she'll feel more like herself." But she really wondered,
knowing Janice Martin's fondness for her late husband.

She poured some meadow tea for Marlena and then for
herself at the table before sitting down, aware of the empty
chair at the head, where Roman always sat. The thought
momentarily crossed her mind that she might've sat next to
Marlena for their visit. But she changed her mind right quick,
imagining Roman's reaction if he unexpectedly happened
indoors. After all, it wasn't too long ago that Marlena had
switched head coverings to the Beachy Amish *Kapp. Roman
frowns upon such higher church folk*, she thought.

"Mammi Janice said something 'bout you having a sewing
class in your *Dawdi Haus* next door," Marlena said. "Is that
right?"

"Well, it's quilting on Wednesday mornings and needlepoint
on Fridays. Maybe you'd like to join us."

"*Denki*, I'll see if I can get all my work done."

"Just come whenever you can. How's that?"

They finished their tea and Ellie ended up savoring two
slices of Marlena's delicious bread, spread with more butter
than necessary, but it wasn't every day she had a chance to
sit and catch her breath like this.

"Are your girls away today?" Marlena asked after thanking
her for the tea and getting up.

"They're over helping their *Aendi* weed the family vegetable garden this morning—my sister down the road and around the corner. She lives in one of the houses near the old mill."

"It's been a while since I've seen that mill," Marlena admitted. "It's real perty with all of those windows, some of 'em gabled. Must be nice and light inside."

Ellie agreed, and after Marlena paid her for the eggs, Ellie walked her out the back door and down the porch steps. She said good-bye and stood there, observing the lovely young woman head for the pastureland between the house and the willow grove. "*Kumme* again soon," she called after her, wondering if Marlena would show up for the morning classes.

A gem of a girl, thought Ellie as she turned toward the house. To think Marlena had left her serious beau behind to come help her grandmother. Although Ellie had heard some gossip at a canning bee last week that Marlena's parents were hoping she'd forget about her boyfriend and turn her back on the Old Order Amish for good.

I sure hope not, Ellie thought.

⁓ ℰ

Marlena was certain Mammi would be restless by now, wondering how long before she'd return. *My grandmother talks confidently, but there's such pain in her eyes.*

Picking up her pace, Marlena took into account the many chores still ahead of her. "I might've stayed too long at Ellie's," she muttered.

She hurried through the willow grove, looking about her and thinking again of Small Jay. Ellie had said his wanderings worried her sometimes, yet Marlena had no spare time to devote to keeping track of the lad, although she surely would if she could. Scanning the area thoroughly, she glanced over near the glistening pond but saw no sign of him.

Rounding the house as she came in from the east meadow, Marlena heard the phone ringing and was glad for her grandmother. Someone to talk to . . . a church friend, perhaps.

She dillydallied, going to the potting shed to sweep the floor, then taking the broom over to the gazebo to sweep that, too. Marlena recalled overhearing her father tell Mamma that, after Dawdi Tim's sudden passing, his four sons arrived at the farm, some of them mighty upset. Apparently, Dawdi had made some unwise business decisions in recent years, so his boys had swooped in and hauled away hundreds of hens and every last one of the nanny goats, and the tractor, too, selling them at auction. Thankfully, her grandfather had owned the farm and, while it was highly unusual to purchase life insurance, it was required by the bank in order to get a loan. So Mammi Janice had nary a financial worry after those debts were satisfied. And being the good steward she was, she'd rented the farmland to an Amish neighbor the Bitners knew.

Carrying the broom back to the white shed, Marlena hung it on the designated peg and made her way toward the house. "Now to pick strawberries," she said to herself.

When she turned around, she was startled to see her grandmother outdoors, moving hesitantly as she came this way. "What is it, Mammi?"

Mammi's eyes fixed on hers, and her shoulders slumped as if an unseen weight was about to crush her. "Your sister Luella's been in a car accident."

Marlena gasped. "Is she all right?"

"She's seriously injured."

Marlena's mind was reeling.

"She was rushed in an ambulance to the hospital," Mammi said, voice trembling as she placed her hand on Marlena's arm. "Honey-girl, let's go an' sit for a bit."

Pulse racing, Marlena followed to the porch, finding it hard to think, let alone to be still. Suddenly she remembered her older sister's baby, and worry squeezed her heart. "Was Angela Rose riding with her?"

"Thankfully, no. The baby was with a friend." Mammi reached down to lift the edge of her apron to her face, fanning herself. "Praise be."

More concerns came to mind. Luella's husband, Gordon Munroe, possibly didn't know any of this, and Mammi's silence surely signaled similar worries. There must be a way to contact him through various military channels, but Marlena didn't know anything about that process or how long it might take.

Nearby, a bee hovered over the red, white, and pink petunias. It was strange to hear the distinct sound of this lone bee, Marlena thought, her heart elsewhere.

"Your aunt Becky is planning to bring the baby here tomorrow."

It was no surprise that her father's youngest sister would step in to help, but . . .

"*Here?*" Marlena sputtered.

Mammi put her hands to her plump cheeks and moaned softly. "Gordon's parents left for a two-week Mediterranean cruise, so they're out of reach."

They sat quietly for a time until Marlena spoke at last, struggling for the words. "Mammi, will Luella be okay?"

Mammi lowered her head for a moment and sighed deeply. When she lifted her eyes again, there were noticeable tears.

Even so, she said quietly, "Let's hold our dear Lord's hand in faithful trust, my dear girl. That's all I know to do."

Marlena nodded, yet it wasn't always easy to trust when things looked so bleak. Oh, she hoped her parents were with Luella at the hospital right now.

Mammi looked over at her, her gaze tender as she blinked back tears.

Aunt Becky's bringing the baby to me. Marlena couldn't fathom why Mamma wouldn't take her. She was unable to decipher such news. "I guess I'm the one they want to take care of Angela Rose," she said in a near whisper.

"Just till Luella's better." Mammi reached for an embroidered hankie from her apron pocket and dabbed at her blue eyes. "Your mother has her hands full with your younger siblings and all the summer canning and whatnot. You know that, dear."

Oh, she knew. And she wouldn't shirk her duty in caring for the little one, even though she'd only laid eyes on the baby once, a few days after Angela Rose was born. Her fancy niece had been dressed in a tiny pink outfit complete with bows. Heaven knew five-month-old Angela Rose needed someone to tend to her.

"Where can we get a crib by tomorrow?" Marlena said, resigning herself to doing what she must as they rose and headed inside to resume their morning chores.

My poor sister!

CHAPTER 3

*S*mall Jay tiptoed, mimicking Sassy as he moved along the road, stepping around a pothole, the cat's leash slack. He'd purchased the bright red leash at Joe Stoltzfus's general store with the coins that jingled in his metal bank, after he'd pried the seal from the base of it. He didn't remember how long ago that was, but he'd had it in his mind for the longest time that there must be a way to keep track of Sassy when he took her outside.

If I could just grow a few more inches . . . maybe then Dat would let me help, he thought. *Someday, when I'm stronger and smarter.*

He swung a long stick in slow circles over his head with his free hand, pretending he could stir up those fluffy white clouds. Why did they sometimes look nearly close enough to touch, especially just after dawn?

"Deacon . . . bishop . . . preacher . . . preacher," he chanted happily in *Deitsch* as he looked over the fields to the farmhouses ahead. It was curious, really, how all the ministers in their church district lived neighbors to each other. He imagined what it'd be like for all four men to go hunting in the fall, coming together for something other than the house meetings every other Sunday.

Small Jay had, in fact, seen the deacon and one of the preachers over at Joe's General Store, not chewing the fat but chewing on black licorice. *Getting it on their beards*, he remembered with a grimace.

He considered what he'd once overheard their old deacon telling his mother. *"Everyone has a purpose in life. A task only he can do."*

Mamma had started to cry, and Small Jay had backed out of the room, feeling sorry for her, wondering why she was so upset. That night he'd prayed, *"Help Mamma not to feel so sad. Make her as happy as I am when Sassy's lickin' my bare toes!"*

"Deacon . . . bishop . . . preacher . . . preacher," he repeated, looking down at Sassy, wondering how long before her little legs and paws would give out. *Might need me to carry you*, he thought, remembering the afternoon his father had pulled him in a wagon over to the pond and showed him how to skip stones. He smiled at the distant memory, wishing he might have another day like that with Dat.

Sassy began to meow; it sounded like crying. He picked her up and snuggled her under his chin. It was time to have a look-see, make sure that stray black-and-white border collie he'd seen down the way wasn't standing out in the road again, where the horses and buggies came tearing down the hill.

He knew the most dangerous spot was right close to where the road met up with the old one-lane bridge spanning Conestoga Creek, before the road came to a T on the other side of the bridge. One turn, to the right, took you past a cemetery on a hilly slope. The other way, to the left, took you toward Brownstown and Joe's wonderful-*gut* store. Small Jay knew that much, for sure, but little else when it came to directions and where roads went. The fastest way for him to get to the store was hitching up his father's pony to the little cart, which he'd done since second grade at the one-room schoolhouse. His mouth watered at the thought of the store's candied caramel apples and jelly beans.

"I must be Joe's favorite customer," he announced, laughing, then thought how sad it was for others who didn't get free goodies. "Why does Joe give them just to me? Why do ya think, Sassy?"

She looked at him, narrowing her pretty yellow-green eyes and meowing like she understood. Small Jay couldn't help but believe she did. It was like they had their own private language.

Tired already from limping along, Small Jay wished he had brought the pony cart, now that his mind was on the Amish general store. He liked to open the front door to make the bell above it ring . . . too high for him to reach up and grab it and ring it for dear life, like he sometimes dreamed of doing. That bell had such a tempting sound. *Listen to me*, it seemed to say. Sometimes, when he didn't see Joe around or standing by the cash register, Small Jay would open the door several times in a row, simply to hear it ring.

Just then the sound of a horse and carriage, *clippity-clop*, wheels clattering against the pavement, caught his attention, and as the buggy drew closer, he knew enough to move farther onto the dirt shoulder of the road.

Glancing over his shoulder, he saw that it was his father's older brother, Uncle Jake Bitner, and waved. His namesake's long white beard was the first thing he spotted as the carriage came near. That, and the sunburned hand resting on the wide-open window.

All too suddenly, the old feeling of terror came and made him tremble—a secret worry that the hitch might break and the carriage come careening down the hill, out of control, and smash into him and Sassafras. Of course, there was a brake on the buggy, but what if the driver forgot in the midst of the fright?

Small Jay held the cat tighter, letting the leash dangle as he stepped off the roadside and waited, his heart pounding in his ears.

"Mighty fine day 'tis, ain't it, young Jake?"

"Hullo, *Onkel*," he said softly, his voice in his toes as the carriage passed by.

Just that quick, his pulse calmed and he felt better, seeing the back of the buggy make its way down the incline to where the road leveled out near the paved bridge ahead.

"All right, Sassy. Safe now." He set her down and wound the leash around his right hand, having tossed his stick somewhere but not remembering when or just where. Sassy sniffed at a patch of grass and sat down, staring at something behind the box-shaped hedge. "What's a-matter?" he whispered as her intent gaze moved from one side of the dark green hedge to the other.

Then he heard the subtle sound of a dog digging and panting from behind the leafy green wall. Right quick, Sassy arched her back and began to hiss and spit. "Oh now," he said softly, reaching down to tickle his cat under the chin. She raised her head to his touch, and he squatted down to do so longer, even though it hurt his bad leg.

Suddenly the gate between the two long hedges opened, and out sprang the border collie. The beautiful dog came right over to Sassy and sniffed, then tentatively nuzzled her nose. To Small Jay's astonishment, she nuzzled right back!

"*Ach*, never seen anything like it." Small Jay couldn't get over the instant attraction between the two. For some reason, the sight of the big dog and his own petite cat made him think of pretty Gracie Yoder, two grades younger in school last year. Gracie was the only girl who'd ever talked to him during recess. True, he was sweet on her, but he wouldn't admit it to anyone but his loyal cat. Now that he was done with school, he wouldn't get to see the soft-spoken redhead much anymore other than at Preaching service twice a month.

"You've made yourself a friend, Sassy," he said, reaching to let the dog sniff his hand, then gently petting its head. He looked down at the dog's collar and saw the oddest name: *Allegro*.

"Ain't heard that before," he said, straightening to ease the weight on his bum leg. In fact, he wasn't even sure how to say it.

As if the collie had heard something on the other side of the road, he turned away and started in that direction. When the dog crossed the road, he seemed to wait for them, panting with what looked like a smile until Sassy walked Small Jay over there to be with Allegro once again.

"Good boy, come home now!" A man with a hoarse-sounding voice was calling to the dog. He called again before he began to play a mouth organ, the sweet strains filling the air.

Lo and behold, the dog obediently scampered toward the man, who looked about the same age as Dat's twin brothers, maybe in his late fifties. Except this man wasn't a speck of Amish. He had the start of a salt-and-pepper beard and a thin, graying moustache. His mostly light brown hair was thick and wavy, unlike Small Jay's twin uncles, who were balding on the top of their heads, and his eyebrows were so thick Small Jay could see them from this distance. But what caught Small Jay's attention even more was the old pair of trousers that looked ragged on the hems, and the drab gray shirt with a black bow tie neatly tucked beneath the collar.

Bow-tie man also had a worn leather *Schnappsack* slung over his right shoulder, and he gripped it with one hand like some fancy *Englischer* women clutched their pocketbooks. The man took a step, stumbled, and then while he was trying to catch his balance, slipped and landed on his backside with a yelp.

Small Jay ran over and tried to say something, but his tongue was all tied up. The poor man was lying there while the dog licked his face, not moving until he turned to look up at Small Jay and smiled. "Slippery here."

Small Jay felt he ought to reply. "Your dog sure likes ya."

Rolling to his knees, then pulling himself up to his feet, the man brushed himself off and nodded. "It is frequently said that a dog is a man's best friend."

Unless your best friend is a cat, Small Jay thought.

Bow-tie man said good-bye, patted his dog on the head, and turned toward the pebbled lane leading to the stone mill—the large four-storied Old Brownstown Mill.

Eyeing the bridge, Small Jay walked over there, first picking up a few stones from the side of the road to toss into the creek. The sound of the *plunk* from high above, on the bridge, made him curious to know how deep the water really was.

Small Jay looked across the road toward the man with his black-and-white dog and directed Sassy to the side of the road, where *Mamm* had always taught him to walk against the traffic. *"Keep your eyes and ears wide open,"* she'd urged.

His father never told him things like that. Yet his mother had insisted this was important.

Small Jay leaned on the cement wall and turned to see where the man and the dog had gone. He was surprised to see them slip inside the abandoned mill on this side nearest the millrace.

When he leaned down to choose a few more pebbles, he noticed a white envelope caught between a bush and the edge of the bridge. "What's this?" He dropped his stones and reached for the envelope, trying to read the name and address centered there: *Dr. B. L. Calvert.* The postmark was Amsterdam, March 1958, but he could not make out the address.

Without thinking, Small Jay pulled the letter from the open envelope and began to read.

> *My dearest darling,*
>
> *I trust you and your traveling companions are doing well. What an ambitious schedule you face!*
>
> *Just this morning, while visiting in Amsterdam, I explored the Rijksmuseum, where you and I have strolled together, marveling at the Dutch Masters. Remember "The Merry Fiddler" that first took our breath away? It is so lifelike, and the violin seems to leap out of the canvas, my dear! It made me recall our passion for violin sonatas. And all the while, I counted the hours until we are reunited.*
>
> *Oh, how I wish I could be with you, but that simply isn't possible, and my prayers follow you always.*

The remainder of the letter was smudged and unreadable. Small Jay looked around to see if someone had dropped it on the way over the bridge. But he saw no one, even farther down the road.

He felt sheepish, having read as much as he had, even though he hadn't understood a few of the words. Quickly,

Small Jay pushed the letter inside the envelope again and returned it to the bushes, just like his schoolteacher had always taught the class to return things that didn't belong to them.

Distracted once more by the call of the creek, Small Jay picked up a handful of stones and hurled the first one over the bridge with all his might, thinking again of his Dat and their fun together. *So long ago.*

CHAPTER 4

arlena awakened early the next morning, her first thoughts of Luella. She knelt at the bedside and offered a silent prayer, asking the Almighty to take care of her sister. With every ounce of trust she had, Marlena tried her best to believe in divine intervention.

Solemnly, she rose to dress, then brushed her waist-length hair. She wondered if taking care of her sister's baby might not be an opportunity to show love for Luella. And to help out—to the best of her ability—as a kind and compassionate Aendi to Angela Rose. Then, surely, once her sister had recovered, they could attempt to mend their fences and forgive each other, the way God intended sisters to do.

"It's long overdue," she whispered as she threaded the twisted sides of her hair into a bun at the nape of her neck.

There was plenty to feel nervous about—an infant she'd had very little contact with was arriving today. And for just how long, she didn't know. Although Marlena had helped with her youngest sister, Rachel Ann, who was now eight years old, Marlena didn't have much experience with babies to draw from like her many female cousins back home.

She did recall the one and only time she'd held tiny Angela Rose, something akin to looking into the face of a wee angel, the bundled weight in her arms ever so light. For that brief moment, she'd experienced the feeling of being responsible for another person—*"the dearest child,"* Luella had called her baby girl.

But Marlena also remembered being glad when her sister reached to take Angela back, relieved because she wasn't sure how to calm her if she should cry. Still, Marlena had blinked away tears that day at this new little girl added to their extended family. *"Dat always wanted there to be more of us kids,"* she'd heard Luella say when they were growing up. But Mamma had been very ill during her pregnancy with Rachel Ann. The midwife had suggested, after the difficult birth, that frail little Rachel might have to be the last Wenger baby—something that was made certain a few days later, when Mamma had to undergo an emergency surgery.

Hurrying downstairs now, Marlena made a nice hot breakfast for her and Mammi—fried potatoes, dippy eggs, and slices of ham. Deep in thought, she said very little as they sat down at the table.

After the meal, Mammi softly read Psalm 24. "'The earth is the Lord's, and the fulness thereof; the world, and they that dwell therein. . . .'" She bowed her head following the reading and prayed a blessing over the day, and over Luella, too. "O Lord in heaven, we give Luella into Thy loving, wise care. We don't know all the ins and outs of her suffering, but Thou dost, dear Lord. Please be all that Luella needs this day: body, mind, and spirit. Guide the hands of the doctors and nurses in charge of her. We ask all of this in the name of Jesus, our Lord and wonderful Savior . . . and our Healer. Amen."

Since her parents joined their new church, Marlena had grown accustomed to hearing prayers similar to this said aloud. That particular issue had been one of many that caused her father to butt heads with two of the ministerial brethren in the Old Order Amish church. But all of that was between her parents and God.

Speaking to the Almighty like a close friend seems downright haughty, she thought.

When the breakfast dishes were washed and dried, Marlena rushed out to pick the day's batch of juicy red strawberries, hoping to beat the sun's intense heat. She'd slipped on her worn-out brown penny loafers to protect her bare feet, something she'd learned from Mammi Janice. Moving slowly through the patch, Marlena enjoyed the earthy smell, eager to see each new bright red appearance, cupping her hand around the vines as she went. A long garter snake slithered boldly past her, out of sight in a jiffy.

On the way back to the house, she carried the bucket brimful of glistening berries, glad to have finished the week's ironing so there was time for baking while her grandmother was in town buying a diaper pail, cloth diapers, and other baby toiletries in case her aunt happened to overlook bringing enough.

A fresh batch of shortcake is in order. In fact, she could just imagine serving the dessert with the fresh strawberries—topped high with whipped cream—to Aunt Becky Wenger Blank, who must have recently learned to drive, since she was bringing Luella's baby on her own from Mifflinburg.

Will she stay the night, too?

While washing the berries, Marlena decided it was a good idea to freeze the excess, since there would be plenty more in the days to come for strawberry jam. *Lord willing.*

Just as she'd finished putting the shortcake batter into the belly of the cookstove, the phone rang. Since Mammi was still away, Marlena hurried to reach for the black wall telephone. "Martin residence."

"Marlena . . . hullo. It's Nat."

Her heart did a leap, and she grinned into the receiver. "Oh, is it ever nice to hear from you!" She'd never heard Nat's voice this way, and she quite liked it.

He paused, then continued. "Listen, I called because I hoped my letter to you arrived all right."

"*Jah.*"

"And . . . along with that, I wanted to say how sorry I am 'bout your sister."

"You must've heard right quick."

"Your father dropped by and asked mine for prayer," he said, sounding more serious. "Our whole family's mighty concerned."

"This means a lot." She was truly taken by his consideration. "I believe she'll recover, don't you?"

"We hope and pray the Lord will raise her up."

"*As a testimony to divine healing,*" her grandmother might have added. But that wasn't an emphasis of the Old Order church. No, the testimony of God's goodness and grace was to be seen in the lives of the People, set apart from the world in every way.

Her lip quivered at the thought of something happening to Luella. She simply could not bear it.

"I miss you, Marlena. I hope ya know."

"Miss you, too." She envisioned Nat holding the phone uneasily, there in his father's barn—this call was quite the exception. Then she went on to say that Luella's baby was coming to stay with her and Mammi. "Till Luella recovers."

"Well, the baby will have plenty of love there, I'm sure."

They said a few faltering good-byes, and it was all she could do to relinquish the telephone, staring at it in disbelief as she hung up.

Nat actually called!

Oh, if only the summer might fly by. She imagined what it might be like if he should come to visit, there in Brownstown. *Unlikely with his father's farm to tend.* So she couldn't get her hopes up.

Still, if nothing else, the notion of such a visit was heartening. *Nat would come to see me if he could. I just know it!*

~～ஐ

After her morning quilting class, Ellie worked in the kitchen with her older daughters and watched her son refill Sassy's bowl with fresh food. "I had seven quilters today," she remarked to the girls, wishing Marlena might have been able to come. She understood, though, having heard from Janice Martin about the impending arrival of Marlena's baby niece.

Ten-year-old Julia quit sweeping in the corner of the kitchen. "Wish I could've gone to your class," she said.

Ellie blew her middle daughter a kiss. "You can in due time, my dear."

Through the kitchen windows, Ellie could see Roman loading the hand-built wooden crib and then the mattress into the back of the market wagon. He hadn't complained about loaning it to the widow for her great-grandbaby while the baby's mother was hospitalized. Ellie shuddered at the young Mamma's plight and offered a silent prayer for a quick mending of limb and spirit. And most of all, for divine peace.

The back door slammed shut, and seven-year-old Sally flew into the kitchen, her brown eyes shining. "Dat needs some help," she declared, ready to turn and run back out.

"Doing what?" asked Ellie with a glance at Small Jay.

"Just steadyin' the crib while he drives."

Small Jay struggled to stand. "I could do *that*."

Ellie sighed, concerned. "Wait just a moment while I talk to your father."

"*Jah* . . . all right!"

His enthusiasm pained her as she went outdoors and paused by the side of the market wagon. "Roman, is this something Small Jay might do?"

Her husband must have caught the tone in her voice. Their eyes met, and he nodded, albeit reluctantly, and gave a long, exasperated sigh. "I'm willin' to give it a try."

She forced a smile. "I'll send him right out."

Back in the house, she motioned for Sally to stay inside and help her sisters.

"What'd Dat say?" Small Jay asked, eyes alight.

"Go on, son. You can help with this chore." She almost said "easy chore," but bit her lip and watched him give Sassy a pat before he began to hobble across the kitchen toward the back door. *It'll be good for him*, she thought, following to the porch. There, she urged him to tell Marlena to simply ask if there was anything else she needed. "Even if it's just extra baby clothes or blankets."

He looked *ferhoodled*. "She's gonna dress a fancy baby Plain?"

"*Nee* . . . didn't mean that. I just want her to know there are extra sleeping gowns and things over here." She was thinking of the leftover items from Sally's baby days, on hand in case Ellie herself had more children. *Maybe someday.*

Small Jay leaned hard on the porch railing, taking the steps carefully. *Always so cautious.* "You won't let Sassy loose, will ya, Mamma?"

"She'll be fine indoors. Now go an' help your father." Ellie watched him head down the petunia-lined walkway until he rounded the corner and was out of sight. *Lord, watch over him,* she prayed, recalling the last time Small Jay had tried to help after Roman reluctantly allowed it, only to suffer exhortations and criticism. Small Jay's lower lip had trembled by the time he returned, fighting back tears yet determined to satisfy his nearly impossible-to-please father. Surprisingly, it hadn't dissuaded him from other attempts.

Ellie shook away the memory and returned to the kitchen, where Dorcas was preparing to make strawberry preserves while Julia and young Sally lined up the one-pint canning jars on the counter.

"Someone's havin' a baby?" asked Julia, her blue eyes blinking.

Quickly, Ellie explained their neighbors' pressing need. "The crib's for Marlena Wenger's niece." More difficult was revealing the sad reason behind the infant's arrival. "We must pray for *Gott*'s help for the little one's mother."

"Oh, Mamma, maybe we can help babysit," Dorcas said. Her blond hair was smooth and shiny clean in her low bun. Today, she wore the white kerchief she'd cheerfully ironed along with a pile of clothes yesterday.

"That's thoughtful." Ellie smiled, grateful for her girls' kindly attitude toward others, including their brother. "I'm sure Marlena will be happy to hear it."

"If need be," Sally added, sounding a bit uncertain.

"Aw, sweetie, you're our baby here," Ellie said, smiling at her youngest.

No need for envy, dear one.

Right away, Marlena spotted the red leash hanging from Small Jay's pocket as he stood with his hands folded there in the back of the market wagon. He looked downright timid while his father removed the sturdy maple crib.

I'm surprised Roman's boy came along, Marlena thought, noticing that Sassafras was missing. It seemed mighty strange, since Small Jay took his cat nearly everywhere.

Small Jay spotted her watching from the front step and waved slowly, offering a hesitant smile. Then, just that quick, he gingerly lowered himself back down in the market wagon, one leg stretched out. She hadn't said more than a few words to him since she'd arrived at her grandmother's for the summer, but when the moment was right, she would. Today the boy was clearly lost in the muddle of things, and she felt sorry for him.

Roman Bitner carried the crib into the house and set it up in her bedroom, on the far wall away from the windows, the ideal spot. She thanked him as he went to get the mattress, which he took time to carry inside and place in the crib before going on his way.

Back outside in the driveway, Marlena caught Small Jay's eye and waved good-bye. He opened his mouth as if he might call something out to her but then shook his head and frowned instead.

Is he afraid he'll fall again? She remembered hearing he'd tumbled off the back of the wagon some time ago; Mammi hadn't been worried, though, saying he'd just gotten a goose egg on his head. Still, Marlena was a bit shocked to see him sitting in the open wagon, especially because he seemed somewhat anxious. *At least he's older now.*

~~~⁀ₑ☉

Aunt Becky's expression was somber when she arrived with Luella's baby later that morning. She carried Angela Rose in from the car in a large wicker basket and set it down gently on the kitchen table. Despite having the crib all made up and hoping she was ready for this responsibility, Marlena felt jittery inside. *I'm scared to death!*

Mammi greeted Becky. "How was the drive here?" Mammi asked, going over to peer down at Angela Rose there on the table.

"Well, the Lord saw fit to let her sleep nearly all the way. A real blessing, considerin' there's only one of me, and both my hands were on the wheel."

Marlena wondered if her aunt had thought to bring along a few soft toys and rattles. In awe of this baby, she watched Angela Rose wave her dimpled hands in the air from her basket while Mammi and Becky talked quietly. Looking into the blanketed little burrow, Marlena smiled down at her. From what she could determine, Angela Rose resembled Gordon. Gently, she touched the baby's forehead. "Hullo there, little one," she said, and Angela wrinkled up her face and began to cry.

"Aw, bless her heart." Aunt Becky reached in and picked her up, kissing her cheek. "She must mistake your voice for Luella's."

"Marlena *does* sound a lot like her sister," Mammi agreed as she moved closer to the pretty little thing now nestled in Aunt Becky's pudgy arms.

"Maybe Angela Rose senses she's not at home," Marlena offered, struggling with a mixture of emotions.

Aunt Becky jostled her tenderly. "She prob'ly needs her diaper changed more than anything." She clucked softly at the baby.

Mammi fixed her gaze on the infant—her own great-grandchild, though Angela looked very English in her pink sleeper.

"I'll go and unload the rest of the things from the car," Marlena offered as Aunt Becky and Mammi took Angela Rose into the next room to be changed.

Marlena was glad to help in this way, needing some time to let things sink in. It was beyond her how all this could possibly work out—adding the care of an infant to her daily routine. Fortunately, it would just be until Luella returned home from the hospital and was stronger.

No more than a couple weeks, surely.

She could hear Aunt Becky and Mammi talking together, Aunt Becky's voice, especially, drifting through the open window on this side of the house. "If she even pulls through, Luella could very well be paralyzed . . . might never be able to hold her precious darlin' again."

Marlena caught her breath. *If she pulls through?* She'd had no idea her sister's injuries were so severe. *Luella simply has to get better. She must!*

She pressed her lips together, refusing to get teary-eyed. *Please, God, let Luella be all right, for her sake, and for her husband's and baby's,* she prayed silently, hoping the Almighty wouldn't see this as a selfish prayer. She sighed, closed the car door, and carried the suitcase into the house.

CHAPTER 5

Marlena was aware of an undertow of apprehension as she sliced the strawberry shortcake for the noon meal, which Mammi insisted Becky stay and eat with them. Her hopes for raising their spirits with the mouth-watering dessert were hollow now, because in the space of a few heartbeats, everything had changed with Aunt Becky's ominous words about Luella.

Presently, Aunt Becky held Angela Rose on her lap, but when she offered a warm bottle, the petite rosebud lips quivered and curved downward. "She's used to bein' nursed, so no wonder she's upset," Aunt Becky said, handing the baby to Marlena. "See if she'll take it from you, just maybe."

Hoping her own anxiety wouldn't make things worse, Marlena teased the baby gently with the bottle's nipple, dripping the warm formula on her lips. Angela let out a whimper that quickly turned to sobbing, as if her tiny heart were breaking.

"*Ach*, she must want her mother," said Mammi, her voice ever so tender.

Concerned, Marlena sighed. She'd heard of some babies rejecting the bottle when their mother was ready to wean. But this?

What if Angela Rose keeps refusing? What'll I do?

Before Aunt Becky kissed little Angela Rose good-bye later on the back porch, she took time to make over her, stroking her round little head. It was clearly difficult for her to leave, and Marlena, noticing the attachment, couldn't help but wonder how often Aunt Becky had seen Luella's baby prior to the accident.

After the car backed out of the driveway and her aunt was on her way to Mifflinburg, Marlena realized they were in need of a playpen to keep Angela Rose safe during time spent cooking, cleaning up the kitchen, and other chores, though at least the little one wasn't crawling yet. "Since we don't know how long she'll be here, maybe it's best we just borrow a couple more items from the neighbors," Marlena suggested.

"Well, dear, I think it's wise for us—for you—to be prepared to care for Angela for more than a few weeks." Her grandmother's blue eyes clouded with tears, and when she looked away, Mammi's shoulders heaved.

"Don't worry, Mammi," she whispered, though she herself felt as worried as she'd ever been.

Mammi nodded her head before she was able to speak. "Luella's truly blessed to have a sister like you."

"Hope I can live up to that." Marlena recalled what Aunt Becky had said. She tightened her jaw and finished washing dishes from the noon meal, looking now and then at Angela Rose, who lay upon several layers of blankets on the kitchen floor, holding a white rattle with a small pink rose on the handle.

Poor little thing has no idea what's going on. Marlena's breath caught in her throat. *How long before she'll bond with me?*

~ ❧

"Did ya remember to tell Marlena what I said?" Ellie asked her son when he walked into the kitchen before supper. He'd made himself scarce after the noon meal, and she hadn't had a moment alone with him to ask about the morning errand.

Small Jay's chest rose and fell repeatedly, like he guessed he was in trouble. "*Ach,* Mamma, I . . . wanted to, but . . ." His eyes darted toward his cat.

She let it drop. Certain things affected Small Jay; things they couldn't really pinpoint. Anything unpredictable could make him freeze up or fall quiet.

Through the back door, she saw Roman walking to the barn, wearing his new straw hat, his strong arms swinging. This wasn't the time to quiz him on what might have set off their son. Besides, it was of no consequence that Small Jay hadn't told Marlena of her willingness to help—Ellie would just have to take herself over to Janice Martin's house after supper to see if there was anything more she could do.

"I wanna take Sassy for a walk," Small Jay announced, pulling the leash out of his trousers pocket, where a couple of cookies also peeked out.

"The meal will be ready in a jiffy," she said, looking at him from her spot at the hot stove. She wiped her sweaty brow with her forearm.

"Won't take long, Mamma. All right?"

"Jake, you *heard* me. Just stay put for now."

He withdrew like he'd been struck. He began to shake his head, most likely out of disappointment. "All right, Mamma."

But something had already begun to happen inside him. Small Jay's pale blue eyes looked dazed, almost vacant. He was sliding into his thick shell, where he often stayed for days, not speaking to a soul.

And I caused it, she thought sadly, at a loss now. She said no more as he reached for his cat and slipped into the next room, on his way to the front of the house. He caressed Sassy as he went to sit at the window with his nose pressed against the pane, far, far away in his safe and bubble-like world.

Ellie was glad she hadn't mentioned those cookies he'd snuck out of the cookie jar sometime earlier. *No wonder he's not hungry.*

Angela Rose's sobs turned to outright wailing later when Marlena picked her up and carried her to the table to sit down for supper. She tried to figure out how to eat with a baby in her arms. "We need a high chair, *jah?*" she said, lightly patting Angela Rose, whom she held up to her shoulder. But there was no point in trying to make small talk with Mammi. Nothing seemed to stop the baby from screaming.

Mammi frowned at the commotion across the table. "She's definitely hungry, and very upset."

"Maybe it's just me." Marlena kissed the top of Angela's silky little head. "I must remind her of Luella, poor thing."

"Here, let me try." Mammi held out her hands and took the baby.

Her grandmother looked so drained. Marlena didn't want to let her take responsibility for feeding Angela Rose. At least not during supper. Besides, there was already too much sadness in Mammi's heart without her having to endure a wailing baby at the table. *Or anytime.*

Angela Rose remained inconsolable despite Mammi's cuddling her. After a time, though, with Mammi's gentle persistence, she gave in and began to suckle, and even Mammi's expression was one of great relief. The peace of the house was definitely at stake.

Once she'd emptied her bottle, Angela Rose was quite content but still blinking her little eyes, wide-awake. Marlena took her from Mammi and rose from the table to walk out to the porch. She patted her niece's tiny back as she prayed silently, stepping out in faith like her grandmother for the second time today. *O Lord, please bring comfort to this little one . . . and healing to her Mamma.*

~~ᥱᴑ

The next time Ellie craned her neck toward the front room, she was relieved to see Small Jay rolling around on the hardwood floor, playing with Sassy, who pawed at him mischievously.

Jah, gut. She felt a measure of relief. The dear boy had such few pleasures.

When it was suppertime, the girls helped set the table while Ellie carried over the succulent pot roast, tender carrots and mashed potatoes, and the large bowl of chow chow. The girls, along with Roman, kept the conversation going after the first unspoken table blessing. Small Jay, however, made not a peep, sitting straight as can be on the bench.

"Son, where did ya plan to go later?" she asked.

"Just to the old mill," he replied quickly.

Roman raised his head, his sunburned face stern. "That far?"

"There's a perty white dog over there . . . named Allegro."

"How do ya know his name?"

All eyes were on Small Jay.

"It's on his collar. And he's got himself an owner who lives in the mill."

Roman chuckled. "The Brownstown Mill's empty, son. Has been for years."

Ellie cringed and asked Julia to pass the potatoes, hoping to distract her husband from further problematic declarations. Things that might send Small Jay back into wherever he went in his mind, especially at mealtime or whenever there were more people about.

"Ain't empty now," Small Jay said softly.

"You're wrong on that, son." Roman was firm. "Furthermore, it's too far to go after supper."

"But it's still light out." Small Jay glanced toward the window, his chin jutted out much like his father's own.

Oh dear. Ellie looked at her girls, all lined up on the bench across from her, eating politely while casting furtive glances at their brother, then their father—like watching a Ping-Pong match. *Their stomachs will pinch up,* she thought, recalling her own mother's admonition when Ellie was but a child that tension impaired digestion.

"How long it stays light this time of year is not the issue," Roman insisted. He glanced at Ellie, then back at Small Jay. "Obedience is what I'm askin' for."

Ellie opened her mouth to circumvent a scene, but their son spoke up first.

"I'll be careful, Dat. Just ask Uncle Jake . . . he saw me near there yesterday."

"That's enough now," Roman said, practically rising to a stand from his chair. "I'll have no more back talk."

Small Jay lowered his head.

Roman reached for another helping of potatoes and gravy, saying no more, and Ellie unclenched her hands, taking a breath. She'd never seen Small Jay so adamant about anything.

CHAPTER 6

*M*arlena wasn't content to see Mammi washing even a few dirty dishes, weary as she surely was. But what could she do, besides walk the length of the house and back with Luella's baby in her arms? Angela Rose was still whimpering in spite of taking six ounces of formula and a small bowl of rice cereal, too.

Wanting to spare her grandmother's sensitive ears, Marlena headed outdoors through the walkways that lined the flower beds, talking softly to her niece, trying to remember the many soothing songs her mother had sung to her when she was little.

While strolling through the front lawn near the tall purple martin birdhouse, Marlena happened to see Ellie's nephew Luke Mast and his younger sister, Sarah, as well as another pretty young woman out riding in the family carriage. They waved cordially, and Marlena waved back, still jostling the fussy baby.

Then she spotted Small Jay walking slowly along the dirt shoulder, near the knee-high grass, going the opposite direction. She couldn't help but smile when Luke stopped to kindly offer a ride. The younger boy stooped to pick up his cat, handing Sassy to Luke at the reins before shuffling around to the opposite side of the buggy and stepping inside ever so carefully.

When they were on their way, Marlena realized Angela Rose had gone limp in her arms and was sound asleep at last, one arm dangling. Holding her breath, Marlena headed in through the front door and carried her niece directly upstairs and placed her gently in the crib. She stared down at the perfect little girl, and her heart went out to her, so much so that she felt nearly compelled to reach down and pick her back up, just to hold her near.

But she changed her mind, given how tired Angela Rose was. Just these few minutes upstairs had made her realize how very warm it was inside, and she had second thoughts about having the crib up there at all. She remembered the door at the end of the hall and went to open it, hoping for plentiful breezes to cool things off, if only for the little tyke's much needed rest. *Mammi's, too, eventually.*

Marlena stood in the second-floor doorway and struggled with her memories of sitting on this balcony with her grandfather. What would he think if he could see her now—trying to care for his great-grandbaby and failing so? Would he have words of wisdom? She remembered he'd said it wasn't the need for more hours in a day that posed a problem for most folk. It was the need for more gratitude. *"Thankfulness is the key."*

He'd say I should be grateful to have Luella's baby thrust upon me.

From where Marlena stood, Ellie Bitner came into view across the rented field. Stepping back from the upstairs door,

Marlena hurried to look in on Angela Rose once again before dashing downstairs, elated their neighbor was coming to visit. *I need all the pointers I can get!*

~~⁓⁓

"Has your cat bagged any birds lately?" Luke Mast asked Small Jay as they rode down the sloping narrow road toward the mill.

"Sassy eats cat food," Small Jay reminded him.

"And what 'bout Shredder, king of naughty barn cats?" Luke glanced at Small Jay, grinning to beat the band. "Has he straightened up yet?"

"*Ach*, he's always in trouble with Mamma." Small Jay didn't know if it was all right to say why, but he went ahead anyway. It was always curious to see folk react to how Shredder—their giant black barn cat with white paws—sometimes got into the outhouse and tore up the toilet paper. Nearly once a week it happened. Sometimes more often. However, Small Jay knew he should be careful whom he told this to, because he'd heard of certain cats mysteriously disappearing.

Luke tapped his wide-brimmed straw hat and laughed. "So *that's* how he got his name."

Sarah sat quietly, not saying a word, though Small Jay noticed her give Luke a couple of sideways glances. The other girl didn't seem to pay much attention.

"Does Shredder have any offspring?" asked Luke.

"Six more kittens, just last month." Small Jay paused. Then, thinking maybe Luke wanted a scary-looking black cat of his own, he went ahead. "I'm sure Dat'll be glad to share 'em."

Sarah laughed softly under her breath.

"*Nee*, we have enough mouse chasers in our barn," Luke

said, pushing his straw hat down. "But if we ever run out, I know where to come callin', ain't?"

Small Jay nodded. He liked Luke's way of talking.

The mill was coming up on the left. "Here's where I get out," Small Jay said as he picked up the limp ball of fur from his lap. "Can ya hold Sassy for me?" He lifted her over to Luke.

"Take your time, now," Luke said, poking Sarah.

But Small Jay was no dummy. Luke was prompting his sister to speak to Small Jay, although coming from a preacher's son, Small Jay guessed it was to be expected. Most folk seemed mighty anxious around him, like they couldn't wait to get on their way. Not Luke, though. Luke Mast talked with him as easily as he would any other fourteen-year-old boy.

"*Denki.*" Small Jay stood beside the buggy while Sassy got handed first to Sarah, then over to him. "*Denki,*" he said again, not sure what else to say.

"Be careful walkin' home, won't ya?" Sarah offered.

Sarah's dainty voice reminded him of Gracie's. Nodding, he recalled the first time Gracie had ever spoken to him. It had been a couple of years ago, in the wintertime, when there were Jack Frost designs on the schoolhouse windows. As the children were bundling up to go out for recess, she'd said just two words: "*Hullo, Jake.*" Even now, knowing she'd used his given name, not his nickname, made him secretly smile.

He waited for Luke's carriage to move forward, then stooped to snap the leash onto Sassy's collar. "Come along, nice kitty," he said, going across to the left side of the road, looking for Allegro.

But there was no sign of the fluffy collie.

He sighed and wondered if he'd risked the trip to the mill for nothing. Dat wouldn't be happy if he knew.

Why's my father always mad at me? The thought zinged through his mind. "Will he ever let me work with him?" he muttered aloud, careful not to move his lips very much when he talked to himself. Eight long years of school had taught him that trick. No sense inviting more attention than what came naturally during the course of a day. Things could be hard enough, yet as he moved through the grades, his skin had gotten thicker, or so he liked to think.

He felt the sun's warm rays on his shoulders as he wandered toward the bridge. And as he stumbled along, a new idea presented itself—as before, he could toss stones into the water below, but today he would make a wish on each stone. And he knew for certain what one wish would be.

The tall grasses along the creek bank nearly concealed the many wild ferns. Small Jay had a bird's-eye view from the bridge, and he peered downward, enthralled by the different hues of greenery. Uncle Jake once said that the reason the Good Lord chose green for the earth was due to its restful nature. Same for the blue of the sky. *"Cool colors,"* his uncle had said, like an artist. Something Small Jay thought *he'd* like to be, if he couldn't be a farmer or a worker.

He caught a whiff of smoke in the breeze and turned to see Allegro's owner sitting on a wide tree stump over near the tailrace. "Let's go an' have a look-see," he muttered to Sassy and limped forward.

He made his way across the grassy patch and called to the man. "Hullo there." Small Jay stood back a bit to determine if he was welcome or not.

"My fine young friend!" The man had on the same dark trousers and gray shirt with the black bow tie. The big brown shoulder bag with its belt-like closure was at his side.

"My cat's come to visit your dog," Small Jay said.

Allegro must have missed Sassy, too, because the collie had already come over to carry out his sniffing routine, same as yesterday.

Bow-tie man chuckled. "I see what you mean, young man."

Sassy purred and rubbed her nose against Allegro's.

"They must not know that one of 'em is a dog and the other's a cat," Small Jay said, pointing and grinning.

"Would you care to join me for dinner?" the man asked, clutching his shoulder satchel. "I'm cooking hot dogs."

"Supper, ya mean?"

"Dinner denotes the evening meal where I live."

"Where's that?"

Just that quick, the light went out of the man's eyes. "Now that you ask, I'm afraid I can't tell you. I mean . . . I don't know." He muttered something under his breath and shook his head. "I apologize for this lapse of memory—mine comes and goes like the hummingbirds over there." He motioned toward three large butterfly bushes with profuse blossoms that attracted both bees and hummingbirds.

"I brought you some cookies. Homemade oatmeal and raisin."

The man's eyes brightened. "Thank you kindly."

Is he lost? Small Jay wondered. "Are ya stayin' in this mill?"

"I am."

"There's a bed in there?"

The man shook his head. "I sleep on the floor. It may not seem like much, but I'm thankful to have located this shelter."

"But . . . on a hard floor?"

"Well, I purchased a blanket at the small store up the road, so I fold it to create a pallet of sorts."

"From Joe's store?" Small Jay's heart sped up at the mention. "Did ya hitchhike there?"

"Thumbed my way . . . similar to how I arrived at the bus station a few nights ago, I guess it was."

"So you've been here less than a week." Small Jay felt mighty proud of himself, figuring this out. But he wouldn't be boastful— his father often read from the Good Book about the importance of being meek.

"Say, now, you're one bright young man. Thank you for jiggling my memory." The man smiled and opened his shoulder bag, removed a small white notepad and pencil, and jotted something down. "These pages are my memory bank." He held up the notepad. "There are more notebooks inside." He bobbed his head toward the mill. "Along with a few other things . . . including two changes of clothes I had the presence of mind to pack."

Small Jay wouldn't say what he was thinking: This here bow-tie man was a person without a home. He was also someone who had trouble remembering important things, same as the bishop's elderly brother, who'd supposedly lost his mind . . . or so the People sadly whispered. But *that* man was Amish and lived with his family, who looked after him. Not so this man, unless he had a handful of folk he was hiding away inside the mill there.

"I'm Jake Bitner," he said boldly and offered his small hand to the man whose own hand was surprisingly smooth, like the surface of vanilla pudding. "My kin call me Small Jay, 'cause I won't grow much taller than what ya see now." He patted his scrawny chest and noticed a smile creep into the corners of the man's mouth.

"A considerably curious name for a person."

"My father dislikes it, tellin' the truth," he revealed, un-certain why he'd admit such a thing to a stranger.

Bow-tie man opened his notepad once again and flipped through one page after another, muttering all the while. "Somewhere it's written here in large letters, so I can see it. Yes," and in that moment, his face lit up. He drew a breath, then began to read from the page. "My name is Boston, and the sound of beautiful music eases my soul." He quickly closed the notepad and stretched out his legs. "I write what I can remember here in my paper memory bank, at least on the good days."

"Is this one of those days?" Small Jay asked, wishing he could shake his hand again to let the man know he understood. "I'll have one of those hot dogs now," he added, not quite sure he'd ever accepted earlier. "I don't s'pose ya have any catsup or mustard, do ya?"

Boston must've found this funny, because he tilted his round head back and laughed heartily. A slight breeze blew his hair across his forehead, and when the man reached up to push back the strands, he must have forgotten what he'd planned to do, since he brought the other hand up, as well, and started moving both in midair, stirring up the atmosphere. "Do you hear the music?" Boston asked, tilting his face.

"*Alsemol*—sometimes." Small Jay bit his lip. He'd never admitted this to anyone, but there were occasional melodies in his head, mostly church hymns.

The man named for a city continued to swirl the air, his smooth white hands moving in careful patterns as he hummed something mighty strange and unlike any tune the boy had heard before. "*Des grebbt mich,*" Small Jay murmured, cover-ing his ears.

CHAPTER 7

*E*llie left the house while Dorcas and her younger sisters were putting away leftovers and washing dishes.

Why was Roman so hard on Small Jay at supper? she wondered, pushing aside her foreboding as she tried to stay focused on her destination—the Martin farmhouse. As her bare feet scraped against a prickly bush, she wished for a path between the two properties. The absence of a footpath revealed what a sorry neighbor she had been to Janice Martin, and she chided herself. *But the urgency wasn't there when Timothy was alive,* she thought, excusing herself. Yet she well remembered how often through the years Janice would stop by in her car with warm desserts and other treats. "I'm embarrassed that I haven't returned the favors," Ellie whispered. Even so, then as now, Roman wasn't interested in making friends with their Mennonite neighbors— or anyone outside their more traditional Amish connections. It certainly seemed as if Roman wanted Ellie to be content at home. *Stuck, like Small Jay must feel at times.*

Momentarily bolder, she turned back to look over her shoulder at their house below. This was the farm inherited from Roman's paternal grandfather, a landscape both physical and otherwise. The land hearkened back to Roman's family's early years, and while Roman's father hadn't been bestowed it, somehow Roman had. It was a splendid place to call home. *Even on days I feel nearly suffocated,* she thought.

It was easy to see Roman's movements from where she stood. He was going back and forth from the stable to the barn and haymow. *Raascht dorum wie verrickt*—Rushing about like mad—hauling new straw into the stable for fresh bedding before nightfall.

Ellie rubbed her sore shoulder, inhaling slowly. She felt freer somehow, standing there and peering back at her cloistered life. And she wondered if this was how her married sister Orpha Mast had felt, too, prior to her and her husband's leaving the Old Order to attend the nearby New Order church. *Roman's cut off our fellowship with them, yet they're family!*

It was then Ellie noticed several long streamers of toilet paper fluttering in the wind, and white snippets all around the outhouse, used by Roman and the other men during their work-day. "That Shredder," she said, shaking her head. "What're we gonna do with him?"

Roman had threatened to take the ornery cat on a long ride some moonless night and drop him off clear out in the country, where there were plenty of field mice to eat. *He'll do it yet,* she thought.

Turning at last, she walked the rest of the way through Janice Martin's rented hayfield toward the spacious backyard, with its neatly edged grass and flower beds, and Janice's renowned kitchen gardens—lettuce flourishing, asparagus nearly done, and bean bushes billowing. There was an appealing herb garden, too, as well as the enormous strawberry patch running along the back fence, where a black crow was perched now, warily eyeing Ellie.

Shuddering at the size of the bird, she quickened her pace. She'd never liked the looks of crows; neither did Small Jay, who as a tot had often trembled visibly at the sight of a flock of them sitting on the English neighbors' telephone wires.

"Hullo, Ellie," Marlena Wenger greeted her from the large porch with an upraised hand. "It's real *gut* to see ya!"

The greeting surprised her. "*Wie geht's*, Marlena?"

"Oh, we're all right, I guess. Would ya like to sit out here, maybe?" the young woman asked. "Mammi's indoors resting while the baby sleeps."

Glad for a chance to get off her feet, she accepted. It didn't take more than a few minutes with Marlena to know the girl felt in over her head with the addition of her sister's little one. "S'posin' your *Grandmammi* prob'ly can't help out much."

Marlena shook her head. "Actually, she's better than I am at getting Angela Rose to take her bottle. Still, I wouldn't think of addin' more to her life right now; the baby's my responsibility. Besides, Mammi's arthritis has been actin' up."

"Well, if you're interested, my oldest daughter, Dorcas, would like to help babysit. Maybe you could use a mother's helper."

Marlena smiled and shrugged. "I'm not exactly a mother, but *jah* . . . that'd be nice."

Ellie named off the other children Dorcas had cared for in the last two years, which seemed to bring a relieved expression to Marlena's face. "Not for pay, mind you."

"That's awful nice. Really 'tis. And I might just take her up on it, too. Perhaps Saturday morning, when Mammi and I go to market."

"Should be fine."

"*Des gut*, then. Please tell Dorcas thank you." Marlena paused and glanced at the sky. "I wonder how long to let Angela Rose sleep," she said. "Aunt Becky mentioned she slept the whole way here, so that's two hours already."

"Well, most babies that age need two *gut* naps a day. You'll know by her cry when it's time for feeding—usually between four and five hours for bottle-fed babies, at least at her age. She'll wake before then unless she's real tuckered out . . . and she just might be that."

"I'm sure it'll all come back quickly," Marlena said. "I helped Mamma with Rachel Ann quite a lot during those earlier years, though she hardly ever had a bottle."

Ellie said she'd assumed as much. Most older daughters helped their mothers with the babies. "But just as important as all the physical care is the loving. Don't forget," she added.

"Well, the odd thing is, this one pulls away." Marlena was clearly uneasy. "She seems to sense that I'm not her Mamma."

Ellie patted Marlena's arm. "The wee one's mother is your sister, ain't so?"

Marlena said she was. "Ya know, my grandmother thinks that might be the problem—Angela Rose misses her mother even more when she hears my voice."

"Then the two of you must sound very similar."

"True." Marlena looked wistful at that, and Ellie supposed she must be thinking of her sister Luella. It had been years since Ellie had seen the oldest Wenger girl; Luella hadn't dropped by Ellie's for visits like her younger siblings.

"Now . . . what else can I share with you?" Ellie asked.

"You've already helped so much, loaning the crib and all."

"I'm thinkin' a playpen and even a high chair might come in handy, too, ain't so?"

Marlena's eyes brightened with tears, and the dear girl nodded her head silently, unable to articulate her appreciation.

Ellie knew better than to say that Roman would be over later this evening or tomorrow morning, for that matter. There was no asking him to do more than he already had. After all, her husband was a busy farmer, or so she'd just have to let Marlena think when Ellie herself showed up tomorrow with the needed items. Dorcas and Julia could help her load things in the back of the family carriage. *If I have to make two trips, I will.*

On the walk home past the willow grove, Ellie enjoyed the soft wind and the color of the evening sky and reminisced about the day Roman had first asked to court her, when they were *Youngie*. She'd sensed his surprising timidity right away but found it endearing. Soon, they began to enjoy each other's company, attending Sunday-night Singings and parent-sponsored activities and extra-long rides in his open black buggy. In only a few months, they were planning their future, yearning to be married.

Folding her arms, Ellie was careful where she stepped. Ah, those early days of their love—she relished every detail. Why, she even recalled where Roman had stood to ask her to ride with him that first time after the cornhusking in the deacon's barn. He'd worn some pleasant-smelling cologne, a fragrance he'd worn every one of their nighttime dates, a mere five months.

She picked her way down through the trees, keeping their house in view, remembering how thoroughly happy she'd been when she'd fallen in love with Roman Bitner. Her bliss continued to their wedding day and beyond, until the night she'd birthed Jake and witnessed the displeasure on her husband's face. His disappointment had squelched her joy like water poured on flames.

Trying now to shake off her anguish over the lasting strain between herself and Roman, Ellie noticed Small Jay walking this way with his cat. Painstakingly, he inched toward the lane that led to the house.

He defied his father. . . . She was sorry this was her first thought upon seeing her son. Goodness, it would never do for Roman to discover him returning this close to twilight. In that moment, she realized that she, too, had disregarded her husband's wishes by going up to see Marlena Wenger.

Slowing her pace to time her arrival after their son's, Ellie sighed heavily. Her sadness was deep in her bones these days, one of the reasons she'd started quilting and needle-point classes for the young women in the neighborhood. She needed to focus on others and forget, somehow, the things that weighed down her spirit. To attract students, she'd even put up a handmade sign on the community bulletin board at Joe's General Store.

As Small Jay crept to the back porch and up the steps, paus-ing at each step, she held her breath. Their boy struggled to get around, yet he was determined to be a help to his father. *A father who doesn't want his disabled son's assistance.* She didn't know what broke her heart more.

Slowly, she counted to one hundred in *Deitsch*, then began to move through the grass and around the pond's southern edge. Her pulse quickened as she saw Roman leaning his full weight into the barn door to shove it closed.

At least she was this close to the house and not just coming down from the pond. Maybe he wouldn't put together where she'd been. "Would ya like some homemade ice cream?" she asked, hoping to set his mind on something other than encountering her there.

"Got some left from yesterday?" he asked, walking quickly toward the backyard.

"If the girls haven't eaten it."

"While you were gone from the house, ya mean?"

She pursed her lips.

"Ellie, what's your attraction to the world, anyway?" Roman raised his eyes toward the Martin farm.

"That's never crossed my mind," she replied quickly. "Marlena's a Plain girl and sweet as vanilla pie."

"Well, she ain't our kind of Amish . . . raised in the Old Order church, sure, but attending the Mennonite meetinghouse with her Mammi and wearin' the Beachy garb. What's a body to think?"

"Just wanted to be neighborly, checkin' how things are goin' with the baby," she said, keeping quiet about her plans to take the playpen and high chair over tomorrow.

"Ellie . . ."

She stiffened, not about to apologize. "My parents taught me kindness and compassion, and that's what I aim to demonstrate."

They headed inside, where Dorcas was already dishing up some strawberry ice cream, as if she'd anticipated them. Had their daughter overheard their arguing?

Ellie cringed and looked around the kitchen. Other than Dorcas, it was empty of children. Sassy was rubbing against the table legs.

Where's Small Jay? Ellie asked Dorcas with her eyes, and her daughter shook her head faintly.

"Girls! Jake!" her husband called. "Ice cream's a-meltin'."

Julia and Sally gathered quickly, their spoons sinking into their ice cream even before their big sister or Dat sat down.

"*Puh!* What'd you two forget?" Roman asked.

Promptly, both girls folded their hands and bowed their heads, Julia's face as crimson as a beet.

Ellie stood still, waiting to make her way to the table. It was then she heard Small Jay clumping down the steps. Sassy meowed, undoubtedly sensing something was up, and Ellie shielded her heart for what was to come.

CHAPTER 8

Marlena had always heard it was unwise to tiptoe about while a baby slept. It was far better to ease the infant into the normal activity of the household—doing things as usual, going about the daily routine.

But after Ellie Bitner left, Marlena felt so exhausted that she found herself moving lightly about her bedroom, hoping the baby wouldn't awaken before she herself had the chance to relax a bit. She looked forward to washing up, though she would not shower until tomorrow morning in the makeshift area partitioned off from the washroom down in the cellar.

She slipped into one of her lightweight nightgowns and made her way silently to bed, where she sat still enough to hear the baby's breathing. Then she reached for her Bible to read a passage like her parents always did at bedtime. *Devout Dat and Mamma,* she thought fondly. Mamma had called just a while ago to see how Angela Rose was settling in. She'd also taken a moment to confide to Marlena that she hoped having the baby there might help Mammi get over her deep grief.

"Especially with you there to bear most of the burden of Angela's care." And Marlena conceded that Mamma might be right. *Who can resist a darling baby?*

Earlier, Marlena had set the room in order, placing the diaper pail near the crib, having put in a mix of water and blue detergent. She had no changing table, so for now she would have to use her bed, with a waterproof pad beneath the baby's bottom. The newly purchased diapers were stacked on the dresser near the crib, along with baby powder and lotion and a number of diaper pins. She'd made room in one of the drawers for the few baby gowns, tiny undershirts, and all-in-one sleepers brought from Luella's house by Aunt Becky. As far as Marlena could see, Becky hadn't brought any little dresses or jumpers, but she guessed that didn't matter. Not just yet.

The temperature upstairs was slightly cooler from having opened the outside door to the balcony earlier. She was surprised the baby was sleeping so peacefully in this heat. Going across the hall to the vacant bedroom, she opened the windows wide and returned to do the same in her room—the bedroom where she and Luella had always slept when the family visited.

Does my sister know who's taking care of her baby? Marlena sat on the cane-back chair, watching Angela Rose's little tummy rise and fall. With everything in her, she hoped all would be well with Luella. And silently she beseeched God yet again to watch over her sister. *And help those in charge get word to Gordon, too. . . .*

Thinking of the years she and her older sister had come here to help with summer gardening and canning, Marlena waited for the sky to turn completely dark before lying on the bed, pondering the baby's seeming resistance to her. Tomorrow, an abundance of garden produce and more strawberries would need to be picked and preserved, and then in two days, market day. *We need to borrow a stroller from someone*, she realized.

She recalled Ellie's thoughtful offer that Dorcas could watch Angela Rose. At least there was that. Even so, it was evident to her how ill-prepared she was to look after Luella's baby for longer than a few days.

Just then she imagined her poor sister lying in a hospital bed. *Is she conscious . . . aware of her situation?* And if so, was she missing Angela as much as Angela was clearly missing her?

Feeling too tired to sleep, Marlena turned over and sighed, mentally composing her next letter to Nat. She wanted to share all of her happiness over his telephone call and the many things that came to her drowsy mind, till at last she fell into a deep sleep.

~⁓෨

Ellie sat on the chair across the room from their bed, wearing her mint green duster. Roman was stretched out on the bed, still muttering things that continued to upset her. How would she ever feel settled enough to rest?

"Small Jay gets by with a lot," Roman said grimly.

"I think he's just forgetful."

"Maybe he hides behind his disabilities. Have ya considered that?"

She wanted to say right back to him that it was wrong to utter such unfounded statements. But she'd said enough already this night. *Too much.* Besides, they weren't going to solve anything now, not as worn out as they both were.

So she would just sit there and wait till his first few snores, then slip into bed. At times like this, she thought back to the days when her husband's eyes were tender, even mischievous, and she missed that Roman. Oh, did she ever.

Down the hallway, faint whispers mixed with occasional giggles. Most likely her two youngest girls were feeling warm and restless, sharing a bed in the muggy house. Small Jay and Dorcas each had their own south-facing rooms, where the breezes came more readily through more windows.

Leaning her head toward the whispers, Ellie smiled, not interested in going to shush Julia and Sally. Such pleasant, familiar sounds.

Some of us are happy. . . .

Ofttimes she could hear Small Jay talking in his sleep, sounding a lot like the way he talked to his cat.

Stretching, she relaxed enough to yawn, thankful for each of her children—though she couldn't help recalling the stressful discussion with her husband earlier, when she'd returned from visiting Marlena Wenger. *I really must count my blessings more and fret far less.*

~~~⌐⌐

Ellie awakened suddenly, rigid as kindling. She shook herself and rose from the chair, creeping to the dresser to look at the day clock. *One o'clock.*

She'd fallen asleep in Roman's big armchair. Not the first time, but definitely the longest. Nighttime breezes were beginning to cool the house, and she was glad she'd thought to leave the upstairs windows open. On such a starry night, there was no chance of rain.

Roman murmured in his sleep. Wearing her slippers, she turned toward the door and stepped into the hall, going to check on the children, as she sometimes did at night.

74

In the first bedroom to the right of the hallway, she leaned on the doorframe, peering in. Her heart caught in her throat at the sight of Julia's blond hair flowing over her slender shoulders. Evidently, she'd pushed the sheet back, or kicked it off. Her long, graceful arm draped over little Sally, who was scrunched down a bit, her chubby hand resting on her pillow, strawberry-blond braids still wound around her head. *Too busy to bother brushing,* Ellie thought, helpless not to smile down at the two of them. Stepping into the room, she went to the bed and lifted the sheet, pulling it up to their waists before leaving the room.

Across the hall, Dorcas was primly tucked in, her white cotton coverlet secured over her slight frame. Ellie felt her forehead, wet with perspiration. Moving to the window, she paused to raise the shade to let in more air, then turned to stand at the footboard. Silently, she asked the Lord God heavenly Father to guide this daughter's every step toward adolescence. *Coming ever so quickly.*

She made her way next door to Small Jay's room. As he always did at bedtime, he'd left his door only cracked open, so his cat wouldn't roam about the house. Roman had been unwavering against having a barn cat, or any animal for that matter, stay in the house, back two years ago. But Small Jay had won the day, and they had all warmed up to Sassafras in a short time, Roman included, and before long her husband had surprised her by agreeing to allow the cat to sleep on Small Jay's bed. Not under the covers, though—that went without saying.

Ellie peered into the room, moving the door open to squeeze through, and saw that the two window shades were up as high as they could possibly go, wound tightly at the top of the window frame. *He stood on the chair again.*

Shaking her head, she wondered why her son was determined to take risks like that, and she thought once more of Roman's remarks.

Sassafras had managed to edge up close to Small Jay's pillow. Ellie stepped near, taking in the tranquil scene, grateful to God for this gentle-spirited child. *Our truest gift*, she thought, deeming him a blessing despite the ongoing struggles.

She turned to leave, but Small Jay moved in his sleep, and she noticed a piece of paper, folded in two, which slipped out of his hand and onto the bedsheet. *What's this?* She picked it up and went to the open window to read it.

This is only for practice. My name is Dr. Calvert, but please call me Boston.

Ellie found this strange, even startling. Where had Small Jay received such a note? And who was Dr. Calvert? She had no knowledge of a Brownstown doctor by that name. Had her son been taken privately to see a physician—without her knowledge? If so, who would do such a thing?

She pushed the puzzling message into the pocket of her duster and, with a troubled heart, cracked the door open the way she'd found it before returning to her own bedroom.

~ e⊙

Marlena dreamed she heard the mournful strains of a harmonica, then awakened to a squirrel pattering across the roof. With a start, she sat up in the moonlit room, uncertain where she was. A baby whimpered, tiny feet thumping against the crib mattress just a yard or so from her bed. In her sluggish stupor, Marlena got out of bed and leaned on the crib railing to look down at Luella's wee one. As before, the wrenching cries rapidly became shrill sobs, even after she reached for

Angela Rose and placed her gently on her own bed to change her diaper. Then Marlena carefully hurried downstairs, her niece in her arms.

I must make up the formula quickly, lest Angela's cries awaken Mammi. Glad for the electricity, she flipped on the soft stove light. Both she and the baby squinted into the brightness, and she was unsure how she ever would have managed to light a gas lantern while juggling a baby.

As she mixed, then warmed the formula, Marlena noticed it was two o'clock. They'd both slept a good portion of the night, something Marlena hadn't expected, given Angela's long crying spell and then nap earlier. Mammi certainly needed *her* rest after such a tiring day, so this was a welcome surprise.

Marlena tested the formula's temperature on the inside of her arm like Aunt Becky had done, then rubbed Angela's little mouth with the bottle's nipple. As before, Angela Rose closed her lips firmly, pushing the bottle away, her face wrinkling. But Marlena tried again, talking to her in a soothing tone. "I know you're hungry, little one."

Angela Rose turned toward her voice, and Marlena held her breath as her niece finally latched on to the bottle, her eyes closing, then opening as she settled into a steady sucking rhythm.

"That's right," Marlena whispered, looking down into the small blue eyes blinking up at her.

Angela Rose raised her dimpled hand to Marlena's lips, which was so dear Marlena willed herself not to cry. "Aw, sweetie, you must surely know I'm not your Mamma." She held her breath, but miraculously Luella's baby did not cry again.

Daring to hope for more sleep, Marlena remembered to lean Angela against her shoulder and rub her back after more than half the eight-ounce bottle had been drained. Angela was moving about and cooing sweetly.

Reaching for the bottle again, Marlena was relieved when her niece snuggled down next to her to take it. Oh, the feel of the cuddly girl in her arms! She got up to turn off the electric stove light, hoping to let the baby's now heavy eyelids give in to sleep once more. As for herself, she was ready to return to dreamland. With that in mind, she carried Angela Rose upstairs and gently removed the bottle to put her back down in the crib.

Immediately, the peace of the house was shattered as the crying began once more.

Quickly, Marlena closed her door and lifted Angela out of the crib. Humming softly, she walked back and forth in the room till she was so weary she could scarcely stand. Needing sleep, she decided to take the sobbing infant to bed with her, now singing "Jesus Loves Me" again and again in English so as not to upset Angela Rose with *Deitsch. An unrecognizable language, for sure.*

It struck Marlena—had Luella ever sung a hymn from the *Ausbund* to her baby? She also wondered what sort of beliefs her brother-in-law, Gordon, had. Would his being in the war push him toward God, or away?

Angela's cries mixed now with hiccups; exhausted though she was, there seemed to be no end to them. Reaching for the bottle again, Marlena gave the last of the formula she seemed to desire, cradling her near as she sat up in bed. All the while, she hoped in earnest for a way to bond with this heartbroken baby.

Is Luella worried about Angela? The thought continued to plague Marlena as she caressed her, the baby's suckling beginning to slow after a time. She'd gone to sleep in Marlena's arms.

Marlena wasn't sure it was the right decision but decided to stay right there for the rest of the night, bolstered up with two feather pillows behind her back, until the sunny brightness of dawn shone on the wide oak leaves that graced the window in shining green.

Sleepily, Marlena looked around the sparsely furnished room—the tall wooden clothes rack, the single maple chair near one window, the crib, and the pine dresser with its modest mirror. She saw that nothing had changed surrounding them, yet she felt strangely different, and it had nothing to do with the lack of rest. Her arms felt numb as she looked into the sweet face of the sleeping babe, but that didn't matter. Truth was, her hope—or was it an unconscious prayer?—had been answered. Maybe the heavenly Father had used her willingness to sacrifice a good portion of sleep.

Leaning down to kiss the baby's soft head, Marlena grasped the precious truth: Her heart had opened wide and gently caught Angela Rose.

CHAPTER 9

Thursday morning turned out to be mild and less oppressive than the day before. The sun shone bright on the corncrib roof as Ellie peered out the kitchen window, then set to work. Roman had said a number of the outbuildings needed to be reroofed, and a whole stretch of pasture fence had to be replaced, as well.

Ellie automatically wondered where Small Jay might fit in with any of those chores, but she knew the enduring truth. Sighing, she mixed up some buttermilk waffles and made scrambled eggs with cheese for her family. Then, reaching into her apron pocket, she felt the note she'd taken from her son's room last night. It was best she wait to talk to him till he was finished eating.

Without Roman around . . .

Later, when they all sat down together, the girls promptly bowed their heads without touching their utensils. Roman observed and nodded his approval before the silent blessing.

After they said amen, Small Jay kept his attention on his

plate, not asking his father the usual—if he might help him outdoors. This was remarkable, and Ellie felt sure Roman had taken notice, too.

Dorcas jabbered about the needlepoint class Ellie was having tomorrow. "Is it all right if I go, Mamma?"

"Me too!" Julia spoke up, eyes pleading.

Ellie smiled, buoyed by the girls' interest. "Dorcas, you may attend, but Julia, I want you to stay here with your little sister."

At this, Julia's face drooped, but only briefly, and she turned to Sally and leaned her head against her sister's. "We'll help Mamma by weeding the garden," she said, which warmed Ellie's heart.

"*Denki*, honey." Ellie meant it for Julia, but Sally grinned across the table at her, as well. "Right now I have a quick trip to make."

Dorcas brightened. "Can I come with you, Mamma?"

Always eager to assist, she thought of her oldest daughter. Ellie agreed, not wanting to make much of where she was going or what she was doing. It felt good to have a calmer atmosphere in the house this morning. Heaven knew it was time for a more peaceful day.

"The vet's comin' any minute now to check on two of the field mules," Roman mentioned as he reached for his coffee mug.

Small Jay's head popped up, blue eyes shining with hope.

Ellie realized she was grinding her teeth. *Will he ask to follow the vet around?*

But Julia preempted her brother. "Can Sally and I watch?"

"*Jah, des gut,*" Roman replied, then finished off his coffee.

Ellie's heart sank for Small Jay. But like him, she said nothing.

~ ℯᎧ

Ellie hadn't had the heart to confront their son after break-fast about the strange note she'd found last night. And once Roman left for the stable to meet with the vet, Ellie and Dorcas loaded up the baby items for Marlena Wenger, then took the family carriage, already hitched to their strongest horse, and left for the Martin house.

When Ellie returned from making the delivery, she could not find Small Jay and assumed he'd taken off walking. She kept the note in her apron and set about preparing for her class tomorrow, uncertain how many young quilters she'd have. Only Amish girls was Roman's wish. *Well, his demand.*

Still, she couldn't think of turning away the young Menno-nites farther down the road—and her own New Order niece, Sarah—if they came, and had respectfully told Roman so. Word about her classes had spread nearly like a wildfire, and it pleased her to have the opportunity to pass along her skills and love of needlepoint and quilting to others. If only Marlena might show up, but the thoughtful young woman had declined coming once again when Ellie was over there just a while ago. Of course, considering the wee one in Marlena's care, it made perfect sense. Besides, Ellie was privately relieved not to have another reason for an altercation with Roman.

Better this way, she thought.

~ ℯᎧ

Marlena lowered Angela Rose into the playpen and then propped her up with pillows. She took time to shake a soft pink rattle within reaching distance and smiled when the little hand grabbed for it. Marlena had quickly decided the kitchen was the ideal spot for the cozy play area, just as Ellie had recommended when she dropped by earlier.

Feeling better today about almost everything, Marlena was pleased to have bathed and dressed her niece without a speck of trouble. No crying fits yet today, either. Even Mammi was complimentary of her handling the baby. *"I believe you're a natural, dear,"* her grandmother had declared with the sweetest smile.

The telephone jangled loudly, and Marlena hurried to pick up the phone. "Hullo," she answered. "Martin residence."

"It's Mamma, honey." Her mother's voice sounded tinny and unnatural over the distance. "Oh . . . my dear girl."

"We've been wondering 'bout Luella. How is she today?"

"I've just had word from Aunt Becky, who called from the hospital." Mamma's breath was coming fast, then became a long, tearful sigh. *"Ach,* Marlena. I'm so sorry to tell you this, my dear. Your sister didn't make it. Luella passed away not an hour ago."

Marlena could not speak, her heart cold with dread. She looked over at Angela Rose and felt even more devastated. *The worst possible news!* Stunned, she moved to sit on the wooden bench near the table and leaned her face into her hand, still holding the receiver.

"Marlena . . . honey?"

"So sorry, Mamma. I feel numb." She moaned. "I can't believe this."

"I know . . . it's just shocking, and so very sudden. We haven't heard back from anyone about Gordon, either—it could take weeks to get word to him, and even longer by mail. Luella's poor husband doesn't even know she was in an accident . . . let alone this." Mamma sighed heavily. "Your father's gone to lie down. He's honestly beside himself."

The silence between them, broken only by her mother's stifled sobs, made Marlena uneasy, adding to the gravity of the horrendous moment.

"What will happen to Luella's baby?" Marlena asked, trembling. Her words seemed somehow unrelated to the overwhelming reality they now faced.

"I'll call Gordon's aunt Patricia the minute I'm off the phone with you. She may know of a way to contact his parents. They're already on the other side of the world, most likely."

"Well, won't *they* want to take care of Angela Rose, once they're home?"

"We must lean on the Lord's wisdom in this. For now, are you able to keep Angela a while longer? I'd guess it'll take some time for them to get a way home."

What could she say? "*Jah*, of course I'll help out till Gordon's parents are back."

"Surely a baby will bring some comfort to you and my mother during this dreadful time."

"Angela Rose is a very sweet baby, Mamma."

"One without a mother." Mamma's words were jolting, and Marlena's eyes pricked with tears. "Once Anderson and Sheryl Munroe learn of Luella's death, I would think they'd try to alter their plans and fly home for the funeral."

"*Jah*, you'd think they'd come for Angela's sake," Marlena said.

Mamma went on to say that the funeral would most likely be this coming Monday, wanting to allow some time out of respect for Luella's husband and in-laws' not knowing. "Your father plans to contact one of our Beachy ministers. Since

Luella grew up Amish, we're hopin' the preacher will agree to have the funeral at the Beachy meetinghouse. We'll let you know where and when as soon as we know."

Marlena felt weak. "Mammi and I will hire a driver, but we probably won't spend the night." Her mother knew that Mammi preferred her own bed, and the baby's things were all here, too. "Now that I've mentioned it, I'm not sure Mammi will even feel up to the trip," Marlena admitted, though for her parents' sake, she hoped so.

Marlena was quiet for a moment; then she asked, "What do ya think Luella would have wanted for her service, considering everything?"

"It's not something she ever talked 'bout, bein' so young and all. And since Gordon's not around to discuss it, what else can we do but make the best plans for our family?"

Marlena pondered that, feeling at a loss to make any suggestions. She knew her parents would never think of having the funeral at the undertaker's, nor would they ask for cosmetics to cover any visible bruises from the accident. Luella may have been English, but such traditions weren't a part of the lives of the People.

"Your father will most likely drive over to their house tomorrow . . . wants to see if there might be a will or last wishes filed away somewhere." Mamma moaned again.

"A person Luella's age doesn't think much about dying." Marlena couldn't imagine the quandary her parents were in— so much unknown, and Luella's husband out of reach.

Shaken to the core, Marlena forgot to ask about her younger siblings before she said good-bye. By then it was too late. Her brothers, Amos and Yonnie, and sisters, Katie and Rachel Ann, would surely be just as shocked at this terrible turn of events.

Going to the playpen, Marlena reached down to cup Angela's little head in her hand and looked into her face. The babe smiled up at her. "Oh, you dear, dear baby," she said softly, tears rolling down. "I'm awful sorry for you, Angela Rose."

Such a beautiful name. In her grief, Marlena ached to return to her own childhood, when she and Luella were still little . . . to try to do things another way, wishing for a different outcome.

~ ❧

Resting his bad leg on a low stone wall that ran along the road toward Brownstown Mill, Small Jay held his cat up to his face, whispering. He enjoyed the familiar vibration of purring in his ear as lively Sassy pushed her little nose into his chest.

"Down ya go," Small Jay said, setting his pet back on the ground and fastening the leash once again. *Dat's right . . . it's a long jaunt over here.*

A short way from where he sat, Small Jay saw Allegro poised at the base of a tall tree, wagging his long tail, evidently waiting for a squirrel, his nose in the air.

"It's Allegro!" His energy surged at the thought of his cat and Allegro playing together again, like yesterday, when the bow-tie man—Boston, he'd said his name was—had set out to write "memory notes" after they'd eaten their hot dogs on the tree stump. Small Jay didn't know what became of the note Boston had pushed into Small Jay's shirt pocket. *"I'm always forgetting my name,"* he'd told Small Jay. *"So I wouldn't be surprised if you did, too."*

In the distance, on the hill beyond the stone bridge and amidst a mass of trees, Small Jay saw a portion of the white church with the tall steeple and spire at the top. He'd once heard that a handful of people walking toward the bridge one fine autumn morning had seen angels in white hovering near the spire. Small Jay didn't know what to make of such a peculiar tale, but he assumed people around Brownstown ought to know whether such things were true or not. It surely wasn't the sort of thing he'd ever ask his parents about. If people saw an angel near a church, well, what better place? Just maybe it was something the Good Lord had permitted to make those who saw it feel better. *Maybe they were sad or lonely, or needed help to believe,* he thought, slowly walking down the incline near the mill.

"Wonder if Boston'll be out cookin' over his fire today," he murmured. Sassy padded forward quickly, as if she sensed they were entering Allegro's territory.

"Hello over there!" Boston called to him, looking even more bedraggled than yesterday as he waved both arms to flag Small Jay down.

Picking up his pace as best as he could, Small Jay was aware that he ought to be on the lookout for horses and buggies. But the sight of the man with his bow tie askew drew him onward.

As he came closer, Small Jay blinked at the sight of a single blanket lying on the ground near the fire pit he'd made last evening. "Are ya sleepin' outside now, Boston?"

The man grimaced. "You must be mistaken, young man. I believe Boston is a city somewhere."

Small Jay shook his head, befuddled. "Remember me? I'm Small Jay Bitner. . . . I visited you and your dog yesterday." He started to mention the meal they'd shared but stopped cold. "I brought ya some cookies. Thought you might need more to eat, maybe."

"Small Jay . . ." The man's lips moved as he pulled a notepad out of his right trousers pocket and flipped through the pages. "Small Jay," he repeated, stopping at a page toward the back of the notepad. "Ah yes . . . I see that name right here. I've been wondering why it was there." He held out the notepad and tapped the page with two fingers. Then, straightening to his full height, the man, who was more mixed-up than Small Jay had thought possible, said, "I am pleased to meet you, young man."

Meet me? He forgot who I am?

Flabbergasted, Small Jay motioned again toward the blanket laid out on the ground near the creek bank. "Ya still haven't answered my question, mister. Have ya moved outdoors to sleep?"

"Begging your pardon?"

Small Jay tried to explain what he had been told previously— that the man was storing his few belongings in the mill, and bedding down inside for the night. He decided not to mention again that the man's name was Boston, just in case the man had been wrong about that earlier. Anyway, Small Jay didn't want to say anything to upset him again.

The man began to hum, and as before, one hand rose into the air, dipping and waving. There was just no talking sensibly to him. And, just as disappointing, the border collie had disappeared. *Is he still hunting squirrels?*

Small Jay felt too jittery to even inquire about the dog, but he wanted to tell the man something that had been on his mind since yesterday. "I'm a lot like you," he confided. "I forget things, too. My brain gets all cluttered up sometimes. My schoolteacher said I'm a child who will never grow up."

The man's face broke into a gentle, even thoughtful smile. "Is that right?" His eyes glistened in the corners. Then, clearing his throat a little, he said, "What a fine cat you have there."

88

"Just a barn cat. But she's my pet, Sassafras."

"Ah, and sassafras is also a mighty fine-tasting tea. Did you know that if you crush sassafras leaves, they smell like root beer?"

He nodded. "Mamma grows it in her herb garden."

The man reached into his pants pocket and drew out his mouth organ. He began to play a sad-sounding tune, one Small Jay did not recognize. While he listened, he noticed the gold ring on the fourth finger of the man's left hand.

When the melody was through, Boston asked, "Would you care to have a seat?"

"*Denki*, but I best not be stayin' long."

"But you just arrived." The man studied him, frowning a bit. "Are you of German descent?"

"I'm Amish."

"You sound quite German." Distracted again, the man put his fingers between his teeth and whistled loudly. He slipped his harmonica back into his pocket, and a minute later, here came Allegro along the trees lining the creek bank. "This is my watchdog."

"Allegro's right friendly," Small Jay said.

"Allegro?" The man's eyes looked cloudy. "That's a musical term. Do you perchance play an instrument?"

Small Jay had no idea what the nice man was talking about, but he wanted to remind him that his dog's name was Allegro. It said so right on the leather collar.

As before, the dog warmed up immediately to Sassy, and bow-tie man must have forgotten what he was talking about, because he got down on his haunches and clapped his hands. "My dog grew up playing with two cats, if I recall correctly. They were quite the trio." Soon he was laughing at the dog and cat as Sassy arched her back against the dog's side. She calmed a bit and the familiar purring followed.

"They seem mighty friendly, ain't?" Small Jay observed aloud.

"Love at first sight, I presume."

"But . . ." Small Jay stopped himself. As confused as he was himself sometimes, he knew this man was thoroughly mixed-up today, when yesterday the things he'd said made fairly good sense—or so Small Jay had thought. "Where's your family?" he asked.

The man pointed toward the dog. "Right there."

"No one else?"

"None that I recall."

Small Jay pondered the sad reply. "What 'bout that ring you're wearin'?" He'd only seen similar gold bands on *Englischers*, and Mamma said it meant they were wed.

"I don't know." The man stared at his hand and turned the band. "But I do know one thing."

"*Jah?*" Small Jay felt his heart speed up some. Maybe a clue was coming.

"The ring is impossible to remove."

Small Jay pondered this. Then, concerned about the man's welfare, he asked, "What have ya eaten today?"

"Crackers and cheese, primarily." The man pulled out one of the oatmeal raisin cookies from yesterday. "I'm saving this for later."

That's all he's got, Small Jay thought. "Say, how about we go over to Joe's and pick up some food tomorrow? I'll bring my pony, Razor, and the cart, so we won't have to walk so far."

The man's smile was filled with pleasure and expectation. "I'll look forward to that, young man."

"Would ya like to jot it down?" Small Jay asked, not certain the man would recall otherwise.

"Excellent thought, my boy." The man reached for his small notepad and removed a pen from his shirt pocket.

Later, as Small Jay walked toward home with Sassy, a notion was forming in his head. When the time was right, and things seemed to fall into place—if they did—he would bring it up to the lonely man with the bright gold ring on his finger. The man who couldn't even remember his own name!

CHAPTER 10

*M*arlena purposely awakened early the next morning
to write to Nat while Angela Rose was still sleeping.
She and Mammi had talked yesterday, sharing their shock
and sadness at Luella's sudden death, but Marlena needed
to jot down her thoughts to mourn properly. And too, it was
important for him to receive her letter tomorrow, so he would
know about Monday's funeral.

Dear Nat,

*Remember how we talked quietly last summer, sitting under
that big maple tree near the old schoolhouse? Well, if I were
there, I'd tell you what my heart is saying this morning.*

*It seems like decades since I talked to Luella, and now she's
gone. And gone where? I wish I knew. Mammi says we must
leave that in God's hands. Yet, while I work, cooking and
cleaning and caring for Luella's baby, I noodle on the fact
that she left the church of her youth and abandoned the Plain
life. What does all of that mean to our heavenly Father? Is
my sister's soul lost for eternity?*

I won't deny that I fret over it. I also wonder if I'm the best person to care for Angela Rose, even temporarily. I can't help but think of her growing up and never knowing the mother who gave birth to her . . . and loved her so. Did you know that her father hasn't even laid eyes on her yet? I wonder how long it will be before Gordon can come home and meet his little girl. She needs him—she is as fragile as a rose petal.

Luella's funeral will be held at the Beachy church in Mifflinburg this Monday morning, and my grandmother and I are going to pay our respects, as well as to offer our support to Dat and Mamma, who, as you can imagine, are beside themselves with grief.

Oh, Nat, it's such a difficult time for our family.

It crossed her mind to ask if he might be going to the funeral, too, perhaps with his family. But she knew better—even so, she wished he would support her in her sorrow, despite his Old Order convictions.

She continued writing, trying to hold back the tears to prevent any stains on her colorful pansy-adorned stationery.

Luella's in-laws are out of the country traveling and unable to take care of their grandbaby just now. From what Mamma says, I'll have to tend to Angela Rose at least until a decision is made for her care while her father's away in Vietnam. No matter what, I will be coming home around Labor Day. I can hardly wait!

Till then, I'll write you as often as I can.

Your girl,
Marlena Wenger

Later that morning, Marlena helped Mammi label the pint jars of strawberry-rhubarb preserves, pricing them for Saturday market tomorrow. Marlena was glad for the simple task while Angela Rose napped soundly in the playpen. It was hard to focus after a night of quietly weeping in the privacy of her room. Many long hours had passed before she could fall asleep.

Mammi's eyes were swollen, too—perhaps they should both just crawl back into bed and weep the day away. But there was a baby to care for and work to be done. Dawdi Tim had once told her that when a person grieved, solace sometimes came through keeping one's hands and mind occupied.

"I can finish up here," Mammi said, her words sounding flat. "Go ahead an' pick the fresh crop of berries while the little one's sleepin'. Ya might want some time alone."

She knows I'm struggling. We both are.

Marlena agreed and rose quickly. She needed her family, and right now she missed Nat's kind understanding and love . . . and oh, how she longed for both.

How was she supposed to feel with Luella gone from them forever? Oh, so distraught and hopeless, knowing too well her sister's reasons for leaving the People behind against the will of their parents. Marlena tried to calm her thoughts, yet she had never experienced such a loss and wished she and her mother might have talked longer. Still, she had been conscious of the effort it must have taken Mamma to make such a call, as well as the cost of long-distance to her father—and surely Mamma'd had other important calls to make. Poor thing, it had fallen to her to tell Gordon's family, once she located them. And, on top of everything else, Mamma and

Dat were the only ones around to plan the funeral for their firstborn.

Help my parents and younger brothers and sisters today, O Lord God heavenly Father, she prayed. *They need Thy comfort and wisdom now . . . just as Mammi and I do.*

Small Jay gritted his teeth when his mother removed from her apron pocket the note from his friend at the mill.

"What do you know 'bout this, son?" Her face had its usual softness, even an unexplained timidity, like she really didn't want to ask this but felt compelled. "Who is this doctor?"

He leaned in close to look at the familiar writing. Boston had pledged that the snippets of things he wrote each day were a memory aid . . . nothing more. Why had he given this paper to Small Jay anyway?

"I don't know." He shook his head.

She went on to say how and where she'd found it. "You didn't go to a doctor without tellin' your father and me, now, did ya?"

"*Nee,* Mamma."

Her eyes seemed to look right through him.

"Son . . ."

Small Jay shrugged, wanting to keep his secret to himself. It wouldn't matter one iota to anyone else that he had a friend who struggled like he did sometimes. He also sensed the older man wouldn't want to be a bother.

"Your father has warned us not to speak to outsiders," Mamma reminded him. "Don't forget he has your best interests at heart."

Sometimes that's easy to forget, Small Jay thought forlornly.

"Be more cautious, won't ya, please?"

Her concern registered with him, but Boston didn't seem like an outsider to him, just a man in need. And Small Jay had something more pressing on his mind. "Can I take the pony cart over to Joe's store?" he asked.

"Today?" Mamma looked surprised. Then at his nod, she added, "Say it correctly, son."

Ach, *what does she mean?* He puckered his brow and looked toward the ceiling. *What did I say wrong?*

"It's important to say *May I* when you're askin' permission. *Can I* stands for whether or not you are able to do something, son. Can you remember the difference?"

He held her gaze and tried to follow her request. "*May* I take Razor and the pony cart over to Joe's?" He purposely emphasized the appropriate word.

"*Jah*, of course you may."

Whew. Was he ever glad she'd noticed his bad grammar and forgotten about Boston Calvert's reminder note, still folded in her hand.

~~~⌒☯

When Small Jay arrived at the mill, he left Sassy in the big pony cart while he tied Razor to a sturdy nearby tree. When he glanced back at his cat, he grinned at the sight of her peeking out of the cart like that. "You silly."

Small Jay went to the mill's side door, where he'd first seen the man and his dog enter a few days before. He couldn't help but wonder if Boston remembered today's outing. Pausing, he looked up to see the historic marker plate high above, reading to himself: *Built by Jacob and Lavina Wolf, A.D. 1856.*

He whistled. "That's gotta be before even Dawdi Bitner was born." In all truth, he couldn't begin to calculate how many years ago this old mill had been built. He even had a hard time remembering how old his younger sisters were. Sometimes the numbers that connected to his life got all tangled up in his brain.

He raised his hand to knock on the door and was startled when it flew open. "*Ach*, you remembered!" Small Jay declared.

"I certainly did—and with some help from this reminder." Boston pulled a scrunched-up note from his pocket.

Small Jay smiled. "Are ya ready, then?"

"Is there room for my dog?" the man asked, stepping out the door with a glance at the pony cart.

"Might be a tight squeeze."

"In that case, the captain will stay with the ship." With that, Boston closed the door soundly behind him, and the border collie began to bark inside.

Small Jay hoped Boston's pet wouldn't be too lonely while they were gone. "Do ya need dog food for Allegro?"

"Grand idea," the man said, not questioning the dog's name.

"And you're Boston, *jah*?" Since things were going so well, Small Jay wanted to clear up the confusion over the name right now.

"Yes, of course. Shall we go?"

Feeling better, Small Jay introduced his black pony to Boston. "Razor likes his sugar cubes."

"Then I want very much to treat him . . . if the store carries such things."

"Joe'll know." Small Jay went to untie Razor and waited for Boston to get into the cart. He handed Sassy over to him till Small Jay was also seated, then reached for the driving lines, and they were off.

When they made the turn onto the two-lane country road,

Small Jay didn't see the soiled letter he'd stuck back in the bushes. *Must've blown away.*

Up the road, a Yankee farmer was burning a brush pile, the dark plume billowing high and scenting the atmosphere. Further along, they came upon two little Amish girls riding in a red wagon pulled by an older boy. Small Jay pointed out cattle, hogs, sheep, and hen houses to Boston, who seemed to enjoy the ride, humming a tune and occasionally murmuring to himself. Sunshine sparkled off the big silo just ahead, like the jewels Small Jay had seen in the Sears and Roebuck catalogue at one of the English neighbors'.

At Joe's General Store, Boston helped him tie up Razor, taking time to stroke the sleek pony's mane. If he wasn't mistaken, Boston whispered something about a sugar cube, which made Small Jay smile. He carried Sassy up the store steps, the leash wrapped around one hand to keep her away from the many trinkets and things inside. Small Jay figured Boston would want to take time to explore the place, though he hadn't an inkling how they were going to pay for much food.

Mamma will wonder what I bought, he thought, remembering that his father liked black licorice. Maybe he'd buy a bagful for Dat . . . if Boston didn't need the money, that is.

"*Willkumm,* Small Jay. Haven't seen ya here lately," Joe Stoltzfus greeted him, an eye on Boston, who ran a hand over his chin whiskers before waving to Joe.

"Hello again, sir," Boston said. "Might you have some sugar cubes for the pony out back?"

Small Jay liked the sound of this and was pleased when Joe nodded his head and darted off to look. "What are ya hungry for, Boston?" he asked while they stood at the wooden counter.

"Beef jerky, some cocoa powder mix, Wheaties, and a half-gallon of milk will be fine. Oh, and dog food."

Surprised at the short list, Small Jay asked if he wanted to buy more hot dogs. "Or maybe some ground beef to make hamburgers?"

"I can easily cool the milk in the creek, but fresh meat won't keep longer than one can snap a finger," Boston replied, explaining that Allegro, or other animals, might be tempted to snatch it right up. "Don't you agree?"

Small Jay didn't think there were any coyotes or foxes over near the mill, but he could be wrong. "By the way, I brought some coins from my—"

"Young man, I have plenty to cover what is needed, sugar cubes included." Boston opened his wallet and flipped through a wad of bills—more than Small Jay could begin to count.

"I might be able to get the pony cart again," he said quietly, "but ya still might want to stock up. It takes a long time to walk over here."

Boston nodded absently, his eyes on the row of shelves behind the counter.

"Some sticky buns would taste *gut* with chocolate milk," Small Jay suggested.

"All buns are sticky when you spread jam on them, wouldn't you say?"

Small Jay flashed him a grin. Boston had him there, for sure.

Pretty soon, Joe returned with the sugar cubes. Boston counted out the amount, thumbing through his dollar bills, and Small Jay couldn't understand how this man had so much money, yet no place to call home. *No place to wash up properly, either.*

Boston also needed a shave, unless he was deliberately

growing a beard, which Small Jay doubted. At least the man didn't stink like some of his father's hardworking men after a long, hot day in the hayfield. No, for now, Boston was getting along just fine, washing up in the creek. Small Jay certainly wouldn't be allowed to go without washing at least every other day during the summertime. *Mamma sees to that,* he thought, wondering suddenly how long it might be before someone from the community might just burst into the store and see him with Boston.

Once he'd made his purchase of black licorice, Small Jay reached to open the door and smiled at the familiar jingle. Then, forgetting himself, he opened the door a second time . . . then a third.

"You sure like that bell, don't ya, Jake?" asked Joe, his expression pleasant. Pleasant with a stiff sort of pucker around his lips, that is—which made Small Jay wonder if he was only pretending to be pleasant.

"Sounds mighty nice."

Again, Boston opened his wallet. "Do you happen to sell such bells here?"

"Ain't any 'cept that one, I'm afraid." Joe was looking hard at Boston, scrutinizing him like the bishop did a wayward church member.

It made Small Jay nervous. "That's all right. We'll be on our way."

Boston stuffed his purchases into his shoulder bag, which he must have emptied out before they left the mill.

"You two travelin' together?" Joe was really frowning now, one hand rubbing his light brown beard.

"I gave him a lift here, is all." Small Jay felt he'd better speak up, or the grapevine might grab hold of his secret and spoil everything.

"I see." Joe suddenly seemed his old agreeable self again. "Have a *wunnerbaar-gut* day, then. Both of yous."

"Same to you," Small Jay said, eager to open the door right quick. This time not to hear the bell ring but to escape.

CHAPTER 11

On the ride back to the mill, Small Jay felt like talking, but Boston didn't reprimand him for talking a blue streak, like Dat sometimes did. "Razor sure likes getting out and trotting fast," he said, gripping the reins.

Boston nibbled on his beef jerky, his hand trembling, but he seemed to enjoy the ride. "I might have gone hungry today, had it not been for you."

Small Jay sat up straighter. Besides his Mamma, few people ever said such nice things to him. His former neighbor, Timothy Martin, had been one. *And more than once*, he recalled. The older man had been the kindest person ever.

The pony was really going to town now, and Boston held on to his side of the cart, his hair blowing back over his ears. "I do so wish to remember this day . . . this amazing ride!" He leaned his head back and closed his eyes.

Small Jay was as pleased as pudding. "We can ride again, if ya want," he told his friend.

"Thank you kindly. I believe I'll take you up on that." Boston was grinning.

Small Jay had always liked the tickle of the wind on his face, and he was glad he'd thought to push his straw hat down under his knees. It was the best way to cool off on such a warm day.

"If you have the time, I'll show you around my place," Boston said as they pulled into the driveway later.

"Your place?"

"My waterfront property. A mansion, young man!"

"I see." Small Jay smiled, reminding himself of Dat just then. "*Jah*, I'd like to see where you and Allegro stay."

The man's eyes widened. "I beg your pardon?"

"Your dog—Allegro."

Sassy had crept into Boston's lap during the ride and was still sitting there, looking content. Boston had to hand her over to Small Jay so he could get himself out of the cart. He carefully heaved his heavy shoulder bag, making no further comment about the dog's name.

Before they went in, Small Jay tied the pony to a tree, and Boston pulled out a sugar cube and gave it to Razor, holding his hand out flat for the pony.

"'Tis the best way, *jah*," Small Jay said, observing.

"I rode a horse once or twice long ago, but don't ask me where that was, or why."

Small Jay listened, not questioning his friend. He found it interesting that the man who always wore a bow tie was so comfortable around Razor. "I sat on my pony's back once without a saddle," he said. "Hung on to the mane for dear life."

As they entered the interior of the large mill, it felt cool and dark inside and surprisingly comfortable. Someone had turned the place into a house with wood flooring and high walls, dividing things up right pretty. There was not a speck of furniture, though.

Over in the corner, near a window, Allegro awaited his master. He whined when he saw them, and Small Jay offered to fill his dish with creek water.

Later, when the dog had eaten his fill of the new chow, Boston suggested they go outside again and sit near the mill-race. "I have a confession to make," he said quietly. "I fear my eyes are weakening . . . perhaps even failing. Can you read to me, young man?"

"I learned in school."

Boston studied him. "How old a student are you, son?"

"I finished up eighth grade last month. I'm fourteen."

Boston didn't say it, but his frown indicated that he, like most people, didn't believe Small Jay was that old. He turned and walked to the nearby windowsill, where letters were stacked high, and removed one of them. Holding it against his chest, he patted it like the letter was a treasure. "Do you mind reading this to me?" he asked as he motioned toward the door.

"I'll do my best. That's what my teacher always said to do." Small Jay wondered why the man didn't wear glasses like some older men, including his Dawdi on his mother's side. But, remembering it was important to be polite, he didn't ask.

"Before you begin, I must say that I don't know the letter's origin, nor that of the others." Boston sighed deeply. "But they must be significant, because they're always in my satchel, including for my . . . shall we say, adventure here?" He stopped and turned to stare at the creek. "Or did I dream that?" he muttered. "Maybe I'm mistaken, thinking I've been carrying them everywhere on all my many trips."

Small Jay's ears perked up. It sounded like Boston didn't know why he'd brought the letters along, or even how they'd gotten here. Yet he had been carrying the bag around since the first day Small Jay had met him. Truly the man was befuddled.

And what trips does he mean?

They sat together near the tailrace, and Boston handed the letter to him. Immediately, Small Jay recognized the handwriting as the same as that on the grimy letter he'd found near the bridge. Had Boston discovered that one and returned it to the rest?

"Go ahead, young man."

"I'm Small Jay," he prompted.

"Yes, of course. Like the bird," Boston murmured, a bright smile on his face.

Small Jay glanced at his newfound friend, more honest than most folk, then looked again at the letter and began to read.

> *My dearest darling,*
> *It has been a long and rather dreary day here, chilly and raining for hours. Perhaps it is because I miss you so that the weather seems bleak. There are days when it seems this time apart will quickly end and you will return soon. Other days, alas, it seems as though you have been gone for nearly a lifetime.*

"What was that last line again?" Boston asked, leaning forward and peering at the letter. "Reread it, if you please."

Small Jay did just that, then paused, waiting.

"Oh, what I wouldn't give to know who penned such tender words." Boston interlaced his long, smooth fingers and raised them to his lips. "Who would write such intimate things?" He reached for the letter and scanned it, apparently looking at the bottom for a name. "Ah, it was Abigail who wrote it. Signed, *Yours for always*."

Small Jay felt as heavy as if a boulder had rolled over him.

"Was Abigail writing to you?" he asked, looking down at the end of the letter.

Boston acted like he hadn't heard him. "To whom is the envelope addressed?" he asked.

"I don't see any envelope. But I could look in your satchel, maybe," Small Jay felt compelled to offer. After all, it was wrong to read letters—love letters, at that—meant for someone else. Even so, he kept his thoughts to himself and waited for further instruction from the bewildered man.

Boston hesitated, then handed over the shoulder bag. But Small Jay found no envelopes, just letters and pages covered with strange dots and squiggles on sets of five lines, odd symbols he'd never laid eyes on before. On one of those pages, the words *"Melody of Love"* were written at the top, with the name Eleanor off to the right.

"Who's Eleanor?" asked Small Jay.

Boston's eyebrows rose, then drooped. He frowned hard, as if trying his best to remember. "Eleanor . . ." Sighing, he said at last that he did not recall.

Just then Small Jay realized with some degree of horror that he saw no sign of Sassy, who had been romping with Allegro along the creek's edge not so long ago.

"Here, kitty-kitty," he called, his heart relieved when she came into view. Poor Sassy was a fright, dirty and with grass in her fur, yet she purred contentedly. "We should be gettin' home with the pony cart. Mamma will wonder where we've been."

Boston's head jerked around. "Mamma, you said?"

"That's right. Why do ya ask?"

Rubbing his hand slowly across his forehead, Boston began to moan. "Oh, what was I saying? My memory is slipping."

Small Jay was about to remind him when the man reached

for his bag and uttered something in what sounded like a foreign language.

"What was that, mister?" Small Jay asked.

"Thank you, young lad." Boston sounded aloof.

"Will ya tell me when you run out of food?" Small Jay said, standing to go.

The man sighed again and looked puzzled at the question, and Small Jay felt a little worried for him.

"Do ya like livin' here?" he asked, trying to get Boston's mind back on the here and now.

With a look of surprise, Boston leaned his head back where they sat and stared up at the large four-story stone structure. His mouth gaped open. "Do I own this place?" He turned to look at Small Jay. "Is this my house?"

"I don't think so. I'm not sure where your home is." Small Jay shook his head, his words choking in his throat. "Maybe Abigail is your wife. She sounds awful nice," he said at last.

Despite his dog, the man seemed so alone, and Small Jay had a strong feeling there was someone, somewhere, who had loved Boston, or who loved him still and might be missing him. *Maybe even right now!*

"My wife left me, so I doubt the letter is from her."

"Left you how long ago?" If he remembered right, the letter had been dated years ago, in 1955.

Boston placed his hand on his heart and shook his head. "My dear Abigail has long since gone, I'm very sorry to say."

Gone to Gloryland? Small Jay wondered . . . and trembled.

~ ✑

That afternoon Mammi insisted on their purchasing a baby stroller for Angela Rose, much to Marlena's surprise. While

Marlena shopped in town with her grandmother, she noticed a renewed vigor as Mammi picked up one so-called "necessary" item after another. It was clear from the purchases, she must think the baby was going to be with them for quite a while. As much as Marlena loved the little one and was willing to do her best to care for her, she truly hoped this arrangement would not last much longer.

"I wonder if my beau has ever laid eyes on Luella's baby," she mentioned as she and her grandmother returned home in Mammi's black-bumper Chevy. "I really doubt it."

"She's a precious child," Mammi said, her words seeming to catch in her throat. "This is all so very sad." She glanced over at Marlena, who held the sleeping baby on the passenger side of the front seat.

Marlena looked down at Angela's tiny eyes fluttering and squinting under the white eyelet sunbonnet—Mammi's idea. She recalled the other pretty things her grandmother had insisted on buying: two little cotton sundresses and a white one with lace edging for Sundays. All rather fancy compared to the way Amish mothers dressed their babies. There were tiny socks with lace edging, too, and a skein of soft white yarn with silver threads woven through for crocheted booties. "It's not possible to spoil an infant, is it?" she asked softly.

Mammi gripped the wheel, her wrinkled knuckles white. "Well, hardly at her young age." She paused, then added, "Not unless ya hold her all night, *jah?*"

"*Ach,* I did that so she wouldn't wake you up, Mammi."

Mammi's eyes had a playful glint. "I guess we'll see how easily she falls asleep on her own from here on out."

"She did last night." Marlena touched Angela's little head.

"I'm just hopin' she'll be content here . . . till Gordon's parents can take her, anyway."

Mammi nodded, her eyes on the road. "It's my earnest prayer that God's will might be done for the child."

Each time her grandmother spoke of calling upon God, it made Marlena feel as if she was missing out on something wonderful, just the way Mammi's face seemed to come alive. Naturally, Marlena had listened to the sermons at her parents' Beachy church about experiencing a closeness with the Lord Jesus. That minister had also talked of being redeemed and delivered from the burden of sin, saying that people could know they were, in fact, saved even before death and the Judgment Day. However, such a declaration was considered the height of pride by her Old Order church. In so many ways, the Beachy Amish sermons were different than what Marlena had grown up hearing, and she still wasn't sure what to think about these new beliefs. She was very sure, on the other hand, what Nat Zimmerman and his family thought of her family's move away from *das Alt Gebrauch*. And this, above all, was the thing that worried her most about being so far away from her beloved.

Will Nat come to Luella's funeral? Her heart leaped at the thought, but she realized that was simply a hopeful dream. Nat wouldn't think of attending a service for someone like Luella, a defiant former Amishwoman, even if she *had* been Marlena's own sister.

CHAPTER 12

*M*arlena was thankful for the overcast skies as she left the house to weed the vegetable garden and the three large flower beds following their return home. She smoothed the dirt around yellow, crimson, and purple dahlias after weeding around mounds of gray-green foliage at the base of each plant.

Oh, she longed for another good soaking rain, which would definitely help the weeding process if she needed to finish this chore tomorrow. But knowing she would be tired after a busy morning at their Saturday market, she kept at it, digging each small weed out by the root.

Glancing at the heavens, she recalled something her Dawdi Tim liked to say: *"A watched sky doesn't rain."* At the memory, she stretched a bit and massaged her neck and shoulders before returning to the daunting task. She wondered how long she would feel heavyhearted like this. *So much has been lost. . . .*

She recalled family summer visits there—the corn and wiener roasts Mammi so loved hosting, the watermelon-spitting contests between her father and brothers, and all the kids playing croquet with the wickets spread around the yard.

Marlena remembered how different it was to share the upstairs guest room with Luella, who'd once confided that she was embarrassed about her Plain appearance when at market and in town. *"I can't wait to get some decent English clothes so people will stop staring at me,"* Luella had whispered into the darkness.

Marlena disliked hearing her sister talk disparagingly about the dresses and cape aprons Mamma sewed in accordance with the *Ordnung*. What had gotten into Luella anyway? Even now, Marlena wondered this.

When at long last she'd finished weeding, Marlena's hands ached, along with her heart. Getting up, she picked her way over her grandfather's stepping-stones toward the house. Her right ankle was sore, and she presumed she'd twisted it in her eagerness to accomplish all the weeding in a single afternoon.

Back in the kitchen, she lathered her hands thoroughly with Mammi's homemade lye soap and set the supper table, grateful for Mammi's help watching Angela Rose, who was napping in the playpen after their busy morning in town. The baby wasn't easy to care for all the time, wanting someone in sight or she'd start crying.

Mammi seemed to like having the baby around nonetheless. She was often the first to reach for Angela Rose when her little lower lip puckered. *And she thinks I spoil her. . . .*

"The weeds are all . . . for now," Marlena declared. "If we get a *gut* rain, I'll be right back out there."

"*Denki*, dear." Mammi looked her way, then fondly toward the baby. "Our little cherub had herself a nice long nap. And your mother called with more details on the funeral Monday morning."

Marlena nodded. "How'd she sound today?"

"Matter-of-fact. She was all business, ya know."

"Prob'ly to keep from cryin'." Marlena looked into the play-pen, where Angela Rose held her favorite rattle. "Did ya get all your sewin' done like you wanted to, Mammi?" she asked, changing the topic.

"Didn't take me long this time. Besides, I managed to get supper in the oven."

Thankful for that, Marlena said, "Something smells delicious."

When it was time, they sat down to the reheated baked chicken and rice, wonderful-good leftovers, and cooked buttered peas, garden fresh, with homemade rolls and apple butter. Marlena put Angela Rose in the wooden high chair so she could be included . . . a circle of three generations. She gave the baby a teething ring, which went right into her rosebud mouth.

And, later, Marlena mixed up more of the rice cereal Aunt Becky had brought, which was lots of fun to feed—they'd forgotten to buy a baby-sized spoon. More cereal ended up on the highchair tray than in Angela's mouth.

When Marlena attempted to wash her face, the baby moved away, crying and wrinkling up her little nose as she arched her back.

After the worst of the mess was cleaned up, Mammi remarked, "It's such a nice evening. Why not take Angela Rose out for a stroll?"

Marlena hadn't thought of that, but a walk during the cooler part of the day might be beneficial. "Will you be all right alone here for a little while?"

"Why, sure. I'll do up the dishes . . . give you a head start on your walk."

"No need to, really, Mammi."

Her grandmother offered a sweet smile; then she touched the baby's dimpled elbow. "I insist." She wiped her brow with the back of her palm. "It's been a couple of hard days for you, dear."

"For you, too," Marlena said softly.

They shied away from talk of Luella, rather discussing whom to call to drive them to Mifflinburg for the funeral. Mammi suggested Dawdi Tim's deacon friend, Vernon Siegrist, before unexpectedly offering to drive them herself. Marlena was quick to gently refuse. They were both too shaken by Luella's death; she couldn't accept her grandmother's thoughtful offer. In the end, they both agreed that it was better to hire a driver for the nearly four-hour round trip.

"I'll telephone Vernon while you're out. We'll see if he's available for an early morning trip this Monday," Mammi said. "The funeral is at nine o'clock."

After a light dessert of fruit cup topped with a dollop of whipped cream, Marlena tied the new white sunbonnet on Angela Rose's little head. She carried her outside and slid her into the stroller. Glad for the heavy cloud canopy, Marlena pushed slowly down the back walkway, wishing Luella might have kept in touch with her, especially after Angela Rose was born.

They moved past the pristine flower beds and Mammi's fragrant red roses—*"red stands for love,"* Mammi always said when the very first blooms sprang to life—and then out toward the berry patch.

Two crows scolded over there, perched on the fence, craning their black necks, then strutting about. She remembered the days, back before her grandfather's illness, when he and

Mammi had kept hens. Oh, the happy days of going to the hen house to gather eggs, eager to get there before the rats did, the miserable critters.

Dawdi had been a high-spirited man, full of fun, quite unlike a few of the sour-faced men at the meetinghouse on Sundays. She'd once caught herself trying to imagine what dear Dawdi would look like without his long, thinning beard, curious about his youthful appearance. He'd had the longest eyelashes she'd ever seen on a man, even as long as Luella's, although her sister had enhanced hers with dark makeup as a teenager, making them appear even longer and thicker.

Marlena stopped walking, wondering why she'd never realized before that Luella had resembled Dawdi in that way—both of them so striking, with fine and well-proportioned features. So fine, in fact, their younger brother Amos had tried to sketch a silhouette of Luella after the supper hour one winter years ago, much to Dat's chagrin.

Walking again, Marlena assumed that was the way of grief— you uncovered facts that had always been in front of you, making discoveries only when it was too late.

Aware of the sultry evening air, she realized Mammi was right; she'd needed this walk. "Let's listen for the birdies again," she leaned down to tell Angela Rose.

As she walked, she spotted the familiar apple orchard where she'd spent busy hours with the amiable Amish neighbors. Rosanna Miller, Benuel's oldest daughter, was closer to Luella's age and as sunny as a springtime sunrise, yet Luella had showed little interest in her, and Rosanna had quickly become Marlena's friend.

Recalling the carefree and sweet-spirited girl, Marlena wondered where Rosanna lived now, or if she'd married yet. In many ways, Rosanna had taken Luella's sisterly place nearly every summer, exploring nearby meadows with Marlena and concocting new dessert recipes and testing them in her mother's old black wood stove. The girls had also liked to swim fearlessly in the swollen creek behind the Mennonite minister's barn while wearing their cape dresses, and once even shared the fright of seeing a water snake within touching distance in the moonlight.

Marlena smiled at the memories, recalling that Rosanna had once said, *"There's a little glimpse of heaven in a buttercup."* She'd been so convincing that Marlena had picked one and slipped it under her pillow.

All the fun Luella missed. . . . Marlena found it curious, the things she recalled these many years later. *I remember the past so clearly.*

Her reverie was interrupted by the sight of Small Jay coming this way with Sassy in tow. "Look, Angela Rose . . . there's a kitty-cat," she said.

"Hullo," the Bitner boy called to them.

"Wie bischt?"

He bobbed his head and a bashful smile spread across his slim face. As was often the case when she first arrived in the summer, Small Jay didn't say much. He waved now and reached for his straw hat.

"Are ya lookin' to catch some lightning bugs?" she asked, moving toward him.

Small Jay shrugged, still fidgeting with his hat. "Just might."

She invited him to walk with her, and they admired the road banks profuse with fragrant honeysuckle. "Have ya met my little niece?"

He shook his head. "Maybe she'll like my Sassy-cat. I hosed

her off a little bit ago." Small Jay explained how dirty she'd gotten, playing near the creek bank down by the old mill. "Not sure she's forgiven me yet."

"Well, she looks right fluffy to me. Why don't ya bring your kitty over closer?" Marlena stopped the stroller and crouched near, running her hand over the plump part of the baby's wrist.

Small Jay put his hat back on and inched over, dragging his leg. He stooped to lift the cat and held Sassy near the stroller, but not too close.

"This is Angela Rose," Marlena told him.

Small Jay looked her over. "*Ach,* she's mighty little. Kinda like me."

Marlena guided Angela's hand toward the cat's soft fur. "See? Doesn't that feel awful nice?" she cooed to the baby. "This is Small Jay's kitty-cat."

Angela lit right up.

"Where'd this baby come from?" Small Jay stared at Angela Rose.

"Well, just north of Harrisburg. She's visiting for a while."

"My sisters'll like her. They ain't so interested in the likes of me, though. They boss me when Mamma's out pickin' peas and rhubarb. 'Specially Julia. Dat says she's full of pepper and spice."

"And my big sister bossed me but *gut* when we were young. But she got married and moved away."

"Ah . . ." he said absently and looked at the sky, then back at her. "Can ya keep a secret?"

"Sure." She straightened and Small Jay set the cat back down on the ground. "But why would ya want to tell *me?*"

"Well, 'cause you listen." He looked timidly at her. "And I could use a big sister."

Marlena pondered that. *Doesn't his dear mother, Ellie, listen with her heart?*

"Promise first not to say a word . . . if I *do* tell ya?" His small face was earnest.

"Is everything all right, Small Jay?" she blurted, uneasy about promising anything.

His head drooped. "Well, not for a lonely old man down the way. He lives in the mill with his dog." Then, as if realizing he'd shared something maybe too soon, he began to shake his head. "*Nee* . . . I didn't mean to say—"

"It's all right," she said, reaching out but not touching him. "You can trust me. Honest, ya can."

His soft blue eyes blinked several times. "Just wonderin' if it's a *gut* idea or not to have my friend Boston meet my parents. I'm hopin' they might let him stay in the empty *Dawdi Haus*, maybe. He can keep cookin' his own food, if they want. He does it now over a campfire."

He went on to explain a little more, but it was hard to understand, really, all this about a stray man living in an abandoned mill and cooking outdoors near the creek. And apparently eating cereal and beef jerky, too. How could Small Jay be so sure about this drifter with the strange name?

"I'd like to meet this friend of yours," she said at last, wondering if it was wise to do so on her own.

"I could take ya tomorrow."

"Maybe after market," she suggested. "I'll see if my grandmother can watch Angela Rose."

Small Jay's eyes shone with unexpected intensity. "You'll go?"

She assured him she would, one way or the other. But she was quite worried about the man Small Jay had supposedly befriended. Might he take advantage of the boy?

Small Jay picked up his cat again and squeezed her till she opened her mouth wide and meowed. *"Denki,"* he said, eyes bright. "I think you'll like Boston, too."

They turned off the main road and walked down the tree-lined lane toward his father's house, so Marlena could confirm that Dorcas was planning to babysit tomorrow. When Small Jay looked worried, she reminded him, "You can trust me, remember?"

His mouth curved up instantly. "I'll try to remember. Ain't always easy."

She pointed out to Angela Rose the red and white geraniums lining the cement walkway, glad she'd heeded Mammi's urging to go for a stroll. But she was still disturbed about this man Small Jay seemed so anxious for her to meet.

Why does he want to spend time with a hobo?

Over in the backyard, Ellie was beating rag rugs at the clothesline, seemingly unaware of Small Jay's comings and goings. Or of his secret.

Did I promise too quickly?

"We leave behind traces of ourselves, Marlena, in everything we do—the decisions we make, the vegetables we sow, the meals we cook . . . and eat," Dawdi Tim had once told her when Marlena was perplexed over a particular choice. She had valued his wisdom and always would. What a powerful influence he had been on her life when she was young and unable to make her own choices about what church to attend. Now he wasn't around to ask any more questions. All the same, she couldn't simply embrace his and Mammi's beliefs from their Mennonite church. From the way they prayed and studied

the Bible to how they lived their everyday lives—much of it differed from the *Ordnung* Marlena had been raised under. *And I would never want to own a car, no matter how black the bumper was!*

Back home at Mammi's, she bathed Angela Rose and gave her a bottle, eventually putting her to bed. Even after the lovely walk, Marlena felt a need to sort through her thoughts and the mixture of sadness and even resentment she was experiencing. Those niggling remnants from the past with her sister that would never be reconciled now that Luella had died. *Oh, if only Dawdi Tim were still alive, I'd sit down with him and talk his ear off.*

CHAPTER 13

*M*arlena had slept lightly, aware of the baby's movements in the crib, every little sound. Thinking of the state of Luella's soul had kept her awake, too, even more than Angela Rose sharing the same room . . . so much more.

In the middle of the night, Marlena had gone down to the kitchen to drink some milk, hoping to get to sleep again before the baby's next feeding. She had nibbled on a cookie while standing at the back door, staring out through its window past the wide porch and the yard, clear out to the dark trees silhouetted against the sky. Luella's death had stirred up things she'd never addressed before, especially their differences in belief.

Now that it was morning, she lifted Angela Rose out of her crib and cuddled her. Then, thinking it might please Mammi, she dressed her in the new pink-and-white sundress with little cap sleeves, almost like wings. "You look so sweet today," she whispered, reaching to pick her up. "Dorcas from next door will take *gut* care of ya while Mammi and I are gone a few hours." She kissed the peachy cheek and leaned her head against Angela's, letting the tears fall. Her cuddly niece, dear as could be, was still a reminder of Luella's deserting her family and faith . . . and marrying a worldly man.

～ℯↄ

The marketplace was already bustling with people when Marlena and her grandmother arrived. Familiar merchants were setting up tables and stands where, within the hour, customers would wait in line for German sausages and home-made breads, as well as produce fresh from the garden—carrots with the greens and soil still evident, and varieties of leaf lettuce, peas, and radishes.

Marlena's mind was occupied with thoughts of Angela Rose, wondering how she was doing at Bitners'. She trusted Ellie to watch over Dorcas, who seemed not only willing to have Angela there but excited, too, as were Julia and Sally. The girls had gathered around Marlena when she'd first arrived, making over the baby, touching her little hands, talking baby talk. Marlena hadn't seen Small Jay, though, and assumed he was occupied with Sassafras somewhere. *Such a kind and loving family*, she thought as she counted out the change for jovial customers, a number of them eager to speak with her. Even though she knew few people in the area, she could always tell which ones were the tourists from their questions about how the jam was made, some even so bold as to request the recipe, which Marlena could honestly say she'd never written down.

"So, it's all up here?" one bright-eyed woman asked, tapping her temple. And Marlena assured her that it was indeed true.

By midmorning, they'd sold nearly all the many pints of strawberry-rhubarb jam, but Marlena knew better than to think Mammi would leave this early for home. Just when she'd spotted another friendly face—one from her grandmother's church—and started to go over to say hello, Marlena noticed Luke and Sarah Mast heading her way.

Immediately she smiled at Sarah, who had always been welcoming to her and her siblings.

"*Wie geht's*, Marlena?"

Moving around the table, Marlena went to greet her, offering a quick smile to Luke, as well. "I'm all right. *Denki* for askin'."

Sarah reached to touch her hand and glanced at her brother, then back at Marlena. "We heard the sad news . . . of your sister's passing."

Luke offered to shake her hand, which caught Marlena off guard. "It must've been unexpected," he said, eyes serious.

She said it was, and looked away—the reality was still so fresh.

"If there's anything we can do," Sarah said, "anything at all, please let us know." Here, she looked again at Luke. "Ain't that right, Luke?"

He nodded. "I 'spect you'll be going to the funeral, ain't?" Luke stood only a head taller than his tall and very blond sister.

Nearly a matched set, Marlena thought, taking note of their blue eyes and the exceptional gold hue of their hair. As New Order Amish, Luke's straw hat brim was noticeably narrow, and Sarah's dark maroon-colored dress and matching cape apron were practically red.

"Sorry?" Marlena said, having forgotten the question. "A lot on my mind."

"Your sister's funeral."

"Mammi and I are goin', but it won't be easy. . . . Luella wasn't in Jesus anymore," she found herself explaining.

"Aw . . . would be ever so hard to bear," Sarah said softly.

Luke stepped in closer. "I've heard your parents are no longer members of an Old Order group." He stated this nearly like a minister might, but since his father was a preacher, she wasn't really too surprised. He had such a brotherly manner about him that Marlena didn't feel put upon whatsoever.

"*Jah*, 'tis true, and I've been goin' with them to the Beachy church back home—out of respect, since I'm still under Dat's roof, ya know. But this summer, I'll be worshiping with Mammi at the Mennonite meetinghouse while I'm here."

Sarah's eyes were intent on her. "Really, now? We have kinfolk who joined that church last year."

Luke removed his straw hat and ran his long fingers through his hair, a smile spreading across his face. "Do ya ever wonder sometimes which end is up?"

"For pity's sake, Luke Mast!" His sister turned, frowning and blinking her eyes at him.

"I meant no harm," Luke said, palms up. "It must be awful confusing, that's all."

"*Ach*, believe me, it can be at times." Marlena felt sure he wasn't poking fun at her.

They talked awhile longer about market next weekend and all the rhubarb Sarah had to do something with, and then they parted ways.

When Mammi saw Marlena returning to the table, she patted the chair beside her. "Such a caring *Bruder un Schweschder*. They seem to look out for each other."

"I've always thought so, too," Marlena agreed. "Makes me wonder what it would've been like to have an older brother." She thought of Luella right quick and cringed at how that must have sounded. "*Puh*, I didn't mean . . ."

Mammi patted her hand. "I know what ya meant, honey-girl. You and Luella were never close like that." She looked away for a moment. "Must make things all the harder for ya now."

Mammi knew? She found this surprising yet almost a comfort, knowing she wasn't the only one who'd realized it.

They spent another half hour socializing, and then Mammi was ready to head home. Considering Marlena still had to pay a visit to Small Jay's friend at the mill, she was glad to be getting on the road. *What sort of name is Boston?* she wondered. Ellie's son often got things mixed up.

On the drive toward home, Marlena recalled that Luella had once snuck home a small transistor radio she'd borrowed from an *Englischer* friend. Boldly, Luella had tuned in to a rock 'n' roll station, wanting Marlena to listen with her. But when Marlena refused, Luella's eyes had flashed. *"You never try anything, Marlena. You're just a no-fun fuddy-duddy!"*

Marlena pushed the remembrance from her mind and asked Mammi if they might stop at the store up ahead so she could purchase a kitchen fan.

"Whatever for?" Mammi looked aghast.

"To keep you and the baby cool when I'm out in the garden and whatnot." Marlena sighed. "We made more than enough at market today, ain't so?"

"It's a luxury we can do without."

So is this car. Marlena hadn't expected her to put up a fuss. She tried not to smile.

"I'd really like for you to have a fan, Mammi."

Her grandmother made several more excuses before concluding adamantly, "That's what windows are for. . . . The Lord sends along His breezes, ya know."

"All right, then, if you'd rather not."

Mammi glanced at her. "I daresay you've become right fancy in your thinkin' since you started going to church with your parents."

"Not at all, Mammi. I'm Old Order, for certain."

"So the fan wouldn't have benefited you, too?"

Marlena groaned and smiled at her. "I guess you've got me there. Even so, I do wish you were more comfortable these hot summer days."

Mammi didn't say another word as she stepped on the accelerator and drove right past the store where fans could be had. And that was that.

CHAPTER 14

By the time Marlena put Angela Rose down for her nap that afternoon, she was breathless and felt flushed. She hurried out the back door, rehearsing what she'd told Mammi about needing to run an errand on foot, without mentioning where or what, trying her best to shield Small Jay's secret. Mammi, who was already tired from market, assured her that was fine; she would just sit at the table and shell a batch of peas Ellie Bitner had left on the porch while they were gone.

Now, as Marlena moved down through the willow grove and scanned the area below the pond, she thought it best to simply wait for Small Jay there. No sense risking being seen near their lane or backyard.

In due time, she heard Small Jay coming along, talking to his cat, and she turned and followed, albeit out of sight, parallel to him in the grove. She could see Ellie's son limping out toward the road, his head turning from side to side. *He's looking for me.*

When he'd finally arrived at the end of the lane, she slipped out of the trees and onto the road. There, they'd be obscured from the view of either house. "I saw ya headin' this way," she explained.

He smiled and nodded shyly. "You remembered!"

"I did say I'd go with you." She matched her pace to his slow stride, wishing for a way to help the poor boy get down the road and back more easily. Mammi's car would be just the thing. Of course, she didn't have the slightest notion how to drive.

"Dorcas sure is high-minded today," he said, "since she babysat for your baby."

"Well, my *niece*."

He shrugged. "I saw her takin' the bottle when I went in for the noon meal." Small Jay said he couldn't get over how tiny she was. "Smaller even than I must've been." His face clouded. "But of course . . . when she grows up, she'll probably be bigger than I am now." He pushed his hands into his pockets.

Marlena felt a tug on her heart. "Sometimes, though . . . small is better."

Small Jay looked up at her. "*Vas?*"

"Sure," she said confidently. "My Mamma says *Gott* ain't hindered by the size of the vessel—that's you or me. In fact, she says that His power is seen even better in those who are weak or small . . . or less fortunate."

Small Jay's eyes widened. "So . . . sometimes small *is* better?"

"Evidently that's the way the Lord looks at it."

Small Jay marveled. "Does that mean He can work through *me?*" Small Jay said, looking up at her just then. "Ya sure?"

"Last Lord's Day at Mammi's church, I heard the preacher read a Scripture verse that said when we are the weakest, the Lord is strong."

Small Jay whistled to his cat. "Hear that, Sassy? God can work through even the smallest of us."

Sassy cocked her head, and Marlena smiled, encouraged by Small Jay's improved mood.

When they arrived at the mill, Small Jay knocked at the door where he said he'd seen Boston going in and out. But there was no response, nor any sign of the border collie Small Jay referred to as Allegro. He knocked again, but still nothing. "Something's wrong—he's *always* here," he insisted.

The boy appeared to be frantic, creeping back and forth from one door to another, knocking, waiting, then knocking . . . resorting to pounding with his small fist, all the while calling, "Boston!" again and again.

At last, when she could stand it no longer, Marlena intervened, lest the neighbors wonder what the world was happening, or lest the poor boy hurt himself. "I'm sure he'll be back later," she assured Small Jay.

But he shook his head and resisted her resolve to head home. Standing his ground, arms folded, he pouted and limped over to a tree stump, sitting there for a time. Then, without warning, he got up and went to the creek's edge and peered down, pointing out the location where his so-called friend kept a milk bottle, a carved-out area where the creek water ran past. "Where'd Boston go?" he said softly now, as if talking to himself. "Where?"

"Maybe just walkin' his dog," Marlena suggested. "Like you do Sassy."

Small Jay brightened at that. "Then he'll be back," he exclaimed. "I wanna wait for him!"

Marlena sighed. Waiting didn't seem like a good idea. "Might not be wise to loiter on private property," she said, looking around.

Clearly dejected, Small Jay finally picked up Sassy, and

they walked toward the road. "I bought my Dat some black licorice yesterday," he told Marlena, who said that was a thoughtful thing to do. "*Jah*, I'm tryin' to do nice things for my father."

Marlena wondered why he was telling her this, but she was glad she could be there to listen to the boy, who talked more like a youngster than a teen.

They had gone only a short distance when a stout neighbor woman came rushing out onto the road, her long black apron flying, her hair wrapped in a triangular blue scarf. "Are ya looking for that rumpled-looking fella? The one with the dog?"

"He's my friend," Small Jay said quickly.

"Well then, you should know that there were several neighbors—Amish and English alike—over there not an hour ago. From what I heard, they ran the bum off, claimed he was trespassin'."

Small Jay's lips pursed at this news.

"Did anyone say where he might've gone?" Marlena stepped forward, knowing it was important to Small Jay and even more curious about the man now that she was certain he was real.

"It's beyond me what he was doin' over there in the mill," the plump Amishwoman replied. "It's anybody's guess where he'll land next. My guess is jail."

Marlena shivered, and Small Jay's face turned pale.

"Jail?" he asked.

"Why sure, that's where a trespasser ends up, young man."

"Was his dog with him when he left?" Small Jay asked timidly.

"Honestly, I don't know. But I can tell ya I had the heebie-jeebies, thinking a drunkard might be wanderin' about." The woman folded her ample arms across her protruding middle.

"*Denki* kindly," Marlena said quickly, anxious to end this conversation.

She breathed a sigh of relief as the gossipy woman headed back to her front yard.

"Why'd she say jail?" Small Jay whispered to Marlena as they continued on their way. "Boston's done nothin' wrong."

Marlena didn't know what to say to that. Trespassing did seem serious enough to get a homeless person in hot water.

They walked silently for a while, and then suddenly Small Jay turned to look toward the hill behind them in the distance. "I wish I could see the angels back yonder."

"Angels?"

"Up there." He pointed to the gleaming church spire and explained what he'd heard a while back.

Marlena had no desire to discourage him, but she suspected Small Jay was confused. Miracles like that rarely happened, and if angels *had* ever been sighted, it would've been all the talk. News traveled swiftly in a rural community. *If so, Grandmammi would surely have heard of it.*

Again, Small Jay turned toward the sloping grade, and together they walked gradually to the crest. "Have *you* ever seen an angel?" he asked when they stopped to allow time for him to catch his breath.

She considered that. "Well, my baby niece certainly looks like one when she smiles."

That seemed to satisfy him. Just then they heard the familiar rattle of carriage wheels and the loud *clippity-clop* of a horse's hooves on the pavement. When Marlena turned to see who was coming, she saw Sarah Mast waving, her other hand holding the reins as she drove alone in her family's enclosed gray buggy.

"Hullo again!" Sarah called, her face sweet with a smile.

"We keep bumpin' into each other, ain't?" Marlena was beyond pleased.

Sarah slowed the chestnut driving horse and pulled off the road, coming to a stop. "Looks like you're goin' my way, maybe? Hop in, if you'd like."

Marlena accepted and held the cat while Small Jay slowly climbed in. "Where are you headed this fine afternoon?"

"Over to help my married sister plant beets." Sarah reached to pet the cat's head. "What're ya doin' this far from home again, Small Jay?"

"Just out walkin'," he said, looking downright miserable. "Went to see my friend who ain't there . . . 'least no more." His voice cracked with emotion.

Sarah's eyebrows rose like she might inquire further. But Marlena wanted to protect Small Jay and pushed past the awkwardness to ask about Ellie's needlepoint class. "I wasn't able to go last time, what with my niece to care for."

"Oh, you really should try an' come to at least the Wednesday quilting class. Bring the baby along. We'll all take turns holdin' her." She explained that there were a number of young women attending now, including some Mennonite and New Order Amish girls, too.

Marlena was so touched by Sarah's cordial invitation and manner, she agreed on the spot, realizing once again how very much she liked Sarah's company. Besides that, she wanted to have something to look forward to after Luella's funeral, which she was beginning to dread.

"How long will you have your sister's baby?" Sarah asked.

"A couple weeks, maybe, if that long. I'm not really sure."

"Well, babies sure have a way of tuggin' at the heartstrings."

Marlena simply smiled. She had already decided she wouldn't let herself become too attached to Angela Rose.

⁓ ᒲᘓ

"Ellie!" her husband called from the stable.

Goodness, she could hear Roman's voice clear in the kitchen, where she was scrubbing down windowsills and mopboards with the girls.

"I need to speak to you," he called again.

She recognized this tone and gave her cleaning rag to Sally to rinse out in the bucket of water. Drying her hands on her long apron, Ellie scurried outdoors and stood on the back steps, waiting for Roman to appear.

He stepped out of the shadows rather dramatically, then motioned to her. So this was to be a private conversation. *Most likely about Small Jay.*

Pushing his straw hat forward, he shielded his eyes from the afternoon sun. "Is young Jake round anywhere?" he asked when she walked over there.

"Not that I know of."

"Well, I'm puttin' my foot down," he announced, a glower on his ruddy face. "I ran into my brother, who's seen Jake loitering near the old mill. Seems there's something strange going on. And I've decided the boy needs to stay round here from now on."

"I understand why you're concerned," she said. "But can't Small Jay be free to choose where he goes so long as he sticks closer to home?"

His sharp gaze trapped hers. "I will *not* have him down there with a drunkard."

"A what?"

"Brother Jake's said word has it a homeless man's been holing up in the former grist mill."

Ellie could hardly believe it. "So you think Small Jay's in danger, then?"

"My brother doesn't lie."

"'Tis true." Jake Bitner was an upstanding man in the church and had even been nominated for preacher on at least two occasions. Ellie knew he would never warn her husband unless he felt there was a reason.

"That's all I'll be sayin' about this," Roman concluded brusquely. He dashed off before she could make another remark.

As Ellie headed back to the house, she knew without asking who was expected to be the bearer of this news.

"Your father forbids you . . ." She tried out the words in her mind, helpless to do anything but Roman's wishes. This dreadful declaration only made her son's narrow little world even more confined.

CHAPTER 15

*M*arlena pushed the screen door open and slipped inside the utility room. The fiery words of the woman near the mill had her worried, and she wished she'd gone to investigate Small Jay's so-called friend immediately.

She was also curious about the angels Small Jay had mentioned and planned to ask her grandmother about that. But in the kitchen, she found Mammi veiled by tears at the sink, scrubbing potatoes. "Aw, Mammi . . . Mammi." She rushed to her side.

"I'm fine." Mammi protested as she rinsed her hands and wiped her swollen eyes with her apron. "What with Luella gone . . ." She stopped. "I 'spect it stirs up more sadness over your Dawdi Tim."

Marlena flung her arms around her. "Why don't ya rest for a while . . . let me finish up here."

Mammi turned to look at the playpen. "The baby was ever so fussy, but she's asleep, at last."

Having Angela Rose here is both a joy and a hardship for Mammi.

"What if I finish makin' supper for ya?" Marlena kissed her cheek and was relieved when her grandmother removed her work apron and headed into the front room to get off her feet.

If only she could pray the kind of openhearted prayer Mammi would send up to God right now if Marlena had been the one grieving so awful hard. But she couldn't find the words in her head, nor in her heart. *So many years of rote praying,* she thought, remembering the remarkable change in her father's prayers—from memorized prayers to fervent ones—after he and Mamma joined the Beachy Amish church. She didn't know exactly what had caused the difference, but she much preferred the way her father prayed now. *Like Mammi.*

Glancing toward the front room, Marlena checked on her grandmother. Mammi surely felt lost without Dawdi Tim, having spent all those years loving him and raising their children together, working this fertile green land, only to have everything end so abruptly.

Marlena took time to scrub off the soil on the potatoes, still searching for some heartfelt yet reverent words to pray. Besides, it wasn't far from her mind that Luella's husband would soon hear the saddest news of his life. How would he take it, not having the chance to say good-bye to his bride before she died? Marlena simply could not imagine such a thing.

She finished washing the pile of potatoes, then dug out each of the sprouted eyes with a paring knife. She and Mammi preferred to cook extra for potato salad or to make fried potatoes with the leftovers. Afterward, she washed down Mammi's electric range and oven, then polished their for-good shoes out on the back porch and left them to dry.

Marlena paused to look in on Angela Rose, still asleep. Later, she hoped to find the time to start another letter to Nat.

If Angela Rose cooperates. The letter she'd sent him yesterday should have already arrived there in today's afternoon mail. Oh, but her return to Mifflinburg for the funeral would only fuel the yearning to see him again.

~⊙

Following the tongue-lashing from Mamma, Small Jay took Sassy upstairs to his room and closed the door. He'd never felt so upset or embarrassed. Not only had Mamma told him he was not to leave the farm anymore to go wandering about, but his father had come inside and interrupted Mamma's conversation with him. *"You're takin' a terrible risk by spending time with a vagabond,"* Dat had stressed. Small Jay didn't know what *vagabond* meant, but the way it was said—and the glare on Dat's face—made him very worried for Boston.

Is des Druwwel? he wondered. "But how can they even know if he *is* trouble?" Small Jay complained to his cat.

He lowered himself onto a chair in front of one of the tall windows overlooking the road, giving in to his urge to just sit and stew. "Where are you, Boston . . . *where?*" The image in his mind was of the poor man suddenly being forced to leave the mill. Small Jay shivered and remembered the sad, sad song Boston had played on his harmonica. *Like Mr. Martin used to play up yonder.*

Tears threatened to spill, but he brushed them away. What would Gracie Yoder think if she saw him bawling like a baby? She'd nearly caught him crying two years ago, when Danny Glick snatched away the ball right as Small Jay was about to catch it during a recess softball game. He'd waited nearly an endless year to be a second baseman, but freckle-faced Danny had other ideas. *"Hop-a-long, you're too small to be playin', let alone on any bases!"* Danny had said the cruel words for Small Jay's ears only.

Hop-a-long, indeed! Later, on the way into the schoolhouse, Gracie had come that close to bumping into Small Jay—almost saw his tears—but he'd had the good sense to look away. *Don't be so* doppich, he'd told himself.

Now, struggling with the painful ache in his throat, he looked over at Sassy. She was taking dainty steps as she stalked over to the dresser and rubbed against first its wooden legs, then the chair's. He didn't much mind her being aloof when it was best for him to sit there alone, what with his parents all *ferhoodled* downstairs. They didn't trust him if they were this vexed. Did they still think of him as a child?

"But I ain't!" He raised his voice just enough to vent his anger.

Boston calls me "young man," he thought. *Not Small Jay.*

He buried his face in his trembling hands.

~♥~

The afternoon sun had slipped behind some hazy clouds, a welcome respite from the heat. Marlena went around opening all the upstairs windows, the house much too warm for Angela Rose. She'd given her a lukewarm sponge bath after supper, dressing her in one of the sleeping gowns Aunt Becky had brought along. The little one smelled so sweet.

Recalling last evening's walk—how much better she'd felt afterward— Marlena decided now was a good time for a short stroll. She invited her grandmother to join them, but Mammi was happy to sit and rock on the back porch, fanning herself.

Marlena placed Ellie's lightweight baby blanket in the

stroller for Angela Rose and set out walking along the drive-way, back and forth. After finding Mammi in such a sad state earlier, she didn't want to leave her there alone on the porch too long. Marlena playfully called "peek-a-boo!" when she and the baby strolled past, which altered Mammi's pensive expression to a smile each time.

Pondering the upcoming funeral, Marlena took in the farm-land around her as she pushed the stroller. Not until that mo-ment had she given much thought to Angela Rose's attire for her mother's service. Never before had Marlena seen such a little one at a funeral, except for occasional nursing infants with their mothers, way back in the kitchen of the hosting house.

Her thoughts were interrupted by a sudden commotion out on the road—cars honking and a horse and buggy being halted with a loud "Whoa!" Curious, she turned the stroller around and headed back down the driveway toward the road.

Lo and behold, besides a buggy there were two cars, one with its bumper blackened, and another one clad in shiny chrome. A small group of Amishmen and English neighbors had gathered. "What the world," she whispered, inching the stroller back.

Another enclosed gray carriage pulled up, and then a hay wagon filled to the brim stopped right in the middle of the road, blocking any through traffic. And at the center of it all was a tall, rumpled-looking man carrying a rolled-up black blanket, a striking border collie standing near.

Uncertain what was happening, Marlena quickly made her way to the back porch with Angela Rose. "There's something strange goin' on down the road," she said. She filled Mammi in, asking if the baby might stay with her on the porch. "I want to take a closer look."

"She's getting droopy-eyed, so she might just fall asleep," Mammi noted. "Be careful, dear."

By the time Marlena arrived at the scene, she remained on the circumference of an emerging crowd. Peeking over a shoulder, Marlena began to put it together: This must be the man from the mill she and Small Jay had attempted to visit earlier.

"The neighbors around the mill have complained," one of the Amishmen was telling the scruffy man in question. "It wonders us why you're stayin' there."

The stranger peered around the circle, looking sideways at his accusers, seemingly self-conscious.

"Rightly so," said another man who leaned against his car. "Are you from around here?"

The sunburned man with a cockeyed black bow tie looked so unsteady, he could scarcely hold his blanket any longer, and after more questions were directed at him, it rolled out of his thin arms and fell to the road, narrowly missing the dog. "Begging your pardon, sir," he said, his brow rutted. "Perhaps I've been in the heat too long."

"Can you tell us your full name and address?" the first man asked, his voice more gentle now.

Marlena moved forward slightly to hear the drifter's response.

Pushing his hand into his pocket and rummaging about, the man from the mill pulled out a notepad. "This is the longest day I've lived," he murmured, sounding exhausted and confused, "but I shall attempt to make heads or tails of this."

"Have ya been drinkin'?" asked another Amishman.

"I do not imbibe."

The questioner seemed to accept this, perhaps relieved by the man's sudden clarity. This poor man, who, in Marlena's opinion, needed a good long shower and a nice hot meal, too.

"Why ain't ya at home, 'stead of sleepin' at the mill?" asked another Amish farmer.

Marlena was surprised to see Luke Mast step forward near his road horse, in front of the hay wagon. His straw hat rested on his straight blond bangs. "I'd be glad to look after this man."

Marlena could hardly believe her ears. *Does Luke know him?*

Just then she heard someone calling, "Boston! Boston!"

She turned and saw Small Jay hobbling down his father's lane as fast as his legs could move. *He must've heard the commotion.*

"Boston!" the lad continued to holler. "I was lookin' for ya!"

Marlena's heart went out to both the boy and the man, and she drew near, wishing she might alleviate Small Jay's obvious fear.

By now, Luke had moved protectively closer to the man with oily hair and disheveled clothes, a leather bag on his right shoulder.

"I wondered where you'd gone, Boston," Small Jay spoke up again. "You had me mighty worried."

The drifter beamed down at Small Jay and slowly reached for his hand. "I was lookin' for you, too," he said softly. "Perhaps that's how I came to find myself here. If only I remembered."

Marlena leaned to pick up the rolled-up blanket from the ground as Small Jay went to Luke and stood on tiptoes, cupping Luke's ear with his hand as he whispered.

Luke nodded immediately, his eyes alight at whatever Small Jay had said. "Come with us now, Boston." He reached for the man's sleeve, then motioned to Small Jay to lead the way.

"Won't ya *kumme* home with me?" Small Jay implored the man.

"Home," repeated Boston, grinning now at Small Jay. "The loveliest word of all."

A few moments passed while those who'd gathered talked right fast in *Deitsch*, rehearsing the scene and what they knew of the man's wanderings in the area.

Marlena caught Luke's eye and smiled her thanks as he held on to Boston's arm, steadying the man. *So thoughtful . . . and confident.* Without thinking, she fell into step with them as they moved gradually up the lane toward the Bitners' farm-house.

When they'd passed the springhouse, Luke asked Small Jay, "Does your father know of your plan?"

"Not just yet." Small Jay looked up at the man he called Boston.

"Well, at least one hurdle is past," Marlena said quietly.

Small Jay stopped walking. "Boston, won't ya meet my friend Marlena Wenger? She's visitin' her Mammi yonder." He pointed toward the house at the crest of the hill.

"I'm pleased to meet you, Miss Wenger. My name is Boston Calvert," the older man said, shaking her hand. Boston's eyes met hers, and for a moment she was sure she saw tears. "I'm grateful beyond words, miss."

She smiled, and they headed onward, the man's dog beside him as they made their way around the house to the paved walkway. And as they went, Marlena wondered how a man could sound so refined and have such perfect manners, yet look so down and out.

CHAPTER 16

*L*uke Mast hadn't waited around once Small Jay insisted he head on home, since his horse and the hay wagon were still parked out on the road. But Marlena wasn't as confident. She really had no idea what Roman's reaction to Boston's arrival might be, and she felt on edge as Small Jay pressed his nose into the screen door and called for his mother after setting his cat inside.

She noticed Boston's hands shaking and wondered if he'd had anything to eat recently. She didn't dare offer to have him stay over at Mammi's, what with the baby there and all. *I'm trusting something works out here with Small Jay and his family.*

When no one came, the boy disappeared into the house, and Marlena considered asking Boston if he wanted to rest a bit on the porch steps. He was teetering now and she worried he might pass out. The man's border collie made whimpering sounds and settled at Boston's feet, his black-and-white head leaning on his stately white paws, eyes alert.

Despite Boston's earlier protestation, she wondered if he had been drinking, but when she asked if he could manage to stand a little longer, there was no alcoholic smell to his breath. If he *was* sober, what was causing his terrible confusion . . . and the shakes?

Ellie appeared just then at the door, wearing a frown. Then, seeing Marlena there with Boston, she stepped outside and smiled. "Well, I didn't realize *you* were out here, dear. Goodness' sake, we can't have yous standin' in the heat." Small Jay stood in the doorway now, and Ellie motioned for all of them to come up and sit on the porch.

Meanwhile, Ellie called into the kitchen for Julia to run and get their father. Small Jay had already seated himself next to Boston on the last available porch chair.

"Mamma, this is my friend Boston Calvert," Small Jay told his bewildered mother. "The man I met . . . at the mill."

"Hullo, Mr. Calvert," Ellie said, making brief eye contact with the bedraggled man. She stood stiffly, her hands on her apron, and turned her gaze to the stable. "Calvert," she said then, her glance returning to Boston. "I believe I saw your name written on a note."

Small Jay's eyes blinked rapidly, but he said nothing.

Ellie shook her head, clearly flustered. "*Ach,* I don't know what's keepin' my husband."

A long silence fell over them.

Finally Small Jay said, "Mamma, can Boston stay with us for a while?" His eyes were pleading. "He's got no place to lay his head."

Boston leaned forward; his hands were shaking uncontrollably now. "May I trouble you, madam, for a glass of cold water?" he asked, his voice faltering. "I would greatly appreciate it."

Marlena took pity on him and hoped Ellie might grant the man's wish. She glanced toward the barn to see if Roman was on his way but saw no sign of him, so she offered to go in herself and get some water for Boston. "I don't mind, really, Ellie."

"*Nee* . . . I'll get it," Ellie said right quick. She reached to open the screen door, which slapped behind her.

"I'd give up my own room for ya, Boston, but the stairs are awful steep." Small Jay leaned down and petted the dog's nose. "Don't know where we could put Allegro, though. Dat's not so keen on havin' animals in the house . . . 'cept Sassy."

"Is Allegro the dog's name?" Marlena asked, finding it peculiar.

"Yes," Boston said, then he began to mutter something about his special letters and reached for the shoulder bag he'd dropped on the porch. His eyes looked foggy as he rooted through the soft leather bag.

Ellie returned with a pale green tumbler of water, ice clinking against the sides.

"Thank you kindly," Boston said, his hand shaking so hard that Ellie had to help hold it for him till it reached his lips.

"I apologize for my husband's absence," Ellie said, standing over Boston now like a worried mother. Her face was pink and her expression strained, like someone worried about stirring up a bees' nest. "If Roman doesn't come in soon, we'll just bring you something to eat out here." Marlena suspected Ellie was going out on a limb by announcing this.

"That is music to my ears." Boston craned his head toward Small Jay and handed him the empty tumbler. "I was quite thirsty. And I do thank you for saving me out there, young man."

Small Jay grinned back at him. "We'll take *gut* care of ya now, Boston . . . you'll see."

At that, Marlena observed Ellie's eyes grow as wide as Dawdi

Tim's old coat buttons. It seemed all too possible that, once Roman appeared, Boston would be sent on his way.

A few minutes later, Sassy came to the screen door and pawed at it, mewing as she peered out at them.

"I'll check your food dish soon," Small Jay promised while Boston looked on, smiling and seemingly getting a kick out of the determined cat.

Meanwhile, Ellie squinted toward the stable, until finally she headed down the porch steps, making a beeline for it as the tail of her long apron fluttered behind her.

She's upset, thought Marlena. Small Jay seemed nearly as nervous as his mother, fidgeting where he sat. Boston, on the other hand, had leaned his greasy head back, relaxed, and was presently snoozing.

"Is your *Dawdi Haus* empty?" she asked Small Jay quietly.

"All 'cept the long table and chairs in the front room for Mamma's sewing classes."

"What 'bout a bedroom on the main level?" She couldn't imagine Boston making it up even a few stairs, at least not tonight. *If Roman will allow a stranger to stay . . .*

Small Jay glanced at the sleeping Boston, then back at her, nodding his head. The boy had removed his straw hat, revealing uneven bangs, and she wondered if he'd accidently moved when Ellie was giving him a haircut. Or had Roman done the hair cutting?

Just then she looked up to see Roman coming this way, young Julia hanging on his arm, both of them talking and laughing. Oddly enough, Ellie was trailing behind. When the three of them were within a few yards of the porch, Roman stopped walking, and his expression changed to cautious.

Quickly, Ellie shooed Julia into the house, then stood near her husband and whispered something to him.

Marlena held her breath as Small Jay rose slowly, laboriously, making his way to stand beside the banister, looking down at his parents.

Marlena was glad Boston, weary as he was, had no knowledge of the obvious push and pull taking place out there on the lawn.

Small Jay started to move toward the porch steps, then paused and waited, his shoulders rising and falling. *He's scared and doesn't know what to do.*

Marlena slid forward in the chair, wondering what was being said between Ellie and Roman. It was ever so awkward to witness Ellie's apparent pleading—it seemed certain Roman had refused whatever she'd asked.

"Can my friend stay here tonight, Dat?" Small Jay's voice rang out at last. "Just till we help him find his real home?"

Marlena swallowed hard, hoping.

Roman, glowering, moved toward the porch, where he eyed the sleeping man. He looked at Ellie, who'd followed him and slipped her arm through her husband's.

"He needs us, Dat . . . honest, he does."

Marlena wasn't sure how to bolster Small Jay's pleas. So she sat still, trying to interpret Roman's demeanor.

Just then Sassy managed to open the screen door and scooted out, heading for the sleeping dog. She stalked over and sat herself down beside the dog's head and began to groom her paw.

"Sure looks like Sassy wants my friend to stay—his dog, too," Small Jay offered, sitting down on the top porch step.

Roman's eyebrows rose as he watched the dog's eyes slowly

open, and then, surprisingly, lean his long muzzle on Sassy's back. "Where'd this dog come from?" he asked.

"It's Boston's," Small Jay spoke up. "Ain't he nice and gentle with my Sassy?"

Ellie gazed at Roman, her arm still tucked into his.

With a little gasp, Boston opened his eyes and shook himself. "Pardon me. I don't wish you to think I find your company lacking . . . not in the least."

Small Jay chuckled. "Dat, this is Boston, my friend from the mill."

Roman stiffened. "Boston, ya say?" He glanced at Small Jay.

"Not named for the city," Boston said. "My mother chose it because of her favorite pie." He slapped one knee and chuckled.

"Boston cream pie?" Marlena said, unable to keep still any longer.

The homeless man gave her an appreciative smile. "Now, I believe that's exactly the name I was looking for . . . thank you kindly."

By now Roman looked not only befuddled but outnumbered. And Marlena hoped the latter was true, because this man Boston was just delightful.

"I best be goin' home. Mammi will wonder where I've gone." Marlena rose and turned to offer her hand to Boston. "I went with Small Jay to visit ya today, but you'd already left the mill," she said.

"I'm certainly pleased to know anyone who is a friend of this excellent young man's." Boston got up with great effort, yet managed to stand straight as he extended a formal handshake to Marlena.

"It's time for evening prayers," Roman said abruptly, walking briskly toward the house.

"But, Dat." Small Jay's voice cracked. "What 'bout Boston?"

"A drifter's place is outdoors, son."

Small Jay continued. "We could bed him down in the *Dawdi Haus*—it's empty, after all."

"You heard me."

Marlena's breath caught in her throat. Surely Roman had a softer heart than this.

"Dat . . . I beg ya. Just one night?"

"Did I stutter, son?"

Ellie rushed up the porch steps and whispered to her husband again, but Roman merely shook his head and waved his right hand in the air as he stepped inside.

Inhaling deeply, Ellie placed her hand on her heart. "If Boston would like to sleep in the haymow, he is certainly welcome."

Bright smiles appeared on both Small Jay's face and Boston's. "*Denki*, Mamma. *Denki!*"

"Tell that to your father," Ellie said. "Now, go on in and get ready for family worship."

"I'd be right happy to sit out here with Boston." Small Jay paused. "If that's all right."

"Your Dat wants ya inside, son." Ellie cast an awkward smile at the man. "I'll bring some food out to ya soon, Boston."

"Thank you kindly," the man said, his face aglow.

Then, before going inside, Ellie fixed her eyes on Marlena, and although Marlena was not sure in the least how all this would turn out, she wanted to believe that Roman Bitner wouldn't be sorry for extending even a small measure of mercy to a very needy man this night.

CHAPTER 17

*D*aybreak on the Lord's Day was accompanied by heavy rain. Marlena went to the crib and reached down for Angela Rose, recalling how her father often referred to such a steady downpour as a gully washer.

She kissed Angela's chubby cheek, whispered, "*Guder Mariye, Bobbli,*" and laid her on the bed to wash her up, talking to her all the while. Marlena blew lip bubbles on her tummy, enjoying the way Angela's wide eyes followed her fingers all around. "I daresay you're a *schmaert* little one." It wasn't the wisest thing to talk so, but hopefully wide-eyed Angela Rose had no idea what she was saying.

Marlena carried her to one of the windows and looked down on Mammi's yellow daisies outside, their graceful petals wide open, drinking up the much-needed moisture. *Perfect for weeding tomorrow,* she thought, *but I'll be in Mifflinburg. At Luella's funeral . . .*

She hated to think of Angela Rose going through life without her Mamma. *Will anyone take my sister's place permanently?*

Downstairs, she spoon-fed some warm rice cereal to Angela

Rose, opening her mouth wide to encourage the baby to imi-
tate her. Her niece sat more solidly in her high chair now that
she was more accustomed to it. Behind them, Mammi made
scrambled eggs. A hot breakfast on a Sunday was still unusual
for Marlena, who'd grown up in a home where cooking was
done only six days of the week. *So much of the past is ingrained
in me,* she thought.

When Mammi was seated, she and Marlena bowed their
heads, and Mammi thanked the dear Lord Jesus for creating
this most wonderful day to worship.

After they'd dished up their eggs and spread strawberry jam
on their toast, Marlena brought up what had supposedly happened near the old church. "Did ya ever hear anything 'bout
an angel sighting?" she asked as little Angela reached out,
trying to touch her face. Marlena caught her hand and kissed
it, making smacking noises, which made Angela Rose giggle.

"Now that I recall, *jah*, there was a *gut* deal of talk back a
few years ago when all that happened." Mammi took a sip of
her warm tea. "And wise folk never reject the possibility of
miracles." She paused for a moment. "But, my dear, I want
to share with ya something our pastor said about that . . .
something I never forgot."

Eager to hear, Marlena set down her toast.

"He said it's less important to seek after miracles than it is
to hunger after the miracle-*giver*." Mammi stirred a spoonful of
honey into her tea before drinking more. "Many folk wear out
the path to a miracle or something they believe is of God, but
they don't bother to seek the Lord and Savior," she restated.

"Oh." Marlena wondered if in some way she was one who
was grasping for a miracle. "I was just curious."

Mammi looked inquisitively at the baby's messy mouth and

chin, and she pressed her lips together, as though trying not to smile. "Just look at ya!" Mammi exclaimed. "I wonder, little one, will this be your first visit to God's house?"

Marlena had thought the same thing. "Did Luella ever attend church once she left home?" she asked.

"Whether she did or didn't, only our heavenly Father knows the cries of our hearts." Mammi rose then and went to get a washcloth.

"Only our heavenly Father knows." Mammi's words went round and round in Marlena's head as she gently washed Angela's chubby little face. She tried to dismiss them when she took Angela upstairs to get ready for church, but she knew for truth she'd much rather know the miracle-giver than see a miracle, including laying eyes on an angel.

In her room, she caught sight of her Bible on the bedside table and wished she had time to sit and read as she often did back home before leaving for the Beachy meetinghouse. Just now, she couldn't get over the way she felt after hearing Mammi's wise words—nearly at the point of tears.

⁓ₑℂ

This being an in-between Sunday, Small Jay had slept in till seven o'clock. When he finally got out of bed, disturbing Sassy, his first thought was of Boston Calvert. Had his friend slept soundly out there in the barn? *With the livestock*, Small Jay thought, knowing the makeshift pallet had been comfortable enough because he'd gone with Dat to see to it, giving Boston fresh straw to place beneath his blanket. Mamma, too, had seemed concerned enough to take a spare pillow out there.

It had been hard not to just go and stand at the back door last evening and gawk; he wanted to know how Boston was doing. Still, Small Jay was mighty thankful to Dat for letting Boston stay at all. Small Jay had tried to tell Dat this, long after his sisters had taken their baths in the galvanized tub and were upstairs for the night. He'd wanted to check one last time on Boston, too, but he figured their guest was just fine, especially after enjoying Mamma's delicious chuck roast and cooked vegetables. Boston had eaten himself full, his eyes lighting up like the Christmas star their *Englischer* neighbors put up on their chimney every year. And Boston had scarcely found the words to express his delight when Mamma brought out a nice big slice of strawberry pie topped with real whipped cream. Small Jay had done the talking for him, though, even giving Mamma a hug for her thoughtfulness.

~⊙

When Marlena and Mammi arrived with the baby, the redbrick meetinghouse was surprisingly full, in spite of the continuous heavy rain. Marlena assumed that the members who'd left their Amish churches over the years to join this fellowship were thankful not to have to hitch up horses and buggies on such a day. *Yet does that make it right to abandon the Old Ways?* The question plagued her as she scanned the pews for a place to sit near the back with Mammi and Angela Rose. The congregation reverently filed in, many carrying Bibles.

Angela took her bottle without a fuss during the four-part congregational singing of hymns, a few of which were new to Marlena. Thankfully, before the start of the minister's message, Angela fell asleep. Marlena's mind was in a haze as she anticipated Luella's funeral right around this time tomorrow.

She followed along as Mammi held the Good Book, trying

to rein in her thoughts during the sermon text—Psalm 28: "'Blessed be the Lord, because he hath heard the voice of my supplications. The Lord is my strength and my shield; my heart trusted in him, and I am helped: therefore my heart greatly rejoiceth; and with my song will I praise him.'"

Marlena felt uncomfortable. The sermon somehow seemed to speak directly to her, especially the idea of *supplication*, or prayerful entreaty. The minister went on to explain how to pray openly from one's heart with a contrite spirit.

Truthfully, Marlena had not expected such a convicting message. At that moment, she was caught off guard by a sincere sense of anguish, in part for not following her parents' and grandparents' wholehearted worshiping and praying. She felt even more sorrowful as she rehashed the what-ifs that shrouded her broken heart—the unresolved matters between her and Luella. Everything was so terribly jumbled up, even intertwined, in her mind.

Marlena *did* yearn to trust God more, just as the psalmist David had. She also desired for the Lord to hear her prayers, yet she was not sure that was possible, not like for Mammi Janice or others. *They have such a tender, joyful approach toward the Lord.*

She sighed, unsure of her own faith. Even so, what if the teaching of Mammi's preacher could become a reality for her?

After the noon meal of cold ham sandwiches, strawberry-rhubarb Jell-O, cottage cheese, and sugar cookies, Small Jay was permitted to go out on the porch and talk with Boston again, just as he had earlier following breakfast. He'd tried to explain that the People gathered every other Sunday for worship, and that the next meeting was to be held at their house, but Boston didn't seem to understand—didn't even know it was the Lord's Day, of all things. But of course the man had no calendar, so how could he keep track of the days of the week?

"I contemplated many things last night," Boston told him presently, while they sat on matching porch rockers. "For one thing, I have never been one to accept handouts. Therefore, if your father agrees, I want to pull my weight here. I prefer to work for my meals and lodging."

Small Jay worried about Boston's ability to do so. "You want me to ask Dat if you can work for him?"

"I will speak to him . . ." Boston paused as though struggling to find the right word. "Well, directly," he added at last.

Small Jay could see by the look of anticipation on his face that Boston meant business. Just maybe, this might make it possible for him to stay longer.

"But before I do"—and here Boston reached down for his bag—"will you read another letter from Abigail?" He frowned hard. "Or is it Eleanor?"

He doesn't remember her name!

Boston shook his head. "I'm all mixed up again today."

"Maybe not," Small Jay replied. "I mean, if you think you are, then you ain't nearly as confused as ya think. *Verschteh*— Understand?"

A grin spread across the man's face. "Quite brilliant, young man."

That brought a good laugh.

"Which letter should I read next, Boston?"

The man shrugged his frail shoulders. "Why don't you

choose one this time?" He opened the satchel wide and encouraged Small Jay to reach inside.

Small Jay felt candy wrappers, snippets of papers, and what looked like a clean pair of folded trousers. Choosing a letter toward the top, Small Jay wondered what had happened to the extra changes of clothing Boston had mentioned. "Did ya leave your other clothes at the mill, maybe?"

Boston stared right through him, like he hadn't heard at all.

"What about takin' a shower? It might be time." Small Jay pointed in the direction of the makeshift shower in the barn, not wanting to hurt the man's feelings. "I'm sure Dat won't mind. Mamma might actually be glad. She sure is when I clean up."

At that, Boston looked worse than *ferhoodled*, which made Small Jay nervous. Was he ill? He looked around to see if Dat was anywhere nearby, in case they needed to run down to the phone shanty to call an ambulance. "Can ya hear me, Boston?" He waved his hand in front of the man's eyes. "Boston?"

The man shook himself. "Sorry . . . so sorry."

"What happened just then?"

Boston was silent, his eyes cloudy again.

Not sure if he should repeat his question, Small Jay began to read the letter dated February 15, 1961.

My dearest darling,

I must confess that I observed the startled look that came over your face yesterday when we met with your doctor. During this difficult time, please cling to the promise of our love and our wonderful life together. We'll focus on what we have, as well as the beauty of God's creation all around our homes here in the States and overseas. Let us be thankful for our many gifts and talents, far-reaching as they have been and continue to be. I'm not ready to throw in the towel and say the best years are behind us. Remember that your doctor hasn't come to a firm diagnosis, though he shares our concern over your pronounced confusion and forgetfulness.

Neither of us can refute that we've suffered our trials, but staying close has made us all the stronger. Never forget what we promised long ago: to take care of each other until the end.

Nothing really has changed. We still possess all that is essential for our daily joy. We have great music, spontaneous laughter, good literature, and most of all, through God's abundant grace, we embrace our deep faith.

I'm writing this note and tucking it into your briefcase, hoping it raises your spirits during your morning break, dear. How I want to see your endearing smile return!

> *Yours always,*
> *Abigail*

Small Jay refolded the letter and handed it back to Boston. "*Ach,* I think this woman loves ya like no other."

"Hmm . . . I do like her choice of words." Boston looked toward the meadow, lost in thought. "How can I meet her?" He wore a mischievous grin now.

"All the letters so far are from Abigail." Small Jay considered that Abigail might be Boston's sister—perhaps even a twin. Even with those other possibilities, Small Jay guessed it was Boston's wife who'd written the love letter. But was she still alive?

"Who's Eleanor, then? Do ya remember mentioning her

just now? You wrote her name on a piece of paper with funny marks on it." He wondered if he should keep prying. "Is she a relative or friend?"

But Boston was preoccupied again. He ran his fingers along his dirty shirt collar and talked under his breath. Then he searched in his bag, seemingly distressed.

"Did ya lose something?" Then it hit Small Jay. The bow tie was missing!

"It must be here somewhere," Boston said.

Small Jay looked toward the barn. "Did your tie fall off in your sleep, maybe?"

Boston's head popped up. "How could you have known what I was thinking, young man?"

Small Jay shrugged and grinned, because he felt even more connected to this wonderful friend. "I don't know; I just did."

Boston's eyes twinkled. "Well, my bow tie can wait. Right now I'd simply like to sit here with you a little more while Allegro naps."

"Sounds *gut* to me," said Small Jay.

They talked further, and Small Jay asked if he'd ever wondered why a pony never grew up to become a horse. Boston chuckled and said he'd wondered that himself on occasion.

"I asked my father 'bout it once," Small Jay confided.

"And might I ask what sort of answer he gave?"

Small Jay wondered if Boston had already guessed how things were sometimes with Dat. The man could be awful quick when his mind was working right.

"Come, now," Boston said. "A smart young man like you. Surely your father had something to say in response."

No one ever talked to Small Jay like this. "I honestly don't remember," he said, not sure where to begin. And next thing he knew, he was telling Boston how he wished he could talk this openly to his Dat. "But I'm like *en Eiszappe*—an icicle—around him. Too frozen to say what I want to."

Boston nodded his head. "Just remember, we're haunted most by the things we never attempt, rather than the things we attempt and fail."

Small Jay let his brain work on that.

"I believe in you, young man," Boston said, reaching over to pat his shoulder. "Therefore, I encourage you to venture forth boldly."

Frowning, Small Jay admitted he didn't understand.

"Step out in faith, as the saying goes," Boston declared. "If you do it in the right spirit, God will be with you."

Small Jay considered this, the idea of freezing up around Dat still skulking like a cat in the back of his mind. But maybe he could do *something* when he saw his father next. *Just maybe.*

Ellie stood behind the screen door, wiping away tears. It was impossible not to detect the friendship developing between her son and this poor homeless man. Small Jay had been craving Roman's attention since he was a toddler, and here was this stranger, trusting their son to read such a beautiful and moving love letter aloud. And to think they were talking of Small Jay's desire to talk freely with his father.

One of the letter's phrases still rang in her memory. *Neither of us can refute that we've suffered our trials, but staying close has made us all the stronger. . . .*

How she wished for a relationship with Roman like that. Dabbing at her wet face, she dropped the hem of her apron and returned to heating the water for the dishes, glad the girls, who were clearing the table, hadn't asked her what she was doing hovering over there. *Eavesdropping, in all truth.*

Later, while Boston played his harmonica for Small Jay, who looked a bit dazed from the music, perhaps, Ellie slipped out to the barn and searched the area where Boston had slept, looking for the man's lost bow tie.

CHAPTER 18

Midmorning that Sunday, Ellie's older cousin Ada and husband Reuben and their four school-age girls arrived to visit. After cheerful greetings all around, the grown-ups sat on the back porch talking and eating watermelon while all seven girls perched like birds on the steps, chattering low. The oldest of Ada's girls, eleven-year-old Lyddie, opened a small white drawstring bag and dumped out metal jacks and two red rubber balls into her lap. Instead of playing jacks right away, however, they started counting them in *Deitsch*, heads touching as they pressed closer, giggles scattered between words.

Just before the game commenced, the youngest girl, Betsy Anne, just six, opened a crinkled paper bag and daintily removed her collection of Royal Crown soda pop tops. Ellie's daughter Sally leaned to see, her mouth wide.

"The king of sodas," said Dorcas, glancing over her shoulder at the adults. "Where'd ya get those?"

Betsy Anne shrugged. "Dawdi likes the taste."

"Fifteen cents at the pop machine near market," Julia added. "Mighty sweet . . . and has a *gut* zip to it."

Ada laughed softly and reached for her pocketbook, where she removed a whole stack of S&H Green Stamps and offered to share some with Ellie, who said she had plenty and thanked her.

Ellie had to smile; she was pleased they were all having such a happy time. She leaned forward to catch her husband's eye, where he sat the farthest away in the row of rocking chairs. He was talking with Reuben, who, like them, had worn his Sunday best, even on this very muggy Lord's Day—black broadfall trousers and matching black vest over a long-sleeved white shirt and black suspenders.

"Have ya seen our son lately?" Ellie asked.

Roman shook his head, pointing toward the barn. "He hasn't been gone but a few minutes."

"We've got us a visitor," Ellie told Ada.

"Oh?"

Ellie explained about Boston as gracefully as she could with all the children sitting within a few yards. "He's asked if he might work round the farm, at least for a little while . . . says he doesn't want to take our generosity for granted." Going on, she revealed that the man spoke kindly, even cleverly, but was often terribly mixed up. "And quite forgetful." Ellie glanced at Roman and leaned closer to Ada so she could talk even more softly. "We suspect it's memory troubles of some kind . . . maybe a medical condition." Ellie didn't feel at liberty to reveal the contents of the love letter she'd overheard that morning, but she had seen enough of Boston to come to this conclusion on her own.

Ada adjusted her royal blue cape apron, which matched her long dress. "Maybe just take him over to see *der Dokder* . . . Isaac King's real *schmaert* 'bout fixin' folk up, ya know. Might be that all he needs is some herbs to stimulate the blood flow to his brain."

"But it isn't senility, we don't think—he's not old enough," Ellie said. "Small Jay says he seems fine one minute, and then gets confused and quite frustrated the next. Boston struggles with his words at times, too. He'll be talkin' and then seem befuddled 'bout how to finish his sentence." She went on to share quietly that Small Jay had befriended Boston nearly a week ago.

"*Ach*, really?" Ada placed her hand on her cheek, looking downright puzzled herself. "Not to be ill-mannered, but how does young Jake know the difference 'tween clear-minded and otherwise, ya know?"

Ellie looked away, refusing to let Ada get the better of her. "I daresay Small Jay's shown himself to be pretty discerning in all this," she said, keeping her tone pleasant.

"'Tis *gut* to hear."

Ellie hoped to goodness there would be no more pointed questions. She happened to notice Small Jay coming across the yard with Boston, who seemed more steady today than yesterday. "There they are," she indicated. Small Jay had finished off his cereal and strawberries right quick that morning to be excused to sit with Boston on the porch while the man finished eating, she recalled. Being around Boston certainly hurried her son up at mealtime.

"He sure looks cleaned up," Ada noted. "Thought ya said he was a beggar."

"I never said *that*." Ellie shook her head, noticing Boston's change of clothes.

"And you're gonna let him stay on?"

"That's up to Roman."

The hum of chatter subsided on the porch as Small Jay

approached with their unlikely guest. "Hello. This here's our friend, Boston Calvert," her son declared, and while Boston offered a wave, he looked around as if disoriented.

"Would ya like some watermelon?" Ellie asked suddenly, rising even before they answered.

"I'll go an' cut some more slices, Mamma," Dorcas said, hurrying to the screen door.

"*Denki*, dear."

"That's one sweet daughter you've got," Ada said.

"*Denki*, Ada. They're all sweet. Just like your girls." *And my son . . .*

Ellie noticed how flushed yet pleased Small Jay looked, like he'd been out in the barn helping feed or water the animals, which got her wondering. *Is this what it'll take for him to get his dearest wish?*

On this visiting Sunday, Small Jay found himself wondering what it'd be like if Cousins Reuben and Ada had birthed sons, as well as daughters. All those girls piled up together there on the porch steps made a barrier to the back porch, and it annoyed him but good. Couldn't they see that poor Boston needed to rest a spell? But no, his sisters and girl cousins just sat there jabbering, unaware. As usual, he wasn't about to say anything, so he and Boston went to sit on the wooden bench that surrounded the oldest tree in the back lawn. It was a bench his grandfather on his mother's side had built out of old wood a few years before he passed away. There in the wonderful-good shade, the grass felt cool against Small Jay's bare feet.

"Sorry there ain't enough chairs to go round," he said while they waited for their watermelon to be served.

"What's that?" Boston looked tired, and Small Jay wondered if he'd been able to sleep soundly in the dusty barn.

"That's Mamma's cousin and family." He motioned toward the adults. "Today's for visitin'. We have Preachin' next Sunday, like I told ya."

"I don't recall that." Boston sighed and leaned forward. "I wonder where my dog's gotten to."

Small Jay looked around.

"Not sure, but I don't see Sassy, either. Maybe they're in the stable."

Boston nodded absently and straightened his bow tie, which Mamma had managed to find in the stable. "The last I saw him, he . . ." He left the thought hanging.

Small Jay felt sorry for the man. Boston sometimes seemed to disappear right in the middle of a conversation, something Mamma said Small Jay himself was known to do.

"Does my hair look shaggy?" Boston asked suddenly, touching his head.

"Mamma could cut it for ya if you want. I know she would."

"Well, at least it's clean now." He craned his neck toward Small Jay. "Thanks for directing me to the barn shower." He glanced toward the outhouse. "And the outdoor facility, too. Which, by the way, has an issue. Someone should know . . . " Boston stopped midthought, same as he'd done several times since the noon meal.

Small Jay gave a little laugh. "I know just what you're talking 'bout. One of our barn cats took to the toilet paper and ripped it to mincemeat. Shredder's in trouble with Mamma, for sure and for certain."

Boston chuckled. "You knew exactly what I meant."

Small Jay nodded and said he'd have to go out there with

a wastebasket and pick up all the snibbles. "This just keeps happenin'." His attention was caught by his sister, who handed the plate of watermelon slices to Mamma. His mouth watered at the sight of the delicious cold treat. When his mother came to serve them, Small Jay smiled up at her as she offered the first slice to Boston. "*Denki*, Mamma."

"This might not be the most comfortable spot for yous." She glanced up at the tree. "But it's nice an' shady."

"We don't mind," Small Jay said, though he was sweating like a pig.

"I beg your pardon, miss. Are you Eleanor's sister?" Boston asked, his slice halfway to his mouth. "You look very much like her."

"I'm Ellie," Mamma said, smiling sweetly, "but that's all right. Lots of folk confuse me with someone else they know."

Boston sighed. "Well, there is no excuse on my part. I do apologize."

Small Jay was truly glad when his mother asked Boston when he'd last been to a doctor. Boston was quick to say he hadn't the slightest remembrance.

"More than a month ago?" Mamma persisted, wiping her brow with a hankie she'd pulled from her long-sleeved black Sunday dress.

"Maybe we could just see if Dr. Isaac can take a look at him," Small Jay suggested as he turned toward Boston, who'd leaned forward to devour the watermelon, stopping now and then to spit the seeds between his feet.

"And what would *you* think of that?" Mamma asked Boston.

"I think this watermelon is the best I've ever tasted." He smacked his lips, Mamma's question clearly flown from his mind, like dandelions gone to seed in a breeze. "Thank you, Miss Eleanor."

Small Jay and Mamma exchanged worried glances.

"Boston really needs to visit Dr. Isaac, Mamma," Small Jay insisted.

The man looked peeved suddenly. "I'm quite present here. Why discuss my wishes in the third person, as if I'm absent?" He paused, frustration adding to the lines on his face. "That's what happened with dear Abigail. She's no longer present, either. And Eleanor is gone, too. They all are."

Mamma bit her lip, and tears filled her pretty blue eyes.

"We should see Dr. Isaac tomorrow," Small Jay said. "Just 'cause Isaac couldn't help me doesn't mean he can't help Boston." He honestly didn't care if his friend was sitting right next to him eating his watermelon clear down to the rind; Boston seemed to be getting worse before their very eyes.

"We'll see what your father says."

"All right, Mamma." Small Jay hoped with all his heart that his parents would help his friend. *Someone has to!*

CHAPTER 19

As planned, Vernon Siegrist arrived to drive Marlena and her grandmother at six o'clock the next morning, just as the sky was brightening. Robins warbled loudly in the tree near the east side of the house, welcoming daybreak, and in the distance, a neighbor's rooster crowed repeatedly. Mammi mentioned to Marlena as they exited by way of the back door that today's washing would have to wait till tomorrow. Caught up as she was with solemn thoughts, Marlena hadn't even considered the weekly chore so ingrained in their routine.

After their initial hellos to Vernon, they settled in for the nearly two-hour drive, no one speaking much. Marlena felt tired from her restless night and the early rising. Angela Rose, however, was wide-awake and babbling in her soft, incoherent language. Marlena had remembered to tuck some small toys and rattles into the diaper bag Aunt Becky had so kindly brought. Wanting to look presentable for the funeral, she hoped her black dress and apron wouldn't be too wrinkled by the time they pulled into the parking lot at the white clapboard meetinghouse. She recalled the first time she'd gone to church there with her parents. In all truth, she'd wanted to stay in bed and fake illness that morning, uncomfortable about leaving behind the Old Order church where she'd grown up, knowing she would miss the familiarity of the service and the flock of worshipers, most of whom were related to Marlena and her immediate family. *And I was missing Nat, too . . . same as now.*

Next to the van window, Mammi looked preoccupied, staring out at the Millers' vast apple orchard. These were the same Amish folk who'd had a roadside vegetable stand ever since Marlena had started coming to visit with her parents. She and Luella had sometimes assisted with English tourists—Marlena more so than Luella—helping fun-loving Rosanna and her family.

As for Luella, she had struck up a friendship with an English girl farther down the road—Olive Hendrickson, one year older. *"We're better suited,"* Luella had told Marlena, smelling of cigarette smoke. Thinking about it now, Marlena was fairly sure Dat and Mamma had known little of Olive and Luella's summertime alliance, or the forbidden things Olive seemed too eager to introduce to an Amish girl on the church fence, if not hanging off the other side.

Yet surely Luella was much more than her shallow interests during *Rumschpringe.* Marlena wondered how her sister's becoming a mother had affected her. *Did she ever yearn for her Plain family . . . including me?*

Marlena hoped so with all of her heart on this, Luella's funeral day. She stared at the quilt-lined wicker basket on the floor of the van between herself and Mammi. She'd brought it along in case Angela got tired of being held during the trip. It had crossed her mind to take it to church yesterday, too, for in the car, but Mammi had said it wasn't necessary. And as it turned out, Mammi was quite right.

Angela Rose represents a part of Luella, Marlena thought while holding Angela on her lap. Again she pondered yesterday's sermon. After the noon meal with Mammi Janice, while Angela napped, she'd taken time to reread the minister's text in the Psalms, even memorizing it.

She reached over to lightly touch Mammi's arm. "What did Dawdi Tim think 'bout churches sendin' out missionaries?" She recalled yesterday's prayer following the sermon. More than a dozen teenagers had gone forward to receive the pastor's blessing prior to leaving to help with vacation Bible school in Philadelphia and New York City churches.

"Why do you ask?" Mammi smiled a little. "Your parents' church instructs young folk that way."

Marlena nodded. A missionary focus was one of the hallmarks of the Beachy Amish-Mennonites, along with permitting electricity and holding Sunday school and home Bible studies. "My old church doesn't evangelize at all," she said.

Mammi folded her hands in her lap. "Well, I can tell you that we attempt to follow the Lord's command to go into every corner of the world and share the Gospel." Mammi turned back to the window, adding, "Your Dawdi was all for spreadin' God's love around."

Marlena pondered her grandmother's words. *Why wouldn't Nat, and everyone who believes in Christ, want to do the same?*

She realized suddenly that she was questioning her old church's traditional beliefs—something the *Ordnung* considered wrong. On this sorrowful day, Marlena did not have the emotional strength to wrestle with such serious thoughts. She must let them rest.

The day had warmed considerably by the time the van pulled into the lot for the meetinghouse. They had arrived earlier than Marlena expected, and she looked around for her parents' horse and buggy, taking note of the carriages already parked at the hitching posts along the back end of the parking area.

"I don't see them yet, do you?" she asked Mammi.

"We'll just wait here." Mammi looked over at Angela Rose, who was sucking her fist. "Our little one's getting hungry."

Marlena wondered where she and the baby might sit during the service. Certainly not up front with her parents and baptized family members, even though it was acceptable in this church to do so for a funeral. And she wouldn't hand off Angela Rose to Mammi, either. That wouldn't be fair. Not at all keen on funerals, she had already decided to take up her responsibility for her niece and see this day through. Like Mammi had said, Angela Rose was their little one, for now. *My main responsibility.*

A few minutes later, she saw the old familiar road horse, Dixie, and the white-top family carriage her father was still driving, evidently resisting the move toward cars that some members now arriving had already made. Marlena's younger sisters, Katie and Rachel Ann, were sitting in the back of the buggy, facing out, and Amos and Yonnie were in the second bench seat, behind their parents. Like Marlena's, her sisters' Beachy head coverings were cup-shaped, with darts on each side. "Look, Mammi, the family's here," Marlena said softly.

Seeing all of them now, so dear, compounded her sorrow, bringing it all back.

Her grandmother reached into her pocketbook and brought out a hankie. *We're going to need each other on this difficult day,* Marlena thought, glad they'd arrived early enough to visit with family before going inside. She fought back a sick feeling of anxiety as she looked again at the meetinghouse that had become her parents' church . . . and hers, for now. *Till I can finally join Nat's.*

"I'm really dreadin' this," she whispered before she and Mammi gathered up the baby's things to exit the van.

"My dear girl, I can't imagine losin' a sister at your age." Mammi gave her a sad smile and reached for her hand. "I'll keep you in my prayers all day long."

She felt a surge of guilt. "I don't mean to be selfish, Mammi."

"Now, now—it's normal to feel this way. I understand."

She thanked her, aware that her parents were getting out of their carriage, followed by her sisters and, last, her gangly teenage brothers. "Let's go and greet them," Marlena said, reaching for the diaper bag and handing it to Mammi, who had gotten out of the van with some assistance from their driver. Marlena scooted across the seat and carefully stepped down with Angela Rose, glad for Vernon's hovering.

The first thing she noticed about her mother was how very pale she looked. Was it the black clothing? Her sisters looked washed out, too, as they rushed to hug her without saying a word. Eight-year-old Rachel Ann clung to Marlena, then touched Angela Rose's head, making over her. *No one looks rosy in black,* thought Marlena, realizing her grandmother also was noticeably pale.

"Can I hold Luella's baby?" eleven-year-old Katie asked, moving in to kiss Angela's cheek. "She's so cute."

Angela reached up and grabbed Katie's white cap string, providing a bit of humorous relief for them all, including eighteen-year-old Amos, whose blue eyes looked bloodshot and swollen. Their other brother, Yonnie, just fourteen last month, stood back away from his sisters, flanking Amos with his arms folded, even though he eyed the baby curiously. *Not as interested as my sisters*, Marlena thought, sizing up her brothers. *Yet Angela Rose is all we have left of Luella.*

She relinquished the baby to Katie and slipped in next to her mother, refusing to cry, even though it was all she could do to keep from it. "How are ya holdin' up, Mamma?"

Her mother looked away for a moment, her eyes red. "I never thought we'd be having a funeral for one of our children. Never thought Luella would pass away before your father and me." She sighed softly. "Thought she had more time, ya know."

"*Jah*, 'tis awful hard." Marlena reached around her mother's shoulders.

"But God is sovereign, and we'll cling to His will today and for always." Mamma's words were resolute, but her chin quivered.

More buggies and a few cars were pulling into the lot. And, talking with Mamma, Marlena realized how very much she missed her family, even though she hadn't been in Brownstown long. Time had shifted with Luella's passing, changing everything.

Katie was touching Angela's cheek and whispering to her, but Mamma kept looking over at them and finally said she simply had to get her hands on her grandbaby. Stepping near, she took Angela Rose from Katie and kissed her little head.

Marlena struggled with tears as she observed the dear way Mamma cuddled Angela Rose.

"How long will ya stay afterward?" Mamma turned to ask Mammi Janice. "My sisters-in-law and other womenfolk have prepared a big meal to serve in the church basement for the extended family. I hope you'll stay around for it after the burial."

Her grandmother looked Marlena's way and nodded. "We'll let our driver know." Mammi glanced over her shoulder, and Marlena knew she wanted her to be the one to tell Vernon, who was still sitting in the van, fanning himself.

Marlena motioned for her brother Amos to go with her. "Mamma hopes we'll stay for the funeral dinner," she said, making small talk.

"*Jah*, a *gut* idea," he said quietly. "I think she wants to talk to you 'bout something."

"Oh?"

Amos shook his head and smiled faintly. "Don't ask me what. Might be something 'bout Gordon's parents. I hear his aunt has been in touch with Mamma."

"All right." She reached the van with Amos and politely told Vernon when to return.

"Yous just take your time, won't ya?" Vernon nodded as he spoke. "A daughter shouldn't die before her parents, that's for sure. Just be a comfort to each other and lean on the dear Lord. He'll get ya through."

Marlena thanked Vernon and assumed he might drive somewhere and settle into a restaurant with air conditioning, perhaps, and have something to eat. It was just too hot to sit out here, even under the row of shade trees along the north side of the parking lot. "We'll see you later. *Denki* ever so much!"

He smiled and turned the key in the ignition, then slowly backed out and headed toward the main road.

Walking back to her family, Marlena couldn't keep her eyes off Angela Rose in Mamma's loving arms. She could tell by the way her mother held her that she really cared for Luella's baby. *We all do*, she thought, refusing to think about whatever her parents wanted to discuss later. If it was about Gordon's family swooping in and taking Angela Rose away until Gordon returned from the war, well, such a thing was too painful to consider on Luella's burial day.

CHAPTER 20

*G*ordon's aunt Patricia just arrived," Mamma whispered when she found Marlena in the ladies' room changing Angela Rose. "Your father wants me to invite her to sit with the family up front. I agree that it's the polite thing to do."

Marlena's heart skipped a beat. "So she's come to represent Gordon and his family."

Mamma leaned near, her breath on Marlena's ear. "Your grandmother and I wonder if she's come for Angela Rose, perhaps. She has a most determined look on her face."

Marlena's hands shook as she fastened a pin in the diaper. "But Angela's happy with Mammi Janice and me. And—"

"No need to panic, dear, but we must remember things *are* likely to change once Gordon's parents are home again. And at some point, Gordon will make clear who should have temporary custody. He may be allowed to come home a short while, but surely he'll have to return to the service."

Marlena reached down for her niece and drew her close. "I don't think I should sit up front with you and the family, Mamma."

"Well, why not, honey?"

"I need to be with Angela Rose," she said firmly. "We'll sit in the back so she's not a distraction, ya know."

Mamma patted her hand. "Considering everything, I think you may be right, Marlena. *Jah*, this is wise."

Considering everything . . . Marlena suspected she was referring to Patricia Munroe. "I'll just slip into the back row, all right?"

"And I'll make sure my mother knows where you and the baby are." Mamma paused to caress Angela's cheek, then left to find Mammi Janice.

I simply mustn't fret, Marlena reminded herself.

———❧———

While Boston snoozed on the back porch, it took Small Jay nearly an hour to pick up the hundreds of paper snippets inside the outhouse and all around it. He caught himself muttering repeatedly, furious at Shredder, who must have been smart enough to hide himself away. "That cat's prob'ly burrowed in the hayloft," Small Jay whispered. "*Gut* thing he's got nine lives."

Small Jay dumped the snibbles down the outhouse hole and remembered something Danny Glick, his former classmate and tormentor, had once bragged about. Small Jay wasn't sure he even believed the tale, but every time he visited an outhouse, Danny's story came to mind—how he'd gotten so *zannich* with his older sister that he'd dropped her best sewing scissors down the hole. "Now, that's mighty angry," Small Jay told himself.

He stared at the shelf Dat had recently built to hold the toilet paper. That was after the last time Shredder caused such havoc, though not nearly as bad as now. "Dat'll have to build one even higher, but then no one will be able to reach it." He left the outhouse, closing the door soundly. "Now, where's that wicked tomcat?"

Frustrated, Small Jay took the time to search the stable area of the barn, as well as the haymow. While there, he noticed Boston's satchel, a little gray kitten's head peering out of the top.

"What on earth?" He shooed the kitty away and then sat down on the black blanket with pieces of straw stuck to it—a one-sided straw tick. Was the Lord God above pleased with this barebones bed in a stable for the poor lost man?

Would Dat wanna sleep out here with the bugs and the animals and barn swallow droppings? Small Jay mused. Just then he spotted a set of pitch-black ears peeking out from behind a bale of hay. "And with Shredder, too!"

Wishing he could move more quickly, Small Jay rose with difficulty but soon gave up the chase before he could catch the troublesome cat. "You'll be a goner yet, if Dat catches ya!" he hollered.

He returned to the straw pallet and reached for the bag that seemed to hold all of the lost man's most treasured possessions.

"This oughta hang on a peg somewhere." He was muttering again, carrying the bag over his shoulder and looking around for an ideal spot. Then, thinking he might just pound a nail into a nearby post, Small Jay set the bag on top of the stack of watering buckets and went to find a hammer and a nail.

~ ❧

Marlena was thankful she hadn't sat in the front row of the Beachy meetinghouse. It seemed more likely she might

177

contain her emotions sitting close to the door leading to the vestibule.

She listened as the dark-haired middle-aged preacher, Brother Simon Ranck, began his sermon. "'For the things which are seen are temporal, but the things which are not seen are eternal,'" he said in English. She still hadn't gotten over the fact that Brother Ranck spoke in English rather than the German of the Old Order Amish service. Her eyes scanned the rows until they settled on the stately figure of Patricia Munroe, where she sat next to Marlena's family—something else that would never be allowed in a more traditional Amish gathering, even at a funeral.

Marlena wiped her eyes with her hankie, glad she was surrounded by three hundred people, as best she could estimate. *Dat and Mamma's relatives and friends all came to support them. . . .*

"If you died tonight, where would you go?" Simon Ranck's words jolted her back to attention. Like her father and all the other men present, Brother Ranck wore his best black frock coat and black vest. "Are you ready to meet your Maker?" Then, with considerably more conviction, he declared, "As we read in Joshua 24:15, 'Choose you this day whom ye will serve.' I urge you not to wait a single day longer. If you're on the fence and ready to jump it, think about eternity. Where do you want to spend it, my friend? I ask you."

Oh, such a worry, to think her sister's soul might be lost. How did Brother Ranck know what to say at such a depressing time? Marlena's father had pleaded with the pastor to hold this service; otherwise, the only option would have been the nearby funeral home. Since Dat and Mamma were no longer members of the house-church Amish, they couldn't have the service at home.

"The Lord Jesus Christ is the only One who knows Luella Wenger Munroe's standing with God," Simon Ranck said now, his expression gentle yet serious. "He alone will be her judge on that Day of days." He paused to take a visibly deep breath. "May this reminder of eternity cause all of us to turn to the Lord and repent of our sins before the clock of our lives ceases its tolling." He bowed his head, and Marlena thought he might be weeping.

She simply could not bear this a minute longer. When Angela Rose started to murmur, pushing the bottle away at this most reverent moment, Marlena was grateful. Quickly, silently, she reached for the diaper bag, put the bottle away, and slipped out of her seat to make her way outside and around the side of the church.

A monarch butterfly landed on a nearby honeysuckle vine, and Marlena moved toward it, hoping Angela might see its beauty up close. "Lookee there," she managed to say. Then, unable to regain her composure, she began to cry. *Brother Ranck must surely think Luella's soul is lost.*

Her throat felt like it might close up, yet somehow, she found the breath to speak. "Oh, dear Lord in heaven . . . please may this not be true. Please . . ." The words were the first prayer of her own that she'd ever dared to speak aloud to the Lord God. Angela Rose chortled as the butterfly flitted to yet another blooming bush, and Marlena followed it. In so doing, she happened to notice an open buggy turning into the far end of the parking lot. Not thinking anything of it, she was startled when the driver pulled right up to where she stood with Angela Rose.

"Marlena . . . I was hopin' I might see ya."

"Nat?" She blinked back her tears and smiled for her beau. "What a surprise."

He was dressed like he was ready for Preaching as he got down from the carriage. "You've been cryin', honey," Nat said, moving near. "Are you all right?"

"'Tis the hardest day of my life."

He glanced back toward the meetinghouse. "What're ya doin' out here, love?"

She told him how Brother Ranck's message had pulled at her heart, and that Angela Rose had become restless.

Nat looked down at the baby and nodded. "You have many responsibilities just now."

Oh, she wished he might invite her to go riding, to take her away from there. "The sermon will be over very soon, and it will be time for my family to view Luella's body," she told him. "I really oughta go back in."

"Wish I could be there for ya." He slipped his arm around her waist. "I really do, but . . ."

"You can't, ain't so?" She knew why. It was against the vows he planned to take when he joined church.

"At least I can be with you now. I wasn't sure I'd catch ya."

"*Denki* for coming, Nat." She put her head down and bit her lip. "The Lord knew I needed to see ya."

He looked startled at this, not accustomed to that way of talking. Then, surprising her, Nat leaned closer. "Aw, love." They moved nearer the bushes, out of view. "My heart's with ya; never forget that, Marlena."

She tried to speak but rested her face against Angela's dimpled cheek.

Nat touched Marlena's chin, lifting her face and drawing near like he might kiss her.

"Angela's brought me such comfort these past few days," she said, glancing down at her niece. "It's like the Lord sent her for that reason, ya know." She felt like she was opening the lid of her heart and spilling it out.

"It's only natural you'd feel attached to her right now, with your sister gone," he said, stepping back. There was something amiss in his voice. "How long do you expect to have her?"

"Well, the other grandparents will decide where Angela Rose will live as soon as they return from their trip," she told him. "Till Gordon's home from the war anyway."

Nat nodded and looked relieved. "That'll be helpful, if they take her, considerin' all you're doing for your Mammi this summer. Truly *gut* news."

"I s'pose," she said a little reluctantly and wondered if Nat noticed her hesitation.

"I guess I'd better get goin'," he said, leaning in abruptly to kiss her cheek. "*Denki* for lettin' me know you'd be here today, love."

She watched Nat climb back into his courting carriage. When he turned to look at her one last time, he waved his hat and smiled at her.

Despite his warm farewell, Marlena was surprised at how he'd seemed to dismiss Angela Rose, even taking a step back from her. *Would he rather I wasn't taking care of my sister's baby?*

CHAPTER 21

*E*llie and the girls finished hanging out the wash on the clotheslines, then hurried indoors to resume washing the woodwork and the floors with lye soap in hot water. When that big chore was finished, Ellie made her way out to the barn, curious as to what Small Jay was up to. She could only hope Roman might take notice of their son's eagerness to assist Boston.

She pushed open the heavy barn door and found her boy standing on a step stool, pounding a nail, his lips puckered with determination. "Your father's told me some interesting news."

Lowering the hammer, Small Jay frowned; then, seeing her happy expression, he smiled. "Is he gonna let Boston move into the *Dawdi Haus?*"

Ellie's heart sank. "Now, son, you know better. But he *did* talk Boston into going to the doctor. How 'bout that?"

Looking somewhat disappointed, Small Jay nodded pensively. Cautiously, he got down off the stool and went to replace the hammer in Roman's large tool chest. When he returned, he reached for Boston's shoulder bag and stepped back up on the stool to hang it on the nail. "See? Now Shredder can't get into it."

Ellie agreed it was an excellent idea and walked with her son to the barn door and helped him shove it open. "Your father's gone to town to run an errand."

"To Joe's store?"

"Could be, but I'm not sure. In the meantime, maybe you and Boston would like a tall glass of cold root beer, since I think Boston's already done with his mornin' chores."

Immediately, her son's face brightened. "I sure would, but Boston might turn up his nose. Homemade's not as sweet and fizzy as fancy folk like."

"I say we find out." She noticed Small Jay looking over toward the Martin farm as they walked from the barn. "Marlena Wenger and her Mammi will be back from Luella's funeral later today."

"The baby, too?"

She found this surprising—he'd never expressed much interest in little ones before. "Well, I believe so. Why do ya ask?"

"Angela Rose smiles at me."

"*Jah*, she's a happy baby, all things considered."

"Looks kinda like Marlena, I think."

"Do ya, now?"

He nodded. "Is Marlena gonna be her Mamma?"

Ellie didn't know how to answer. "*Gott* will provide," she assured him. Then, glancing toward the porch, she smiled to see Boston in a rocker, just waking up from a nap. "Here we are, son. And look who's had his forty winks already."

Boston's gaping mouth slowly closed, but he had a relaxed look. "Young man," he said, his eyes widening.

"Boston has somethin' to tell ya," Ellie told Small Jay. "A little surprise."

This seemed to boost the boy's pace, and Ellie stood back as Small Jay moved toward the porch steps, reaching to grip the railing.

"Have ya got somethin' up your sleeve?" Small Jay asked, hobbling over to sit in the rocking chair next to Boston.

Mischievously, the man raised his shirt sleeve and peered underneath. "Indeed I do. Your very kind mother has offered to sew a suit and some new shirts for me," Boston announced.

"Does that mean you're coming to Preachin' next Sunday . . . here, at our house?" Small Jay paused and shook his head. "Wait . . . ya mean you're gonna dress like Dat and me?"

"I certainly am," Boston admitted.

Small Jay clapped his hands. "Mamma, was this your idea?"

It was Ellie's moment to head for the kitchen.

"Mamma?" His voice had never sounded so lilting. "Is Boston stayin' on with us, then?"

"Just till his family is found," she called over her shoulder, heartened at the joyful response.

"*Ach*, Mamma, 'tis the best news of all!"

"I'll be back with the root beer," she said, ever so thankful her son had such a good friend. She wondered how long it would be before Boston trusted them enough to share the story of his life. *If he remembers.*

She thought again of Roman and how he'd hemmed and hawed but eventually volunteered to help her get Boston to the doctor today. It was a marvel, nearly a miracle. Most of all, she was glad Roman had agreed to let the man work there in exchange for his very humble bed. *If Roman can learn to accept*

Boston, why not Marlena Wenger . . . and my sewing students?
she wondered, feeling a sliver of hope.

The private family viewing was in progress in one of the
rooms just off the vestibule when Marlena returned inside.
Already she could hardly believe that Nat had been there;
he'd come and gone so quickly.

She stood in the vestibule with Angela cuddled next to her,
knowing she really ought to go in to see her older sister one last
time, if for no other reason than to comfort Mamma and Dat.
Yet she wouldn't think of taking Angela Rose along, and she
was reluctant to give her up with Gordon's aunt somewhere
around. *Maybe I should just remember Luella as she was.*

Marlena stepped near the windows in the entrance area,
drawing strength from the sunlight streaming down like an
English bridal veil. *Was my sister's beauty her downfall?*

Something Dawdi Tim had sometimes said came to her
mind. *"Pretty is as pretty does, yet what good's a pretty dish when
it's empty?"* Marlena considered those words with a sad heart.

The first person to emerge from the viewing room was
Gordon's aunt, one of the few *Englischers* present—a tall, lean
woman wearing black from head to toe, including dark lace
veiling over her auburn hair. Marlena stiffened as the woman
looked her direction and, lifting her thick brows for a split
second, walked quickly toward her.

"I was hoping we might have an opportunity to meet," she
said. "I'm Angela Rose's great-aunt Patricia."

Marlena introduced herself, as well, and was glad the
woman didn't offer to shake hands. Angela Rose was

squirming and becoming quite fussy, undoubtedly tired of being held.

"There is certainly a strong resemblance between you and Luella." Patricia managed a brief smile. "You'll be interested to know that I've finally received word from my brother and his wife—Gordon's parents." She continued talking as if she were somehow in charge of the moment. Or if not that, the baby's future, at least the part that was to unfold under her watchful eye. "Anderson and Sheryl hope to hear from Gordon by the time they're back from their travels, and they'll decide what to do from there." Here, Patricia touched the baby's tiny hand, and Angela began to cry nearly on cue.

"She's tired, as you can imagine," Marlena explained.

"Poor dear, I'm sure she is," Patricia said. "Such a dreadful day." She stepped back a bit and sighed. "I spoke with your parents regarding the baby's care—I've spent quite some time tasking myself over this matter. I'm too busy at work to care for Angela, so for now, I believe you and your grandmother are a better option." She went on to make a point of saying that she was single, as well.

Marlena nodded as the woman continued to converse with such composure that Marlena wondered whether Patricia Munroe had experienced even a speck of sorrow this day.

"*Nee* . . . it's all right, really," Marlena tried to assure her mother after the family had left the small viewing room, again politely refusing anyone's offer to take Angela Rose so she could step in to pay her last respects. "I'm fine, honest I am. Anyway, it's time for the burial service," she said.

Mammi Janice came to her rescue and gently guided her outdoors, where the long, shiny hearse was parked near the entrance, waiting to take her sister's body to the cemetery. Marlena noticed Patricia making her way across the parking lot to her car and wondered if she, too, would join the procession.

Glancing over toward the honeysuckle vines near where she'd seen Nat, she was still surprised at his impromptu visit. To think she'd walked outside within minutes of his arrival! Yet the joy of seeing his handsome face had diminished when she considered his cool response to Luella's baby. *I really enjoy caring for Angela Rose. And for as long as need be.*

Seeing her parents and siblings heading outside now, she could not comprehend, for the life of her, how it had come about that Luella was to be buried in a plot in their family's row. It wasn't necessary to know, of course, but it *was* true to her father's compassionate nature. *Dawdi Tim would've done the same thing,* she thought, even though everyone knew Luella had cut her Plain ties.

"What if Gordon Munroe doesn't agree with his wife's burial location?" Marlena whispered to Mammi as they waited for the casket to depart from the church.

"It's all in God's hands, dear."

That seemed to be Mammi's unswerving answer to everything, and it was one Marlena knew Mammi Janice also believed.

～～ ⌒

Nestled against Marlena, Angela Rose fell asleep during the ride to the cemetery in the plain-looking limousine. Katie and Rachel Ann sat on the other side of Mammi, leaning forward repeatedly to stare at their sleeping niece, till Mammi eventually patted their knees and they quit, wearing more serious countenances as the ominous-looking motor vehicle took them to Luella's final resting place.

It was harrowing, really, what with the casket in the hearse just ahead of them. Marlena assumed her sisters and brothers were also shuddering at the thought. Avoiding eye contact with her parents, Marlena tried not to think about the strange situation—the family unified one last time. She sighed and looked down at Angela's pretty little face in such sweet repose, oblivious to the weight of the moment.

Marlena relived Angela's sudden arrival in Brownstown last week—all the crying and resisting, *rutsche* and fussing. And oh, the anguish in her pretty eyes. It broke Marlena's heart to think this baby, asleep now in her arms, might have to go through yet another uprooting.

Heeding the urge to pray, feeling desperate now, she opened up her inner being to God like Mammi did every day, except in a silent prayer. *Dear Lord God, wilt Thou be our helper, especially for Angela Rose's future? My mother and grandmother always say to trust in Thy wisdom, O Lord, and I really want to do that right now . . . more than anything else on Thy green earth. In our Lord Jesus' name. Amen.*

After a generous hot meal shared with the extended family, her mother mentioned a box she'd packed for Marlena with a few of Luella's personal items. "Why don't ya take it back to Brownstown and look through it when you're ready."

Surprised, Marlena wanted to ask about it but kept still.

"According to Gordon's aunt Patricia, there's nothing in there he would care about. Of course, I got her say-so first."

The intensity in her mother's eyes seemed to indicate her

need to create a bridge of sorts between Marlena and her sister, and Marlena hoped Mamma wouldn't be disappointed.

"There are even some postcards Luella received from one of the neighbor girls in Brownstown. You might remember Olive Hendrickson?"

Marlena couldn't believe Luella and Olive had kept in contact. "Really? That's a shock."

"Evidently Olive was a *gut* friend these past years," Mamma said.

Marlena hadn't forgotten the time Olive and Luella had gone hiking all over Olive's grandfather's land and came across an old wooden footbridge spanning the gorge. Luella had talked a lot about it.

"You're sure it was Olive who wrote to Luella?" Marlena said, still surprised.

"*Jah*, the English girl who lived not far from the Millers'."

"I never would have guessed," she said in a low voice.

What else don't I know about my sister?

CHAPTER 22

$\mathcal{F}$ollowing the noon meal of baked chicken and mushrooms, and mashed potatoes with gravy, Ellie sent Dorcas and Julia out to the woodshed to carry in armloads of kindling to fill the woodbox. Meanwhile, Sally stayed put to wash dishes. And when the kitchen was all redd up, Ellie and her three girls went out to the hen house to gather eggs. She observed the delicate way young Sally reached for each egg and placed it in her metal basket.

The girls talked of their fondness for their unusual guest. Julia cheerfully suggested they start calling him "Onkel Boston," which brought a stream of giggles from Dorcas and Sally.

"He must have a family *somewhere*," Dorcas observed.

"*Jah*, maybe." Julia smiled sweetly. "But if he doesn't, we could adopt him."

Always our little dreamer, thought Ellie.

Later, as they wiped the eggs with a wet cloth, Julia told on her little sister, pointing out that Sally had recently boasted she was getting old enough to gather eggs more often. "She said she never cracks a single one, Mamma."

"My girls are growin' up to become responsible young ladies," Ellie replied.

A long moment of silence passed, and then Julia asked hesitantly, "What 'bout Small Jay? Will *he* ever grow up?"

"Well now, Julia."

"I just mean so he can help Dat round the farm, is all. He surely seems to want to." Tears sprang into Julia's eyes. "I'm awful sorry if it came out all *ferhoodled*, Mamma."

"Oh, my dear, of course you are." She gave her a smile, wishing she'd initially been less quick to respond. How she loved her daughters, who, like Small Jay, had gone out of their way to make Boston feel welcome.

~___ᘓℭ

After Roman came in from cultivating the fields and had washed his hands and face at the well pump, he accompanied Boston Calvert to the gray family buggy and waited till he was settled inside. Small Jay stood near the carriage with pleading eyes. *He wants to come along,* Ellie knew. But Roman sent him back into the house with his sisters, and the corresponding looks of disappointment on both her son's face and Boston's were not lost on Ellie. Witnessing the growing bond between them yet again only made it harder for her.

As they rode, Roman talked about the barn, which also needed to be cleaned thoroughly for the upcoming Preaching, including hauling away manure and stacking hay. Boston was quick to volunteer his "assistance," as he said. As usual, his choice of words made Ellie even more curious about him— clearly this was a man with a higher education than eight years, like their Amish scholars. Maybe even a college education. Roman, however, seemed out of sorts and grumbled about all the time it had taken to fetch several runaway cows earlier. Even when Ellie stuck her neck out and tried to assure him that they wouldn't be gone long, he continued to grouse about the day's remaining work.

Then, changing the subject, she said, "By the way, Small Jay did a real *gut* job of cleanin' up the mess Shredder made." She wanted to bolster her case for giving their son more tasks around the farm.

"I noticed your young man out there, as well," Boston chimed in, which made Ellie smile. "He was scrupulous in his work."

"That cat," Roman muttered. "Shredder seems to have disappeared."

"Maybe he suspects trouble," Ellie suggested.

Roman harrumphed. "No question 'bout that!"

She didn't care to know what her husband had planned for the feline. Instead, Ellie turned the topic to setting Boston's mind at ease about Dr. Isaac, who was well-known in the Plain community. "He treats mostly Amish and Mennonite patients, and with much success," she added.

Her remarks seemed to register enough that Boston nodded his head. Later, though, when the man's head drooped to his chest, Ellie wasn't sure if he had been going along with what she'd said or had already been in the process of falling asleep.

⁓☙

The visit with the folk doctor went as well as Ellie had expected. Boston seemed to like Dr. Isaac, who, not surprisingly, had a tincture and an herbal tea on hand to offer Boston. "They just might help you." Boston promptly handed them off to Ellie for safekeeping, concerned about forgetting when to take them.

They returned to the horse and carriage, where Roman awaited, his head back, mouth wide. Evidently her husband had fallen asleep during the hottest part of the day.

The sky was clouding up in the west as they headed toward home down the stretch of road that wound past the Martin farmhouse. Ellie looked but didn't see any sign of Janice and Marlena—perhaps they hadn't returned yet from Mifflinburg. She wished she had a wristwatch like the Mennonite girls who came to her sewing classes, but she assumed that, if they weren't home, they were at least heading this way. Even though she didn't know Marlena all that well, she felt sensitive toward her, and she asked God to be near Marlena and her family on this difficult day.

As they neared the turnoff into their lane, Roman began to fish for information about Boston's former whereabouts. "No man's an island, ya know." He glanced at Boston. "Surely your relatives are lookin' for ya, sir."

"My dog is the last remnant of my family life," Boston said with a shrug. "He's my faithful companion . . . all I have."

"Well," said Roman, "if you want, one of the English neighbors can drive ya to the police department in Lancaster City. Someone might have filed a missing person's report there. What would ya say to that?"

Ellie held her breath, pleased and surprised that her husband had offered this.

"I wouldn't say that *I'm* the one missing," Boston said.

Roman chuckled at that.

"As long as you're with us, we'll get you feeling better, the Lord willin'," Ellie said, patting the little paper sack.

"Did the doctor say that stuff would remedy his confusion?" Roman asked, his brow furrowed.

"Well, not in so many words, but he did say the tincture and tea can't hurt."

Roman huffed. "There's a world of difference 'tween that and a cure," he pointed out.

Ellie supposed her husband was right, but she could still hope, couldn't she? Besides, Dr. Isaac had never steered them in the wrong direction before. *He just couldn't cure Small Jay.*

"If you'd like, I can take ya over to the Hendricksons' place down the way," Roman said, leaning forward to look at Boston, his gaze probing.

"Do I know them?" Boston asked.

"No . . . but they could get you to the local authorities. Surely the police have been alerted if you have family somewhere frettin' 'bout where you've gone."

"But since that would be an exercise in futility," Boston interjected, "I'd rather resume my work earning my keep, if you please."

Ellie swallowed her hopeful sigh, knowing as rigid as Roman was, he would never seek out worldly folk, not even to report a possibly missing man. It simply wasn't his way.

As they pulled up to the house, she rejoiced silently to see her dear boy standing at the mailbox, slipping a letter inside and putting up the little wooden flag. Then, turning, he stood there, no doubt waiting for Boston's return.

Our precious gift, Ellie thought of Small Jay, clearing her throat to keep the tears at bay.

~⊘

After his father unhitched the horse and buggy and returned to field work, Small Jay and Boston took turns sweeping the porch and the sidewalks leading to the house and *Dawdi Haus.*

Allegro sat eyeing them on the lawn but hurried to Boston's side when the man took a seat on the back porch.

"How about I read another letter to ya?" Small Jay volunteered. "All right?"

Boston agreed. "But first I want to relay the discussion during the ride back from the doctor . . . if I can remember all of it."

"Take your time. I have all day, ya know. Dat doesn't think I can do much work round here."

Boston looked puzzled. "And why is that?"

Small Jay shook his head. He wasn't about to tattle on his father.

Thankfully, Boston let that slide and told him what Dr. Isaac had said, as well as about the possibilities for locating any family Boston might still have.

"Maybe your love letters will tell us where you're from," Small Jay said softly.

Boston smiled. "There may be some truth to that, young man."

"What if you just listen while I read and tell me if something jumps out?"

"Jumps out?"

"Jogs a memory," Small Jay clarified with a glance down at Sassy, curled up at his feet.

"Love letters, you say?" Boston teased from his willow rocker. He pulled his harmonica from his shirt pocket and began to play the same sad yet pretty tune that Small Jay had heard many times before.

"Did Dr. Isaac give ya anything to take?"

"Why do you ask?"

Small Jay knew that most of Dr. Isaac's remedies needed

time to work. Still, he hoped for a better outcome for his friend than himself. "Just wonderin', is all."

Mamma came and sat in one of the rockers, too, with Sally sitting herself down on the floor of the porch in front of her so Mamma could brush her long hair. Sally counted the brush-strokes in *Deitsch* as Allegro rested quietly, taking it all in till he must've spotted a squirrel. Then, with a great spurt of energy, he shot toward the meadow.

"Boston's got another letter for me to read," Small Jay told his mother.

Mamma looked up. "Would ya like some privacy, Boston?"

"The more the merrier, as the saying goes." Boston smiled over at Sally, who stopped counting and suddenly looked bashful.

Boston held out the satchel for Small Jay to retrieve a letter. "By the way, thank you kindly for the ideal spot on which to hang my worldly goods." He chuckled a bit.

"You're welcome," said Small Jay. "I thought it would be better, what with Shredder lurking about."

Boston laughed again, then grew more serious. "I suppose you're right. I need to keep the letters safe if I hope to have them to jog my memory."

Small Jay nodded, still hopeful that would happen. No matter what, he also enjoyed these glimpses into Boston's past life.

This letter began like all the others, *My dearest darling*, but it had been written nearly a year after the last, in the winter of 1962. *If I remember correctly*, Small Jay thought, wondering if he might not try some of Dr. Isaac's memory aids for himself.

Mamma tilted her head and had a sober look on her pretty face as Small Jay continued to read.

I have been taking time to sort through some of our musty old books upstairs, and I found a thought-provoking old poem that nicely expresses the way our marriage works. See if you agree, my dear:

> *"They were so truly one, that none could say*
> *Which of them ruled, or which did obey:*
> *He ruled because she would obey; and she,*
> *In so obeying, ruled as well as he."*

Interrupting him, Boston asked Small Jay to read the poem again, word for word.

Small Jay did as his friend requested, then noticed Boston cover his face with his smooth hands. "What's a-matter?"

Boston remained silent for a long time, which made Small Jay's heart pump faster. *Is he sick?*

Away in the pasture, Allegro was racing through the grass, a ray of sun shining down, making his black-and-white coat gleam. Small Jay wished Boston's pet was there with them on the porch just now, because the poor man looked like he needed some comfort.

Leaning down, Small Jay reached for cuddly Sassy, picked her up, and laid her carefully on Boston's lap.

Small Jay and his mother, and even Sally, exchanged worried glances. At last Boston sighed and placed both hands on the cat's back, stroking her. "This letter reminds me of Abigail's book collection," he said quietly, his brow wrinkling. "What is such a thing called?"

Small Jay looked toward his mother. "Mamma, do you know?"

"A library, maybe?" she asked.

Boston's eyes widened. "Ah yes . . . and for a strange and wonderful moment, I could see that very comfortable spot in my mind's eye." He described it for them: the wall-to-wall shelving rising from floor to ceiling, the fireplace on one wall. "There was even a beautiful ladder that matched the shelves perfectly." He scratched his head, the cat still in his lap.

"What type of wood?" Small Jay asked.

Boston rubbed his beard and looked at the sky, clearly aggravated that he couldn't readily recall that detail.

"Was it oak or maple?" Small Jay suggested.

"No . . . I recall reddish hues."

"Cherrywood, perhaps?" Mamma ventured.

Boston nodded emphatically. "That, my dear lady, is the correct wood. Thank you."

"So Abigail had a cherrywood library," Small Jay said, smiling.

"Now if we just knew who Abigail was, that'd be *wunnerbaar-gut, jah?*" Mamma said.

"*Jah,*" Boston replied unexpectedly.

"If ya keep talkin' like that, better watch out, or they'll make ya deacon," Sally chimed in. "When ya get your new black suit an' all."

"Oh now, you," Mamma corrected her, laughing.

Small Jay finished reading the rest of the letter aloud, and when he was finished, Mamma asked if Boston minded if she looked at the poem.

"Help yourself, dear lady," Boston said, motioning for Small Jay to hand it to her.

"Please, call me Ellie," she reminded him, her eyes twinkling. She read the letter, her lips moving like she was reciting it to herself. "Where's the envelope?" she asked when she'd finished and refolded the letter.

"If I knew, I might know where I'm from," Boston said as he tucked the letter into his shoulder bag.

Just then Sassy started and hissed loudly. Small Jay turned and spotted Shredder on the hunt, crouching low in the grass just beyond the woodshed, waiting as he was known to do. Then, when his prey was in sight, he silently pounced and snatched a good-sized rodent. *Maybe a rat,* thought Small Jay. "Looks like Shredder's still around," he announced.

While he was almost glad to see the old black cat on the prowl again, he also felt unexpectedly torn, much like he'd felt when he wrote the letter to Luke Mast that he'd mailed a little while ago. He felt the same way, too—arguing with himself—whenever he thought of Boston's finding his family. Boston's people would surely want to pull his friend away from here, back to his other life.

His real life.

CHAPTER 23

While Marlena bathed Angela Rose after a light supper of cold cuts, bread, and strawberry jam, she realized again how glad she was to have stumbled into Nat outside the meetinghouse that morning. She supposed Nat and she were a little unaccustomed to each other, having been apart for two weeks now. *Like a wood stove needs regular polishing,* she thought, recalling how awkwardly he'd bussed her cheek there in the private haven near the honeysuckle vines. The encounter had been peculiar, and her excitement at meeting him had been lessened by his relieved reaction to the idea of Gordon's parents coming to take away Angela Rose.

Later, when she'd slipped the little cotton gown over Angela's head and was giving her a bedtime bottle in the kitchen, cuddling her more than usual, she mentioned to Mammi that she was going to sort through the box her mother had sent with them.

"Yet tonight, dear?"

Marlena did feel particularly spent from the emotional day. But she wanted to sort through the large box and get it over with, though she didn't feel right admitting it to her grandmother. And there was a part of her that was also curious about the postcards from Olive, especially. "Do you remember the Hendricksons, Mammi?" she asked.

"I've seen Isabelle Hendrickson many a time at market over the years, and sometimes walking their dog up the road."

"What do you know about her daughter Olive?"

"Just that she lives near Philly somewhere and teaches in an underprivileged neighborhood."

"Her mother told you this?"

"*Jah* . . . and they're ever so proud of her." Mammi looked at her inquisitively. "Why're ya askin'?"

Marlena filled her in on what Mamma had said about the postcards, all the more eager to open the box. She also thought of asking Mammi's opinion of Gordon's aunt but decided against it. There had been enough talk for one day.

Marlena kissed Luella's drowsy babe before laying her down in the crib. She leaned over the railing to pat her soft little back, wanting to tell her many things, especially that her Mamma had loved her very much. "Maybe there's something in the box for you, a keepsake for when ya grow up," she whispered.

When she was sure Angela was asleep, Marlena reluctantly headed downstairs to see what mementos her mother thought were important enough to pass along. Mammi had since gone to sit on the back porch for some fresh air, and undoubtedly to ponder the day, leaving Marlena alone in the warm kitchen with her awaiting discovery.

Ellie yearned for a tender relationship with her husband, like Abigail's with Boston. She had found herself listening with great interest today as Small Jay read the letter from Abigail. *Surely Boston's bride of many years.*

Now Ellie tried to recite the poem about unity in marriage, remembering the last two lines especially well: *He ruled because she would obey; and she, in so obeying, ruled as well as he.*

The more she pondered the poem, the more she wanted to follow its advice, in hopes of creating a happier bond with Roman.

"*Kumm yetz*—Come now!" Roman called the children into the front room for family worship.

When they were seated, he took time to say that the Bible reading this evening would be from Luke in the New Testament and Proverbs in the Old. Then he began to read, "'He answereth and saith unto them, He that hath two coats, let him impart to him that hath none; and he that hath meat, let him do likewise.'"

Roman glanced at Ellie and held her gaze before turning back to the middle of the Bible to read from Proverbs, chapter nineteen, verse seventeen. "'He that hath pity upon the poor lendeth unto the Lord. . . .'"

Ellie noticed the verses he'd chosen were short and to the point and easy for even the youngest of them to understand. As Roman took the lead in kneeling and folding his hands to pray silently, she wondered if maybe he had chosen them purposely. *Bless our union, O Lord God,* Ellie prayed, departing from the usual rote prayer. *Wilt Thou soften my husband's heart toward me?*

Afterward, the girls headed upstairs to dress for bed. But Small Jay lingered.

"What is it, Jake?" asked Roman, still seated.

"If we're supposed to have pity on the poor, like ya read, Dat . . ." He looked away, working his jaw now.

Ellie encouraged him by nodding her head.

"Well," Small Jay went on, "if we follow the verses, then why isn't Boston sleepin' in a real bed, same as us?"

Roman drew in a quick breath and ran a hand through his hair. "Listen here, son, I've taken him to the doctor, and your Mamma's sewin' him clothes—she even went and bought him a straw hat like mine, to keep the sun off. The spot we gave him outside is comfortable, cooler even than in here."

It sounded to Ellie like her husband was arguing with himself.

Small Jay's face fell. "I just thought—"

"There's little more we can do, son."

"But what if he's an angel, and we don't know it?" Small Jay said softly. "The Bible says we can entertain angels without knowin'."

"It's mighty clear that Boston's not an angel. Now, it's time ya took yourself off to bed."

There was ever so much on Ellie's mind to say to Roman, but she held back. She knew all too well that he preferred she not speak up to him.

Roman waited till their son was out of earshot to say more. "What is it about this Boston? Why isn't anything we've done for him *gut* enough for our boy?"

She didn't have the heart to tell Roman what she thought— that Boston might be filling a place in Small Jay's heart intended for a father. "Well, he's never behaved like this with anyone before, comin' out of his shell an' all. Our son's maturing before our eyes, Roman. He wants to help Boston."

"And *we* aren't? What more can be done aside from getting the police over here to cart him away?"

"I know you, dear, and you'd never do such a thing."

Roman bowed his head into his knees. "*Nee*," he murmured.

She remembered the poem, likely Abigail's way of affirming whoever the letter was meant for. Ellie tried now to adopt the same tone as Abigail. "Roman, you were awful kind to take Boston to see Dr. Isaac today. Very kind."

Roman's face looked more relaxed when he looked up and met her eyes. "I didn't mean to . . ." He tugged hard at his beard, making his bottom lip protrude. "I don't know . . . I guess it really isn't just Boston stayin' here that's so trying."

"What then, love?" She felt certain she knew the whole of it—what was eating away at him.

Roman rose suddenly with a groan and walked the length of the house to the kitchen. She could hear the water running in the pump sink and wondered if her husband was washing his hands or running water over his head.

~ ❧

Marlena found what Mamma had chosen to pack of Luella's ever so surprising: several cape dresses, along with aprons, too. "Things my sister stopped wearing when she left home," Marlena said to herself.

There were also bright-colored floral and striped dresses, and even a few scarves, as well, all modern and in the latest style. And two sets of embroidered pillowcases Luella had sewn as a girl.

The postcards and letters Mamma had mentioned were in the bottom of the box, secured by a rubber band. Seeing how thick the stack was, Marlena removed the rubber band and flipped through them, glancing at the back and seeing that each was written to Luella from Olive Hendrickson. Marlena could hardly believe she was looking through Luella's personal mail.

After putting them in sequential order, she began to read. It seemed that each time Olive and her family were on vacation, Olive sent a postcard to Luella. In some cases, there were letters with postcards tucked inside. Only occasionally were the messages written from Olive's home—those featured details about school grades, plans for college, and a note about meeting a boy . . . and later, the joyful message: *I'm getting married. How I wish you could come to the wedding!*

One of the last letters in the pile described Olive's tour of the Loretto Chapel in Santa Fe, New Mexico. A postcard of the chapel was enclosed. Olive and her family had been deeply touched by the story they were told of a passerby on a donkey, who'd ended up staying in the chapel for months to build a staircase for the choir loft—one with no visible means of support. Before the anonymous man's arrival, everyone had thought it would be impossible to fit a staircase into the small space.

> *I really felt something, Luella. Something real and powerful—like I was seeing the result of a miracle. Anyway, I stood in the middle of all those tourists and found myself lifting my heart to heaven. I can't explain what I was feeling, but seeing that work of art, and being told that the creator of the incredible staircase was an answer to many prayers—you know he disappeared, never to be found?—well, I'm telling you, it stopped me in my selfish tracks. Okay, I'll just say it: The story made me want to believe in God with everything in me.*
> *Do you have any idea what this means?*

Marlena reread the postcard and wondered if Olive's experience was something akin to how the people must have felt seeing the angels near the Brownstown church steeple. She considered Olive's reaction to that miraculous staircase, not forgetting what Mammi Janice had told her: *"Wise folk never reject the possibility of miracles."*

Not many months after the Santa Fe letter and postcard, Olive wrote again:

> *I want to help those who need it most, Luella. Life's too short not to make a difference in this world. My husband and I have decided to commit to giving a year to missions, if we're selected.*
>
> *P.S. I've never felt so happy!*

Marlena stared at the postcard. "Luella never mentioned her continuing friendship with Olive," she whispered, picking up the brightly colored dresses. What could she do with these worldly dresses, and the Amish ones, too, especially since Luella had been much taller and thinner than Marlena? She wondered if any of Olive's correspondence had rung true for her sister. Had the more recent letters and postcards made any impact on her life?

Searching again through the box and suddenly feeling energized, Marlena yearned to read more from Olive. But she found only the loud dresses and the pillowcases.

Going to the back porch, she sat with her grandmother, who looked so peaceful there with her big Bible open on her lap. "I feel like I never really knew Luella." Marlena folded her arms.

"Why's that?" Mammi rocked harder, as if trying to rouse herself.

Marlena told of the correspondence from Olive, particularly the insightful moment in New Mexico.

"Plenty-a folks' hearts are moved, even changed, by signs and wonders," Mammi said, turning to her. "But remember what the Lord Jesus said to Thomas? 'Blessed are they that have not seen, and yet believe.'"

Marlena hadn't heard or read that verse in years. Momentarily she wondered what Nat would think of Olive's so-called enlightenment in Santa Fe, or the possible miracle that precipitated it. She made a mental note to ask him when she returned home at the end of summer.

She was aware of the sounds of twilight—a train rumbling in the distance, crickets and birds calling between trees, and the echo from a mouth organ in the direction of the Bitners' place.

It saddened her to dwell on Luella's funeral, but what had taken place at the burial service was both special and beautiful. She had been standing back away from the freshly dug grave, holding sleeping Angela Rose, when, at the designated time for the final prayer, her father stepped forward, next to Simon Ranck. But rather than the preacher, her father had begun to speak. *"We have brought up our daughter in the fear and admonition of the Lord, and do now commit her soul to our loving heavenly Father, who sees and knows all things, including the intent and longing of the heart. . . . Dust to dust, ashes to ashes."*

He paused, head still bowed so low that his beard pressed against his black vest and frock coat. *"The Lord bless you and keep you, the Lord lift His countenance upon you and give you peace."*

Marlena had been astounded at such a departure from

anything she'd ever witnessed at a burial. *Was Dat's blessing as much for us as it was for Luella?*

Presently, Mammi closed her Bible and rose to go inside, and Marlena followed. Instead of preparing for bed, she headed upstairs to look in on Angela Rose before going to open the balcony door at the end of the hall. She stepped outside and could see much of the fertile land her grandfather had carefully tended for years. *Dawdi took the care of God's earth seriously,* she recalled. *Like a calling,* he'd said.

Marlena thought again of Olive Hendrickson's lovely postcards and felt the lack in her own sisterly connection with Luella. Even here at Dawdi's tranquil farm, meaningful conversations between them had been few and far between. Pondering these many things, Marlena found herself missing what might have been.

CHAPTER 24

The next day was a quiet one for Marlena and Mammi, although busy with washing. On Wednesday Marlena awakened at dawn to the happy sound of babbling mixed with babyish giggling. She slipped out of bed and peered down into the crib and saw that Angela Rose had managed to free her little feet from the drawstring gown. The little darling was sucking on the toes of her right foot.

"Now, that's *one* way to start the day. Just how do those little piggies taste, huh?" she asked, kissing the bottom of one foot. "Can I have a bite?"

Angela reached up to touch Marlena's nose with her slobbery fingers, laughing right out loud.

"*Ach,* such a tease you are!" She picked her up and, after dressing her for the day, carried her downstairs to see Mammi Janice, who was already cooking eggs.

She relayed what Angela had been doing with her toes, which seemed to trigger a bit of baby talk from Mammi. Squelching her own silly laugh, Marlena observed the playful

209

interaction between the two; she couldn't remember her grandmother carrying on so with any of her grandchildren.

Later, at one point during breakfast, Mammi took the spoon and played like it was a buzzy bee, leaning her head forward and frowning when Angela Rose's tiny mouth refused to budge. After repeated tries, Angela's mouth finally popped open, and she took her warm rice cereal at last.

"She's a stubborn one, ain't so?" Mammi said.

Marlena agreed. "Not surprising, I guess." Yet she couldn't help smiling. Was Mammi's new exuberance a hopeful sign that she was overcoming her loneliness for Dawdi? The truth was, Angela Rose had brought delight into their shared sadness.

It won't last much longer, she thought suddenly. *No matter how much we love her.*

~~⁀◌~~

At Mammi's prompting, once her niece was down for a nap, Marlena set out to the Bitners' house for the hour-long quilting class. She noticed Sarah Mast hurrying into the lane on foot and was happy to see her. *She's going too!*

She observed the lively energy of a handful of other young women just ahead of her. Two of them wore the floral-print dresses so typical of Mennonites like Mammi.

Sarah turned around and burst into a smile. "Hullo, Marlena. Looks like you're joining us today."

"*Jah,* I told Ellie I'd come if I could, and today's the day." She caught up to Sarah. "I didn't have time to cut any squares, though."

"Well, I'm sure that won't matter." Sarah waved to the others and commented to Marlena how warm it already was this morning. "And it's still only nine o'clock. Say, how's your little niece? Thought you might have her along."

"I did think of it, but she's starting to get into a *gut* napping schedule, which is a blessing."

"Maybe sometime you'll bring her, then?"

"We'll see." *If she's still around to bring . . .*

Ellie was standing in the doorway of the little *Dawdi Haus*, smiling her welcome. The cozy place was situated on the south side of the main farmhouse and surrounded by colorful annuals of many varieties, as well as pots of bright pink geraniums on the porch. Ellie showed them into the front room, smaller in scale than her own and with a large rectangular sewing table set up in the middle of the floor.

"The quilting frame will go there, once we're ready to work on a big quilt, but for now we're just talking 'bout patterns and piecework," Ellie said after she introduced Marlena to the other young women. Most of them were neighbors Marlena had come into contact with here and there, but she knew no one as well as Sarah Mast.

Ellie's instructions were clear and thorough; she was a good teacher and took time for the benefit of the girls there who weren't Amish to describe layouts for the Double Nine Patch quilt and the Diamond in the Square. She also gave ideas for making a crazy quilt, although it wasn't necessarily an authentic Amish style. "Even so, some of us like to experiment with designs and loud colors," she said with a wink.

The girls sitting across from Marlena smiled in unison, as if recognizing this as a shared secret desire.

"And we mustn't forget tied quilts, which are fun to make and quick, too." Ellie glanced at Dorcas, who was nodding her head. "Just ask my daughter here how easy they are to make up."

Dorcas turned pink in the face.

Later, while Ellie displayed some of her own quilts, pointing out the intricate stitching on the backing, Marlena had an idea. "What about a keepsake quilt?" she asked quietly. "Has anyone here made one?"

Ellie said she didn't know of any particular pattern. "It's an interesting idea, though. Why don't ya draw a sketch of what it might look like?" she suggested. "And bring it to class next week."

After the group dispersed, Marlena was delighted when Sarah asked to walk with her as far as her grandmother's house. She told her about getting some of Luella's dresses, both Plain and worldly. "I wasn't sure what I'd do with them, considering everything, but I'm thinkin' now of making a crib quilt for her baby."

"That's a *wunnerbaar-gut* plan, Marlena. I can't wait to see the piecework all laid out."

"It'll take some doin', cutting the pieces from the dresses." Marlena smiled. "Well, you know . . . we're all busy this time of year."

"Is your Mammi able to help some with pickin' garden vegetables or canning?"

"She does what she's able. Since Angela Rose arrived, she's been spelling me off when the baby is napping," Marlena said. "Like today."

"I'd be happy to help with Angela sometime, or bring over supper—whatever ya need," Sarah offered.

Tears sprang to Marlena's eyes. "*Denki*."

"Well, I'll drop by sometime and we can decide what day

is best." She asked if Marlena was coming to the needlepoint class on Friday. "You'd love that, too."

"I'm sure I would." Marlena meant it. "Must be mindful of all that's needed of me just now, ya know."

"Well, I hope to see you before next Wednesday. All right?"

"Sure, come by. Mammi thinks so much of you and your family."

"Oh, and before I forget, Luke wanted me to invite you to visit our church sometime, if that'd interest ya."

Marlena had to laugh a little. "What's one more church, *jah*?"

"*Nee*, I'm sure that's not what he was thinkin' at all."

Marlena hadn't forgotten Luke's good-natured comment about the several churches she'd attended. "Mammi likes going to her meetinghouse, of course, and it's *gut* for me to attend with her. But thanks anyway."

Sarah nodded and waved. "Something to think about, if you want to learn more about our small New Order Amish group."

Why would she suggest it? Marlena wondered as she turned into the driveway. She wouldn't think of letting Mammi go alone to church. Still, she thought it was awful nice of Sarah to invite her. *Luke too.*

⁓⊙

After the students had gone home, Ellie and Dorcas swept down the walls in the front room, then washed them thoroughly. That room and the one directly behind it were the two largest downstairs, where the actual gathering would take place on Sunday morning. *Only three days after today to get everything in tip-top shape*, Ellie thought, feeling like she was racing the clock.

As she worked, Ellie couldn't stop thinking about the poem in Boston Calvert's letter. She felt compelled to put those words into action, especially today. There had been even more girls from outside their Old Order community at this morning's class, and she was now on edge about Roman's reaction.

There's no question he'll disapprove.

Had Roman observed any of her students coming or going? She knew for sure both Small Jay and Boston had seen the young women filing into the *Dawdi Haus*. While she was welcoming her students, she'd seen her son and Boston making their way toward the well pump, Boston playing his harmonica. Small Jay had called to her when the music stopped and held up two big Thermoses, saying they needed some cold water for the men who were working in the hayfield.

Boston seemed to be quite disoriented—he'd called her Eleanor yet again. Small Jay had mistakenly thought the prescribed tincture and tea were starting to help the man's memory, but that was not at all true, nor to be expected after only a day. The sad truth was there were good days and bad ones for poor Boston.

And who is the Eleanor he refers to occasionally? Was she Boston's daughter or a niece? He spoke of her nearly in the same breath as Abigail. Ellie remembered how Boston had repeatedly interrupted Small Jay that morning while her son read another letter. The man had appeared to be upset and confused, though unable to say why. But oh, her son was doing so well with his pronunciation of English words, and reading cursive, too. Marlena really wished Roman might overhear him reading sometime. *So smoothly.*

Ellie hadn't been able to stay around for much of that particular letter, rather going out with the girls to pick lettuce, kohlrabi, radishes, peas, and cut rhubarb before her quilting students arrived. *Always plenty of rhubarb this time of year!* But what details she'd heard kept nagging at her. Abigail had thanked Boston for *"writing your exquisite melody."* So now Ellie assumed Boston knew how to play *and* write music, of all things. Yet when Small Jay had asked that very question, Boston brushed it off as if he had no knowledge of any such thing. Still, did that mean anything on a day when he couldn't even remember his dog's name?

Ellie went now to wash the soil from her garden vegetables at the well pump between the house and the stable. When Roman wandered over, she decided she would not talk up to him when he broached the topic of her quilting class. *If he does.* She purposed in her heart to be kinder to him from now on. *Like when we were first married.*

Sure enough, Roman restated his staunch position: "Ellie, I've told ya before, I'm not keen on ya havin' close fellowship with women from other churches."

She nodded and realized it was time to show her submission to his wishes. "If you're unhappy with certain students from other Plain groups comin' to my classes, I could give up teachin' to please ya, Roman." She swallowed her sadness, secretly hoping he might back down.

"Would ya, now?" He went to sit on the nearby wooden bench.

"*Jah,* if it would make ya happier. You ain't so much these days."

He was silent for a time, folding his hands, his arms resting on his legs as he hunched forward. Then, just when she was convinced he wasn't going to say another word, he glanced up. "Well then, Ellie, let it be known you won't be teachin' anymore."

Her heart crashed to the ground. Stunned, she set the large bowl of vegetables down and said nothing. She washed her hands in the cold water from the pump, splashing it onto her cheeks and into the crooks of her elbows. The welcome chill cooled her from the heat and humidity and kept her tears locked up so her husband could not see her bitter disappointment.

For pity's sake, what have I done?

CHAPTER 25

At noon Small Jay walked out to the porch and gathered up Boston's dinner plate and utensils to carry inside to Mamma, then returned to his friend.

"Your mother is one remarkable cook," Boston said, patting his stomach.

"*Jah*, for sure." Small Jay had his mind on other things. "Mamma says we can take the pony cart down to Joe's again."

"What does Eleanor need at the store?"

Small Jay didn't correct him. He'd tried doing that before and apparently it just made things more maddening for Boston. Coming closer, Small Jay whispered, "I need to run a secret errand. Once I get the pony hitched up, I'll tell ya all about it."

Boston frowned. "You have a pony?" His eyes looked so glazed over, Small Jay wondered if it was a good idea to take him along.

"Wait here and I'll come back for ya." He smiled at the man, feeling downright sorry for him. "Maybe you could have yourself forty winks on the drive, *jah*? A little snooze, ya know."

Boston's face relaxed into a smile, and he leaned his head back against the rocker and was asleep nearly that quick.

It took only a short time to hitch up; then Small Jay walked out to the outhouse. There, he removed the rock he'd pushed in front of the door and inched it open just enough to see Shredder sitting there, the yellow-green eyes shining like the cat had expected him.

Small Jay noticed there was not a single piece of torn paper anywhere. "Prob'ly 'cause of Dat's clever idea," he muttered. Out of necessity, his father had enclosed the shelf, making it impossible for the cat's claws to have a heyday again with the paper. However, this didn't mean that Dat wasn't still eager to wring Shredder's furry neck.

Small Jay removed Sassy's collar, already snapped to the red leash, from his pocket and talked softly to the wicked creature while he slipped the collar around his neck. "There now, let's take ya for a nice walk to the pony cart. I want ya to meet the mouth organ man." He had it all planned now, right down to the minute. "My father's gonna have a fit if I don't get you out of here."

He could see Allegro nosing around the barnyard. Shredder hissed loudly, then hacked up a hairball, which made Small Jay laugh.

Shredder strained against the leash, twisting and turning to bite it like a puppy might. It was obvious Shredder wasn't used to being confined, and as Small Jay tapped Boston gently on the knee to wake him up, he was glad they didn't have far to walk. As soon as they were all piled into the pony cart, Small Jay asked Boston whether he wanted to hold the ornery cat or take the reins.

Boston reached for the driving lines, and they were off.

"Which way shall we turn, young man?" he asked, seeming more alert again.

Small Jay pointed to the left, and quickly Razor pulled them down the hill, past the old mill, across the stone bridge and the mighty creek below, and over toward Joe's store. To attempt to control Shredder's wild movements, Small Jay had wrapped the leash tightly around his hand till he had a powerful-good grip. Even so, Shredder scratched at Small Jay's arms and legs.

"Keep goin'," he told Boston as Joe's store came into view. "Where we're headed first is up a ways yet."

Just then Shredder began to howl. "*Sei schtill*—Be quiet! I'm savin' your life, cat." *One of many lives, if you're lucky*, he thought, tightening his hold on Shredder all the more.

When they arrived at the Mast farmhouse, Small Jay asked Boston to wait there in the cart. "I'll be right back," he said, taking the lines from him and tying the pony to one of the pickets on the whitewashed fence. "Come along, Shredder. I want ya to meet your new master."

Luke must have seen him coming and waved as he approached. "I got your note 'bout Shredder. I'll be glad to take him off your hands."

"Just a warning, the second he's let loose, he'll scram. If you've got some catnip, that'll help."

"Oh, we've got plenty." Luke smiled. "And some cats like sweet cream, too, *jah?*"

"Not sure about this one."

Luke leaned down to size up Shredder. "By the looks of him, I'd say he prefers mouse meat."

"He *is* a barn cat."

"Ain't like your civilized Sassafras."

"*Nee,* Mamma would never let Shredder in the house. *Niemols!*" He'd *tear up everything in sight,* thought Small Jay with a grimace.

"Looks like he'd like to scratch my eyes out," replied Luke.

"He will, too, if I don't take him off this leash."

"Maybe his name's his downfall. Ever think of that?" Luke tilted his head as he scrutinized the cat. "He needs a name he can live up to. He's mighty tall, even when he's sittin'. And grand, too. Like he thinks he's the king of the world."

Small Jay wasn't sure what Luke meant.

"Maybe King's a better fit." Luke reached for the leash.

King, thought Small Jay. He followed as Luke led Shredder, or King, around to the back of the house. In short order, the unruly cat was eating out of Luke's hands, so to speak, licking up the fresh cream Luke had poured into a bowl there on the warm sidewalk near a purple-martin birdhouse.

Feeling mighty good about this, Small Jay figured everything was going to work out fine. He remembered to thank Luke, then added, "Keep that cat collar and leash. It's all right with me." With that, he backed away slowly, gritting his teeth and hoping King Shredder would stay put. Then he turned to head down the driveway to the pony cart.

Boston's chin was resting on his fist as Small Jay untied Razor. He crawled into the cart just as Boston was waking up.

"Now off to Joe's store," Small Jay said and explained that he'd given Sassy's collar and leash to Luke Mast.

"Ah, so you wish to purchase a replacement?" Boston asked as they made the turn onto the road.

"They'll help Luke keep that ornery cat in tow till he gets used to bein' round his new home . . . I hope."

Boston yawned.

"Luke was kind enough to save Shredder's life, so it's the least I can do." *King Shredder,* thought Small Jay, grinning to himself.

In Joe's parking lot, they got out and tied up Razor to one of several hitching posts. Small Jay asked if Boston had any sugar cubes left in his pockets.

"What are you referring to, young man?"

Small Jay reminded him of his purchase last week, but Boston didn't seem to know a thing about it, and Small Jay decided to drop it. *It's like he just plain doesn't remember.*

They made their way up the front steps, and suddenly Boston stopped. "Now, wait a minute. I do believe I gave all those sugar cubes to your father's mares over the last few days. You see, son, when I have trouble sleeping, I go and talk to the horses for a time."

"And feed them sugar cubes?"

"That's right." Boston waved him on into the store with the very welcoming bell over the door. "So I may need to stock up."

Small Jay smiled. *He remembered!*

~~~

All afternoon, while Ellie cleaned and scrubbed the house, she felt like a *Dummkopp.* Why *had* she opened her mouth to Roman, offering to give up something she held so dear?

Three of her younger sisters and four female cousins arrived to help finish washing all the windows inside and out. They also spent hours weeding and edging flower beds—peonies, chrysanthemums, and painted daisies—and even used the push mower on the lawn. A couple of them went to the cellar and swept the place out good and washed down the cement walls, too, then dusted and reorganized the glass jars of preserves, fruit, and vegetables from last year's canning season. Things were coming together nicely, and it was only Wednesday.

I should have time to write letters to my students tonight, so they receive them in Friday's mail, Ellie thought dejectedly. Suddenly it struck her that some might not get their mail delivered in time, and what then? Her needlepoint class was scheduled for this Friday morning, after all.

She groaned loudly, catching herself too late, and her cousin Lizzie wanted to know if she was all right. *How can I be?* But Ellie just kept shining windows, her arms beginning to play out. Her attempt to be respectful to Roman's wishes had ended in the worst possible result. Yet she knew she'd brought it upon herself.

How will I get word to my students in time?

<hr />

"Dat, has Shredder turned up yet?" wide-eyed Sally asked at supper. She was having trouble cutting her meat, and Julia leaned over to help.

Ellie was pleased to see her girls looking out for each other. She noticed Small Jay paying no mind to the table conversation, lost as usual in his own world of thoughts.

"That's one *duckmeisich Kaader*—sneakin' tomcat," Roman declared, his tumbler of root beer in hand.

"He just up and disappeared?" Dorcas paused in her eating. "Mighty handy, ain't so?"

Our perceptive girl, thought Ellie, wondering what Roman would say to that.

"We've had enough talk 'bout that ornery cat. It's time we start preparin' our hearts for the Lord's Day comin' up," Roman said, changing the subject.

Dorcas nodded humbly.

"*Jah*, and dessert's a-waitin'," said Sally. "Ain't so, Mamma?"

This brought out the sunshine all around the table, and Ellie was somewhat relieved.

~ ℮

In the middle of their supper, the phone rang and Mammi Janice motioned for Marlena to answer it. "Martin residence. This is Marlena."

"I'm sorry to interrupt your meal," her mother said.

"That's all right. We're almost finished." Marlena glanced at her grandmother and mouthed that it was Mamma. "It's always *gut* to hear your voice."

"Yours, too, dear." Her mother paused a second. "I know you remember meeting Patricia Munroe at the funeral. Well, she called a little bit ago with news that Gordon is officially missing in action."

"Oh no. They can't find him after all these days? I thought they were tryin' to—"

"It's more serious than that," Mamma interrupted. "Patricia said the transport plane he and other soldiers were flying in was shot down."

Shot down?

Marlena gripped the phone. "Are ya sayin' Gordon's just lost, then? Not . . ." The lump in her throat kept her from saying what she was thinking, hoping it wasn't true.

"I asked Patricia the same thing."

"Well, he and the other soldiers have to be *somewhere*."

Her mother explained what little she'd been told. "It's such a difficult area to search, and in enemy territory, too. Gordon may have been captured. We simply don't know . . . and might never know."

"Do his parents know this yet?"

"*Jah*. They'll get back from the Mediterranean as soon as their ship reaches port and they can arrange for a flight home."

Marlena's mind was spinning. Gordon was feared dead— undoubtedly his parents would be coming for Angela. "Oh, Mamma, after Luella's accident . . . now this . . ." Her voice failed.

Her mother was silent, too.

Marlena's lip quivered and she turned away to hide the tears springing up. "Honestly, I don't see how we can possibly give Angela up," she said softly into the phone.

"Believe me, I understand. But Patricia will be callin' back in a few days, once Gordon's parents are finally home and settled . . . ready for Angela Rose. So I'll let you know when they arrive."

After they said good-bye and hung up, Marlena filled Mammi in on the call, but she had no desire to finish eating supper. She wandered to the front room and out to the front porch swing, feeling almost as sad as when she'd heard of Luella's passing. That Gordon had been lost in battle and might have died was terrible news indeed, but foremost in her mind now was the idea of surrendering her little niece to people who hadn't even bothered to come to their own daughter-in-law's funeral. Surely they could have gotten home from Europe somehow.

Marlena bowed her head and wept. She tried to process this latest jarring news and realized her mother hadn't said anything about stepping forward to take Angela Rose herself. Surely she and Dat hadn't resigned themselves to

Anderson and Sheryl Munroe bringing up Angela as a fancy *Englischer*?

Marlena tensed up at the thought. Considering they'd lost Luella so completely to the world, wouldn't her parents want to do everything possible to keep their flesh and blood in the Anabaptist way of life?

CHAPTER 26

That evening, Ellie heard Boston playing his favorite melody on his mouth organ again, beautiful yet heartbreaking. She and Roman had quietly slipped out the front door to the porch while the girls did up the supper dishes. Roman had suggested they spend some time alone, something that rarely happened anymore.

Together, they relaxed on the old glider, Ellie on one side and Roman on the other. She felt glad it was just the two of them; so many things were on her mind.

But it was Roman who was first to speak. "I've been thinkin'," he said, eyes fixed on their sprawling front yard. "Wasn't sure ya knew that Jake's been helpin' Boston do some of the chores." He folded his arms across his old white work shirt. "Chores Boston is doin' in exchange for room and board."

Ellie wondered what to say.

"Strange as it seems, the boy's able to do more lifting and whatnot than I thought . . . and for longer, too," Roman said. "More strength in those arms than I would've guessed."

Ellie was heartened but held back.

"Jake's mighty fond of Boston. Which ain't gonna be so *gut* when Boston leaves."

"*Jah*, when that day comes, it'll be hard for our son," she agreed.

"I really think we should figure out a way to help Boston get back to his family or friends—move this along, ya know. Someone must be out there wonderin' what's become of the man."

"I've thought that, too," Ellie replied.

They talked about what they were willing and able to do under their church ordinance as far as searching. Getting the authorities involved, or not.

"Jake told me just yesterday that he's gathering snippets of information . . . I think that's how he put it," said Roman.

"He said that?"

Roman nodded and glanced at her for the first time since they'd sat down. "The boy's surely not bright enough to do somethin' like that, is he?"

Since her husband scarcely ever asked her opinion, Ellie felt tongue-tied for a moment. "Well, he's smart in some ways but struggles in others, as we both know."

"But what sort of clues—or snippets—could he be getting from Boston?"

"Maybe they're from the love letters," she admitted.

"The *what?*"

Ellie told him about the clutch of letters in Boston's satchel. "He says he doesn't know who the letters are from, exactly . . . what his relationship to the woman might be. Boston really doesn't remember much at all, I'm afraid." She continued, telling Roman that both she and Small Jay thought the letter writer, Abigail, was Boston's wife. "But she might be deceased now. On the other hand, he also talks 'bout a woman named Eleanor, but Small Jay and I really can't figure out who that might be."

"I guess that explains some of what Jake's sayin'."

Ellie smiled a little, pleased to hear Roman talk this way after all the years they'd been at loggerheads over their son. She ventured out on a limb and asked, "Since Boston's workin' for ya, have you given any thought, maybe, to lettin' him sleep next door?"

Roman's eyes locked on hers. "What 'bout those sewing classes you're havin' over there?"

"But . . ."

A long silence passed between them. Then Roman said, "Well, never mind, I daresay Boston can sleep over there."

Ellie's heart leaped up.

Roman continued. "I nearly forgot you're quitting your classes."

"I do plan to, but there's a hitch with this Friday." She described her quandary.

"How's that a problem, Ellie? Just tell any of the girls who might show up for the last class."

She nodded compliantly but was annoyed when Roman got up right then and went into the house without even looking her way or saying more.

I brought this on myself.

By the time Ellie managed to compose herself and return to the kitchen, the place was spotless, and the girls were out playing hide-and-seek in the backyard. *Roman's allowing Boston to sleep in the* Dawdi Haus, she thought, watching her husband put up a rope swing on one of the sturdiest limbs on their old oak tree for the girls. Ellie stood behind the screen door now, listening while Boston played the lovely tune over and over. Small Jay sat transfixed next to his friend the harmonica player, keeping him company there on the back porch while Allegro and Sassy snoozed at their feet.

It was hard not to simply ask Boston if she might just sit down and read through all the letters he kept in his bag—one after another. The fact that he wanted someone to read them aloud caused her to wonder. *Does he realize how personal they are?*

Ellie wondered how she'd feel if such special correspondence belonged to her. She pondered this till the tears welled up. If *she* were the one suffering with a waning memory and was lost from home, would she realize the letters might be the only tangible link to her beloved . . . or to her family?

She was certain Small Jay believed this. Even so, it was beyond her how on earth their son could make heads or tails of it all.

───༄───

Marlena found her grandmother sitting outdoors in the gazebo with her Bible after Angela Rose was asleep for the night.

"I've been doin' nothing but praying while you put Angela to bed," Mammi said before Marlena even brought up the phone call again.

"Our family needs prayer," she said, sighing. "Guess we'd better start getting Angela's things packed and ready."

"I've wondered if Gordon's parents might try to come home sooner if something has happened to him." Mammi's voice sounded so frail. "We must pray earnestly for them. *Ach,* receiving such news . . . their son over there in a terrible war. No wonder they want their grandbaby with them."

Marlena nodded. She certainly couldn't deny them such a comfort. Angela Rose would bring Gordon's grieving parents some much needed solace. "If only they had the dear Lord to lean on just now," she said quietly, more to herself.

"Well, they *do*, my dear. He's closer than a brother, our Good Shepherd, everything their hearts long for."

"Do ya think they understand how to reach out to Him?"

"That's what we're here for, Marlena. To point the way and be the light they need." Mammi wiped her eyes. "We'll do all we can to show kindness when they come. They may never experience God's love otherwise."

She should have known her grandmother would talk this way. Mammi always did.

"The Lord Jesus says ever so gently, 'Come unto me, all ye that labor and are heavy laden.' He offers rest and peace. Think of that, honey-girl. Rest and peace during this awful sad time." Mammi dabbed her eyes with her hankie. "Come . . . oh, come unto me, He says. Don't wait a minute longer, He pleads."

Marlena had never seen Mammi so moved.

"If we sow seeds of compassion, we harvest love. If we sow kindness, we receive kindness, Marlena. And the Lord calls us to be witnesses to that compassion and kindness, too, remember."

"This must be the reason your church—and others—sends missionaries to other countries."

Mammi nodded her head slowly. "I just wish someone had put their arms around poor Luella to let her know how precious she was to us . . . that we cared for her and wanted the best for her." She turned her head toward the Bitners' farm, looking that way for the longest time. "I don't mean that none of us did, mind you. It's just that once she was gone from the family, who knows if she remembered how much God loved her."

Marlena thought of Olive's correspondence with Luella.

"Do ya hear that music?" her grandmother asked. "I hear the same melody nearly every day now."

"It's Small Jay's friend Boston. Is the tune familiar to you, Mammi?"

"I don't recall ever hearin' it before."

Marlena didn't say what she was thinking, but the melody sounded like a sad yet sweet love song. Maybe the sweetest she'd ever heard.

CHAPTER 27

*Y*ou *can do it . . . you can do it,* Small Jay told himself as he tried to lift the weighty leather harness up and onto their biggest driving horse on Thursday. But it kept falling to the ground, no matter how hard he strained. He'd wanted to surprise his father and muttered his frustration under his breath.

Boston came to his rescue just outside the stable, at the very moment Small Jay thought of calling for help. "'*Many hands make light work,*' my grandmother Calvert liked to say." With the Plain haircut Mamma had given him just that morning, Boston looked nearly Amish. His bangs were straighter than even Small Jay's as they marched across the man's creased forehead. And with the new straw hat sitting just so on his head, well, Small Jay liked the effect just fine.

"I 'spect Dat told ya the surprise, *jah?*" Small Jay said as he and Boston fastened the harness around the mare.

Boston nodded his head so vigorously, his straw hat slipped forward. "And I can't thank you enough, young man."

"Wasn't my doin', really." *Dat wouldn't have agreed if it was me asking.* "Mamma's the one to thank."

"Your good-hearted mother is laundering my clothes, as well." Boston started to go about his sweeping again once the harness was carefully in place. "Since it's not clear how long I'll be here, it's especially kind of your father to go to the trouble of supplying a bed for these old bones."

Small Jay felt so happy, he could hardly think straight, which he figured he rarely did anyway. "Mamma will be clearin' out all her sewin' things from the *Dawdi Haus*."

"I can hardly expect that."

"After tomorrow, she's quittin' her classes." Small Jay knew this because Mamma had mentioned it at breakfast, a flat sort of look in her eyes. Dorcas had wrinkled up her face and opened her mouth to object, but Mamma put a quick stop to it. "You'll have the *Dawdi Haus* all to yourself," Small Jay told Boston. "Not much furniture but the bed, though."

Boston dusted off his black broadfall trousers and straightened to his full stature, his eyes soft on Small Jay. "I've sincerely come to think of you and your family as my own." He paused, sputtering a bit. "And I have *you* to thank for that, young man."

The lump in Small Jay's throat ached so that he couldn't have said anything in response even if he wanted to. In his bedtime prayers, he had been sneaking in some requests to the Lord God ever since he'd brought Boston home. "Just think, tonight you'll be sleepin' on a real mattress," Small Jay told him, feeling mighty good about saying so.

"Instead of a straw pallet," Boston said, sounding mighty clear in his thinking today. "And very soon, a new Sunday suit, too. Blessings abound . . . and I am rejoicing."

Small Jay joined with his friend's deep laughter, and for a brief moment, he almost wished Boston might stay put in Amish country all the days of his life.

~

To help out her grandmother that morning, Marlena called Vernon Siegrist to drive her to Joe's General Store while Angela Rose giggled in the playpen. They were in need of additional canning rings and lids for all the strawberries she'd picked before breakfast to make more jam for Saturday's market, as well as a few odds and ends like new needles and some modest white buttons for a nightgown Mammi was making for herself.

The day was already hot and sticky, and Marlena fanned herself with the tail of her black apron as she rode in the large van. Vernon had indicated there would be more stops for passengers along the way, which was all right. She never much cared for being the only passenger; most trips passed more quickly when there was someone to talk to.

She noticed that Vernon was taking the long route, heading up the hill from Mammi's farmhouse past Rosanna Miller's parents'. Marlena looked carefully as they drove by, wondering if she might see any sign of her former friend. She gawked again when they passed Olive Hendrickson's family home, too. She'd thought of letting them know of Luella's passing. *The neighborly thing to do,* she decided, making a mental note.

Letting herself sink into the bench seat, she relaxed fully, as she did each night when she fell into bed—though since leaving home for Brownstown, she dreamed fitfully at times, often of Nat Zimmerman. Sometimes the dreams were peaceful as she was wrapped tenderly in his embrace; other times they were worrisome, and she'd wake up breathing fast, like she'd just run from the barn to the house and back in a single minute. She tried to let those fretful dreams fade away, but the gentle dreams she enjoyed reliving, hoping Nat would wait for her, as they'd planned.

And she dreamed about Luella, too, particularly since her death. But in those stark and wordless imaginings, Marlena reached out to a sister she could never quite touch. And when she awakened, her heart was ever so heavy.

Up ahead, Marlena could see Luke Mast waving Vernon down at the end of his lane. Not expecting to see him, she watched as Vernon slowed a bit, then stopped along the shoulder.

Luke leaped into the van and brightened when he saw Marlena there, and right away asked if it was all right to sit next to her. She scooted over to give him plenty of room, surprised that he hadn't taken the seat up with their driver, like most men did.

"Sarah said she saw you at the quiltin' class at your neighbors'." Luke smiled warmly.

Marlena nodded. "Your sister's really wonderful."

"She thinks you are, too, Marlena."

They talked about the recent lack of rain and how warm the days were. Then, comically, Luke began to tell her about one of their Jersey cows. "For some particular reason, she didn't seem interested in bein' milked this morning. My brother called her a mule head, which wasn't the best way to strike up a conversation with a dairy cow, ain't?"

A mule head? She covered her mouth so she wouldn't laugh too loudly. "What was she doin' that she didn't wanna be milked?"

"No idea. It was the oddest thing, her bein' so contrary like that. Sarah had to go and get her attention."

"Did she manage to get her in?"

"Took a while, but we finally did." Luke explained that he'd also gone out to help coax the reluctant cow.

"That happened sometimes at my grandparents', too, back when Dawdi Tim was still alive." She told how her grandfather liked to whistle with his fingers between his teeth. "It was a signal his dairy cows obeyed, believe me."

Luke listened, seemingly interested, unlike her brother Yonnie, who rarely paid attention when Marlena told stories.

"So Sarah said she invited ya to visit our church sometime." Luke's comment came out of the blue.

Marlena told him what she'd said to Sarah.

"Well, if you ever change your mind about it, you'd be welcome, that's for certain."

"I appreciate that, Luke."

"There are a *gut* number of *die Youngie* who attend, just so ya know. Not to boast, but the New Order Amish church is really growin', and not just in this area but in Ohio, too."

"I'm curious 'bout something," Marlena said. "How does your minister sound when he prays?" It was a bold question, but she really wanted to know if they prayed the way Mammi Janice did. *Dat and Mamma, too.*

Luke turned to her. "Why do ya ask?"

She didn't think she should say what she really felt—that she yearned for the kind of relationship her parents and grandmother seemed to have with the Almighty. Talking to the Lord God as if He was their dearest friend seemed like a big part of it.

"It's all right, Marlena." He gave an encouraging smile. "Say what's on your mind."

Her neck grew warm, and she wondered what Nat might think of this.

"Are ya searchin'?" he asked.

"Not sure that's what I'd call it."

Luke studied her thoughtfully. "You asked about our pastor's praying style."

"*Jah.*" She so wanted to pursue this.

"What is it you want to know?"

She went ahead and shared everything, all that her soul longed for in wanting a closer relationship with God. "Maybe I'm all mixed up—too many churches in my life. Could that be?"

Luke raised his hand to remove his straw hat. He took his time answering, running his tan fingers through his thick blond hair. "Not necessarily. Sounds to me like your heart's hungry."

"My Mammi talks like that, too. 'The cry of our hearts is to follow in the Lord's footsteps,' she says."

"And ya know, she's right. Nothin' else can fill up that longing. I know . . . I felt this way, too, a few years back."

Luke's answer intrigued her. "Honestly, though, it seems arrogant to talk to the Lord the way some folk do when prayin'."

"Reverence is important, *jah* . . . but so is honesty." He went on to say that as his bond with the Lord Jesus grew over time, he began to feel comfortable praying aloud rather than using only the silent rote prayers he grew up with. "It took a while, though."

"Were you raised in the Old Order church, then?" she asked.

He nodded.

"I guess I'm torn between that teaching and what I've come to enjoy at my grandmother's church," she admitted.

"I'd really like to talk with you 'bout this another time," Luke said as the van slowed to pick up two Amish ladies who were laughing and gesturing as they talked while waiting along the road.

"*Denki*, Luke."

He got up and moved to the very last bench to make space for the womenfolk.

Marlena contemplated everything he'd said and realized it lined up with Mammi Janice's own vibrant faith. So wasn't it time for Marlena to settle things, to embrace the answers to the cry of her heart?

CHAPTER 28

When the mail arrived Friday morning, Marlena was so anxious for a letter from dear Nat, she dashed out to the road while Angela Rose was safely settled in the playpen. Angela had been pushing up, trying her best to get up on all fours. *She will be soon*, thought Marlena.

She fingered through the mail and found mostly letters for Mammi—three from her older sisters in Hickory Hollow and Strasburg, and a couple of circle letters. But there were two for Marlena—one from her sister Katie and the other from Nat Zimmerman. Smiling, she had to decide which to open first.

At the sound of a buggy, Marlena spotted one of the neighbors coming down the hill in a gray family carriage and waved. She decided to read her sister's letter first, because she wanted to savor Nat's later, when she had plenty of time to read it slowly.

Dear Marlena,
  How are you? Thank goodness you got to come for Luella's funeral. Even though it was a hard day for all of us, it made me happy to see you and Angela Rose. Oh, that little one

brings a smile to my face! I loved holding her in the parking lot when we first got there.

Mamma says we might not see her very much from now on, but I'm praying we will. Preacher Ranck always says God knows the desires of our hearts.

I really hope we get to see our little niece grow up, don't you?

Marlena could almost hear her younger sister's voice. "I feel the same way," she whispered into the humid morning breeze, recalling everything Mamma had implied Wednesday evening about Gordon's parents' possibly coming for Angela Rose. But Mammi Janice had sounded rather accepting of it, so she guessed she ought to be, too. *"Always take the high road,"* she often said.

Angela was beginning to fuss now, and Marlena hurried inside and placed Mammi's letters on the kitchen counter. "Here's your mail," she said to her grandmother, who was preparing to can more jars of strawberry jam for tomorrow's market day.

"Looks like you have some letters, too, dear."

"*Jah*, one from Katie and one from my beau."

"Your little sisters were so kind to me at Luella's funeral," Mammi said, telling how Katie and Rachel Ann had wanted to sit on either side of her on the front row of the women's side of the church.

"I miss them," Marlena said.

"Well, and they miss you, too, don't ya forget." Mammi looked at her attentively. "I can't tell you how much it means, havin' you here . . . giving up your summer back home to help me."

Marlena waved her hand. "I'm just glad it worked out." She slipped the letters into her apron pocket and stooped to get *rutsche* Angela out of the playpen. Taking her upstairs for a diaper change, Marlena wondered when Gordon's parents would arrive—this Lord's Day? On Monday?

It was hard to be cheerful as she took care of Angela when likely there were only a couple days remaining.

Later that afternoon, after picking the ripened produce in her grandmother's garden, Marlena came close to dozing off while Angela napped in her arms; she wanted to spoil her just a little more. In her haze, she remembered walking through her mother's sweet corn crop with Luella, their brothers, and several older girl cousins, combing row after row for weeds. *"Redding up the corn,"* her brother Amos had called it.

Luella had kindly shared some of her cold lemonade with Marlena on that scorching day when Marlena complained that her tongue was turning thick, she was that thirsty. *Luella let me drain her Thermos and never once made a fuss about it.*

The pleasant memory gave her pause, and she drew in a deep breath. Were there more such memories buried somewhere in her heart?

Mammi called up the stairs to ask if everything was all right. Still holding Angela Rose, Marlena got up and went to stand at the top of the stairs.

"Ach, sorry," Mammi said, seeing her with the baby. "I didn't realize . . ."

"I'll be down right quick," Marlena said, worried that losing Angela Rose to her English grandparents might set Mammi back emotionally.

"The jars are ready to fill, when you're ready," Mammi said, turning the corner and stepping out of sight.

Marlena went back to the room and put Angela in her crib. Then, opening the right-hand dresser drawer, she dropped the letters inside and headed downstairs to help Mammi make jam for market.

<hr>

"All right with you if Dorcas runs up to Janice Martin's to ask about babysitting tomorrow?" Ellie asked her husband midafternoon. He'd lingered at the table after coming in for some cold meadow tea to wet his whistle.

"Don't see why not."

"I'll let her know, then." She was glad Roman seemed all right with it.

She hadn't told him how things had gone when she'd announced to her class that she wouldn't be continuing. Such sad expressions on all the faces!

Instead, she mentioned the girls' response to Marlena's baby niece last Saturday. "They really enjoyed having the baby here," she told Roman.

Roman nodded, his eyes fixed on some distant point out the window.

"As for market, I'll be takin' some preserves and a few other things myself, but you'll be around, I s'pose, in case Dorcas and the girls need anything."

He said he would. "And Jake and Boston? Will they be goin' with ya?"

"I'd thought of takin' Small Jay along, *jah*."

"Leavin' Boston here?"

"Guess I thought he would be workin' in the stable, groomin' the horses, maybe."

Roman shrugged and said that was true. "But I doubt Jake

will want to go." He sighed. "Seems to me the boy'd rather stay and help Boston."

Ellie was conscious of the ticking day clock. "There are other young men at market," she volunteered. "Luke Mast goes with his sister to help their mother."

"They're New Order, though, remember, Ellie."

"Hmm," she murmured, realizing she'd put herself smack-dab into that corner.

"Not car-drivin' Amish, though," he added. "That's one *gut* thing 'bout them."

She knew now wasn't the best time to bring up what she thought about all the splinter groups of Amish—more, seemingly, each year. Seeing Roman sitting there, so relaxed and rather pleasant, she couldn't bear the thought of a stressful word coming between them.

"Ya know, I've got Boston's harmonica tune stuck in my head," Roman said just then.

"It's so appealing, ain't?"

"Perty, if ya really listen. Like it needs words."

She'd never heard Roman say such a thing. "I've wondered that, too."

"Boston plays it all the time. Must be mighty special to him."

Hearing this, Ellie actually had to look away. She didn't know what had gotten into her husband . . . but she liked it. "I'll go out and find Small Jay and let him know it'll be just the two of us for market tomorrow."

"Might ask him first if he'd like to go or stay. How'd that be?" Roman was grinning and looking right at her.

My husband's asking me?

Roman was certainly chock-full of surprises today.

243

CHAPTER 29

*M*arlena helped Mammi clean the house, then stopped to make supper. She'd washed another pile of diapers yesterday but needed to wash more soon, in anticipation of Gordon's parents' arrival.

While she and Mammi chopped cucumbers and tomatoes for a garden salad, Marlena talked freely about yesterday's unexpected visit with Luke Mast. "He suggested we finish our discussion another time," she confided.

"Well, wasn't *that* nice of him," said Mammi. "Maybe he wants to be more than just a friend."

"*Ach*, Mammi . . . that's not what I meant." Marlena told her they *were* friendly but there wasn't any romantic attraction.

"I see," Mammi replied, keeping a straight face.

"My heart belongs to Nat Zimmerman."

Mammi's eyes twinkled. "You may be interested to know that Luke Mast has always reminded me of your Dawdi Tim when he was that age."

"He does?" Marlena didn't think they looked anything alike.

"It's his disposition—Luke's mannerisms—not so much his looks, I s'pose."

"Oh, maybe so." Marlena wondered why Mammi mentioned this, but as she thought about it, she could see what Mammi saw. *Jah, I sure can.*

When supper dishes were cleaned and put away, while Angela Rose chewed on a teething ring, Marlena took time to cut out pieces from Luella's dresses. She decided to balance the solid-colored fabric with florals or prints. *Half Plain, half fancy*, she thought, realizing her sister had been Amish longer than English. This brought her some solace as she measured random sizes and pieces of fabric, looking forward to making a crazy quilt like one Ellie Bitner had shown the class. If she could just take another look at the method, that would help greatly. *I'll just have to wait till the next class*, she thought as she stopped to bathe Angela Rose in the deep kitchen sink.

"Tomorrow's market day," she told the little one, smiling into her face while lathering up her silky hair. She kissed the tiny nose, which made Angela giggle.

Then, just as she'd wrapped her in a towel, Dorcas Bitner appeared at the back door. "Hullo there!" Marlena called to her. "Come on in."

Mammi came from the front room to welcome Dorcas, as well, evidently setting aside her circle letters for now.

"I dropped by to see if you'll be needin' a babysitter tomorrow," Dorcas said as she walked over to Marlena and Angela Rose. Dorcas reached out her finger, smiling at Angela, who grabbed hold and tried to suck on it. "She must be teethin', *jah?*"

"She *has* been drooling a lot," Marlena said, then apologized for being too busy to let Dorcas know sooner. "I'm so glad ya dropped by." They made arrangements for tomorrow morning.

"My sisters are lookin' forward to seeing Angela again." Dorcas retrieved her finger and leaned down to kiss Angela's forehead. "Such a sweet little one."

Marlena didn't have the heart to tell her this most likely would be the last time Dorcas would babysit. "She likes seein' you. Just look at her smile."

Mammi, who'd spread out Marlena's piecework on the kitchen table, motioned for Dorcas to come look, and Dorcas hurried over. "I'm makin' a quilt from my sister's dresses to give to Angela Rose as a remembrance of her Mamma," Marlena explained. "It's one way to use up some old dresses, ain't?"

Dorcas nodded, awful solemn just then.

"I can hardly wait for your mother's next quilting class."

Dorcas looked like she didn't know what to say. Was it the fact that the fabric was from Luella's dresses, or was it something else?

Seemingly uncomfortable, Dorcas finally said she could let herself out, then turned and left, nearly stumbling toward the back screen door. "I'll see ya tomorrow, then."

Marlena said good-bye, curious why she'd left so abruptly. Then, eager to read Nat's letter, she put away the pieces and took Angela upstairs to get her ready for bed. She dressed her in one of the soft cotton gowns, then sat in a chair to give Angela her bottle, wondering all the while what Nat had written.

It took longer than usual to get Angela Rose settled, but finally, when she was asleep and in her crib, Marlena went out to the second-floor balcony and sat down in Dawdi Tim's old chair. She was grateful for her darling's letter, missing him so.

My dearest Marlena,

It was wonderful seeing you again following your sister's funeral. Sad as the circumstances were, I wish we could've spent longer together. Lord willing, there will be plenty of time for that when you finally return at summer's end. Till then, I must try to be patient.

I hope things are going well for you with your sister's baby. Are her Englischer grandparents coming for her? Or perhaps she's even gone by now. I'm glad that we agree that's the best place for her. You've done so much already!

But there's more on my mind, dear, than your many responsibilities. Some of what you shared with me in your last letter really surprised me. I know you're there to help your grandmother, but I prefer that she go on her own to the Mennonite church. Couldn't you attend the Old Order Preaching with the neighbors you mentioned, the Bitners? And it doesn't seem wise to pursue friendship with any New Order Amish, even Sarah Mast, no matter how friendly she might be. Truth be told, the thought troubles me.

Marlena gasped, unable to read further. "*Troubles* him?"

She wished now she'd had the courage to share about her spiritual longings in her recent letters. Nat was clearly upset, and it bothered her that he was attempting to say what was best for her without knowing the whole picture. She felt especially frustrated that he was intruding on her close relationship with beloved Mammi. "*Puh!*"

The burning aggravation drove her back indoors to the bedroom, where she dropped his letter into the drawer and decided not to read the rest of it right now. *I'd really better not. . . .*

Ellie cut ample slices of her strawberry pie and asked Julia to help her carry the dessert out to the porch, where Boston was already making music, entertaining Roman and Small Jay.

"What other songs can ya play?" her husband asked as he and Small Jay rocked together side by side.

"Let me think," Boston said. "Ah, yes . . . do you know this one?" And he began again.

Right away, Small Jay's eyes grew big. "'In the Garden,'" he said, humming along.

"'While the dew is still on the roses,'" Ellie sang softly. *Boston knows this?*

After that hymn, Boston played two others that he said were tunes from his childhood. To Ellie, they sounded nearly angelic, they were that awe-inspiring.

Later, as Boston stopped to catch his breath, Roman asked when he'd learned to play. "As a youngster, I studied the violin, and after that the piano. So it was easy for me to pick up the harmonica and make music." He held the mouth organ out for Small Jay to try. "Wipe it off first, if you'd prefer."

Ellie was amazed by Boston's apparent clarity tonight. This was the first she'd known about his musical ability as a youngster, and she wondered if he still played the other instruments. She recalled again the letter that Abigail had written, thanking him for writing *"your exquisite melody."* She might have asked about it, but here came Dorcas, waving and returning from the visit to Marlena.

"She must be goin' to babysit tomorrow," Ellie said, motioning toward her.

Roman didn't acknowledge this, but Dorcas was full of chatter. "That's one precious baby up yonder," she said. "Oh, and I saw the pieces Marlena's been cutting out there on the kitchen table, Mamma."

"Does she know you've quit your classes?" Julia asked unexpectedly.

"*Nee*, and the other Wednesday quilting students must not know yet, either," Dorcas said, trying to smooth things over, bless her heart.

Ellie was silent, unsure what to say. The thought of not seeing Marlena anymore at class or otherwise was disappointing, yet when Roman looked over at her, she put a smile on her face, just for him.

~~~

Small Jay walked next door to the *Dawdi Haus* with Boston to see where Mamma had him set up to sleep. In the largest of the rooms downstairs, he spied the big table. "Wonder why Mamma won't be teachin' classes anymore," he muttered to himself.

"I'm sure your mother will tell you if you ask," Boston replied.

Small Jay knew she'd probably try to explain if he asked . . . unlike Dat, who was less predictable. Did Boston know that? Small Jay considered Boston to be mighty wise sometimes for such a confused man.

After Boston said good-night, Small Jay left by way of the squeaky back door, slowly making his way down the few porch steps and around to the main house.

Small Jay was surprised to see his father still sitting outside and thought he might test Boston's advice from the other day.

"*Venture forth. If you do it in the right spirit, God will be with you.*" Boston had sounded so sure of himself.

At once, Small Jay's chest felt tight. Certain no one was around, he went up the porch steps and eased himself into the rocking chair next to Dat. "*Denki* for lettin' Boston sleep next door," he made himself say, though the words sounded pinched, like they were stuck under his tongue.

"Boston seems happy enough," Dat said, crossing his leg over one knee.

Small Jay considered that.

"Cat got your tongue?" Dat looked over at him.

Small Jay nodded, but he could not let this moment pass. His heart sped up. "Remember when we used to go fishin'?" He glanced at the glassy pond in the meadow behind them. "Over yonder."

"Been a *gut* long time."

"I think so, too." Small Jay breathed deeply, trying to get some air into his lungs. Maybe that would help him calm down. "What if we went again sometime?"

His father's eyebrows rose. "Well, we sure could."

Oh, Small Jay was just dying to ask when, to get it set in his mind that he hadn't dreamed this. But he didn't press, instead soaking up what his father had given him just now.

Boston's suggestion worked, thought Small Jay gleefully. *Dat knows I want to go fishing with him, and he didn't say no!*

~~~ ⁊

A slow-moving car was coming this way as Marlena walked up the hill toward Hendricksons' house. The mosquitoes were out thick and biting, so she hurried her pace, wanting to get there and back before too long.

Mrs. Hendrickson came to the door, inviting her inside, smiling and wearing a short-sleeved top tucked into a graceful floral skirt. "How nice to see you again, Marlena. Goodness, last time was your grandpa's funeral, if I'm not mistaken."

Marlena remembered, and they reminisced for a time about the large crowd that had come to pay respects to a man who'd grown up in this area. Then Marlena told her the reason for her visit. "I have more sad news, I'm sorry to say. My sister Luella passed away suddenly last week, and I thought you . . . and Olive might want to know."

"Oh, my dear, what a shock! Whatever happened?" Mrs. Hendrickson lowered herself into the nearby chair, sighing.

Marlena mentioned the accident, leaving out the details.

"I know Olive will be terribly upset about this. Is there anything we can do for you, Marlena?"

Marlena thanked her and said she was doing as well as could be expected. "I've been staying with my grandmother to help out this summer."

"I'll definitely phone Olive right away tonight." Mrs. Hendrickson paused to fan her face with a hankie. "You may not know this, but Luella and Olive were fast friends for years. Their letters flew back and forth until Olive moved to Philadelphia—she lives there now. I believe they've been in touch since."

Marlena didn't know if she ought to mention the many postcards and letters now in her possession, but Isabelle Hendrickson seemed to have more on her mind.

"Olive always had such nice things to say about your sister."

Marlena smiled. "I'm takin' care of Luella's baby for a while."

"What a blessing for the little one. What's her name?"

"Angela Rose."

"Oh, do bring her over sometime. I'd love to see her!"

Again, Marlena felt hindered by the lack of a good response, knowing too well that Angela wouldn't be around to do any visiting. "Well, I'd best be getting back to Mammi."

Mrs. Hendrickson said she understood and was glad for the visit, then rose from the chair and accompanied her to the front door and clear out to the road.

"I'm glad Olive was such a close friend to Luella," Marlena managed to say.

"Yes, they were nearly like sisters in some ways. So this news will be very difficult."

Feeling numb now, Marlena waved woodenly and headed back down the hill, toward the familiar farmhouse.

⁓ ᦉ

Mammi was already upstairs in her room when Marlena returned, so she knocked lightly on her door. "It'll be an early morning tomorrow," she said softly.

"*Jah*, how's Isabelle?"

"She was shocked about Luella."

"Undoubtedly." Mammi sounded tired.

"I'll leave ya be, Mammi. *Gut Nacht* now."

Mammi said the same, and Marlena turned toward the room she shared with Angela Rose, who was still sleeping peacefully. Marlena knew how easy it would be to fall into contemplating Mrs. Hendrickson's reaction to Luella's death. Instead, she went to her drawer and quickly removed Nat's letter, ready to finish reading. Thankfully, the remainder was full of typical talk about his family and the farm there. *Nothing else worrisome.*

She felt she ought to write back, to let him know that she

252

was struggling terribly right now, trying to understand the longings of her heart. *Surely the Lord God wants us to seek after Him. . . .*

Once she was ready for bed, Marlena found some stationery and began to share her innermost thoughts with her beau as never before. She kept her letter polite, yet she made it clear that she truly enjoyed her grandmother and her church. *And I'm learning many new things from the Bible, things I've never heard before now.*

Yet she did not write anything more about Sarah and Luke Mast. *I'm not willing to give them up as friends*, she thought, finding it unbelievable that Nat would even suggest such a thing.

CHAPTER 30

*S*mall Jay hoped Boston wouldn't be too lonely while he and Mamma went to market Saturday morning. Their driver was Lois Landis, a Mennonite neighbor, and while Mamma did the talking on the way into town, Small Jay did the watching. He enjoyed seeing all the other neighbors' cows—some Holsteins, others Jerseys—and young, scampering goats, too, out on the grazing land.

A few times he caught himself counting, then remembered he wasn't alone. Mamma looked his way as if she might remind him to keep his thoughts to himself, but she simply smiled a sympathetic smile.

She knows me but good. . . .

The closer they got to market, the more he wished he'd stayed home with Boston to help curry the horses. The work wasn't easy for a man like him.

Small Jay had overheard his father talking to Boston again that morning, asking where his family or close friends might be located, sounding concerned. But Boston had been more baffled than usual by what Dat was saying, and Small Jay's former notion that Boston's memory was clearer in the mornings didn't seem to be true after all. Still, he hoped the folk medicine Dr. Isaac had given Mamma for Boston might help before too long. Boston had been faithfully drinking the medicinal tea each morning, and taking the tincture at the noon meal.

When they arrived, the driver helped Mamma by carrying in her delicious preserves. Mamma herself brought a large canvas bag of her tatted doilies and other handiwork. Small Jay had always been interested in her embroidery but knew he ought not to say anything, lest Dat shake his head at him. *Women's handiwork.* Truth was, those items brought a good price, and Dat should be happy for the extra money, especially now that he had an extra mouth to feed with Boston. *Even so, Dat'll miss him when he goes back to wherever he came from,* thought Small Jay, hoping maybe then *he* might step into Boston's shoes out in the stable, grooming the horses and whatnot all.

At that moment, Small Jay noticed a dozen or more scooters lined up against a wall and wondered how long before he, too, might be allowed to ride one down to market, or over to Joe's General Store.

When can I prove I'm old enough?

Inside, clusters of customers were already waiting at the homemade popcorn booth, and the half moon pies just two tables away were popular, too. He was glad to arrive early, as Mamma liked to do, because once he'd helped set out the preserves, he could wander about, visiting with other Amish boys, usually younger. Most were youngsters outside the Brownstown Amish church district—some slipped him nickels or dimes, feeling sorry for him, he guessed. Luke Mast had never done that, though. Luke and his mother had always treated Small

Jay very kindly, even respectfully, which made him feel like standing taller, head high. Of course, he'd never want to give in to pride . . . though he *had* been sorely tempted. Fact was, Luke just brought the good out in people.

Wandering about, change jingling in his pocket, Small Jay headed straight for the chocolate chip cookies at Gracie Yoder's aunt's market table. While his own mother's cookies tasted even better than Nellie's, he liked to think he was helping the Yoder family in some small way. And, too, he hoped he might get a glimpse of Gracie there. *She's probably home babysitting her twin sisters today.* He'd heard through the grapevine that Gracie's mother depended on her a lot.

Small Jay's mouth watered at the smell of the oversized chocolate chip cookies even as he eyed the peanut butter ones. But he only had enough for one, because he'd spent most of his birthday money on a new leash and collar for Sassy and two batches of licorice for his father. *Better that Dat has treats, since he works so hard.*

Even so, Small Jay wished he could surprise Mamma and buy her a cookie, too, what with all the standing ahead of her today. She had packed a nice lunch for both of them, but Small Jay doubted there were cookies this big in his lunch pail. He thought of breaking the cookie in half, right down the middle. Jah, *that's a wonderful-*gut *idea.* He could just imagine the smile on his mother's heart-shaped face.

After making his purchase, Small Jay stopped halfway back to Mamma's long market table, freezing in place. Just ahead of him, three tables away, stood Gracie Yoder with her mother and a makeshift double stroller, where Gracie's identical baby sisters sat, shaking matching rattles and drooling. Staring, he guessed they were about the same age as Angela Rose. And oh, did he ever want to walk over there and talk to Gracie, but like always, his knees locked up and he stood there, stock-still, unable to move or speak.

He thought again of Boston's advice. He wracked his brain, but his mind was blank. He supposed he might still be standing in that very spot when he was all hunched over and gray, not budging a single inch for decades to come.

Small Jay never would have admitted it, but he felt tormented. Here was the girl of his dreams, beautiful, petite Gracie Yoder, and all he could do was stare at her.

Then Boston's words came to him, tickling his ears. *"Venture forth boldly!"*

Of course that meant Small Jay must pick up his feet and walk over there, put a smile on his face, and let her know he thought she was simply wonderful. But the notion turned his mouth to cotton. He couldn't even swallow!

"We're haunted most by the things we never attempt." Boston's words flew back now, strong and clear.

Small Jay was so tired of being dragged down by his own disbelief, being too afraid to attempt something big.

It worked just fine with Dat last night, he remembered suddenly. *So why not now, with Gracie?*

He filled his lungs with air and stepped forward, moving now. It was all happening. He could see Gracie quietly listening to their mothers as the two women conversed. Now and then, Gracie would smile down at her baby sisters, touching their chubby cheeks with her fingers.

But in that instant, she looked up, right his way.

Now, he told himself. *Do something!*

Small Jay raised his right hand, his arm ever so heavy. And he waved.

Time seemed to stop as he held his breath. Then, wonder of wonders, Gracie Yoder waved back. And smiled!

His legs trembled. But instead of moving forward to talk to her, he turned and headed for the water fountain one aisle over. The cotton in his mouth needed drenching—and he needed air. "I did it," he managed to whisper.

Glory be!

⁓ ℯↄ

Marlena kept thinking about Angela Rose—the baby powdery smell of her, the adorable grin—as Mammi sold jar after jar of strawberry jam at market. Marlena made change and gave bills of sale to patrons, all the while hoping Dorcas Bitner wouldn't be discouraged about losing her weekly babysitting job once Angela was taken away by her paternal grandparents.

After a while, Marlena saw Sarah Mast and her mother walking the aisles—"stretching our legs," Sarah told her with a smile. It was then Marlena learned that Ellie Bitner was disbanding her sewing classes. "The news came rather suddenly, too," Sarah informed her.

Marlena was sorry to hear it and wondered if it had anything to do with what she'd heard from Mammi about Roman's being finicky, not wanting his family rubbing shoulders with others who were attending a more progressive church. *"He's never gotten over Ellie's sister and family leaving the Old Order church,"* her grandmother had observed.

Mammi encouraged Marlena to visit with Sarah for a bit, so the two of them wandered about. "How are ya comin' along with your piecework for the baby's quilt?" Sarah asked.

"I've only had a little time here and there. Really, I've just started."

"Would ya like some help with it?"

Marlena said she would and felt comfortable enough to share that Angela Rose would most likely be leaving to live with Luella's in-laws. "No doubt I'll be able to focus more on the quilt then, even with all the gardening and canning."

"Oh, you'll miss the little one. How soon?"

Marlena looked away and pressed her lips together.

"*Ach,* this is hard for ya." Sarah touched Marlena's arm.

Sarah hadn't continued, or brought up Luella's passing, and Marlena was glad. It was bad enough feeling like this in public, barely able to rein in her emotions. If she'd been back at Mammi's house, she would have much preferred to go and sit in the gazebo or on the second-story balcony and quietly gaze out at the clouds or the horizon. Truly, she never knew when the heaviness of grief might crash down upon her.

She and Sarah ended up strolling outside, leaving behind the flurry of activity. "Luella and I didn't get along very well when we were young," Marlena eventually admitted. "But I honestly believe the Lord wants me to take care of her baby, perhaps as a way of forgiving my sister." She inhaled slowly. "Does that make sense?"

Sarah nodded.

"But even though I feel strongly 'bout it, everything seems out of my control now," Marlena admitted. "I'm afraid Angela will be gone very soon."

Sarah studied her, eyes squinting. "I understand why you feel that way. But none of this is out of *God's* hands."

"I'll try to remember." Marlena appreciated Sarah's kindness and her sympathy. "I don't know how to thank you," she said, biting her lip.

"What if I drop by next Wednesday mornin'?" Sarah asked. "Would that suit ya?"

"I'll be home and . . ." She paused, not sure she could voice the words.

"Will Angela Rose be gone by then?"

Marlena nodded her answer, tears coming fast.

"All the better, then." Sarah gave her a smile. "Laying out her quilt might just keep your thoughts occupied. And I'll bring along a delicious dessert, too."

Marlena agreed. "You're a *gut* friend, Sarah. *Denki.*"

~~ও

On the ride back from market, Vernon had Mammi sit up front to make it easier to get in and out of the vehicle. Marlena sat behind her, next to Ellie Bitner and her son, who were also sharing the ride with a few others. Ellie explained that she'd had to call for a ride with another driver this morning, since Vernon's vehicle was full.

As they talked, Ellie offered no reason why she'd canceled the sewing classes, only said she wasn't able to continue. Marlena decided not to bring up her plans to work on Angela's crib quilt with Sarah Mast. Besides, Ellie seemed rather detached, and Marlena assumed she was worn out from the day. Either that, or Ellie was less willing to talk openly with Marlena. *Maybe it was Roman who put a damper on things.*

During the trip, they passed a young Amish boy on a scooter clear in the middle of the right lane. Vernon slowed up and steered the van around him, into the oncoming lane. Farther up the road, five barefoot Amish youngsters strolled along, two with fishing poles slung over their shoulders. Small Jay pressed his nose against the window, staring out.

"There are quite a few children out playing today, or tending roadside vegetable stands," Marlena commented.

"Well, it's so warm," Ellie replied. "And this time of year, the youngest neighbor kids go from one vegetable stand to another. Say, I've noticed the Millers down the hill have a big produce stand out again this summer."

"Do ya ever see Rosanna?"

"Oh, haven't ya heard? She's gone fancy and owns a restaurant in Maryland—just think of that. *And* word has it she wrote a book about growing up Plain."

Marlena stared at her in astonishment. "Truly? My friend Rosanna?"

"I got it straight from her mother," Ellie confirmed, nodding.

Marlena shook her head. "Who would've thought Rosanna could sit still long enough to write a book."

Ellie *tsk-tsk*ed. "Guess we never really know what's goin' on inside another's head, *jah*?"

Marlena let Ellie's gossip roll right off and thought of Luella. More than anything, right this minute, Marlena longed to lay eyes on her sister's darling little Angela Rose.

CHAPTER 31

Until the ministerial brethren arrived that Lord's Day morning, Small Jay waited with his father and uncles in a line of men in the front yard of the Bitners' farmhouse. Boston stood with them, too, looking nearly the same as the others in his new white shirt and black suspenders, trousers, and vest. The only difference was the graying moustache, which Small Jay had forgotten to tell him to shave. Even Boston's short beard contributed to his Plain appearance—a few weeks' growth, nice and thick. Boston's straw hat sat flat on his head, parallel to the ground, just like Small Jay had suggested.

When the bishop, two preachers, a visiting minister, and the deacon took their places at the head of the long line, the oldest men began to move up the front porch steps and into the large room, made larger by removing the wall partitions, which Dat and his brothers had done yesterday. As they filed in, Small Jay and then Boston removed their straw hats like the other men, placing them on a wooden bench. Today Small Jay had permission to sit with Boston in the back, with the

262

other unbaptized men, and facing the women and girls and little children. The preachers would take turns standing in the narrow gap between the two sides of the congregation.

Small Jay spotted Luke Mast's cousin Paul, a couple of years older. Seeing Paul made Small Jay wonder how Shredder was getting along. *Well, King.* He guessed no return of the black cat was a good sign. Small Jay craned his neck to spot his father, rows ahead. *He thinks Shredder up and ran off. And all the better!*

Across the way, Small Jay could see Mamma and his sisters sitting together in the same row amongst the womenfolk. Then, goodness, he spotted Gracie's mother right behind Mamma, and Gracie, too, holding one of the twins. *Right in my view,* he thought, smiling as he bowed his head, trying to be reverent. Slowly, he inched to the right on the wooden bench, thinking it might remedy the distraction. Now hopefully he wouldn't be looking in Gracie's direction for three and a half hours. *Though I wouldn't mind, especially after yesterday at market. . . .*

As it turned out, halfway through the first of two sermons, Boston fell asleep and nearly lost his balance when his head bobbed forward. He would surely have tumbled off the bench if Small Jay hadn't reached for Boston's elbow. The young man nearest him gave Small Jay a look, and, mighty embarrassed, Small Jay slid down on his backside, trying to make himself smaller.

At last all was well again. Oh, did he ever hope neither Gracie nor the preacher, for that matter, had noticed the disturbance.

But as the sermon progressed, Boston remained sound asleep, leaning now against Small Jay, who shivered in horror as the man began to sniff and then snort like a pig. Small Jay shrunk lower with each embarrassing sound, his face reddening when he noticed Gracie stretching taller in her seat, eyes wide, moving her head to get a better view of the commotion.

Boston's grunts grew louder, becoming a garbled throaty snore. *En Schnaixe!* Annoyed, the minister paused in his preaching, and Small Jay assumed it was up to him to poke Boston. Well, he did just that, but only lightly the first time, which bought only a momentary reprieve.

The second time the same thing happened, Small Jay jabbed Boston in the ribs. Unfortunately, this created even more of a scene when Boston gasped for air and burst into song—an unrecognizable melody, at that.

"Take him outside," one of the more devout teen boys whispered, tapping Small Jay on the shoulder.

Small Jay had never felt so self-conscious, and he did as he was told and quietly spoke to Boston about leaving.

Awake now, Boston rose with Small Jay. "What an exceedingly short sermon," Boston declared loud enough to be heard in the entire men's section. This was met by a wave of muffled snickers from *die Youngie* nearest them.

Freckle-faced Danny Glick caught Small Jay's eye and pulled a face. *I'll never hear the end of this!* Small Jay thought, mortified as he led Boston to the kitchen area and out to sit on the back porch. From there, he could hear the preacher resume his sermon. "Ain't a sin to fall asleep in church," Small Jay said quietly.

Boston looked at him, bemused.

Small Jay continued. "One of my uncles has a way of makin' his church naps look downright pious. You honestly can't tell he's sleeping, 'cause he props his head up with his hand."

"Like this?" Boston demonstrated.

Trying not to smile too broadly on the Lord's Day, Small Jay nodded. He wondered if Gracie Yoder would think well of him for helping Boston. Or would she be shocked that Boston had come to Preaching service at all?

Such thoughts beset him while he sat with Boston, who promptly fell back to sleep, his right fist propping up his jaw. Small Jay strained to hear the preacher. Not succeeding, he thought of every rote prayer he'd ever learned from Mamma and then added one of his own. *O Lord God, if it is Thy will, let my father realize that I'm a hard worker. Open his eyes to see that I ain't a little boy anymore. Also, may Dat not be so sorry he's only got one son . . . 'specially one like me.*

Marlena felt like she was on pins and needles during the ride home with Mammi and Angela Rose from the Mennonite meetinghouse, just waiting for Gordon's parents to arrive and pierce through the fiber of her heart. Mamma hadn't written or called yet, and the hours were marching by. Marlena didn't know whether to pack Angela's things or wait till the Munroes came. She felt uneasy not knowing how to plan.

Just east of Mammi's house, she pointed out the many gray buggies parked along the side of Roman Bitner's place. "Looks like our neighbors are hosting church," Marlena said as they turned off the road toward Mammi's.

"Such a lot of work for Ellie and her family to prepare," Mammi said, pulling slowly into the drive and turning off the ignition.

"Her daughters are still young, but I'm sure they helped with the cleaning and the food for the shared meal."

"Can't say I miss the days of hosting such a large crowd . . .

'least not at my age." Mammi shook her head and glanced over at Marlena as she slipped the car key into her purse. "Did ya know your Dawdi and I hosted Bible studies here at the house? Sometimes we were packed to the rafters."

Marlena wasn't sure she'd ever heard this. At the time, though, it might not have been something her parents wanted her or her siblings to know. *Might've triggered too many questions about attending Bible studies*, she guessed. Back in those days, Marlena's parents wouldn't have dreamed of going to such gatherings.

Mammi looked over at her. "You must be stewing 'bout Angela Rose, honey-girl. I can sense it."

"I just wish Mamma would've called by now to give us some idea 'bout when."

"I 'spected so. But every extra minute is a pleasant one, *jah?*" Mammi glanced at Angela Rose, who sucked on her fingers. "A gift of sorts."

They headed inside, and Marlena got Angela settled into Ellie's loaned high chair before making ham and Swiss cheese sandwiches for them. She took the strawberry Jell-O from the icebox.

Mammi prayed the blessing, asking the Lord to bring calm to Marlena's heart and fill the house with peace.

"I felt God's presence strongly in church today," Marlena confessed.

"Oh, honey . . ." Mammi's face beamed.

"I truly believe He's callin' me to take care of Angela Rose, Mammi. I just don't understand what it all means . . . 'specially not right now."

"Well, we must take one step at a time and keep clingin' to His hand. That's a *gut* reminder for me, too."

Marlena nodded and smiled at Angela, who was patting her tray with one dimpled hand and waving her teething ring with the other.

"Can I ask ya something, Mammi?"

Her grandmother nodded. "Of course, dear. What is it?"

"Well, we Plain folk live and breathe to serve the same Lord God heavenly Father, don't we?"

"*Jah*, and seek to please Him in all that we do and say," Mammi said.

"Then what 'bout the difference in things like the length and color of our dresses, or how we get around town? What does the Lord think of all that?"

Mammi glanced toward the window, then back at Marlena. "Seems to me, things like that—whether or not Amish or Mennonite farmers use tractors out in the field or to fill silo, or what sort of *Kapp* a woman wears—well, I don't see how any of that'll matter much in heaven." She smiled and fanned her face. "Here's what I believe's really important. Do we follow God's ways with all that is in us? Have we opened up our sin-sick souls to the grace and redemption of our Lord and Savior, Jesus Christ?"

Marlena felt the now-familiar tug in her heart. And as she thought on what Mammi had said, she realized it sounded quite a lot like the way her friends Luke and Sarah talked, as well.

How'd I miss this my whole life?

After the dishes were washed and Angela was already napping, Marlena's mother phoned. "I just knew it was you," Marlena told Mamma.

"Why, 'cause my mother's praying 'bout it?" Mamma asked, her voice almost teasing.

"The Lord seems to answer Mammi Janice's prayers, that's for sure."

Mamma laughed softly, agreeing. "Well, dear, as you might imagine, Gordon's parents are devastated by the news of their son being missing in the midst of that war. Right now they're in shock . . . and tryin' to sort things out. Patricia called to ask on their behalf if you wouldn't mind keepin' Angela Rose for a while longer."

Marlena's heart skipped a beat. "I'd love to, Mamma. I really would."

"Oh, honey, that's so *gut* of you. If needed, you and I can set up a nursery for Angela here when you return home at summer's end."

"I think I'd do almost anything for Angela."

"I believe you would, dear." Her mother paused a second. "Which leads me to the next thing. Maggie Zimmerman wanted to talk privately with me yesterday at market."

Nat's mother?

"Evidently Nat's been talking to his father 'bout your attending the Mennonite church there."

"*Ach*, no, Mamma."

"It does seem Nat and his parents are worried you're being heavily influenced toward a higher church."

One that isn't as humble and traditional as the Old Order Amish, thought Marlena. "*Jah*, I can understand why they'd be concerned."

"I'm not sure who's more upset, Nat or his parents."

"Maybe all three," Marlena said, her heart pounding in her ears. *If they only knew the whole of it . . .*

"From what Maggie said, I honestly suspect her son's frettin' the most."

Nat had never been enthusiastic about her leaving for the entire summer, and his last letter had left no doubt about the reasons behind his concerns. "Even so, Nat knows this arrangement won't last forever. He and I've already discussed it."

Mamma shifted away from that subject and talked instead of how much Katie and Rachel Ann missed Marlena. In turn, Marlena asked about her brothers, as well.

Then, after a time devoted to a few everyday things, her mother said, "It seems only the dear Lord knows how long you'll have Angela Rose now. Are ya sure you can manage with everything else you're doin' there . . . for my mother?"

Marlena assured her that she was just fine. "Angela's little face brightens up every time she sees me, Mamma. She's beginning to respond to me in a way she doesn't with anyone else."

"I daresay she's bonded in a short time. That's *gut* . . . and bad."

"She *needs* me, Mamma."

Her mother sighed into the phone. "I hope you won't be heartbroken in the end."

"That's kind of you, Mamma. And thanks for lettin' me know about Gordon's parents' request. I feel so sorry for them, I do. But I can't say I understand them . . . not wanting their granddaughter with them, at least not just yet." Marlena fought back tears, trying to imagine what Luella would think if she knew. *And Gordon, too!*

"Your father and I are prayin' for you every day, Marlena."

She thanked her mother, said "I love you," and then they hung up.

Marlena sighed as she thought of Nat and his parents, but presently she cared more about the news regarding her niece.

She headed upstairs to see Angela Rose, who was beginning to stir in her sleep. Despite all the uncertainty, Marlena wouldn't think of turning her back on this precious baby, seemingly so alone in the world. "I'll take *gut* care of you, for as long as the Lord permits," she promised the little one.

CHAPTER 32

Mamma's words played continuously through Marlena's mind while Angela napped. She did not want to harbor any frustration toward Nat or his parents, but she couldn't deny that she was feeling drawn toward things that would only confirm their fears. *Even so, Nat and I are going to be married,* she thought. *Aren't we?*

When Angela Rose opened her little peepers and grinned over at Marlena seated on the bed, she went to her. "We're goin' for a Sunday afternoon stroll, little darling. And I have a surprise for ya." She dressed Angela in the navy blue baby bonnet she'd purchased on the sly at Saturday market. "There. Now you can easily pass for an Amish baby." She picked her up and kissed her soft, warm cheek.

"You'll fit right in with all the other little ones out havin' an airing today," she said, carrying Angela downstairs to tell Mammi where they were going.

"I surely hope you can find some shade somewhere. It's mighty warm out there," Mammi said.

"I know just where to go," Marlena assured her. And she did, taking the main road a short distance, then turning onto the tree-lined back road that eventually led past the old mill where Boston had stayed. She'd decided not to go all the way down the hill in this heat, however.

Still pondering her mother's phone call, Marlena knew better than to let things simmer, lest her frustration turn to anger. She began to pray like Mammi, whispering her cares to the Lord above, laying them all out like quilt squares. She also pleaded with God to steer her footsteps—for always. "And give my beau Thy understanding."

She felt sure that if Nat could just experience either her parents' church or Mammi's here, he'd appreciate the second thoughts she sometimes had about joining their more traditional one. "How can I move ahead with baptism back home, dear Lord? How . . . after what I'm learning?"

She recalled the verse Mammi had read before breakfast that morning, from John chapter seven, verse thirty-seven: *"If any man thirst, let him come unto me, and drink."*

After closing the Bible, Mammi had gone on to say that her own spiritual thirst was quenched once she believed and made the decision to drink from the living water. *"I'll never thirst that way again,"* Mammi had said with tears spilling over her wrinkled cheeks.

"More than anything else, I want the living water that Jesus offers," Marlena said into the air now as she pushed the stroller.

Tears threatened, and she let them fall. And the more she prayed, the harder she cried.

272

Small Jay and his father had gone walking along one of the shady field lanes the mules crossed daily, except on the Lord's Day. There, the corn was waist-high to Dat.

"I heard something at the shared meal today, Jake. And I'm gonna ask ya about it straight out."

Small Jay turned to look at his father.

"The grapevine has it you snuck Shredder over to Abram Mast's."

Small Jay was surprised to hear this; he'd mistakenly assumed this would be about Boston's outburst in church. "*Jah*, I did," he fessed up.

"Supposedly Luke got a letter . . . one you wrote yourself?"

Small Jay nodded solemnly. "*Is des Druwwel?*"

"*Nee*, you ain't in trouble." Dat stopped walking and looked down at him. "Just wonderin' why ya didn't come to me first."

Small Jay shrugged, feeling like he'd done something wrong. "I figured Shredder was done for."

Dat shook his head. "Not a *schmaert Kaader* like that."

"Well, he seemed *dumm* to me. He kept doin' the same thing, Dat. He never learnt."

His father burst out laughing. "I like that, Jake . . . I certainly do. Mighty discerning."

Small Jay nearly asked right then why his father never used his nickname, but it had been such a long time since Dat had done anything with him like this, he didn't want to spoil the moment.

"Next time there's something on your mind," Dat said, starting to walk again, "will ya look to me first, son?"

He felt he ought to pinch himself to see if what he was hearing was true. "I'll remember."

"*Des gut.*" Dat put his big hand on Small Jay's shoulder.

He felt mighty pleased as he realized that it must be all over the place about the letter he'd written to Luke, and Shredder going to live over there. Maybe even half of Brownstown had heard about it.

Swallowing several times, Small Jay noticed Dat had matched his own stride with his as they walked slowly back toward the house. Truly, it was nearly the best day of his life.

~⁀☉

Marlena stared up at the tall rattling windmills as she pushed the baby stroller, recalling how, as a little girl, she liked to see the sun bounce off Dawdi's, squinting up as she pointed to it. "*Perty Windmiehl*," she'd say over and over, grinning through missing front teeth.

Marlena also remembered both her and Luella helping Mammi Janice by pushing the old lawn mower, their small hands side-by-side on the wooden handle. At one farmhouse along the road, she noticed a pair of black field boots on the porch steps, and a long fly strip hanging near the door. Seeing the boots reminded her of trying to walk in Dawdi's old ones and toppling out of them, giggling all the while. *Seems like just yesterday . . .*

Marlena gazed out across the lush hayfields, still daydreaming. After this sacred day of respite, haying would commence. Men would be cutting once the early dew dried tomorrow, swirls of insects flying out from the remaining tall hay. Rabbits and groundhogs were discovered in there, too, sometimes before it was too late.

She saw mothers out walking now—Amish and English alike—pushing baby carriages or pulling wagons filled with youngsters shielding their eyes from the sun. Some of the women called "hullo," and she waved back.

As she walked, Marlena considered how endearing and inquisitive Luella had once been before she'd turned sullen in her teens and quickly became disinterested in anything that wasn't English.

While brooding over the past, Marlena saw Luke Mast coming this way. His head was down as he walked on the opposite side of the road, his lips moving like he was talking to himself.

Should she speak first? He had been such an attentive listener the last time they'd met by happenstance in the van. Now, though, Luke was intent on working something out, so lost in thought he appeared to be.

She wiped her face, drying her tears, and just then he looked up. "Hi, Luke," she said.

"*Wie bischt*, Marlena?" He smiled and crossed the road to her.

"I'm all right, and you?"

He glanced at the sky. "Sometimes it's easier to pray out here with the birds and the breezes, ya know."

"I'm finding that to be true, too."

He nodded and met her gaze. "There's somethin' real inspiring about sharing one's heart with the Creator when surrounded by His creation." He leaned down to smile at Angela Rose and tap gently on the top of her little blue bonnet. "This is your niece, ain't?"

"*Jah*, and I'll tell ya she's one happy little girl today."

"Happy's always *gut*." He crouched down. "Are ya catchin' any perty butterflies today?" he asked Angela.

She let out a baby-sized giggle.

"Hey, I think she likes me." Luke chuckled. "I've got two nieces your age, little one," he said, making a silly face for Angela.

Marlena had to smile. "She's wearin' her Amish bonnet for the first time . . . dressed part English and part Plain."

Luke glanced up at her. "What's it matter at this age?"

Marlena was surprised. "'Course, I guess Angela Rose really is half Amish and half English, considerin'."

"Bring her over and we'll teach her to milk cows next."

Marlena laughed. "I'm thinkin' she might be a little young yet."

"You've got a point there." Luke stood up, eyes twinkling. "Well, I'd better let ya get back to your prayin'."

Luke removed his hat and fanned his face, then put the hat back on. "Would ya mind if I walked with yous a little ways?"

She shook her head, guessing he wanted to finish their conversation from the other day. But as they went, she quickly discovered he had other things on his mind. It seemed he needed to get something off his chest about a young woman he was fond of, but who was in love with someone else. "And she's prob'ly in the dark about how I feel," he said, folding his arms as they walked.

"So it might be best not to say anything," Marlena said, "considering ya want to respect that, *jah?*" Luke hadn't asked for her opinion just yet, but she'd given it anyway.

"That, and not make a fool of myself." He shrugged. "I've considered any number of things, but I want to do what's respectable."

Marlena recalled seeing the pretty brunette riding with Sarah and Luke. *The day Aunt Becky brought Angela Rose to Brownstown.* Of course, Marlena wasn't going to embarrass Luke and mention her. "Does your sister Sarah know how ya feel about the girl you're sweet on?"

"No one knows. That is, no one but you."

Why's he telling me? She felt pleased that he found her to be trustworthy. "I'll keep mum on this."

He nodded. "Now ya know what I was praying 'bout before."

Fleetingly, she thought of telling him about Nat Zimmerman's concerns as to where she went to church, wondering what he might think of all that. But it was enough that Luke had already shared so freely.

Chapter 33

*T*he very next evening, Roman surprised Ellie by urging her to invite Boston to join them at the supper table. Happily, she complied.

After the silent prayer of thanksgiving, there was some lighthearted talk about Boston's ever-increasing beard and moustache. His thick eyebrows rose at the children as he remarked that he hadn't seen a single upper lip sporting hair anywhere at yesterday's Preaching service. Then the topic of his bow tie—missing yet again—came up when Small Jay asked about it, but Boston didn't seem worried.

"Do the men of your community ever wear ties to adorn their Sunday shirts?" he asked.

"Some church districts allow it," Roman spoke up, "but ours is considered a low church, so we're more traditional—and simple and modest."

"What do you consider a high church?" Boston asked, eyes serious.

"Some call it progressive," Roman told him. "They go softer on the *Ordnung*, allowing telephones, holding Sunday school on the between Sundays, even lettin' some members drive cars, of all things."

He's thinking of my sister Orpha and her husband, Abram, thought Ellie, wondering how far Roman would take this conversation.

Boston bobbed his head, his expression playful, and asked if it was permissible to request seconds. Roman said it was fine, and then he, too, helped himself to more of the ham loaf and mashed potatoes and gravy.

At the end of the meal, Boston offered hard candy to everyone, beginning with young Sally. "I purchased it at Joe's store the other day with your young man here."

Sassafras came meowing over like she wanted some, too, and Boston patted her little head while the girls thanked him repeatedly.

Ellie noticed how quiet Small Jay was. Quiet and pensive. *So far, this has been a different kind of summer for him . . . for all of us.*

When the chatter died down, Roman mentioned that the farrier would be coming tomorrow to scrape the horses' shoes and to check if they needed new ones. Immediately, the girls asked if they could go out and watch. Roman paused a moment, his eyes lighting on Small Jay. "Don't ya think it's your brother's turn this time?"

Small Jay made a little gasp. "I'd like that, Dat. I would!"

Ellie smiled at their boy and her husband, then nodded her approval.

"Maybe Boston would like to go with ya, too," Roman said just before folding his hands and bowing his head, ready for the second silent prayer.

Ellie followed her husband's lead, thanking God for their

scrumptious meal, and for Roman's budding interest in their son.

~~⁀ꙅ

Between baking two loaves of bread and doing all the ironing Tuesday morning, Marlena also took time to play with Angela Rose, thrilled at her progress in trying to push onto her knees. "You can do it, sweetie," she encouraged her, clapping when she'd get up on her hands and knees, only to flop down on her tummy again. Marlena was careful not to applaud when Mammi was around, guessing she might frown on it. Even so, Marlena knew firsthand that her own mother had coddled Katie and Rachel Ann till they were each two years old, the age when training in character development and yielding to authority began in earnest.

So I'll spoil you for a little longer, she thought, enjoying Angela Rose's dovelike cooing.

The mail came early that morning, and Marlena spotted a letter from Nat. She couldn't open it fast enough and begin to read.

My dearest Marlena,

How is your little niece faring? Truth be told, I was surprised to hear your sister's baby is still in your care. No doubt, though, you're eager to return Angela Rose to her rightful place with her father's family. An Englischer *child belongs with her people, after all.*

I've looked to my own father for some advice concerning several things, Marlena. And since you and I are planning to join church together, I do expect you to stop attending Mennonite services there in Brownstown. Frankly, it gives

*everyone here the wrong impression, and Dat says nothing
good can come from flirting with the edges. It's essential for
our future as man and wife that you hear me out on this, or
we'll need to discuss our future together.*

Marlena reread the last lines, attempting to comprehend.
Not only did Nat seem certain that Angela Rose did not belong
with her, but he was clearly displeased to hear that Marlena
planned to continue to attend church with her Mammi—so
much so that her beau seemed to be giving an ultimatum.
Yet, why now? Surely this was all due to his father pressing
him. Marlena recalled what her mother had mentioned when
she'd called.

Distressed, Marlena wasn't sure why it was so necessary for
her to quit going to Mammi's church now, when she would
only be in Brownstown a couple more months. Oh, in her heart
of hearts, Marlena realized she was reluctant to stop attending
any sooner—the words the preacher said each week were a
bright spot in the midst of her grief and confusion over first
Dawdi's and then Luella's death. *How can I possibly give that up?*

"Or Angela Rose, should it come to that," she whispered.

And all the rest of the day, Marlena felt covered by a dark
and dismal cloud.

~ༀ

Wednesday morning, when Sarah Mast was dropped off by
her mother in the family carriage, Marlena had already decided
to pour her melancholy about Nat's letter into a sketch for
the baby quilt's design. Thoughtfully, Sarah brought along a
few crazy quilt sketches, one of which her cousin had made.

The two of them laid out the piecework and took turns

holding Angela Rose. Later, they had some of Sarah's wonderfully moist midnight chocolate cake while Mammi Janice embroidered pillowcases on the back porch, humming hymns.

"Luke mentioned meeting your young niece Sunday, out on the road," Sarah said in passing. "He said she was a very sweet baby."

"Oh, and she is."

Sarah wiggled her fingers at Angela. "I s'pose it's hard not to dote on such a perty baby. But you don't want her to become vain."

"You're right 'bout that."

Sarah studied the drawing Marlena had decided on, and then showed her how to number the pieces on her sketch. "Do ya know what color binding and backing you want?" She asked if Marlena wanted the top and bottom ends to be bound in a different color than the sides. "There are lots of ways to do this, Ellie says."

"I'm still deciding," Marlena told her, so glad she'd come.

They discussed scalloped edges and decorative bindings, but it was Sarah who asked if Marlena wanted a quilt more in keeping with a "lower" church like the Old Order, or something that would be acceptable to her grandmother's church.

Hearing it put that way, Marlena realized again what a quandary she was in, not knowing where her niece would grow up—as an Amish child or an *Englischer*.

"Angela Rose's situation is uncertain at this point," Marlena shared with Sarah. "Honestly, it makes me feel awful sad, thinkin' of losing touch when her father's parents come for her." She still felt too frustrated with Nat to talk about him just now.

"I hope you and your family will be permitted to see Angela

from time to time," Sarah said. "She *is* your blood kin, of course."

Marlena nodded and thanked her for being such a supportive friend.

At the appointed time, Luke arrived for his sister. Seeing him from the window, Marlena recalled how fervently he'd prayed along the road the other day. She realized just then that she hadn't even asked Nat to join her in prayer about the challenges facing them, whether about Angela Rose's future or their own. *That's just what I'll write in my next letter to him.* She hoped this request wouldn't cause further conflict, but he needed to know how important prayer was to her. *Nevertheless, if he loves me, we'll work something out.*

CHAPTER 34

*S*mall Jay had memorized a few of the melodies Boston played on his mouth organ each evening, and sometimes, when his parents weren't within earshot, Small Jay liked to hum along. It was the very best time of day, and he often counted the hours till they sat on the back porch and ate ice cream to cool off.

Small Jay was glad Boston had suddenly been included with the family at mealtimes, though he still wasn't certain how such a thing had come about.

As for the letters, little by little, Boston had been adding what tidbits he remembered as Small Jay read aloud—stopping him to mention new things, like a big black piano in a sun-strewn parlor with an antique music stand nearby.

According to Boston, there were only a few letters left to be read. More and more, Small Jay had been getting the feeling that Boston might wake up one morning and remember where he belonged. There were times when he felt sure Boston's memory was slowly getting better, at least here and there. *Maybe Dr. Isaac's cures are working.*

That weekend, Mamma asked Boston if he'd like to go to market next Saturday with her and Small Jay. "I think you'd enjoy yourself," she said, a light in her eyes.

"Is it permissible to nap at market?" Boston asked jokingly. "Napping seems to be what I do best."

Mamma refuted that but said she'd make sure there was a chair for him behind the table. "We'll only be able to stay till a little before noon, since I'll have some baking to do," she added.

Small Jay's mouth watered at the thought of freshly baked pies and cookies, though he was mostly happy that his English friend could finally experience the marketplace for himself. *Maybe he can spend some of those dollar bills in his wallet on more candy or delicious fudge.*

Marlena hadn't waited long to answer Nat's letter. In fact, she'd already sent hers, hoping to hear something back from him right away. She prayed his heart might soften toward her desires and toward Angela Rose. How could he be tentative toward any baby, let alone this one who was so dear to Marlena herself?

She had been loving in her reply but made it clear how she felt about Angela Rose—and how she believed God was calling her to care for her as long as needed. She was also firm about going to church with Mammi Janice for the duration of the summer. *Why must Nat make things so hard—put me in a corner over this—when surely he knows I'm honoring my grandmother?*

Meanwhile, Mammi had come down with what she called *"der Schnuppe"*—the sniffles—and a fever. Marlena felt certain the illness had been brought on by all the stressful events of late.

When Sunday rolled around and Mammi was still too sick to get up for church, Marlena decided to go on her own. She dressed around and got Angela Rose ready, too. "We'll let Mammi rest awhile," she whispered.

After breakfast, she slipped the diaper bag over her shoulder and carried her niece out to the roadside. There, Marlena began to walk down the hill toward Bitners', thinking that perhaps one of the New Order families might see her and offer a ride to their house meeting.

After all, Luke and Sarah did invite me.

In a few minutes, Marlena spotted Abram and Orpha Mast, Sarah's parents, and waved for them to stop. Unlike the more traditional buggies around the area, their buggy wheels had rubber strips, the only noticeable difference. It turned out that Luke, Sarah, and two of the other children had gone in another carriage, so there was ample room for Marlena and the baby.

Orpha was brimming with smiles as Marlena got situated. Orpha wore a dress that was nearly as red as one of Luella's fancy dresses, but she had not a stitch of makeup on, and her shoes were black and quite conservative. "Sarah's ever so pleased to help ya work on the baby's quilt," Orpha said, making room on the front bench seat. "It's really nice of you to make such a unique remembrance for the baby."

Babbling sweetly, Angela Rose reached her busy little hand toward Orpha's bright sleeve and held on as the horse pulled them forward.

"Sarah says she's a happy little one, and I can surely see that."

Marlena smiled. "Angela's a real *gut* baby, too. Growin' fast now."

"How soon will ya start stitchin' up the new quilt?" asked Orpha. "The way Sarah talks, it's unlike most of ours round here."

Marlena vouched for its not being authentically Amish in pattern or color. "It's a crazy quilt like you've never seen before."

Orpha laughed softly, and Abram glanced at her, then at Angela Rose, who still gripped Orpha's sleeve. "This is your older sister's baby, *jah?*"

Marlena sighed and nodded. "Luella recently passed away, so I'm lookin' after her for a while."

"Sarah mentioned something," Abram replied, his pale blue eyes solemn. "Awful sorry for such a small one."

They're polite, not asking where the father is. . . .

Orpha added, "She seems at ease with you."

Marlena recalled again how terribly upset Angela had been her first days there. And it struck her that most folk just went about their daily chores and never gave much thought to the ties that bound a family—how very fragile they could be.

One never knows what change a single day might bring.

Marlena remembered the verse she'd read that morning even before getting out of bed: *"Boast not thyself of tomorrow; for thou knowest not what a day may bring forth."*

Each person at the New Order house meeting was so welcoming, though not nearly as many were present as the crowd at Mammi's meetinghouse. Marlena wondered if their friendliness was in hopes of gathering more converts, as some said. Even so, she believed they were genuinely glad to extend a hand of fellowship to her, and in the midst of her qualms about her and Nat's plans for marriage, the experience was a paradise of peace.

As with the Old Order church, the women and children sat on one side of the long, open room, the men and older boys facing them on the opposite side. Much of the service was similar to what she had grown up with, except that English was spoken in more than half of it. She also noticed this minister making eye contact with the congregation, whereas in her former church, the preacher stared at a wall or fixed his gaze on a window.

Like Abram Mast, the men here wore their hair shorter than her father or Roman Bitner. And the women's cape dresses, for the most part, were louder in color—red, turquoise, and Kelly green.

Marlena liked the fact that they held Sunday school for adults and children on the between Sundays, as Orpha had explained on the way there, saying that each person took turns reading the Scriptures at those house gatherings. They also discussed the particular passages, something never done in an Old Order setting.

What made Marlena most curious about this offshoot of the traditional church was that the young people were required to be baptized *before* they were permitted to date. *"That way, the dating partner knows for sure they're settled in their beliefs,"* Sarah had said during one of their times together.

After Preaching and before the common meal, Marlena spotted the same attractive brunette she'd once seen riding with Sarah and Luke. . . the young woman Luke had confided about to her.

Orpha, and later Sarah, offered to hold Angela so Marlena could enoy the simple meal of homemade bread, cold cuts, and strawberry pie. During the meal, Orpha's four sisters-in-law and a few of her same-age cousins came by to smile at Angela Rose, talking to her, which helped Marlena feel accepted, too.

Naturally, she knew better than to expect Luke to seek her out. She had seen him eating with his older brothers and a number of other young men she didn't know, and he never once looked her way. She did notice him glance at the tall brunette several times, however. *I hope he knows I'll keep his secret,* she thought, glad she'd had the idea to worship there.

"Your grandmother doesn't mind your bein' here, does she?" Orpha asked, suddenly looking serious.

"Well, she doesn't know yet," Marlena admitted. "But she won't mind when I tell her."

"'Tis *gut.* Wouldn't want to cause ya any trouble."

Ach, if she only knew! Marlena gave Orpha a warm smile.

CHAPTER 35

The following Wednesday, Marlena welcomed Sarah Mast for a second time to work on hand sewing the crazy-quilt pieces. They talked casually as they sat around Mammi's kitchen table—Sarah told of helping her mother and sisters, putting up forty-five quarts of canned green beans. And Marlena said she and her grandmother had done the same, only fewer quarts, while reciting Scripture verses. *Nat wouldn't be pleased if he knew the latter,* she thought.

Sarah kept looking at Angela Rose in her playpen. "She's becoming so active. I wonder if she'll walk early."

"Well, my mother says it's important for a baby to crawl for a *gut* long time before learnin' to walk."

Sarah agreed.

Mammi, who was feeling better, suggested that Angela be permitted to lie on a blanket on the kitchen floor while the girls worked. Marlena gave her a rattle and a teething toy to keep Angela occupied.

"I've been wanting to dress her more like Mammi and me,"

Marlena confided in Sarah when Sarah commented on the baby's little dress. "Not necessarily to push too quickly in that direction, though, considering everything."

"You've been mighty busy, I see."

Marlena said she'd managed to squeeze in an hour or so lately each day to sew. "I hope to make several small dresses in all—pale blue, soft pink, and mint green."

"Do ya plan to have Angela longer, then?"

Marlena said she really didn't know. "But she doesn't have enough dresses, and she'll outgrow them fast."

Pleasant conversation occupied their time as the two young women pieced together the colorful quilt. Marlena mentioned having also spent time redding up Mammi's pantry, organizing things. She'd painted the porch railing outside and accomplished a lot of garden work, as well as kept Mammi's house clean—and all this just since she'd gone to the New Order Amish church that past Lord's Day. She thought once more of Luke and realized she hadn't given much thought to his dilemma, but she had offered up a prayer for divine wisdom and comfort.

It must be difficult, caring for someone who has no interest in him.

~~~oO

On Friday, Mammi asked if there was any more word from Patricia Munroe about Gordon's parents. But none had come. Were they having second thoughts? Marlena knew from Mamma that they had been reluctant for Gordon to marry Luella in the first place. Was that partly behind their hesitancy now?

As each day passed and Nat's response to Marlena's last

letter did not come, she became more vexed, even though she tried her best to relinquish her anxiety to God. She found herself trying to second-guess what Nat might be thinking, but she wanted to give him the benefit of the doubt. At times, she was just about sure that all would be well if she could only talk face-to-face with him about Angela Rose, as well as her growing faith.

How can such things put a wedge between us, unless we allow them?

───⌒○

It was already very warm early Saturday morning as Ellie headed to market with Small Jay and Boston, tickled to treat him to his first such experience.

At her market booth, Boston began to play one tune after another on his harmonica, drawing an inquisitive crowd. Youngsters and their parents watched with bright-eyed amusement, some of them tapping their toes. The music, so skillfully played, created a pleasant shopping atmosphere for the tourists and locals alike. One male customer, who'd come all the way from London, England, to tour the back roads of Amish farm country, suggested Boston get a job playing every Saturday.

Meanwhile, Small Jay assisted Ellie in ways he hadn't before—greeting customers and bagging up jars of preserves, along with her handmade items. Ellie wished with all of her heart that Roman could witness this transformation for himself.

Small Jay's finally getting more attention from Roman, she thought, recalling several times recently that her husband had told of his encounters with Small Jay and Boston as the pair worked side-by-side.

It was hard for her to make sense of what she felt whenever Roman shared these observations—such a sense of relief after all these years. And Roman held the reins in his hands and heart.

~⸮

Driver Vernon Siegrist regularly kept the radio turned off when the van was full of Plain folk. Today, however, he'd turned the music on right away when they were getting in, a treat for Small Jay, to be sure. The soft music provided a nice background for the womenfolk's chatter.

Slowly, one Amishwoman after another got off the van as Small Jay sat with Boston, heading home for the afternoon. Mamma seemed extra pleased because she'd run clean out of her homemade wares. Small Jay knew she would have liked to stay around and visit with many of the womenfolk there, but as planned, they'd left a bit early, not wanting to tire out Boston. Aunt Orpha had been one of those who stopped by and commented on Boston's lovely music that morning. Even Luke and Sarah had dropped by to say hullo.

Small Jay tried to mind his p's and q's as he gazed out the window, noticing a pond in the distance. He wondered just when his father might suggest they go fishing, but it wasn't something he would bring up again. He'd said that he wanted to and felt sure his father would follow through. Or so he hoped.

Reliving the market experience today, Small Jay realized how much better things had been with Boston along. The one lack was Gracie Yoder, who hadn't been present this time, at least that he knew. Gracie's aunt Nellie often wandered down to talk with Mamma, and if Nellie had been there, Small Jay was sure she would've dropped by to see Mamma and to soak up Boston's music. But there'd been no sign of either Nellie or Gracie.

Glancing now at Boston, he noticed the man's eyes were half closed, his head forward. His shaved upper lip and straw hat made him look so very Amish. If Boston stayed on indefinitely with them, would he eventually want to take baptismal instruction and join church? If so, he'd have to go through the two-year or longer Proving time, but Boston sure didn't seem opposed to dressing like the People or working hard. *As hard as he's able*, thought Small Jay. *Kinda like me.*

While he sometimes daydreamed about Boston living permanently amongst the People, he also had a feeling that Boston might not really want to be Amish at all. He wondered if the man ever had glimmers of memories about his former life. Did he miss Abigail, for instance, the woman responsible for so many letters to her "dearest darling"?

Presently, Dat's farmhouse came into view, and Small Jay pointed toward the east-facing *Dawdi Haus*, where Boston had been spending his nights. "Home again, *jah?*" Small Jay said softly.

Boston nodded and smiled drowsily, then turned around to thank Mamma for inviting him today. "A delightful experience, to say the least. I met some fine folk."

A few minutes later, Boston pulled out his billfold and offered to pay Vernon for the round trip. Mamma intervened and said *she* wanted to pay, but Boston insisted until Mamma backed down and let Boston give some money to Vernon, who thanked him heartily.

Boston leaned back then, waiting for Mamma to slip out

of the van from the seat behind them. Small Jay realized how quiet it had become, and he sat very still, listening to the radio music, knowing it would be a long time before he heard such fine radio melodies again.

Boston climbed out next with Vernon near. Vernon waved at Dat and hurried across the yard to visit, but Small Jay felt like staying put. That's when he began to recognize the melody of the song on the radio and found himself humming along.

"Ach, I *know* that tune," Small Jay said to himself. *But how?* he wondered. Then it struck him: *That's Boston's melody! He plays it every night!*

Small Jay got up and leaned his head out the open van door. "Boston, come back right quick! Somethin's on the radio you oughta hear."

Boston turned and frowned, then walked back this way. All the while, the radio was playing what sounded like Boston's favorite song.

"Just listen," he said as Boston poked his head inside.

Then a smile spread across his face as Boston stepped into the van and slid over next to Small Jay. "Well, what do you know?"

Silently, they sat listening, and Small Jay observed a flicker appear in the man's eyes, along with a kind of settling into place, and he turned to smile at Small Jay.

"That's Eleanor Frank, one of the finest soloists in the country," Boston said, his hands moving and dipping now as he liked to do.

"Is that a piano I hear?" Small Jay asked, captivated by Boston's strange expression.

"Ah yes . . . I recall making this recording." The man placed his hand on his chest and hummed lightly. "What you're hearing is my accompaniment, young man."

"On the radio?" Small Jay was confused.

"Oh yes. You see, I was Eleanor's pianist for a number of years." Boston gazed out the window, a faraway look in his eyes, like he was beginning to remember more. "Eleanor and I toured all over the country and in parts of Europe, too . . . a long time ago. It's hard to remember precisely when."

"She warbles like a songbird," Small Jay said.

"A most lyrical high soprano." Boston's smooth hands began to sway and lift once again. "I believe I was living in Arlington, Virginia, when we recorded this album. Sometime later, this popular single came out of that."

Small Jay made a mental note of everything Boston was saying—the music seemed to be prodding the man's memory. It was the oddest yet most wonderful thing. "Where's Arlington?"

"Near Washington, D.C.," Boston replied without missing a beat, as if he knew right away. Then, as the music wafted along, he began to tell of being a well-known pianist and composer of music, one who played with the top American orchestras and around the world, too. His wife, Abigail, couldn't always travel with him because of her work, but she wrote love letters to Boston when he was touring as Eleanor's accompanist. "I wrote the song 'Melody of Love' specifically for Eleanor's vocal range. But it was about Abigail." He sounded so proud of himself and happy, too.

"Where was your house then? Did ya live there recently? And where's Abigail now?"

Boston wrinkled his brow for a moment, as if struggling to recall everything just asked. Small Jay was sure it was a lost cause; Boston hadn't remembered details like this in the longest time.

Then a smile appeared on the man's lips, and he quickly rattled off his address. Small Jay swallowed hard and began to repeat the important information over and over in his head while the woman sang Boston's heartbreaking melody.

I have to talk to Dat right quick, Small Jay thought, worried he'd forget the address and everything else if he didn't hurry.

After the last note was sung, a man with a deep voice began to talk, telling how the song had been sweeping the nation because its composer, Dr. Boston Calvert, had disappeared from his home earlier that summer.

"That's *you*, Boston! The man's talking 'bout you!"

Goodness, he must be famous. . . .

Boston, meanwhile, was trying to locate his harmonica in his trouser pocket. "That was the Boston who could remember . . . *me* before my memories flew the coop like so many chickens."

When he'd found his mouth organ, Boston began to play the lovely song once more as great tears stained his face.

Small Jay wanted to weep, too, because of sudden joy and a creeping sadness that mixed up inside of him like a rag rug with many colors. But he was a child no longer. Small Jay climbed out of the van, determined to handle Boston's revelations in a way that might make his father proud.

CHAPTER 36

As soon as Small Jay revealed to his father what had taken place, Vernon agreed to drive Small Jay, Boston, and Dat over to the Hendricksons' to place a collect call to Mrs. Abigail Calvert in Arlington, Virginia. They planned to use the address Boston had recited so effortlessly as a way to get the correct phone number from the operator. Soon, very soon, Boston would know for sure if his wife, or any other family members, were waiting for his return.

"Why don't I put you on the phone, Jake, once we know if Abigail's even there?" Dat said at the neighbors' house while Boston sat expressionless in a nearby chair. "Do you remember what day you met Boston at the old mill? How long ago was that, son?"

Small Jay said he didn't recall for certain, but he *would* like to talk to Abigail. In his mind, he felt he knew her at least a little from reading her letters aloud to Boston.

The right connection was made, and someone answered the phone. From the sound of Dat's side of the conversation, not only was Abigail Calvert alive and well, but she was thrilled to know that her husband was safe and had been found. Dat gave her the information he had about Boston and how to locate their farmhouse, as well.

When Dat paused to listen to what Abigail had to say, he nodded at Small Jay, literally grinning. *The first he's ever looked at me like that,* Small Jay thought, gritting his teeth to keep back the tears.

When at last his father handed the phone to him, Small Jay said, "Hullo, Abigail. This is Boston's friend Small Jay Bitner."

"Your father says you're responsible for helping my husband in many ways. I want you to know how very grateful I am to you."

Oh, was her voice ever pretty. As beautiful as the first rose of summer, and as sweet as her letters. "Boston's sitting right here smilin' at me . . . I believe he wants to talk to ya."

"Before you go, Small Jay, I wonder . . . did Boston happen to tell you how he managed to get so far from home?" Abigail asked, her words mixed with tears. Small Jay knew this remarkable woman was crying because she loved Boston. She'd missed him so and had been terribly worried.

"Maybe he'll remember all of that when he sees you again," Small Jay said with a glance at Boston. "He does remember a few things when he hears his music . . . I found that out just today."

"Oh, please do put my darling on. And, young man, I don't know how to thank you adequately. This phone call from your father and you is an answer to my every prayer. Thank you so very much."

Small Jay blushed, at a loss for what to say. He placed his hand on Boston's shoulder. "It's Abigail," he said quietly. "She's a very happy lady, and she says she can't wait to see ya."

"Do you mean my wife did not forsake me?"

Small Jay held up the phone as Dat stood near.

"This is Boston," the man said, leaning his head near the receiver. Then he began to whimper, then sob. "Oh, my dear, dear girl . . ."

Small Jay stepped back to give him some privacy, wondering how long before Abigail would arrive there to take her beloved husband home.

~~~

After market, Marlena went to Bitners' to get Angela Rose. There, she met Dorcas's grandmother, whom she offered to pay for being there to oversee Dorcas. But Mammi Bitner refused, and Marlena walked back to her own Mammi's with Angela Rose, pushing the stroller up the hill. Tired after a hectic day selling their jams and jellies, she smiled remembering Boston's serenade at market and the way he took such an interest in people's response to his music.

Presently, the phone rang as she put Angela in her crib upstairs. When Mammi didn't answer on the second or the third ring, Marlena wondered if she'd gone out on the porch or slipped away to the garden.

By the time Marlena had hurried down to the kitchen and picked up the receiver, she was out of breath. "Martin residence," she answered.

"I received your letter, Marlena," said Nat.

Not hello or how are you?

She caught her breath, surprised that he'd called to tell her. "I'm so relieved to hear it, Nat. I've been praying 'bout things here lately," she said softly. "And hope you have been, too."

"Listen, I don't understand why this is so hard. Couldn't your mother take the baby . . . or your grandmother, maybe?"

She fell silent. Then she said, "Mammi's honestly in no shape to do that."

"And your mother?" He sounded miffed. "Won't ya try and look at this from my point of view, Marlena?"

"I've tried, believe me," she said. "Besides, that's not what I've been prayin' the most about."

"How much longer do ya think you'll have your niece?" He ignored what she'd said. "'Cause it seems to change nearly every week." He paused a moment. "We *are* a courting couple, after all."

"I know that, but tellin' the truth, it really doesn't matter to me how long Angela's with me."

He breathed audibly into the phone. "Another month, then . . . or two?"

She bit her lip. "What if it's a year or more?"

Nat paused, a long silence that seemed to last forever. Then he said, "That's too long. So's six months. We'll be officially engaged by then. How can we court properly with a baby around?" He went on to explain that he had everything all planned out. "And there's no room in any of it for an *Englischer*'s child . . . especially not the child of a wayward person like your sister."

She stepped back, gasping. "So that must be the *real* problem, then."

He was quiet again. Then he said more thoughtfully, "It's all of that . . . and also what I wrote in my letter."

"Where I go to church," she said flatly.

"You never told me when you left that you planned to attend the Mennonite church with your grandmother. And then when I ask you to stop, you won't."

"I just assumed you'd know that I would go to church with my Mammi out of respect and all," Marlena continued. "But over time, it's become more to me than that—I'm learning things about the Lord I never knew before, things I need to hear with Luella gone." She paused to take a breath.

"As for Angela Rose, she's my sister's baby, Nat. I know things weren't so *gut* between Luella and me, but her daughter needs me. And I want to take care of her . . . and for as long as God allows." Her lower lip quivered.

"How can ya be willin' to throw away our future for someone else's baby?"

"If it's the Lord's will, then I want to be here for Angela. I feel certain He's asking me to do this."

The silence on the other end of the line stretched out so long she wondered if the line had gone dead. Then Nat spoke again. "How can you say that, Marlena? It simply won't work."

She'd never felt so hemmed in, but he'd obviously made up his mind, without room for compromise. "Do ya mean to say that this is the only choice I have . . . that I must choose between you and Angela Rose?" Marlena was incredulous—she had been so sure Nat would understand once she'd explained.

"You'd honestly choose the baby over me, even though you likely won't keep her in the end?" He sounded equally astonished.

"*Jah*, 'cause you're unreasonable, Nat. I never knew it till now." Surprisingly, she didn't feel anger toward him. Rather, she felt terribly sorry for him. How could Nat be so blind to the importance of giving her niece a loving home, however temporary? And why couldn't he demonstrate some patience in this, or feel some appreciation for her growing faith?

Marlena shook her head in disbelief as they said good-bye

and she hung up the black wall phone, feeling almost dizzy, her heart dangling as if from a phone cord.

From the second-floor balcony, Marlena could see a shiny black car turning into the Bitners' long lane after supper. She noticed Boston sitting on the back porch in one of the rocking chairs. The entire Bitner family lined the walkway as though anticipating someone's arrival.

When the car rolled to a stop, a tall, thin man dressed in a charcoal gray suit and a black hat stepped out of the car and hurried around to open the door on the opposite side. The passenger was a middle-aged woman, her blond hair swept up. She wore a cream-colored suit, the graceful skirt falling just below the knees as she moved with poise toward the Bitners.

Almost in unison, Roman, Ellie, and their children moved toward the woman, and Boston rose and walked down the porch steps, making his way around the walkway as the Bitners made an opening for him.

"Who's *this*?" Marlena whispered, intrigued.

What she saw as she inched closer to the railing made her weep, especially when Boston opened his arms wide and the beautiful woman walked toward him. *Can this be the woman Ellie's talked about—the one who wrote love letters to Boston?*

Ellie kept wiping her eyes as she watched the tender reunion unfold.

"Oh, my darling," Abigail said as she and Boston embraced. "Just look at you! Have you converted to Amish?"

He beamed down at her and removed his straw hat now. "When in Rome, you know . . ."

Abigail looked into his face, pleading for forgiveness, and then quickly explained what had transpired that critical evening, nearly a month ago. "I thought you were having one of your better days, my dear, so I slipped out to the grocery store. When I returned, you were gone, Boston . . . vanished from our home." She said again how terribly sorry she was to have frightened him so.

Boston slipped his arm around her waist. "I must have gotten my old leather satchel, the one I'd often take on my musical tours, and left the house in search of you," he said softly. "After a time, I was certain you'd left me . . . or worse."

He thought she'd passed away, Ellie thought sadly, glad that Boston was remembering more details. Was it Abigail's arrival that triggered this, just maybe?

"I think I purchased a bus ticket, though I don't recall the trip. There's a ticket stub in my shoulder bag."

"Well, bless your heart," Abigail said, shaking her head. "And somehow, you ended up out here."

Boston nodded. "There must have been a taxicab somewhere, as well. I vaguely remember walking along serene country roads that reminded me of my childhood. When I stumbled upon an old stone mill, I tried the doors and found one open." He glanced at Small Jay as if wanting assistance.

Allegro came bounding across the yard just then, wagging his tail as he made a beeline to Abigail, who leaned down and petted his head, clearly glad to see the border collie—as delighted as Allegro himself seemed to be.

Small Jay looked at his father and Roman nodded, encouraging him to go ahead. "My cat and I met Allegro first . . . he led us to Boston." And to the best of his ability, he told Abigail all that had transpired.

Abigail remembered her manners and apologized to Ellie and Roman before introducing herself. "You must be Roman Bitner," she said, extending her hand and thanking him for the phone call.

Ellie shook the woman's slight, well-manicured hand, too, and marveled at the attention Abigail gave to the children as she leaned down to speak to each one. "With all of my heart, I thank you for taking care of my husband," she said, placing her right hand on her heart now. "I really don't need to know all the details of Boston's journey here. It's enough to know that he is alive and well."

"We're just so glad we found you," Ellie said.

"How might I reimburse you for your trouble?" Abigail asked.

Small Jay stepped forward. "Boston was never a bother."

"That's right. And we hope you'll bring him back to visit us—both of yous must come again for a visit," Ellie said, meaning it. "You've truly been a godsend."

"What a lovely family you are," Abigail said, her brown eyes smiling. Then she reached for Boston's hand and led him to the waiting car. "We mustn't keep you dear folk any longer."

Ellie waved as Boston turned back once more, looking over kindly at Small Jay. "If my bow tie turns up, young man, it's yours to wear . . . perhaps to market." Then he winked.

Small Jay seemed to understand, and when Boston held out his hand, Small Jay shook it firmly and seemed to grow two inches before their eyes.

"Take care of Miss Sassy, won't you?" Boston said.

They all took notice of pretty Sassafras sitting right next to Allegro, near Abigail's feet. The dog shifted and whined, restless.

"Thank you, each and every one," Boston said finally, then

followed Abigail to the car, the strap of his satchel slung over his shoulder. Allegro got up and scampered behind them as Sassy meowed and complained.

The children offered more waves and good-byes, and Ellie noticed little Sally's lips tremble as she tried to be brave.

"I can hardly believe he's leavin' us," Ellie said to Roman.

He moved closer to her. "She'll take *gut* care of Boston, *jah?*" When he smiled at her, Ellie thought he might actually wink.

"There's no doubt in my mind," Ellie said, touched by her husband's nearness.

Once the driver had pulled out of the lane and onto the road, Roman stepped over and placed his hand on Small Jay's shoulder. "Boston has you to thank, son." He paused and reached to shake Small Jay's hand. "We all do."

Small Jay ducked his head.

"I sure could use such a *schmaert* worker in the stable tomorrow. What do ya say, Jake?"

Ellie could no longer suppress her tears. She watched Small Jay grin at his Dat and nod his head without speaking.

CHAPTER 37

Later that evening, Roman held the shortest-ever family worship Ellie could recall. After the silent prayers, he sent the children off to bed. She could hear the girls chattering about how nice Abigail was to her "dearest darling" as they hurried up the stairs. Small Jay carried his cat up behind his sisters, trying to keep his distance from their giddiness.

When Ellie and Roman were alone in the front room, he suggested they go out and sit on the front porch swing. "All right with you?" he asked.

She wondered what was on his mind—they hadn't often taken the time to be alone together in recent years. When they sat down, Roman began to relive aloud that first afternoon the man from the mill had come into their lives. Ellie listened, enjoying his voice and the pleasant breezes.

Roman didn't talk for long, but neither was he gazing at the hayfields. His eyes were on her, and when he reached for her hand, it took her breath away.

"I'd like to think you'd take care of me thataway . . . like Abigail does Boston," Roman said.

"Jah." Ellie nodded. "The Lord willing and we live that long." Suddenly she wanted to wrap her arms around his suntanned neck. But goodness, they were out on the *front* porch, of all things, behaving like they were youngsters.

"Ever think we'll see Boston again?" Roman asked.

"Hmm . . . I don't know. But Jake surely would enjoy that."

"Jake's goin' to miss him." Roman smiled. "We all will."

Ellie leaned back and sighed. "Ya know, that Abigail's quite the letter writer."

Roman chuckled. "Where'd that come from?"

"Let's just say I learned a lot from hearin' our son read to Boston."

"I daresay his comin' was a *wunnerbaar-gut* thing." Leaning over, Roman bussed her cheek. "And I've been thinkin' . . ."

A delightful shudder slipped down her back.

Roman told her about a discussion he'd had with his brother Jake in the past few days. "He seems older and wiser, and he's been kind enough to point out some of my 'inconsistencies,' as he puts it." Roman turned to look at her. "So after thinkin' some—and plenty of prayer—I've decided it makes no sense to allow an *Englischer* like Boston into our lives, and even treat him like family, while holdin' your sister Orpha and her family at arm's length."

Ellie blinked, looking at him. "What do ya mean?"

"Well, just because we don't have full fellowship and agreement with certain surrounding church districts doesn't mean we can't be friendly and hospitable to one another."

Had Roman's brother planted all this in her husband's thinking? Ellie found it remarkable and somewhat hard to take in, considering how adamant Roman had been about keeping to themselves.

"And those sewing classes of yours . . . They brought ya such joy . . . and to your students, too. I saw the young women talkin' and smiling as they came and went." Roman wrapped his arm around her shoulder. "I've thought it through, love. I want ya to feel free to be the teacher you are, Ellie. Won't ya start up those classes again?"

"Are ya certain 'bout this?" she asked, wanting to give him an out if he was looking for one. She didn't want to contact the girls again only to have Roman pull the rug out from under them.

"Never more so," he said.

Ellie smiled through her tears and couldn't hold back any longer. Inching forward, she kissed him sweetly right then. He drew her even closer and kissed her back, and my, oh my, if anyone had happened along the road just then, Ellie wouldn't have been the wiser.

~⁓ℰ◯

To Marlena it was a miracle that she didn't break down or disclose her deep disappointment over Nat to her grandmother as the days passed.

Their big garden burst forth an abundant yield, and Marlena poured herself into the harvesting, canning, and freezing of produce, ever grateful, like Mammi, for God's outpouring of provision and love. At each meal, they gave thanks for the summer showers and the sunshine, and then again, during family worship, when Mammi read the Bible aloud to her and little Angela Rose. Dawdi Tim had always said, *"It doesn't matter what a farmer believes or where he goes to church. Truth is, he's dependent upon the Lord of the harvest for plentiful sunshine and the necessary rainfall."*

For seven Wednesdays, Sarah Mast came to help Marlena stitch up the crazy quilt for Angela Rose. They had discussed various designs for the stitching on the backing, including the most popular—stars, baskets, impatiens flowers, and hearts—but Marlena had quickly decided on heart-shaped quilting. *The love I've gained from opening my heart to Angela Rose—and the Lord God—more than compensates for my breakup with Nat. For surely his ongoing silence means we're through. . . .*

While Marlena's pent-up tears sometimes threatened during the day, she saved them for after she'd put Angela to bed. With God's help, she coped, did her chores, and took good care of her little niece, knowing that she was doing exactly what He expected of her.

By mid-August, her mother's frequent letters were a reminder that Marlena's return home was forthcoming. In a short time, they would give back Ellie's loaned baby items. Marlena also began to recognize that her first thoughts each morning were no longer of Nat Zimmerman and what she'd lost.

I've forgiven him, she thought, realizing she hadn't yet mentioned the breakup to anyone, not wanting people to feel sorry for the loss of a beau who'd turned out to have priorities so unlike her own.

With the potato harvest fast approaching, Marlena decided to thoroughly clean Mammi's house—an early fall housecleaning. She washed everything from the top down like she and Mamma always did before hosting Preaching, back when they attended their former church. And while she beat her grandmother's rag rugs and swept and dusted, Marlena couldn't get the local New Order group out of her mind, still recalling the Scriptures the minister had read and referenced. *And their exceptional friendliness.* Because of that, she looked forward at summer's end to returning to Mifflinburg to a similar type of preaching at her parents' new place of worship. *I won't be joining my childhood church with Nat,* she knew for sure.

She understood now that she'd primarily looked forward to joining the old church for Nat's sake. *Just so we could marry.*

But now there was oh, so much more to her decision. Things had come to a head this summer with Mammi, and Marlena had realized she needed a faith that fed her soul . . . and traditions that helped answer the cry of her heart.

~⁓ᛒ

Whenever Marlena glanced at the crazy quilt hanging over the crib railing, she felt pleased. It contained something of both Luella and herself, two sisters at odds but linked by one darling baby girl. She was also struck again by the blended motifs of the Plain and the fancy. And she couldn't have completed it in less than two months if Sarah Mast hadn't helped.

Someday, Angela Rose will know that I used her Mamma's dress scraps.

And secretly, Marlena hoped that the extra time Gordon's parents had requested might just extend into a lifetime.

CHAPTER 38

A week before Marlena planned to leave Brownstown for home, the phone rang. Patricia Munroe was on the line. "Your mother felt strongly that I should be the one to contact you, Marlena," she told her. "I have some wonderful news."

Marlena listened, wondering what on earth.

"My nephew's alive! Gordon was wounded but escaped and was rescued. He's well enough to fly back to the States."

"Oh, what a blessing for your family!" Then, realizing what this meant for Angela Rose, Marlena began to tremble.

"Gordon will come for Angela Rose, of course. I'll contact you soon to let you know when he'll be there."

"I'll have Angela ready." Marlena could scarcely get the words out.

"We are incredibly grateful to you, and to your grandmother, Marlena. I know Gordon is thankful, too. You've been very generous with your time."

"Well, it's been a joy to care for her."

Thankfully, Patricia didn't linger and said good-bye, then hung up.

Every sorrow of the past months encompassed Marlena, and she slumped down into the chair at the foot of Mammi's kitchen table, unable to quell her tears.

Patricia called again that afternoon to tell when Gordon would be coming. And afterward, Mammi gently insisted that Marlena must not try to be strong and carry around such heart-ache alone. "Trust our dear Lord Jesus for the peace to bring this to pass with a gentle spirit, my dear. It could be a testimony to Gordon," Mammi reminded her.

"*Jah*," Marlena said, praying that her heart would come to match her grandmother's wisdom.

Sarah Mast dropped by hours later with a hot noodle and turkey casserole she'd promised. When Marlena accompanied her back outside to the waiting horse and buggy, she found Luke sitting high in his courting carriage, holding the reins.

"You have been so helpful to me this summer," Marlena offered, smiling. "*Denki* ever so much for the dinner, Sarah. And I appreciate your listenin' ear, too—both of yous."

Luke grinned suddenly and quickly looked his sister's way, waiting till she was seated to glance back at Marlena. "We'll miss seein' ya round here, Marlena," he said, his tone earnest.

"*Jah*, do come back and see us anytime," Sarah said, lifting her hand to wave.

"Oh, I wish you lived closer," Marlena said, meaning it for Sarah, but Luke chuckled, and she felt her face go rosy.

Sarah gave her brother a playful prod. "Can we keep in touch?" she asked Marlena.

"I'll write ya, for sure," Marlena replied, glad at the prospect.

Luke, still smiling, gave her a slow nod, then backed up the horse.

Standing there, she really wanted to call to them—to spend more time. How very dear they'd become to her. *A brother and sister in the family of God!*

When she'd watched them head all the way out to the road with more cheerful waves, Marlena returned to the house, where she set to packing some of Angela's things, including bibs and sleeping gowns and handmade booties. She left out the clothes the baby had already outgrown. *So many in the space of less than three months.* Last of all, Marlena carefully folded and wrapped up the crazy quilt, memorizing the random pattern of the pieces from Luella's former dresses.

I pray Angela will cherish this special quilt for always.

~⁕~

The front doorbell rang on the designated Friday afternoon prior to Labor Day weekend. Gordon stood on the porch, his face solemn, wearing tan walking shorts—his left leg bandaged heavily at the knee and a large gash in his forehead. He looked different from when she'd first met him following his marriage to Luella. Marlena couldn't help but think of Luella and how glad *she* would have been to see her young husband back from the war. "Won't ya come in?" Marlena welcomed him into the front room.

Angela was crawling this way, and when she looked up, she rolled up to a sitting position and began to cry. She whimpered through her tears, making babbling sounds that sounded a little like "Maw-ma." Then, crawling quickly to Marlena, she puckered up her face and raised her little arms to be picked up.

"Wow . . . she's that big already?" Gordon said.

Marlena reached down for Angela Rose, knowing this would be her last chance to hold her. "Your daddy's here to see ya, sweetie. See?" She tried to turn her around to look.

But Angela clung all the more, pressing her chubby face into Marlena's neck and sniffling.

"She's a shy one sometimes," Marlena explained. "In a little bit, she'll warm up to ya, though."

"Maybe it's the bandages," Gordon said thoughtfully. "And she's never seen me before, since I had to leave before she was even born." He kept his distance, as though hesitant to intrude farther into the room. Tall with deep dimples on either side of his smile, he was very good-looking, and Marlena understood why Luella had been attracted to him.

"Have a seat, if you'd like to stay awhile," she offered.

He glanced over his shoulder at the car in the driveway. "My parents are waiting, so I'll have to take a rain check, if that's okay."

"Would they like to come in, too?" Marlena said, aware that Angela Rose was quivering against her. *Does she sense what's coming?*

"Thanks, you're very kind," he said but declined. "If you're ready, I'll start carrying things out to load up the trunk."

She said she was and watched with apprehension as Gordon reached for the diaper bag and the suitcase Aunt Becky had brought. Marlena hadn't bothered to pack the little dresses or the Amish bonnet. *Angela won't need them now.* She thought again of the pretty crib quilt and her own initials embroidered into the right-hand border, *MAW*, for Marlena Ann Wenger.

While she awaited the inevitable moment, with Angela Rose still snuggled against her, she pleaded with God to help her not cry when the time came. It might make the parting harder for the little one.

Mammi wandered into the front room just then, and her red eyes proved that she, too, was heavyhearted.

"Does it seem like we're handin' her over to the world?" Marlena had to know.

"We'll keep her in our daily prayers," Mammi whispered, patting Angela Rose softly. "Oh, little honey-girl, I pray the dear Lord Jesus will go with you all the days of your life. And may you surrender your life to Him at an early age."

"I prayed that, too," Marlena said and walked to the window to let Angela see the car and her father opening the trunk. "You're goin' home with your daddy, my little angel."

When Gordon came again to the front door, Angela began to cry all the harder.

"I wasn't expecting her to respond like this." He tilted his head to smile at her and touched her little back. Then he asked, "Is there anything I can do to repay you, Marlena? I don't know how my parents or I would have managed without your willingness to help."

Marlena glanced at her grandmother. "We love your little daughter dearly. You don't owe us anything. Really, it's been a joy and an honor to have her for these few months." She bit her lip as tears came. "*Ach*, it's hard to say good-bye to her. It truly is." She leaned her head against Angela's, then kissed her. "*Ich liebe dich, mei Bobbli*. I will miss ya for always."

Angela Rose looked up and patted Marlena's face, still whimpering, then pressed her button nose against Marlena's.

"It's obvious the two of you are very attached to each other. I'll do my best to let you know how she's doing from time to time." Then he added that he wanted to make it possible for

Angela to see Marlena and the rest of Luella's family every so often.

"Oh, if you would, we'd all love that. I know I can speak for my parents and siblings, too."

Mammi nodded her head and dabbed a hankie at her eyes.

"Well, I'd better not prolong this. Thank you again." He reached for Angela Rose, who tensed up. Her cries escalated to heartbreaking sobs.

"The dear Lord be with ya," Marlena said, watching him head out the door and across the front lawn toward the car. She couldn't bear to stand there any longer. It felt like her heart was being taken away.

But Mammi bravely stayed put at the window, telling her later that Gordon had given his howling baby to his mother in the backseat before driving quickly down the road.

⁓ ᥱᎧ

Late that afternoon, Ellie walked barefoot to the mailbox and found a letter addressed to Mr. Jake Bitner: *AKA, Small Jay.* She smiled, noticing the Arlington, Virginia, return address, and hurried out to the stable, where Roman was showing Small Jay how to curry their largest road horse, rubbing the brush in deep circles into the muscular part of his body, away from his frame.

"Lookee what came in the mail." She held the letter high.

Small Jay stretched up to reach it. "Must be from Boston and his perty wife."

"Must be." Ellie grinned as he opened the envelope.

"It's a card. And it says, 'You saved the day.'"

Roman stopped what he was doing and leaned over to look. "Ya know, son, I believe they're right."

Small Jay read the rest of the card aloud, including the personal note at the bottom. "I think it's from Abigail," he said. "Listen to this. 'Boston's doctors are trying a new therapy, and he's written another song, which is just as outstanding as his others. On the days Boston's memory is fairly clear, he fondly recalls his time with you and your family, and even makes me smile with talk of a cat named Sassafras—*like the tea*," he says. We very much would enjoy hearing from you, Jake. Your friend, Abigail (for Boston Calvert).'"

Ellie smiled. "A very nice note."

"I oughta tell Sassy 'bout this," Small Jay said. "If only Boston had kept the envelopes with his love letters, ain't so?"

"Well, but then we might not have gotten so well ac-quainted," Roman wisely observed.

"True." Small Jay stuffed the card into his pants pocket and picked up the mane comb, returning to the driving horse.

Ellie appreciated that Abigail had sent such a considerate card. "Lord bless her for that," she whispered as she made her way back to the house. Halfway there, she noticed a big black cat sitting in front of the outhouse, looking pleased as pie. "Shredder's back? Oh, wait'll Roman hears this!"

CHAPTER 39

"Oh, Mammi, that was just awful," Marlena said once she'd pulled herself together after Gordon left with Angela Rose.

Her grandmother cut a sliver of honeydew melon for her, fresh from the garden. "You were just wonderful to Gordon, dear. The Lord was with ya, I know." Mammi opened her arms to Marlena. "Never forget you did a very *gut* thing for your sister's wee babe this summer. Luella couldn't have asked for more."

How can I dismiss what I felt the Lord wanted me to do?

Mammi tilted her head and smiled thoughtfully. "There is no sorrow bigger than the grace of God." She carried a large basket of dozens of cucumbers out to the back porch to peel. "Take your time eatin' the melon, Marlena."

Marlena pondered Gordon Munroe's visit and all that had just taken place. When she finished eating, she opened the utensil drawer and found a paring knife and went to help Mammi with the chore. "After this, do ya mind if I take a walk? Will you be all right here alone, Mammi?"

"Well now, I'll have to be." Mammi glanced up at her. "You'll be leavin' for home soon, honey-girl."

"I *could* stay longer if you'd like."

"But would ya want to?" Hope sprang into Mammi's eyes.

"I'm in no hurry to get back . . . now."

A peaceful expression spread across Mammi's face, and Marlena felt good about pledging more time. *She still needs me.*

Later, Marlena headed through one of the fields. The alfalfa was ready for its third cutting, and in the next big field over, thousands of cabbages were ready for harvest.

Out there alone with the soil, the air, and the sky, she pushed her way to the willow grove and let herself cry. She purposely rejected imagining Gordon's drive home, fretting that Angela had cried all the way, nor did she wish to relive the scene in Mammi's front room, where Angela had clearly been frightened of her own father. *Dear little girl.*

Looking over toward the Bitners', Marlena knew she had to cling to Dawdi Tim's wise words even as tears rolled down her cheeks. *I mustn't worry. I will be stronger once the storm is over.*

Overhead, the willows swayed slightly. *Like a heavenly green fountain,* she thought as she watched Small Jay and his father harness one of their big road horses, working together at last.

She'd heard from Ellie that Boston's wife had come to take him home to Virginia, and that Ellie would start up her sewing classes again next week. *Maybe Mammi and I could go and make a wall hanging from the material in Angela's little dresses.* The classes, and the good fellowship, were something to look forward to, something to distract her from her grief.

Turning south, where the pond seemed to mingle with the

nearest trees, Marlena walked toward the road. Someone was pushing a stroller, headed this way. Drawing closer, she saw Sarah Mast and quickly wiped her wet face with the back of her hand.

"Hullo there, friend," Sarah called. "We meet again." Then she must have realized that Marlena had been crying. "Are you all right?"

She put on a smile. "It's been a hard day, is all."

"Come, let's walk together. By the way, this is my oldest brother's baby, Lena Mae."

Marlena moved toward the stroller and smiled for the wee girl, who grinned back at her. *Just a little older than Angela.* Tears came again, and she fell into step with Sarah, telling her about Angela Rose going home with her father and grandparents a little while ago.

"Oh, that *was* hard for ya. I'm so sorry."

"Well, I knew it was comin', but knowing didn't make it any easier. What a wonderful thing, really, that Gordon was found alive." It was good to talk to someone like Sarah and not have to hold back as she did when sharing with Mammi Janice, protecting her. "Honestly, I hardly know what to do with myself. Oh, there's plenty of work ahead—I don't mean that. It's just that right about now, I'd be thinkin' ahead to Angela's supper in a few hours, ya know. Then we had a sweet ritual after family worship . . . her bath, and then I'd sing a hymn while she took her bottle, rocking and lovin' her as best I could." Marlena stopped her recitation for fear she'd start crying again.

"It'll take time to make new daily patterns," Sarah said gently. "Not that I know anything 'bout the kind of sadness you're sufferin'."

"Well, there's actually more you don't know. No one does, although I think my grandmother might suspect by now. And my parents surely know, too." *Actually*, she thought, *they must be relieved.*

Sarah didn't probe, instead just kept pushing the stroller up the hill, near fenced pastureland where mules and cows grazed. A farm stand stood nearby in all its late-summertime glory.

Testing the waters, Marlena said, "Have ya ever harbored a secret about a relationship?"

Sarah looked at her. "It's been two years now, but *jah*, I suffered a heartache."

Marlena pressed ahead and began to share her loss of Nat Zimmerman, keeping his name to herself. "I lost my beau because of my growing faith in the Lord . . . and because of Angela Rose. But I'd do it all over again . . . make the same choices, if I had the chance."

Sarah shook her head, looking shocked. "You had to choose 'tween him and Angela Rose?"

"I know it sounds just awful. But that's all over now. Besides, I love my little niece."

"Well, ya must've loved your beau, too."

"Sometimes I question what I felt for him, tellin' the truth." She confided in Sarah that she believed if he'd sincerely loved her, he'd never have put her in such a bind.

Sarah said she'd pray for her. "The Lord alone understands your former beau's situation. And sees his heart."

"I believe that. And I hold out no hope of getting back together, even now that Angela's gone. We don't see eye to eye spiritually anymore."

"Sounds like you've made a clean break. You know your own mind, Marlena. *Des gut.*"

"My Dawdi Tim used to say, 'Storms make a strong tree, just like trials make a strong Christian.'"

Sarah had tears in her eyes, too, as she reached for Marlena's hand while gripping the stroller with the other. And they walked that way for a little while, a sweet comfort.

"My brother Luke's taking our Ohio cousin to the train just now," Sarah said, making small talk. "You may have seen her with me at Preachin' the day you visited."

"A tall brunette?"

"Jah, that's Cora Sue. Sweetest girl, really. I wish she could stay longer than just summer's end."

Their cousin?

Luke's hush-hush revelation resurfaced in Marlena's mind. *I must've been wrong about who he's sweet on.* But she breathed not a word to Sarah, wondering who the very fortunate young woman must be.

───❦───

"Dat's gonna teach me to drive the team," Small Jay told his mother that afternoon before supper.

"To hitch up, too?"

"Says so."

Mamma looked like she might burst. "Such *gut* news, *jah?*"

"I had to pinch myself on the way inside." He showed his arm. "See here?"

"You're becoming a young man, son."

Like Boston had called him. He took off his straw hat and ran his fingers through his thick bangs, glad they'd grown out so Mamma could even them out just today. "Boston hardly ever used my nickname, ya know."

"Maybe it's time we all call ya by your given name." Mamma's thoughtful expression touched him. "If you're ready."

He considered that. "Well, I don't feel so small no more." He patted his chest. "If Dat thinks it's all right, then Jake's fine." He thought then of Gracie Yoder and wondered if she'd ever referred to him as Small Jay to others. *Does she even think of me?* he wondered, recalling Boston's comical aside about wearing the lost bow tie to market. *To impress Gracie, maybe.*

Truth was, that bow tie was long gone. Besides, you didn't really need a bow tie or sugary-sweet words to catch a girl's attention. How many times had he thought back to that wonderful-good moment at market? Sometimes he wasn't sure if he hadn't just dreamed it. Well, he hoped not. Oh, did he ever.

"Dat's never ever called you Small Jay," Mamma was saying, "so I guess it's up to your sisters and me to catch up, ain't so?"

He was suddenly full of love for dear Mamma and mighty glad no one was around to see him go and give her a hug. Something he told himself he'd never do again. *Grown men don't hug their mothers,* he knew.

Then Jake Bitner straightened to his full height, turned, and headed toward the stable, where his work was waiting. *And Dat, too.*

~⊘

Marlena considered heading back to Ellie's to set a time for returning the baby furniture, once she'd washed everything down good. But Sarah wanted to stop at one of the farm stands, and they stood and visited for longer than they'd intended. Now it was time to hurry home to help Mammi finish making supper.

As it turned out, Sarah caught a ride with her father, who'd seen her with the stroller and stopped to pick up both her and the baby in the family buggy. Abram Mast waved cordially at Marlena.

"I'll come over and see ya again soon," Sarah said as they rode away.

Marlena waved until Sarah was out of sight; she so appreciated her friendship. Walking back toward Mammi's, she hoped she wouldn't have disturbed dreams tonight. Sighing, she realized anew that Angela Rose wouldn't be waiting for her with sweet drooly smiles when Marlena walked into the kitchen.

O Father, Thy will be done on earth as it is in heaven. . . .

CHAPTER 40

*I*n an attempt to soothe their sadness, Marlena awakened early the next morning to make waffles and bacon. She didn't need to ask if her grandmother had slept well; she could see by the deep lines beneath her eyes that she hadn't. As for herself, Marlena was anxious to wash down the crib and haul it over to Ellie's. It had stood all night in her room as a shadowy reminder of the baby she'd grown to love . . . and lost. Each time she'd rolled over, she had to turn away, heartbroken by the sight of it.

Neither she nor Mammi spoke of Angela as they ate, though Marlena could think of nothing else. *Did Gordon feed her the rice cereal she loves? Is she getting to know her father? Is she still crying?*

Every imaginable question crowded in, and she tried not to glance at the spot where the high chair had been. Last evening, she'd taken time to clean it, then set it out on the porch, thinking she could easily make it fit in Mammi's big trunk to deliver it to Ellie.

The telephone rang, startling them. "Who'd be callin' this

early?" Marlena said, reaching for the phone. "Hullo, Martin residence."

"Yes, hello, is this Marlena Wenger?"

"Who's callin'?"

"It's Gordon Munroe."

"Oh, of course." *Does he want to share something about Angela Rose . . . maybe an update?*

"I'm sorry to bother you, but do you have a moment, please?"

"Is everything all right?"

He paused, and she could hear Angela whimpering in the background. "It's obvious my daughter misses you very much."

"And I miss her, too. Oh, you have no idea."

"Last night, I stayed up reading a package of letters Luella had written to me. They arrived at my parents' address . . . sent there when I was classified as MIA." He stopped again, drawing a breath. "Marlena, I'd like to talk to you about one letter in particular."

She glanced at Mammi, then turned to look out the window. "All right."

"Not now, though . . . not by phone. I'd like to drive back down there today if it will suit you."

She heard the urgency in his deep voice. "*Jah*, that's fine."

He thanked her and said good-bye.

"*Ach*, mighty strange," she told Mammi after she'd hung up. "Gordon's comin' to talk to me 'bout one of Luella's love letters."

"Well, isn't that something."

"I should say so." She couldn't guess in the least what was up, or what she could possibly offer.

~⊙

327

When the doorbell rang out front, Marlena was busy peeling a mound of potatoes. She stopped to wipe the perspiration from her brow and looked at the kitchen clock. She knew this couldn't be Gordon Munroe, not unless he'd pushed the speed limit.

Drying her hands on her apron, she walked through the house and saw that it *was* Gordon after all. "Come in," she said, opening the screen door, deciding not to comment on how quickly he'd arrived. "We can sit in here, if you'd like. My grandmother's resting a bit on the back porch."

"I appreciate your taking time to see me today, Marlena." He was holding a letter-sized envelope as he sat on the settee nearest the windows. "You've certainly had your share of losses recently. I'd like to offer my condolences to you for your grandfather . . . and for Luella, too. I'm sorry I didn't think to say anything yesterday."

"Dawdi Tim was an inspiration to many people, 'specially to his family," she said, sitting across from Gordon.

"I wish I'd known him. And I definitely didn't know your sister for nearly as long as I'd planned to." Gordon looked away, a glint in his eye. "Luella talked quite a lot about your grandfather Martin. In fact, in one of her letters, written not long before she died, she said his opinion mattered more to her than anyone's."

Marlena nodded. "I felt that way, too." *Just had no idea Luella did.*

He opened the letter in his hand. "I'd like you to hear your sister's words directly, if you don't mind."

Folding her hands, Marlena listened as he began to read.

Dearest Gordon,
I miss you and pray for your safe return to me.

Angela Rose is such a dear baby, and she brings me so much happiness—I wish you could see her growing little by little. Oh, and does she ever look like you! She also reminds me of Dawdi Tim Martin, with those beautiful eyelashes. Dawdi even had the longest arms ever. He would boost me onto his big horses and lead me around the barnyard.

I've been thinking about the summers Marlena and I spent in Brownstown lately. Did I ever tell you how Dawdi read the Bible to us in English? Afterward, he would close the Good Book so reverently and talk about Jesus, as though He was a brother or a very close friend. I still can't get this out of my mind. Well, my heart.

Now, I don't know if you'll understand or even approve, but I've made my peace with God recently—a long time coming. And I've been taking our baby to church with me every Sunday morning. It's very different than the Amish church I grew up in, but I'm learning more about the heavenly Father who loves me no matter how badly I've hurt my parents . . . and my siblings, most especially my sister Marlena. When I look at our little daughter, I feel compelled to teach her these tenets of Scripture, too. Being a parent has opened my eyes to what's really important.

Honestly, I regret leaving my Plain life behind—not that I have second thoughts about marrying you, Gordon. It's just that being in the Amish church gave me the best start I could have had, if only I hadn't strayed from the simple gifts of integrity, kindness, and embracing peace—all the wisdom I learned there.

You might wonder where I'm going with this, dear. With you half a world away, battling a war I don't understand— and me here alone with Angela Rose—I've been wondering if

*we shouldn't have a will made in case anything might happen
to you or to me. Along that line, I can't think of anyone I'd
rather choose to mother our baby than my sister Marlena.
Without question, she is the very best choice to care for Angela
Rose, if it ever comes to that. I just know she would show
her the tenderest love.*

What do you think of this idea?

While he was reading, Gordon paused several times to regain his composure. When he finished the letter, his face was
wet with tears. "Do you understand now why I had to see you?"
He wiped his eyes with a handkerchief.

Marlena was deeply touched by her sister's words, but she
was not clear why Gordon had felt such a need to rush here.
"I guess so . . . but I'm a bit puzzled, since Angela has you,
Gordon."

He nodded and refolded the letter before slipping it back
into the envelope. "The military life is not conducive to raising
a young child—not for a single father," he said. "I'm home for
a bereavement leave, but I'll be expected to return to battle.
And, as you must know, my parents are well past their child-
rearing days. As long as they can visit Angela Rose, they will
respect my wishes for her care."

"It would be a very big change for their lives, *jah*." She
sighed, trying to grasp all that Gordon was implying just now.
"But I'm single, too, and there's no romantic prospect that I
know of."

"But do you love Angela Rose?"

She nodded. "More than you know." She thought of Nat's
ultimatum and bit her lip. "I'd do anything for your baby girl,
believe me."

He tapped the letter on his knee. "Obviously Luella recognized that, as well."

Knowing her sister had named her in the letter made Marlena sigh. It was truly a surprising compliment to realize Luella had seen her in that way. *She must've understood me better than I thought.*

"If you're willing, I want to honor my wife's memory and sign over full custody to you, with the understanding that I'll send you money every month to help with Angela's needs." He stopped for a second, folding his hands. "Of course, I would also like to visit my daughter occasionally, as my schedule permits."

Her tears were her answer, and Gordon gestured toward the door, saying he needed to return to the car quickly. Oh, Marlena wanted to call for Mammi and tell her right then what this visit was all about. But, still in awe of what her ears and heart had just heard, she rose and walked to the front door, pushed open the screen door, and stepped out onto the porch, filling her lungs with God's fresh air. *What an amazing day, indeed!*

Then, hearing the most precious baby cries ever, Marlena turned and saw Gordon's aunt Patricia handing Angela Rose up to him from the car.

Hurrying down the steps, her skirt tail flying, Marlena outstretched her arms. "Oh, my darling!" she called. "You're here . . . my precious baby."

And then, scarcely aware of anything but that Gordon had passed his daughter into her embrace, Marlena wept the happiest tears of her life.

CHAPTER 41

Late that September, before the harvest, corn leaves shimmered all over Brownstown farmland. Marlena first noticed the glints of gold when Mammi drove to purchase additional dress material for Angela Rose. As they sped past the rows of corn, Marlena caught a sprinkled reflection of dazzling sunlight, like thousands of tiny mirrors.

God's calling is sure, she thought, thrilled to have Angela Rose in her care for always.

"You seem to enjoy sewin' more than ever," Mammi said as they rode.

"It's nearly like making doll clothes, she's so small." Marlena smiled down at Angela Rose, dozing in her arms. "'Cept she's a lot more fun."

"Enjoy it now, 'cause these days won't last at the rate she's goin'."

They laughed merrily, and Marlena knew it was ever so true. These were the days to cherish, while her niece-turned-daughter was still small.

Every dawn is different, thought Jake that Saturday as he walked with Dat in the early morning darkness along the familiar road toward the old mill. This dawn was the first he'd go fishing with his father.

Over the one-lane bridge and on down the creek bank to the opposite side, they carried their fishing poles without a sound except their shoes on the road.

Silently, they opened the tackle box and began baiting their hooks in the light of Dat's big flashlight.

"Mighty quiet this time of day," Dat remarked, his voice a mere whisper.

Only a few yards away, Conestoga Creek rippled past, and Jake's mouth watered at the thought of the pan-fried bluegills and carp Mamma would be cooking up for dinner this noon. Maybe even a catfish—though, thinking of Sassy just then, he wished whoever'd named the latter hadn't put the word *cat* in there. Sassy had meowed and fussed when Jake left her in his room back home. *"Just Dat and me this time,"* he'd gently insisted.

They cast their lines, then perched themselves on the leaf-strewn grassy bank.

"What would ya think of goin' hunting with me this fall, son?"

"This fall?" Jake sure hoped he'd heard right.

"Why not? Grouse and pheasant huntin' starts soon enough. Thought I'd get ya ready by teachin' ya to shoot," Dat replied, leaning forward when he had a pull on his fishing line. "If you're willing."

Jake waited to answer, lest he scare away Dat's catch. He

turned to look at his father, still taking in his words, and watched him reel in a nice-sized bass. "You think it's time, then?" Jake asked, his heart pounding.

"I say you're more than ready," Dat said, nodding his head emphatically.

I think so, too! Jake sat up a little straighter, and when his line tightened and jerked, he leaped right up and reeled the fish in faster, even, than Dat had.

Triumphantly, he held high his catch for Dat to admire just as daybreak brightened the sky, the sun's rays brilliant over yonder green hills.

———

In October, Marlena's entire family came to visit for several days, and the reunion was a joyful reminder of earlier gatherings when Dawdi Tim would set up the cider press in the barn. Everyone helped to make apple cider, and Marlena couldn't help but remember Luella working with her, washing the apples from Benuel Miller's orchard up the hill. *An assembly line of love.*

Privately, Dat suggested that Marlena ought to remain with Mammi Janice through the winter and possibly into next spring. "I think the baby might need some constancy 'bout now," he said while Mamma and her mother sat in the kitchen, looking at old photos and reminiscing. Marlena didn't even need to stop to think—she eagerly agreed.

Subsequent family visits were the high points of that fall and winter, and Angela Rose took her first timid steps on Christmas Eve, putting the biggest smile on Mamma's face, and even winning some applause from Dat.

Each month, Marlena received airmail letters from Gordon

as he finished his first tour of duty. He included generous checks for Angela Rose's needs and kindly requested regular updates—his fatherly affection for his daughter had not ended when he surrendered Angela Rose to Marlena's care. As a surprise for him, Marlena purchased a small camera to take pictures, which she enclosed in her return letters, something for which Gordon seemed grateful.

On Angela's first birthday in January, a package arrived from Gordon—a journal-like letter chronicling the events of the past year. *"Prayer, and my love for Luella and our baby, gave me the will to live,"* he'd written. Gordon also asked if Marlena would please save the letter till Angela was old enough to read it for herself and understand and appreciate the painful ordeal her father had suffered in the war and in the loss of his wife.

The following spring, Marlena's fascination with the New Order Amish church became a genuine pursuit of their beliefs. Attending that church held in Amish homes satisfied her soul's deepest yearning. No longer was there a smidgen of doubt in her mind—she belonged to the Lord Jesus.

It was during this special season of new life that Marlena began to realize that Luke Mast must be planning his Sunday afternoon "prayer walks" to coincide with her own long strolls with Angela Rose.

Hope sprang into her heart that verdant springtime.

"You see, Marlena, *you* were the young woman I was talking 'bout last summer," he told her, blue eyes shining.

His revelation took her breath away.

"It might seem now like I was speaking in some sort of code, which I guess I was." He gave her a sincere smile. "I needed to know how you felt about my pursuing someone who was already promised."

She recalled his confidential sharing and how certain she had been that Luke was talking about the brunette she'd seen riding with him and Sarah. *But, of course, that girl turned out to be his cousin.* Hearing him reveal that Marlena had been the object of his affection all this time made her blush.

"So when I heard of your breakup with your beau, I knew I should wait for a while longer to tell you how I feel," he added.

Sarah must've told him, Marlena thought, all the more thankful for their sisterly relationship.

Luke went on. "I wanted to give ya time to recover from Luella's passing, too. That was mighty heavy on my heart."

He was so sympathetic and understanding, Marlena found herself looking forward to their weekly walks and the way he kept their conversation flowing in such a fun-loving manner. Equally important, Luke was gentle with Angela Rose, even offering to carry her around after the shared meal on Sundays, or holding her dimpled hand as they walked together, his steps made short to accommodate Angela's tiny ones.

Marlena also noticed Luke continue to befriend Jake Mast, who'd abandoned his youthful nickname. Truth be told, Luke's bighearted manner with everyone—so like Dawdi Tim's—made him a favorite with all ages amongst the People. *Sarah's handsome older brother is everything a young woman might desire in a friend. And more,* Marlena caught herself thinking.

So they agreed to be just that, taking their time to get to know each other. "Lord willing, next September you could take baptismal instruction," Luke suggested. "And after that, I'll court you in earnest, if you're ready."

Marlena approved, appreciating his willingness to take things slow for her sake, as well as Luke's obvious fondness for Angela Rose. Mammi, too, thought it was better that she didn't rush into a new dating relationship, given all Marlena had been through . . . though Mammi let it be known that Luke Mast would be a mighty fine choice for a husband, "Someday."

But by the time Marlena realized how very attracted she was to Luke—and how ready she was for rides in his fine courting carriage—summer was beginning. Thankfully, there was plenty of time for their romance to unfold.

Their summer as friends seemed to pass leisurely. And not only did Marlena feel completely at ease in Luke's presence, she'd begun to feel lonely when she wasn't with him. She also discovered that his favorite dessert was caramel cake, so she baked it for him on several occasions—things were even sweeter when his eyebrows lifted and that winning smile appeared on his suntanned face.

Their courtship, which followed their baptism into the New Order Amish church, took a turn one fall evening when Luke insisted on having Angela Rose along on one of their buggy rides. Surprising Marlena, Luke stopped over at his parents' farm and hopped out of the highly polished black buggy with twenty-one-month-old Angela and, after offering to help Marlena down, walked with them both toward the house.

"Are your parents expecting us?" She felt giddy seeing Sarah wave from the kitchen window just then. Luke was known to spring things on Marlena, and he seemed to enjoy the air of mystery.

"Thought I'd show ya the house where I grew up," he said, stopping in the large front yard, standing on the thick roots of a majestic oak tree jutting up from the ground. He smiled mischievously and tickled Angela's chubby cheek, then reached for Marlena's hand in the secluded, shady spot. "This is the wonderful-*gut* house," he said and glanced over his shoulder at the large white clapboard farmhouse, "where I'll be bringin' my bride . . . and her little one, to live one day." Luke looked down at Angela, then back at Marlena. "If you'll have me, dear."

Her heart swelled with love for this, her truly adoring beau.

He raised her hand to his lips and kissed it softly. "Will you let me love you all the days of your life?"

Tears sprang to her eyes, and she couldn't speak. He opened his free arm to her, and she nestled against him. "I will," Marlena said at last, thankful to God for bringing Luke into her life.

He smiled handsomely and, reaching for her hand, motioned toward the house. "I want my parents and Sarah to hear this first," he said with a wink. "All right with you?"

She agreed. "Then I'd like Mammi Janice to be next."

They were united in this plan, and when Angela Rose clapped her little hands, completely unaware—surely—of what had just taken place, Luke chuckled, a spring in his step when he took his "two girls" into the house.

Luke held the screen door for her and called for his mother to come right quick. "I've got the best news!"

Never was there a sweeter day! Marlena thought as she stepped inside.

EPILOGUE

*I*t was soft-spoken Jake Bitner who first told pretty Angela Rose about the bow-tie man he'd met at the old mill a decade ago. Luke and I had just celebrated our ninth wedding anniversary and were hosting a Thanksgiving dinner for our families, including dear Mammi, who'd ridden over for the day in Bitners' family carriage. Their unmarried son, Jake, now twenty-four, drove the horse-drawn sleigh with his three single sisters all bundled up, including nine-year-old Esther, born a year after Abigail came for her dear Boston. Dorcas and her husband and baby boy joined us at our home, too.

Angela Rose and Esther Bitner, close in age, sat next to each other on the long wooden bench and folded their hands and bowed their heads as Luke pronounced the blessing over the feast. My dear husband thanked God for the struggles that make us strong and for the blessings of an abundant harvest.

After the amens echoed, Luke reached under the table and squeezed my hand. I must've blushed because Mammi Janice caught my eye and beamed over at me.

The next day, while our baby son napped snug in his cradle,

I sat down with Angela Rose and her younger sister—Luke's and my daughter, six-year-old Emma—to show them how to make quilt stitches on a practice sampler. Little Emma screwed up her face, having a hard time, but Angela managed to put three on her needle right away. She was so excited as she tried to get stitches that I decided to tell her the background behind her favorite quilt . . . the one I'd sewn from her Mamma's dresses. Emma wandered off to play with her homemade faceless dolls as I shared.

"I want to tell you a true story, honey-girl. I have a feelin' you'll tell it to your own children on chilly autumn nights as you sit around the fire, and they'll retell it to their youngsters one day."

Angela's eyes were wide with wonder beneath her white *Kapp*. "My mother, Luella, was fancy like my first father, ain't so?" she said.

"For a time, *jah*." I explained that Luella had grown up Amish, then left to become an *Englischer* and married Gordon before he'd gone off to war. "But she never forgot what it meant to be Plain, and she wrote about it in one of her love letters to your father . . . before she died."

"Can I read the letter someday, Mamma?"

"Let's ask your first father when he and his wife and little boys come for their Christmas visit, all right?"

That seemed to satisfy Angela, and I leaned over to kiss her.

"I'd like to make a crazy quilt, too," Angela said, returning to her stitching again. "Will ya teach me, Mamma?"

"I surely will. And ya know what I think? My sister Luella would've been very happy if she knew of your interest in quilting."

Angela Rose smiled up at me. "So I ain't too young, then?"

"Well, my Dawdi Tim used to say, '*Listen for God's voice when you're young, and quickly answer His calling.*'"

My darling girl nodded her head. "And do it with all your might, ain't?"

⁓୧ එ

That night I gathered my daughters to me as we sang "Jesus Loves Me" in *Deitsch*. Then I tucked them into bed with a prayer.

I headed across the hallway to Luke but thought I heard the breathy strains of a harmonica and stopped to listen. *Where's it coming from?*

Lured by the music and the rising moon, I walked to the end of the hall and looked down over the fenced pastureland. The mules' coats were thickening up for winter, and it wouldn't be long before more snow and sleet clattered against the windows.

The solitary melody seemed to drift back to me over the years. And as I sat down to nurse my young son, rocking him to sleep and stroking his fuzzy little head, I hummed along with the hushed refrain.

I was brimming with ongoing thankfulness for Luella's precious love-gift, and for all that God had brought my way—dearest Luke and our darling second daughter . . . our newborn son, too. My gratitude blended with the unexplained music . . . and a heritage of enduring wisdom.

The light of the moon accentuated the white church spire in the near distance, and seeing it, I smiled and remembered. "Wise folk never reject the possibility of a miracle," I whispered.

AUTHOR'S NOTE

*T*he rural setting of Brownstown, Pennsylvania, is a reminder of some of my happiest childhood memories.
It is the blissful location of my uncle Amos and aunt Anna
Jane Buchwalter's home, where they raised their four children.
Their large white clapboard house was situated within yards
of the picturesque stone Brownstown Mill, built in 1856 as a
lumber mill, though it later served as a grist mill and woolen
mill, owned by DeSager, before being renovated into offices
and boutiques. Presently it is a private residence. And the
topping on my research came when Sarah Hartman Shanely,
a fan of my books, contacted me to say that she had grown
up in the mill after her parents purchased it in 1994. What
a small world! I'm so pleased at Sarah's eagerness to answer
questions about her beautiful childhood home.

My sister and I and our cousins looked forward to exploring
this area, especially near Conestoga Creek and the one-lane
bridge not far from the historic mill, where we tossed pebbles
into the water below like Small Jay Bitner in this book. We
also ice-skated on that creek during the winter, and fished

and played in it—often up to our waists—in the good old summertime.

Buchwalter family gatherings were held in the three-story house surrounded by Amish and Mennonite farmland, the familiar *clip-clop* of driving horses hitched to buggies regularly coming from the road in the predawn hours on visiting and Preaching Sundays.

As occasionally happens, the splendid setting presented itself to me first, eventually giving way to three cherished story threads for this novel, as well as a cast of endearing characters. Marlena Wenger, however, had been in my heart for some years, waiting her turn as one of my gracious leading ladies. I sometimes think Marlena is, perhaps, one of the most tender-hearted protagonists I've written to date. Perhaps you agree.

As is always true, there are a host of remarkable people who helped to bring this book to its completion. They are the following: David Horton, my fine acquisitions editor and wonderful friend, who was keenly interested in this storyline from the outset; Rochelle Glöege, my brilliant line editor, who partnered with me in delving into medical treatment for mental disorders in the '60s (which was woefully lacking!); Aleta Hirschberg, Nan Best, Sarah Shanely, Dale and Naomi Hartman, and David Buchwalter, for period research; Dale Birch and Dave Lewis, for relevant aspects of the Vietnam war; and Erik Wesner, for helpful input into Amish settlements near Mifflinburg, Pennsylvania. (Don't miss Erik's new book, *50 Fascinating Amish Facts*.)

I'm grateful to my husband, David Lewis, for his brain-storming help (so fun!), double-checking Plain facts and tradition, and reading the hundreds of pages of rough drafts; our granddaughter Ariel for suggesting the name Anderson for Gordon's father; Jim and Ann Parrish, Donna De For, Noelle Buss, and many other prayer partners for consistent and faithful devotion to prayer; Steve Oates for driving me all over Mifflinburg during the fall 2014 book tour; and Amy Green, my adventuresome publicist, who reminded me on a sunny September afternoon how daring it is to wade across Conestoga Creek.

Many thanks also to Hank and Ruth Hershberger for answering Amish-related questions and offering correct *Deitsch* spellings; Barbara Birch for expert proofreading and always warm encouragement; and to my numerous cheerful and cooperative Amish and Mennonite friends and relatives, who read my drafts but choose to remain behind the scenes.

Finally, abundant thanks to you, my devoted and caring readers. You are so very dear to my heart, and I am sincerely appreciative of your interest in my work.

Soli Deo Gloria!

Beverly Lewis, born in the heart of Pennsylvania Dutch country, is the *New York Times* bestselling author of more than ninety books. Her stories have been published in eleven languages worldwide. A keen interest in her mother's Plain heritage has inspired Beverly to write many Amish-related novels, beginning with *The Shunning,* which has sold more than one million copies and is an Original Hallmark Channel movie. In 2007 *The Brethren* was honored with a Christy Award.

Beverly has been interviewed by both national and international media, including *Time* magazine, the Associated Press, and the BBC. She lives with her husband, David, in Colorado.

Visit her website at www.beverlylewis.com or www.face book.com/officialbeverlylewis for more information.

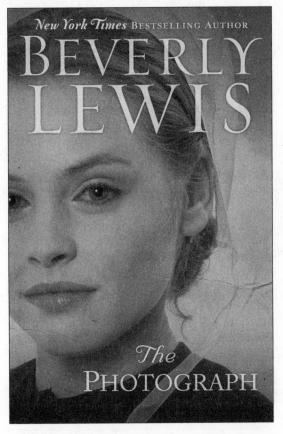

The Photograph

The Next Novel From Beverly Lewis

AVAILABLE SEPTEMBER 8, 2015

◊BETHANYHOUSE

Stay up-to-date on your favorite books and authors with our free e-newsletters. Sign up today at bethanyhouse.com.

Find us on Facebook. facebook.com/bethanyhousepublishers

Free exclusive resources for your book group! bethanyhouse.com/anopenbook

anopenbook

More From Bestselling Author
Beverly Lewis

To find out more about Beverly and her books, visit
beverlylewis.com or find her on Facebook!

When two formerly Amish sisters return home for their parents' landmark anniversary, both are troubled by the past, and the unresolved relationships, they left behind.

The River

Jenny Burns has always had an "old soul," but her quest to join the Amish world will challenge her spirit—and her heart—in ways she never expected.

The Secret Keeper
HOME TO HICKORY HOLLOW

Desperate to find her daughter, Kelly is thrilled when her private investigator finds a prospect. But her "chance" meeting with the girl's guardian, Jack, takes an unexpected turn when he asks her out on a date. If she comes clean about her motives now, will she lose both a daughter *and* a chance at love?

Child of Mine (with David Lewis)

◆ BETHANYHOUSE

Stay up-to-date on your favorite books and authors with our free e-newsletters. Sign up today at bethanyhouse.com.

f Find us on Facebook. facebook.com/bethanyhousepublishers

anopenbook

Free exclusive resources for your book group! bethanyhouse.com/anopenbook

More From Bestselling Author
Beverly Lewis

Bible verses and inspiring illustrations complement this lively tale of a brother and sister spending a day and night remembering all they know about their heavenly Father. The last page also offers suggestions for parents as they seek to teach their children about God.

What Is God Like?

Rich illustrations beautifully capture life on an Amish farm in this delightful picture book featuring a young girl who tries to be just like her beloved mother…with humorous and touching results.

Just Like Mama

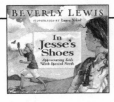

Gently showing children how to accept and be kind to those who are different from them, this sensitive yet realistic story follows Jesse's sister, Allie, as she struggles to understand and relate to her autistic brother—and to the kids who make fun of him.

In Jesse's Shoes

◊ BETHANYHOUSE

Stay up-to-date on your favorite books and authors with our free e-newsletters. Sign up today at bethanyhouse.com.

Find us on Facebook. facebook.com/bethanyhousepublishers

an open book

Free exclusive resources for your book group! bethanyhouse.com/anopenbook